Praise for *Daughters of the Wild*

"This is a powerful and exquisite novel, rooted in the mystical vine, which guides everything the characters do.... Magical realism at its finest."
—*Booklist*, **starred review**

"Saturated with magic and mysticism, this novel is a luminous and blisteringly real exploration of the bonds of motherhood, the limits and expansiveness of love, and the possibility of transcendence."
—**Jessie Chaffee, author of** *Florence in Ecstasy*

"*Daughters of the Wild* is a gorgeous, different, and completely engrossing book. Burian's writing is transporting—and exactly what I needed right now."
—**Jessica Valenti, author of** *Sex Object: A Memoir*

"A magical, gripping exploration of women's power and the ties that bind. I won't forget the complexity and the strength of these characters."
—**Danielle Lazarin, author of** *Back Talk*

"With prose as luminous and transformative as the psychoactive plant at this novel's core, this is a book about dignity, intuition, and the sustaining vine of friendship. A perennial read."
—**Courtney Maum, author of** *Costalegre*

"Writers like Karen Russell, Joy Williams, and Gabriel García Márquez spring to mind, but Natalka Burian's voice is her own: lyrical, spunky, and defiantly untamed. It's a voice we'll be reading for a long time to come."
—**Adam Wilson, author of** *Sensation Machines*

Also by Natalka Burian

Daughters of the Wild
A Woman's Drink: Bold Recipes for Bold Women
Welcome to the Slipstream

NATALKA BURIAN

the Night Shift

PARK
ROW
BOOKS

PARK
ROW
BOOKS™

ISBN-13: 978-0-7783-3304-3

The Night Shift

Park Row Books
22 Adelaide St. West, 41st Floor
Toronto, Ontario M5H 4E3, Canada
ParkRowBooks.com
BookClubbish.com

Printed in U.S.A.

Recycling programs
for this product may
not exist in your area.

For every
New Yorker,

past,
present,
and future.

the
Night
Shift

I remember how the darkness doubled.

I recall lightning struck itself.

I was listening, listening to the rain.

I was hearing, hearing something else.

—TELEVISION.

One

Waking up late still felt wrong to Jean Smith. She had set her alarm for 6:30 a.m. every weekday—and some Saturdays—since 2001. She took promptness seriously, and the early wake up allowed her plenty of time to get to work a few minutes ahead of time, despite subway delays and dropped contact lenses. Now that her job on the Upper West Side belonged to someone else, Jean thought that her body would continue rising with the dawn. Instead, she had settled into the morning routine of a high school junior on summer break.

She reached for her phone and saw that it was almost eleven. *I'm sure my body needs it*, she thought, trying to reassure herself and dispel the vague guilt that loomed over a wasted morning. Jean trusted her body above all things.

Her old boss, Dr. Goldstein, had sent an arrangement of lilies earlier in the week. They languished in a corner, browning at the edges, but were still fragrant in a decaying, funeral way.

Jean knew she should throw them out, but she couldn't shake the finality of the gesture; once the flowers were gone, all evidence of her former life would be, too. So much of Jean's time in New York had been contained in Dr. Goldstein's office and she wasn't sure if, all of a sudden, overnight, she could be a completely different kind of person.

She plucked the tiny florist's card from its plastic fork and read the message for the dozenth time. *Dear Jean, I'm so sorry to see you move on, but I wish you nothing but the best in your future endeavors. You will always have a place here if you need it. My best, Myra.* Even though the note was written in the bubbly, immature hand of a stranger, Jean could almost hear Dr. Goldstein's rich, low voice dictating it.

Jean startled and dropped the card when the buzzer rattled through the apartment. She waited a minute; sometimes these things were a mistake—another person's birthday flowers or udon noodle delivery—but the buzzer was insistent. Jean didn't live in the kind of building with a buzzer that actually worked the door downstairs, so she walked into her unlaced sneakers by the threshold and descended the three flights of stairs to the street.

Two women stood on the step, their noses to the glass. One was very old, hunched with a face like a creased flour bag. The other was a middle-aged mom in a butter-yellow cardigan, with a heavy gold necklace at her throat. Neither of the women wore coats, and somehow this made them look more like apparitions than anything else. Jean squinted into the cold light of the vestibule, assured that there had been some mistake. These women weren't here for her. But, as she pulled the door open, their supplicating faces beamed squarely at her.

"Hello," the middle-aged mom said. "I'm so sorry to bother you. This is going to sound a little strange, but my mother used to live in your apartment, and it would be—gosh, it would be wonderful if she could come up to take a look." Her vowels were wide and flat, obviously Midwestern.

Jean stood back, like a slapped person. This was the last thing she had expected to hear. She tried to collect herself, looking into the wrinkled, powdery face of the old lady, wrapped neatly in a babushka-style scarf ablaze with poppies.

"I promise we won't take long. I'm sure you have things to do, but we're only here for the day…"

"I guess so. Why not?" Jean tried to sound friendly and magnanimous as she motioned them into the vestibule. The daughter was tall—almost as tall as Jean, a shared feature that made Jean simultaneously warmed and suspicious.

"I—I think it's worth mentioning that there isn't an elevator."

The middle-aged woman smiled. "Oh, we know! Mom remembered that. Didn't you?" She patted her mother's liver-spotted hand and clasped it tight. They scaled the stairs slowly. The daughter watched patiently as the old woman's sensible orthopedic shoes found the flat and rise each time.

"So, where are you visiting from?" Jean asked, not sure how she was meant to behave. Maybe she should have been solemn and silent, but the daughter, at least, didn't seem like the solemn, silent type.

"We're here from Chicago. For a funeral, actually."

"Oh, I'm so sorry," Jean said, fidgeting where she paused on the landing, waiting for them to catch up.

"Thank you. Here, Mom? Right here?"

The old woman nodded down the hall, grasping at the railing. Jean held the apartment door open, standing awkwardly beside the COME BACK WITH A WARRANT–emblazoned welcome mat her roommates had purchased at a yard sale.

The old woman looked so tenderly through the doorjamb that Jean was forced to avert her eyes. The visitor maneuvered herself through the apartment by bracing herself against the walls and finally sat at the little kitchen table. She spoke rapidly to her daughter in a gnarled Eastern European dialect.

"Oh, Mom." The daughter beamed. "She said the bathtub used to be right here." She pointed to the awkward space where Jean and her roommates had wedged the coffee table. "And she and her three sisters slept in that corner over by the window. Isn't that just amazing? Mom lived here until she got married." She turned back to her mother, and they spoke quietly for a while, their language like a zipper—smooth but toothy. In a long pause, they sighed like twins and stared as though counting every wall and window.

"Can I get you something? Water? Or maybe coffee?" Jean asked, wondering if she should make some excuse to leave and give them privacy, but was also about ten percent convinced this could be some kind of scam, and, if she left them alone, she would return to an empty apartment.

"Oh, no thank you, dear. We should get going. Isn't that right, Mom?" The woman smoothed her mother's forehead, loving but purposeful.

"Thank you," the old mother said to Jean, her voice marbled with a heavy accent. Jean nodded deferentially. The woman's gaze was harsh; Jean felt like she was being poked with a sharpened stick.

"I can't tell you how much this means to us," the daughter said, revealing extravagant crow's feet when she smiled.

"Of course—it was nothing." Jean tried to force a smile to match, but couldn't do it after watching the old woman silently catalog her former life in that apartment, under all of the landlord's cheap fixes and the debris from Jean's and her roommates' lives.

"Well, we won't keep you. Let's go, Mom, and leave this nice girl alone." Jean walked them to the door, where the daughter paused, pressing a carefully folded twenty-dollar bill into her palm. "We really appreciate your kindness."

Jean opened her mouth—wanting to demur, to decline the money—but she was in no position to be declining anything. "It was no trouble at all. Have a safe trip home." Jean locked the door behind them, and felt a pinch of guilt between her eyebrows, worried that maybe she was supposed to do something else for the old mother.

Jean thought about their unexpected visit all day. She thought about the old woman as she scrubbed the dishes and set them on the drying rack. Jean wondered if the old woman had stood in the exact same spot—as a girl—not much younger than Jean, and scrubbed the dishes, too. Jean thought about the old woman when she crossed the street to the Dream Clean. She thought about her when she pulled her clump of wet laundry out of the machine like a birthed lamb from its mother. Where had the old woman washed her clothes? Jean thought about the old woman packing all of her things and leaving the apartment on her wedding day. Jean flinched in the mirror, tweezing her eyebrows.

She had a compulsive thought that the old woman had left something in the apartment, and now, like the pea under the mattress, everything tilted toward discomfort. But the truth was that Jean was off, and not because of her apartment and not because of the old woman. Jean was off because she had blown up her whole life.

She had allowed panic to creep in at Dr. Goldstein's office and had ruined everything. Dr. Goldstein's curiosity was perfectly normal—even predictable considering her line of work. But when she asked Jean about her mother, Jean reacted like a person waking up in a tub filled with ice post-organ harvest. She had felt shocked, frozen, violated—all thanks to a few prying questions. Now Jean was dislodged into the great river of New York City with nothing—not a raft, not a door, not a pool float: nothing but a hastily acquired job that she was, on a cellular level, wholly unsuited for. Jean sliced the old woman from her thoughts and dressed for her new, unsuitable job in a haze of self-loathing. She took off in the afternoon, before her room-mates came home from work, leaving the drying rack sparkling with clean dishes.

It was only four hours into her shift at the bar, and Jean had never been so tired. She didn't really smoke, but she stood out-side on the sidewalk, her nose and fingers tingling from the cold, holding a lit cigarette anyway. It had rained earlier that night, and the gingko leaves stuck to the pavement in irregular gold coins. She squinted through the smoke at an alley cat sauntering in and out of the deli across the street. Jean envied that languid animal and its free rent.

The only acceptable kind of break from her new job at the bar, Red and Gold, was the smoking kind, so Jean took it. She had to get outside, at least for as long as it took for the cigarette to burn to its end. It was only her first week, and though she was getting used to being on her feet and smiling a lot more than she ever had before, she couldn't get used to the feeling of being entirely, bodily, wrung out. The flow of work, though, that feeling of jumping onto a moving train, was addictive.

The door creaked open, and the sound of the Stooges thun-dered out into the street. Her co-worker Omar pressed the door back into the jamb with the bottom of his foot, seal-ing the sounds of the bar inside. He was slight, sharp-jawed, handsome—and he was much better at his job than she was at hers. Omar nodded in her direction but didn't look her in the eye. "Hey, you're up," he said, lighting a cigarette of his own.

"Already?"

"Already. The clock stops for no one, newbie."

Jean dropped her cigarette in the ash can and bent to stretch her calves the way she had when she ran high school track. In one way, it was nice to be reminded of her physicality, to be re-minded that her body could hurt because of something she had decided to do. It was evidence of a choice she had made. If Jean knew anything, she knew the value of making her own choices.

"I'm going to get a coffee. You want one?" Omar's voice was soft, the voice people used when they were approached by a dog in a stranger's yard. Jean winced, remembering when Omar told her he had to change the way he talked to everyone since September 11.

"No thanks, I'm okay. See you in there, I guess." She pulled open the misaligned front door, face-to-face with a paper turkey printed in autumnal colors, the kind of decoration elementary school teachers tacked up in their classrooms.

The decaying interior of the bar was the opposite of her last job. Her old office had smelled like vanilla Glade Lasting Mist. Red and Gold just smelled. It was soon enough after the mayor's nonsmoking ban for people to remember when bars smelled like smoke. The regulars still talked about it, still grumbled about having to go outside to smoke. "Fuck that guy," everyone said, as they shouldered out into the weather. But not Jean—she was grateful for that ban, for those precious minutes in the cold night air.

Jean slipped beneath the pass and scanned the room, satisfied that no one was watching her, and then inspected her ragged nails. Her palms were chapped from the constant dishwashing, and she wondered if the cuts and creases from all of the bottle caps she pried open would scar her skin forever. She wondered how permanently, in general, this particular job would mark her.

A large group of friends had coalesced around the pool table in the back, all skinny jeans and T-shirts from Goodwill emblazoned with commemorative text from Bar Mitzvahs and family reunions. It was somebody's birthday, and the group had contracted and expanded throughout the night. Jean knew they would be hard to get rid of at closing, but they made the room feel lively in a way she was grateful for.

Jean turned her focus to the row of customers seated at the

bar. The first lesson she learned in Dr. Goldstein's office was just as—if not more—relevant at Red and Gold. "Everyone you meet is wearing an invisible sign that says 'Make me feel important!'" her former boss had said. The more important you made someone feel, the easier they were to manage in Dr. Goldstein's office; the more important you made someone feel at Red and Gold, the more they tipped. It was a skill Jean had sharpened to an almost involuntary degree. In the same way some people were natural athletes, or good at learning other languages, Jean was good at making people feel important.

"Can I get you all something else?" she asked the drooping couple seated in front of her, her tone equal parts sympathetic and commiserating.

"I got it." Mitch, the other bartender, elbowed her aside. Jean slunk back, suppressing a spike of anger. He still didn't trust her to do the job, didn't believe that she could secure the tips that he could.

After three nights in a row, Jean had begun to understand the tides of custom on her shifts. Red and Gold was settling into a lull—when people went to shows at the venue around the corner—but they could expect one more frantic rush before closing.

"Listen, I shouldn't have done that," Mitch said, putting a hand on her shoulder. He had the waxen complexion of a person whose skin rarely saw the light of day, and this vampiric pallor still shocked Jean a little every time he stood too close.

"I really don't care. It's fine." Jean tried not to shrug off his touch. Instead, she pushed her hair behind her ears—hair the texture and color of tree bark, her mother used to say.

"No, it's not fine. You're new, and I should let you learn." Mitch looked down at her; it was no small feat, since Jean was tall, too. He wore a tiny black vest over a white T-shirt that settled tightly over his impressive potbelly.

"Thanks," Jean said. "That's very generous of you."

"Ha! You're making fun of me, right?" Mitch slapped her on the back, like a cartoon dad.

"Right." Jean forced another smile, adding it to the parade of forced smiles she had produced that night. Jean hated that a young woman smiling was a cue that everyone understood. She hated, even more, that it was one she had to rely on so heavily in order to pay her rent.

Mitch cracked open a line of PBR cans and pushed them across the bar. "You're sweet, but not fast enough for the weekends. You'll get the hang of it. Nobody's new forever."

"That's the truth," Omar said, dropping a tub of used glassware in front of her. Jean hauled it to the sink and sank the glasses into the steamy dishwater.

"You had a nine-to-five before this, right?" Mitch asked.

"Right." Jean dunked another batch into the electric blue liquid.

"What happened? You didn't like it?" Mitch watched her closely.

"No, I liked it. It just wasn't for me anymore."

"What does that mean? I bet you had insurance and everything. Did you have dental?"

Jean didn't tell him that she had to quit because she was teeming with emotional problems. She just shrugged. "I did, yeah."

"Oh man, that is *the* dream! You know how many cavities I have in here?" Mitch gritted his teeth like a jack-o'-lantern. He winked at a pair of men at the end of the bar and made them another round.

"Yeah," Jean agreed, wiping her hands dry. "This has been an adjustment. Especially financially." She frowned at the crowd of clean glasses.

"If you want more work, my cousin said they're looking for help at her restaurant." Omar's voice was so quiet, Jean had to lean forward to hear each word. "Just a few hours, but it's good pay. Early in the morning, helping her in the kitchen. Only prep, nothing fancy. You can go right when we close, so it could work out well for everybody. It's hard to go from nine-to-five to a couple weeknights over here. You interested?"

"Yeah, of course—that would be great." Jean felt a genuine rush of gratitude. Rent was looming and she keenly missed her beautifully regular and, comparatively, abundant direct deposits from Dr. Goldstein's office.

"What? You're giving out jobs and you didn't ask me first? That's cold, Omar," Mitch said, feigning insult and ignoring the girls with matching side-swept bangs and overly glossed lips who leaned toward them expectantly.

"You're lazy, man," Omar said with a smile. "I'll take you over there after work," he said, turning to Jean.

"Tonight?" she asked, rolling one of her ankles looking for some small moment of physical comfort, like dodging under an awning in the rain.

"They need somebody to start now. If you meet my cousin tonight, you'll probably just get the job."

"Sure, okay, sounds good. Thanks." It didn't sound good at all, but she really needed the job. So, leaving Mitch to close up, Jean buttoned her denim jacket and followed Omar into the night.

"The shift starts at two and you have to finish up before they open for service in the morning. Between here and there you can get a little break, a little breakfast, you know, whatever you need."

"How far is it?" Jean struggled to keep up. Her legs had never been so stiff. Between working all night on her feet and the cold, she was having trouble matching Omar's pace. It was humiliating to be so unaccustomed to physical labor. It felt dishonest, like she had cheated her way out of an important, character-building rite of passage, like losing teeth or shaving her legs for the first time.

"Maybe fifteen minutes. It's downtown. You want to take the train?"

"No, it feels good to walk," she lied.

"Sorry, I know I walk fast. But hey, the faster you walk, the less chance you get hit by that can of soda some racist throws at you. You ever work in a kitchen before?"

Jean wasn't sure what to say to that; she keenly understood that not a single observation she had to offer would be of any value. "No. Have you?"

"A lot, yeah. I basically grew up in my uncle's restaurant. It's easy. You don't have to talk to customers. That's the best part."

"Sounds amazing."

A gust of bitter late-autumn wind stabbed through her jacket, and the skin on her face and hands stung with cold. She was going to have to dig out her winter coat and hope that the zipper worked through another winter. She was grateful for Omar's silence, because her face was too cold to talk. Omar stopped in front of a locked gate, skimmed with graffiti. Jean tucked her bare hands into her armpits and waited as he texted.

The gate rumbled up halfway, and Omar motioned for Jean to duck underneath. It seemed impossibly gymnastic for her sore, frozen body to bend like that, but somehow, it did.

A young woman with overplucked eyebrows greeted her on the other side. She was short and curvy, and had a bleached blond buzz cut.

"Hey, Lu," Omar said, closing the gate behind them. "This is Jean. She just started at Red and Gold." He turned to Jean and said, "Lu runs everything over here. She's fancy."

"Hello," Jean said, unsure of the degree of formality required of her. She put her hand out, the way she would have done at any other job interview, and Omar's cousin shook it, examining her through narrowed eyes. Her hands and forearms were wrapped in matching winding lines, all part of an elaborate tattoo Jean couldn't make out.

She dropped Jean's hand and turned to Omar. "You hungry?" she asked him.

He nodded.

"There's still croissants from yesterday. Help yourself." Omar disappeared, turning on an overhead light that illuminated an immaculate, minimalist café. A neat row of empty vases lined a long zinc counter, and a series of skillfully photographed Mediterranean landscapes marched across the electric white walls.

"Wow," Jean said.

"Yeah, they spent a lot of money in here," Lu said, following Jean's gaze. "The restaurant is next door. A Michelin star and now they think they're the shit." She rolled her eyes. "They expanded over here because it was so busy. We make all the pastry for the restaurant, too."

Jean nodded and adjusted her posture, trying to project a sense of alertness that she did not possess.

"You have any experience?"

"Um, not really." Jean's eyes dropped to Lu's hands, almost mechanical in their neat clasp.

"That's okay," Lu said. "I actually prefer that. Working with these little shits who think they know everything makes me dizzy."

"You want a coffee, Jean?" Omar called.

"Yes please—just milk," she called back, suddenly aware of yelling so close to Lu's face. "Sorry," she murmured. Jean was conscious of her tallness, which made her hollering seem worse somehow.

Lu waved the apology away. "You start at two and end at six when we let in the morning shift. It's not rocket science. If you pay attention, you'll be fine."

Jean nodded and forced her eyes to open wider. The coffee would help, she thought.

"So, what happened at your last job? Omar said you quit?"

Jean couldn't tell her the truth. If she tried to explain, it would sound ridiculous and Lu would surely throw her out. Her boss had asked a few personal questions about her mom so she had to quit? She couldn't tell Lu that.

"I was an assistant," she said instead. "To a psychotherapist. She's older, losing her eyesight, you know, in her eighties, and…"

"She retired?"

"Something like that," Jean fibbed, relieved.

"Can I call her for a reference?" Lu asked.

Jean froze, but after a moment she nodded, continuously, as though nodding along to a song. Dr. Goldstein would give her a great reference. After all, she'd worked for her for a long time. Jean had started while she was still a student, before her academic life deteriorated. Dr. Goldstein was kind enough not to ask too many questions when Jean left school for good, her schedule opening up like miles of empty road. As long as Jean did her job well, Dr. Goldstein didn't pry.

But, when Dr. Goldstein showed a growing interest in her past, in her parents, it sent chills down her spine. Jean wasn't some patient—it wasn't Dr. Goldstein's, or anyone's, place to figure her out. Jean didn't want to be figured out at all.

So she did the responsible thing—gave two weeks' notice and trained her replacement, a grad student named Arpita, who sat all floppy, like a child. She had done everything right. Dr. Goldstein would never begrudge her a decent reference. Would she?

"I guess this is a big change for you." Lu leaned back and gave Jean one more appraising look.

Jean looked Lu in the eye, wishing hard that they were sitting down. "Nothing wrong with change."

Lu grinned and Jean felt herself, involuntarily, match the other woman's smile. It felt strange to smile for real. "Good answer. You're hired. Just don't be late. I fucking hate it when people are late. Go wash your hands and I'll get you started on the biscuits."

"What? Now?"

"Yes, of course now."

Two

Jean woke up and reached for her phone. It had died early in the morning, while she was learning how to pipe uniform eclairs. She winced at the time. It was already late afternoon, which meant she would barely have time to shower, eat something, and get to her opening shift at Red and Gold.

Her roommates, an overly polite couple who went to visit one or the other's parents in Long Island every weekend, were both at work. One, Molly, was a paralegal, and the other, Christine, worked as a medical assistant. They were neat and generally quiet, but most importantly, they left Jean alone. She desperately wanted to be able to have her share of the rent on time, so they would continue to leave her alone. Jean hobbled to the bathroom and turned on the shower. Her arms hurt from the bakery and her legs hurt from the bar—her bad hip ached from both shifts. She stood over the sink and swallowed a few Advil.

In the shower, she helped herself to some of Molly's deep conditioning treatment, just to stand under the hot water a little longer. She briskly towel dried her short hair and caught the glow of her phone signaling a missed call. There were a few missed calls from a number she didn't recognize, and, as dutifully as if she were still taking messages for Dr. Goldstein, Jean got a pen, prepared to make notes. She played the solitary voicemail tacked at the end of the flurry of calls.

"Oh, hi, Jean, sorry to bother you. It's Arpita. From Dr. Goldstein's office? Can you call me when you get this? It's not exactly urgent, but maybe a little bit—like medium urgent? Thanks so much, and really, really sorry to bother you."

Jean called back and left a voicemail on Arpita's cell phone. She probably should have tried Dr. Goldstein's office, or even Myra's home phone, but she was too tired to think about having to talk to her old boss, to pretend cheer and ease when she felt like she'd been run through a meat grinder. She dressed quickly and slung her bag over her shoulder. She wrapped an extralong scarf around her face, hoping that it would compensate for her inability to locate her winter coat.

The sun hung at peak gleam, beautiful, making the day as warm as it would get, casting a maximally flattering light across every building and face Jean passed. She stopped at the deli next door for a coffee and tinfoil-wrapped egg and cheese sandwich and caught the bus down Second Avenue. Gliding down the street in that perfect light made everything seem fine. Whatever this phase of her life was, Jean would get used to it. People could get used to anything—that was a fact she knew too well, all the way down to her screw- and plate-studded bones.

It was funny, Jean thought, the way people her age talked about where they came from—it was such a binary, either all fondness, like Molly and Christine, or a full blackout, like her. To stop herself from thinking about it more, she unwrapped her breakfast sandwich and devoured it, focusing only on her body, bite after bite, adding, not subtracting, to the person she had become in this enormous city.

Jean felt much better by the time she arrived at Red and Gold. A New Wave record twinkled down out of the speakers like confetti. The Advil and caffeine were working, and Jean was optimistic about starting a fresh shift at the bar.

"Oh hey! You must be the new girl," a voice called out from the dim back room.

"Yeah, I'm Jean," she answered, squinting to identify the source of the voice. A young man studded with piercings sat in a corner booth, counting out cash for the register.

"Just give me one second; I already fucked this up twice. Math is not my forte, man."

"Sure, sure—I'll just go set up."

Jean shucked off her jacket and scarf and stowed them away behind the bar with her bag. She started slicing lemons and limes into uniform wedges—her favorite part of the job. The small triumphs accumulated quickly, turning a just-okay day into a good one, almost by magic.

"Sorry about that," the young man said, approaching her on the other side of the bar, like a customer. "I'm Iggy."

"Nice to meet you." Jean gave him an efficient look, the kind she used to give Dr. Goldstein's patients, sorting them into two categories: trouble, or not. *Not*, she decided.

"You settling in okay?" he asked. He joined her behind the bar and stocked the register with the thrice-counted change.

"Sure," she said. "The last few nights have been great."

"A lot of Mitch, huh?"

"He's not so bad," Jean said.

"Thursdays can get a little wild—it's the weekend for all of the college kids, you know?"

"I know."

"You in school?" he asked.

Jean shook her head. "Not anymore."

"Where'd you go?"

"Doesn't matter—I didn't finish." Jean made an uneven cut and almost sliced into her thumb.

"Me neither," Iggy said. "Never had the temperament for it. It's a lot of time to do for a lot of debt. My parents wanted me to be a lawyer, but I was like 'sorry, man, I have to object,' you know?"

"Oh, I know." Jean nodded.

Iggy laughed. "What did your parents want you to be?"

"Gone," Jean said, tacking on another ubiquitous smile to soften her reply.

Iggy was right; Thursdays were wild. There was a fight, a group of underage kids Iggy had to eject, and an onslaught of vodka soda orders of medieval battalion proportions. Jean liked the frenetic tempo. There was no time to worry about being nice enough or striking the right tone; all she had to do was make ten thousand vodka sodas. When her right arm started to protest, Jean scooped ice with her left. She sank into the work, like she used to sink into running, and didn't even care that she couldn't slow down long enough for one of her fake smoke breaks.

Working with Iggy was different than working with Mitch. Jean understood, instantly, why a person would put someone like Iggy, and not someone like Mitch, on a shift where they served one million vodka sodas. Iggy was quiet and fast. Mitch's chattiness would have been a disaster on a Thursday night. Iggy was also tactful. He broke up the fight with ease and sent the underage kids on their way with unexpected kindness. By 1:00 a.m. her feelings about Iggy had tipped from "not trouble" to unadulterated fondness. Getting to know someone this way was so emotionally economical. Jean thought, for the first time, that maybe she was in the right place after all. Maybe the emergency job she had taken out of desperation was actually the perfect job for her.

Even though her shift was technically over, she agreed to stay a half an hour longer after a pleading look from Iggy for help with the last rush. She buzzed from the work, the cash in her pocket, and the celebratory shot she and Iggy had taken just before she left for the bakery. Jean realized how hungry she was and stopped for a slice of pizza on the way. She knocked on the bakery gate, wiping away the grease on her lips from her dinner-breakfast with the back of her hand.

Lu lifted the gate, her face set in a furious scowl. "Jean," she said coldly. "Want to explain why you're late? Didn't I say that was literally the only thing I give a shit about?"

"Oh, Lu, I'm really sorry. The bar was so busy, and I had to stay a little later. I'm so, so sorry—I'll stay later here, too," Jean stammered. Her heightened mood plummeted, like a bird shot out of the sky.

"You can't stay later. We open at six. You better hope you finish what we need to finish. If you don't, that's it. If you're late again, I'm sending you home for good. Understand?" Jean nodded, and Lu crossed her tattooed arms over her chest. "Everybody gets one, and this is your one." Her voice was flat and stern.

"Sorry," Jean murmured once more.

"Stop apologizing! Just come in and do your job." Lu stepped aside and let Jean through the gate.

Jean's night at the bakery was the exact inverse of her night at the bar—it was quiet, tense, and the feelings she had for Lu were not fond. Jean skipped her break, refusing even a trip to the bathroom, so furiously she concentrated on every single pain au chocolat. Jean raced through her tasks, completing each one more quickly than the last. She had always been good at making everything feel like a game, even if she was playing against herself. It was what Dr. Goldstein would call a coping mechanism. If you were playing against yourself, the only person you could disappoint was yourself.

"I'm not mad at you," Lu said, the first time she had spoken outside of a series of terse commands about flour and butter measurements. "I just have certain standards and I expect everyone to follow them."

"I understand," Jean said. The lights blazed overhead, bright as the sun.

"Look, it isn't an easy job, and I'm sure working at the bar isn't easy either. If it's too much, just tell me. No hard feelings, okay?" Lu slid a tray of bombolini into the deep fryer fragrant with oil, one at a time. Jean froze, momentarily mesmerized by the bronzing dough.

"It's not too much. I like working here," Jean said. "It's nice to have some quiet after the bar." She didn't add how badly she needed the money. "I'll figure it out. I won't be late again."

"I hope not," Lu said, lifting the sizzling doughnuts from the fryer and motioning for Jean to roll them through a soft drift of sugar. "I like working with you. You're fast and you don't talk too much."

"Thank you," Jean said, and an involuntary smile spilled across her face—not even the full force of her contrition could stop it.

"Oh, and I called your reference. Never got back to me—maybe she already packed her suitcases for Boca Raton."

Jean squelched a wave of unease and smiled. "Yeah, probably." Jean stayed quietly working until the morning coffee shift knocked on the gate.

Three

Jean's job at the bakery was calming in the same way her job at the bar was energizing. While there, she couldn't think about anything outside of work in any meaningful way, which, for Jean, was perfect. At Red and Gold and at the bakery, all she could think about were Red and Gold and the bakery. Jean was eternally present, with not a moment to spare to consider the past or the future. Even the exhaustion was fascinating. Jean loved learning something new that her body could do, identifying and surpassing the limits she had once believed were fixed.

On her first day off in over a week, Jean felt the opposite of relieved, relaxed, or restful. She made rent, and happily turned over her share to Molly and Christine. She even had enough left over to provide a small cash reserve in case she was late to the bakery again and got fired. She wished she was more certain that wouldn't happen so she could just buy a new coat. For the last few back-to-back shifts, Jean had taken a taxi from Red and Gold to Lu's, but she couldn't keep doing that. It was already adding up uncomfortably quickly. Maybe she could find a bike somewhere, or borrow one.

Molly and Christine were in Long Island for the weekend, and instead of enjoying her empty apartment, Jean felt the urgent need to escape it. To be out. She hauled her filthy clothes to the Dream Clean and deposited her first check from the bakery at her bank's branch in Union Square. She bought a pair of gloves at a pharmacy, lingering, inexplicably, in the dental hygiene aisle. All of those clinical minty greens and blues reminded her of hospital rooms and all of the other things she wanted to forget. Jean decided to get out of there and take a walk. She couldn't shake the feeling of being idle and unsettled.

When her phone buzzed in her jacket pocket, she almost believed she had willed the distraction into existence.

"Hello?" she answered, her relief immediate as a patch of shade on a hot day.

"Jean? It's Arpita."

"Oh, Arpita—hi! How are things going up there?"

"Things are fine… I think." Arpita paused, and Jean waited, not sure if she should interrupt. "It's just that, Dr. Goldstein, you know, seems a little…"

"A little what?" Jean stopped and huddled against the side of a Blockbuster Video. A fluffy black-and-white dog paused to sniff her feet and then walked on.

"A little off? But it's hard to tell if this is just how she is, or if something's wrong with her, you know? I thought I would just check in with you to make sure everything sounds normal."

"Okay." Jean pressed a finger into her other ear to eliminate some of the noise from the street.

"Jean? Are you there?"

"Yeah, I'm here—can you hear me?" Jean wandered a few steps down the block.

"I can now, yes. I said, do you think something's going on

with her son? Like something, I don't know, untoward?" An ambulance raced down the avenue and Jean waited to speak until it passed.

"Dr. Goldstein's son? Jeffrey?" Jean was confused, unsure whether she had heard Arpita correctly.

"Yes, him. Jeffrey."

"I mean, I don't really know. I only met him a couple of times over the years." Jean had spoken to Jeffrey on the phone more often than in person, and he'd always seemed like somebody's regular, painfully square, middle-aged son.

"Only a couple of times? Really." Arpita's tone slanted toward suspicious.

"Why? What's going on?"

"He just, well, he seems to be around a lot."

"Is he visiting his mom?" Jean thought about the last time Jeffrey had been to New York. It was a long weekend, and he had taken Dr. Goldstein to the opera.

"I think so."

"What's wrong with that?"

"I don't know how to put this delicately, but he seems kind of creepy to me." Arpita lowered her voice.

"Creepy how? Did he say something to you?" Jeffrey had never seemed like an obvious racist, but 9/11 had revealed the worst in people. "Oh God, did he do something?" A bus rumbled by.

"No, no, no, not creepy with me. More like creepy with Dr. Goldstein."

"What do you mean?"

Jean felt herself moving along the street in search of a quieter place, walking into a mostly vacant park.

"He just seems really pushy."

"You mean like physically pushy? Like elder abuse?"

"No, more just emotionally aggressive." Suddenly, Arpita

sounded restrained, as though someone were in the room with her.

"Honestly, I don't think there's anything to be done about that. I mean, he's her son, right? And he'll go home eventually. Right?"

Arpita sighed. "Okay, I guess that's true. Sorry to bother you—thanks for talking this out with me."

"Sure, no problem—call me anytime. Take care." Jean hung up feeling stranger than before. The wind picked up and she ducked into a Dunkin' Donuts for shelter. She bought a coffee drink exploding with whipped topping and sipped from it as she walked. Jean tried to push back her restlessness. She imagined sealing it away into the sidewalk with every step. Her dissatisfaction didn't vanish, no matter how hard she stamped. The coffee grew cold quickly, and she threw it in a nearby garbage can. She looked up and saw that her legs had transported her back to Red and Gold. Jean jammed her frozen hands into her pockets. The cartoon turkey taped to the door stared her straight in the eye—a dare. She walked in, for the first time, as a customer.

It was still early and the bar was mostly empty, apart from Mitch, Iggy, and a mismatched couple at a table in the back. Jean had noticed them before—the woman was tiny and sharp-eyed. She seemed sober no matter how much she was served, but her companion was epically sloppy. A faller-downer, Mitch called him.

"Hey! Jean Jeanie!" Mitch greeted her with a two-armed, exuberant air traffic controller's wave. She ducked her head, a little shy to be on the other side of the bar, and sat down next to Iggy. "Can't stay away either, huh?"

"Hey, man, I'm just picking up my tips!" Iggy toasted the air with a dented can of Tecate.

"Just stopping by." Jean shifted a little, glad she hadn't removed her jacket and scarf. She could feel her face reddening. She really should have thought this through a little more.

"You want a drink?" Mitch said, all gentle and perceptive.

"Yeah, sure whatever."

The faller-downer shuffled to the jukebox in the corner and Mitch winced, setting a Tecate in front of her. Glenn Danzig screeched out of the speakers, and Mitch caught Jean's eye as he shook his head. "My man is keeping his feet! It's going to be a good night." Jean smiled and shuddered from her first sip of the too-cold beer. She was still thawing from her walk down Second Avenue.

"You know, Faller Downer is a former nine-to-fiver, like you."

"Oh yeah?" Jean loosened the scarf around her neck.

"He was a finance guy, if you can believe it," Mitch continued, staring at the customer's unsteady walk back to his companion. "Walked away from it all. Pulled the plug after 9/11. Were you in the city? For that?" Mitch turned to Jean.

She only nodded—Jean wished everyone would shut up about it. She had carefully packed away the horror from that day and couldn't understand the people that kept unwrapping and comparing their own, similar horrors.

"What are you up to tonight?" Jean asked Iggy, talking too fast.

"I know the doorman at Transmission. You want to come? A lot of my friends will be there." Iggy looked down at his drink while he spoke.

"What's Transmission?" Jean asked, reaching for her beer.

"What? Jean Jeanie's never been to Transmission? You're kidding. It's a party they have every week—you have such a bad haircut, I figured you were one of those Transmission kids. You know, it's part of the whole look over there."

"Ouch." Jean put her hand to her hair, feeling around the shape of her shorn head. "I did this myself—do you know how hard it is to cut the back?"

"No offense!" Mitch said, holding his hands in the air. "It's cool, really."

"Sure it is." Jean smiled, turning back toward Iggy. The half a beer on her empty stomach produced a welcome glow of confidence, and Jean beamed that effervescent feeling straight at Iggy. "Okay. Let's go."

Another beer and two slices of pizza later, Jean and Iggy strode back up Second Avenue against the gusting wind. "It's the remnants of Nicole," Iggy said.

"Who?"

"The tropical storm."

"Oh, right." Jean walked quickly, pushing forward through the gale. "Are you from somewhere with lots of hurricanes?"

"Not really. I just like weather." They crossed the street, suddenly divided by a clot of tipsy college kids. As they neared Union Square, the streets grew denser and louder. People desperately wielded their umbrellas, and Jean edged closer to Iggy.

"Why do you like the weather?" Jean winced as a slap of rain smacked across her cheek.

Iggy cracked a smile. "It's stupid, but I like that nobody really knows what's going to happen. It's always changing—kind of the only reliable adventure you can get as an adult. And we're here, before I say any more embarrassing shit." He stepped into a narrow doorway and ran up a flight of stairs, motioning for her to follow. Iggy paused on the landing where a line had gathered and looked Jean in the eye. "I'm really glad you came tonight."

"Me too." Jean could feel the music through her feet on the stairs and the hum of voices in the air. Iggy pushed a path to the entrance, and shook hands with the doorman, waving Jean through.

Iggy nodded at the bartender over the heads of the customers waiting to order. The bartender, a dead ringer for Jennifer Lopez, winked in friendly acknowledgment. "Babe," he called out over the music. "This is my friend." When he pointed at

Jean, she felt a great jolt of surprise. "Take care of her." The bartender barely glanced at her and vaguely nodded. Jean jammed herself into the free space, leaning against the bar.

"I'm going to see if my friends are here yet—get a drink and come meet us, okay?"

Jean nodded, grateful for the opportunity to collect herself and settle into the night. The bar was full, much fuller than Red and Gold even on her busiest shifts—the space was also much, much larger. In this bar, people came to dance.

Girls in cocktail dresses and boys in skinny ties flung themselves toward and away from each other. Kids in artfully cut up T-shirts strutted through the crowd, while the somber DJs looked on from a dim corner. The music was elastic and sunny—mostly British, all of it great for dancing. Jennifer Lopez set a shot in front of her with an efficiency that Jean coveted. Jean watched the room turn to liquid around her; people on the dance floor, people at the bar, people in line for the bathroom, people pressed up against each other and the wall—they all transformed into a soft whorl of energy.

When she looked at them like that, it was easy to dive in. Jean pushed away from her spot at the bar and dove. She had never been a dancer, but something about the night and the music, and her nocturnal new life, made it easy. She wasn't self-conscious, thanks to all of the drinks; instead, she was filled with a ferocious delight. The arms of that galaxy of dancers opened up for her, and the way her body moved within that embrace surprised her. Jean had rarely felt so good. It made her a little sad to think about just how rarely. Maybe it was time to go home, she thought. But, within that small dip in her mood, someone grabbed hold of her shoulder.

"Hey, there you are!" Iggy hollered.

Jean responded with a relieved smile and a wave.

"Let's get another drink," he said, hooking his elbow into

hers and pulling her out of the crowd. "Are you sure you haven't been here before?"

"First time," Jean said. She suddenly felt where the sweat had erupted over her body and fanned at her face.

"What do you want?"

"Whatever."

Iggy called their order over an oblivious couple making out against the bar. "Here, come meet my friends." He pressed a cold glass into her hand—a vodka soda.

"Funny," she said.

Iggy led her through a narrow corridor and into a little side room that opened onto it. It was just big enough for a booth where Iggy's friends were gathered. There couldn't have been more than five or six, but Jean was overwhelmed by their volume.

"Guys, this is my friend Jean. She works with me at Red and Gold."

A cavernous *Ahh* opened around her as the friends made sense of her among them, and, for the second time that night, Jean dove into the opening they made for her. Iggy scooted her into the booth, where she was crushed shoulder to shoulder with an Asian girl with bobbed dark hair. A white, freckly redhead with long blunt bangs regarded her from across the table, twisting the straw from her drink into a ragged, red plastic heart.

"It's Jean, right?" the girl with the bob asked.

"Right." She took a long sip of her watery vodka soda.

"Cool—very old-fashioned. Are you named after somebody?"

"Nope," Jean lied. "What about you?"

"Claire." The girl stuck her hand out in a comically abbreviated way, like a raptor, thanks to their close quarters. "Not named after anyone either. How long have you been in the city?"

"A few years," Jean said, although she knew exactly how many: eight.

"Where from?"

"Pennsylvania. Nowhere interesting," she added quickly. Jean was used to stringing up these deterrents in all of her first conversations with people.

"Not like Luke over there." Claire smiled in the direction of a young man staring over at them from across the table. "He's from the city, born and raised!"

"Wow," Jean said, planting her gaze directly into her drink to avoid the carnivorous stare of born and raised in the city Luke. Jean steadied herself against the obvious currents of friendship at the table. She felt an unsettling lurch over being the odd one out—she didn't often feel lonely, but something about the booth and the comfortable companionship with Iggy had changed her equilibrium.

"Jean," Iggy shouted. "Will you please tell Claire she can't audition for the Bad Girls Club?"

"What's the Bad Girls Club?" Jean shifted to face Claire.

Claire rolled her eyes. "Jesus Christ, Iggy! It's just a job." She lowered her voice, dipping into confiding tones as she spoke to just Jean. "It's a reality show—I'm an actress. It's shitty, but this is the kind of work that's out there. I just want to audition for a role that isn't a geisha or a dry cleaner."

"If you do it, you'll always regret it, C." Iggy banged his hand on the table like a gavel and Jean jolted in her seat.

"Don't get me started on the stupid shit you've done, Iggy." Claire threw a discarded lime wedge across the table in his direction.

"Listen, we've all done things we regret." The redhead with the heavy bangs stared directly at Jean when she said it. Jean looked around the table, certain there was something she had missed.

"I need the bathroom. Sorry." Claire winced sympathetically at her and pointed toward the corridor.

"I'll go with you," the girl with the bangs said. They jostled out of the booth and soon Jean was sandwiched between Luke and Iggy. Iggy's attention was turned away, absorbed in conversation with an androgynous friend wearing heavy plastic-rimmed glasses.

"So, do you like working at Red and Gold?" Luke asked. He moved a little away from her on the bench instead of a little closer, which immediately made Jean like him better.

"So far, so good," she said, offering a thin smile over the rim of her glass. "What about you? How do you know Iggy?"

"We're in a band together."

"Oh yeah? I didn't know Iggy was in a band."

"Yeah, Ig is great. He's been playing the guitar since he could walk, practically."

"What do you play in the band?"

"I'm the singer," he said, like it was a joke. Jean felt an involuntary smile bloom across her face.

"I know, right? You want to go dance?" He nervously rearranged his faux hawk in the dull gleam of the framed Siouxsie and the Banshees poster hanging over them.

"Sure," she said, with a shrug. She set her drained glass on the table and leapt over Iggy without asking him to get up, an acrobatic move that revealed her athletic past.

"Whoa, you're really tall!" Luke said, once he'd extracted himself from the booth. Jean looked down at his voluminous, expensive haircut from a few inches. "Amazing," he said, like a person eating a plum for the first time, half carnal, half sweet. Despite her better judgment, Jean liked the way he said it.

"Let's go." She led them back out to the dance floor.

Jean's night grew blurrier and blurrier the more she danced. She forgot about her jacket, shoved into the booth with Iggy's friends, all strangers to her. She forgot about her wallet and keys. Jennifer Lopez kept serving her shots. When last call murmured through the crowd like a game of telephone, she and Luke dodged the rush of dancers securing one more for the road and returned to find Iggy and most of his friends gone. Only the redhead and Claire remained, talking close and holding hands on the table.

"Hey, where'd everybody go?" Luke asked.

"You know—everywhere, home—" The redhead let her sentence hang in the air between them. "Not the *long way.*"

"Oh, right," Luke said knowingly. "How many days is that this week? Four? That's too much." He shook his head in Claire's direction.

"Don't look at me! I didn't go with them," she said. "Ig says that's where he gets his best song ideas." Claire shifted her gaze to Jean. "Looks like you two are having fun."

Jean looked down and noticed that she and Luke were holding hands. She tried to let go, hoping that their fingers would organically detach, but Luke's grip remained sure and confident. *Uh-oh*, Jean thought.

"What's the long way?" she asked. She felt all of their attention at once.

"Oh, you know," Claire said, defying physics by rolling her eyes while keeping her gaze locked on Jean.

"Should we get one more drink?" Luke asked them.

"Why not?" The two girls stood up, and Claire handed Jean her jacket. Jean felt suddenly chilled and pulled her arms into the sleeves, finally detaching from Luke.

"I should probably go," she said, then remembered she should thank the bartender. "Actually, there's somebody I need to find." Luke's disappointment burned like a flashlight in the dark.

"Just hang out for one more," Claire said, and pulled her toward the bar where a group of kids in trucker hats congregated, tripping over their feet.

"So," the bartender said. "You have fun?"

"So far so good—thanks for everything." Jean was aware of scraping her words together into some approximation of steadiness. It felt amazing to be so uncontained. She staggered under the freedom of all of that space. She dug in her jacket pocket and set a now-damp twenty-dollar bill on the bar for Jennifer Lopez. "I really appreciate it," she told her, sincerely.

"Anytime. You want another?" the bartender asked.

"No thanks. I have to go." She shook her head and mussed her hair a little, catching a glimpse of herself in the mirror behind the bar.

"Can I walk you?" Luke asked. "Do you live far from here?"

"Not too far." She waved to the bartender, and the two girls, and let Luke follow her out. He was so small and harmless, she thought—why not? She felt him come up close but jammed her hands in her pockets so he couldn't grab one again. She didn't want this to get too cute.

"So, where is your place?" Luke asked. She liked how fast he had to walk to keep up with her and felt a flash of heat.

"A few blocks up. Where do *you* live?"

"Brooklyn."

Not perfect—she was tired and didn't particularly want to go to Brooklyn. But it had been such a long time since she'd gone home with someone. And Luke seemed particularly benign.

"Okay, let's go. To Brooklyn," she said. Luke leaned in and stood on tiptoe to kiss her.

Jean lost some of her courage in the cab on the way over the bridge—the heat in the back was broken, and shivering, she curled into herself beneath the seatbelt's restraint. She had time to regret not already being at home in her bed with a glass of water. But when they tumbled out of the taxi and Luke reached for her, she felt okay, even good again. She opened her arms and half dipped him like a starlet in a black-and-white movie. They fumbled down the street and into his dark apartment.

The fucking was twinkly, blurry, easy, and just right.

Four

When Jean woke up, her jaw was clenched in terror. Nothing felt right—the smell, the light, the temperature—everything was distorted. It was a sweaty, unpleasant realization. She had stayed out all night and gone home with a stranger. An incongruous feeling of triumph stirred in Jean's chest. The realization that she was capable of something so out of the ordinary softened her sudden, jolting return to consciousness.

Luke lay beside her, still asleep, still shrunkenly handsome. Her mouth was dry, and a wave of nausea crashed over her as she sat up to look for her pants. Luke made a sound she was embarrassed to hear—half moan, half whine.

"Where are you going?" he asked.

"I have to go to work." Jean found her pants and slipped them on, inspecting the room quickly as she hunted for her jacket. The floors were new, the heat was central, and the windows were huge—the opposite of her apartment.

"You have to work right now?"

"I mean, I have to take a shower and change."

"Take a shower here." He reached up with both arms like a reanimated corpse in a zombie movie. She couldn't tell if he was stretching or supplicating.

"I like having my own shampoo and everything." Jean knew she was talking too fast, a bad habit when she was nervous, but she was suddenly desperate to be outside, in the cold. "Where's the train over here? Where even are we?" She added the "we" to be kind. She could see in the morning light, thanks to her many hours of training in Dr. Goldstein's office, exactly the kind of person Luke was. She remembered the night in his bed with bracing clarity—it had been fun and messy with lots of laughing. In her quick attempt at emotional calculus, Jean arrived at a sum that Luke was genuinely positive.

"The L. Two blocks," Luke muttered and flopped back into his pillow.

"It was really great meeting you," Jean said, and added an affectionate hair tousle to the top of his head.

"Unexpected but great, yes."

Jean sat on an original Eames chair in the corner strewn with clothes to tie on her boots. "See you around?" She waved at his prone form.

"Definitely." He flipped like a hungover pancake and flashed her a sleepy smile.

The train ride back was filled with late, anxious commuters. Jean felt invisible, like an enchantment had been cast over her. Their eyes skipped over her slouched, disheveled form, latching onto the brightly lit Dr. Zizmor ads or the books they held close to their bodies. The man next to her noisily slurped a cappuccino with the lid off. She was desperate for a coffee of her own. Her head hurt more in the artificial light of the train car than it had outside. She climbed out of the subway station only a few blocks from her apartment. She knew Molly and Christine could still be home, getting ready for work, so she stopped in the bagel place on the corner. She sat by herself for a luxurious half hour drinking a milky sweet coffee and eating a soft sesame bagel with cream cheese, fresh from the oven. Jean felt the gaze of an older blond woman seated in the corner, but tried to ignore it. She was certain that she looked even more disheveled than she felt.

Back at her now-empty apartment she discovered a note on the counter beside the coffee maker. Molly's exquisite handwriting swooned off the page.

J—Sorry we missed you last night/this morning.
My mom wants to know if you want to come over
for Thanksgiving. You can stay for just dinner
or the whole weekend.
Think about it and let me know.

Jean crumpled up the note and threw it in the bathroom garbage can. Molly's mother had extended an invitation to Thanksgiving for the last two years that Jean had been roommates with her daughter. Jean had declined both invitations, as surely as she would decline this one. Jean planned to celebrate Thanksgiving like she celebrated every other holiday, with a good book and a two-packet hot chocolate. It had become her thing—festive in its own private way. Any family gathering on a holiday was a woozy fun house version of the painful holidays she had endured as a child, and she refused to put herself in front of a mirror like that again.

She opened her ancient laptop and discovered an email from Dr. Goldstein. Jean clicked it open.

Dear Jean,
I hope this finds you well. I've been meaning to call you
to check in, but Jeffrey has been visiting and it's been

quite busy here. I haven't had many spare moments. I
wanted to ask if you remembered seeing my patient
files from 1968–1978. It seems as though they've gone
missing and Arpita isn't sure where to look.

On another note, I would love to hear your voice.
Please do call when you can. It's been very difficult.
Yours,
Myra

Jean shivered under the endearments embedded in the text.
She sent a swift reply with her guess about the missing files' location, and closed with a promise to call, which she didn't in-
tend to honor. She had hoped that Dr. Goldstein would be the
type to be able to move on. Boundaries! She was a therapist;
she should know. Jean closed her laptop a little too forcefully
and tried to take a nap.

Later that night at work, Jean waited for Iggy to come in. He
was covering Mitch's shift, but hadn't shown up. It was Monday, so Jean mostly stood around, just waiting to close so she
could get to the bakery on time. The few customers she served
sat quietly and drank slowly. One of the regulars, a middle-aged
man with an accent she couldn't identify, sometimes came in
with Olympia Dukakis—the only excitement Jean could expect.

Iggy made a theatrical entrance, almost two hours late. "Well,
well, well," he said, with a wide smile. "I heard you were up to
no good last night."

Jean covered her face with her hands. "Oh my God! What
about you? Why did you desert me?"

Iggy rested an open palm over his heart. "What? You were
the deserter, man."

"You left me with your friends and just took off."

"Um, excuse me, I very much did not. I found you said bye,
etcetera, but you were, you know, busy." Iggy pressed together

the tips of his index fingers in the universal sign for smooching and Jean blushed. He walked around the bar and grabbed his own beer, but cracked it open only when he was seated on the other side, like a proper customer.

"You really said bye?" Jean's stomach twisted. Not remembering something seemed as absurd to her as growing gills and breathing under water. "Are you sure?"

"Oh, I'm very sure. So, you and Luke, huh?"

"Stop it!" Jean threw a cocktail straw at him. "He's very sweet, but it was absolutely a one-time thing."

"Poor Luke. A once-in-a-lifetime thing for him."

"I'm sure Luke does okay."

"I don't think he's going to forget it—not the way he was talking about you today at band practice…"

"Ew, seriously stop! I'm begging you."

"I'm just saying, Jean, maybe give him another chance?"

Jean flicked another straw over the bar. "I see you're taking the night off, then?"

"Ow! My eye!" He squinted around the mostly vacant bar with one eye closed. "I think you've got it under control, killer. You really want to split these tips?"

"I guess not," Jean grumbled.

"But seriously, what happened last night?"

"Nothing—you're such an old gossip."

"Old? I'm only twenty-seven."

Jean's mind spun acrobatically trying to redirect their conversation, desperate to talk about anything else. "Wait a minute," she said, struck by a bolt of inspiration. "You didn't tell me before that you were in a band."

"What? Oh yeah. I'm in two bands."

"Okay, so even more information you've been hiding. Tell me about these two bands." Jean was back in comfortable territory, much happier to be listening than to be explaining anything about herself. As Blondie crooned overhead and Iggy talked, Jean started to relax.

"We're playing on Sunday—you should come. It's your day off, right?"

"Sure, I'll come. Where is it?"

"Ludlow Lounge, at eleven."

"P.m.?"

"Um, yes p.m. Who's the old grandma now? Oh, I realized last night I don't have your number." Jean hated giving out her number; the fewer people who could be in touch with her the better. But, since technically Iggy was her co-worker, she felt a professional obligation to share it. She typed it into his boxy maroon Nokia, thinking about maybe replacing the last digit with a different one. She glanced at the tiny digital time.

"Shit, I'm going to be so late again," she said.

"For the bakery? Do you go in every night?"

She nodded. "Pretty much, except for Sundays. I can't keep taking cabs over there, but I can't be late. Maybe I can try closing a little early?" she suggested weakly. "Just tonight—I mean, it's Monday. No one would really care, would they?"

Iggy's face was careful, somber. "Probably not—but that only helps you out tonight." He paused, alternately staring intently at her and at his clasped hands on the bar. "This might be a stupid question, but have you heard of shortcuts?"

"What, like the movie?" she asked, recalling a film class from another lifetime.

Iggy shook his head. "No, no, no, like *shortcuts*." He lowered his voice, although it made no difference in the mostly empty bar.

"*No,*" she replied, replicating his tone, thinking it was some kind of joke.

"Seriously?" he said. "You don't know?" He mumbled something to himself. "I mean, I thought everybody knew about shortcuts."

Jean shook her head, sinking into that familiar feeling of being left out, a kid outside a closed door. She winced a little at the pain this still caused her.

"Hey," said Iggy, gently. "I didn't mean it like that. You're a smart cookie. It seems like something you would know about. Something you especially would *really, really* know about." He stared at her meaningfully, as though he was waiting for her to confess she'd just been messing with him.

"Well, I don't."

"Huh. If you don't already know, you're going to think I lost my mind."

"What do you mean?"

"It's like these doors." Iggy paused, his face contorted in confusion. "You really don't know?"

"Jesus, *no*, I don't!"

"Shh," he said.

"What, is it like, illegal?" It was probably drugs, she thought.

"I mean, kind of." Iggy sighed and looked up at the ceiling as he spoke, as though he were embarrassed. "There are these doors. All over the city."

"Yes, there are lots of doors."

"Shh, my God." He scanned the near-empty bar.

"I thought you said everybody knew about this." Jean yawned and shook herself a little.

"I mean, I thought *you* did. Cool people, not everybody."

It was definitely drugs, then, Jean thought. She shot herself a lukewarm Coke from the soda gun and swallowed it quickly, hoping the sugar and caffeine would get her to the next shift at Lu's.

"So, there are these doors all over the city, and if you go to the right one, it takes you to a totally different place. Like chutes and ladders."

"*What?*" Jean leaned forward and inspected Iggy's face to check the size of his pupils.

"Like secret passages."

"Okay," she said slowly.

"I'm just saying, there's one kind of close to here that you could definitely use to get to your other job on time."

"Sure there is," she said, with a slow smile.

"There is!" Iggy barked out an uncomfortable laugh. "Look, I'll take you over tonight, if you don't believe me." He drew a long sip of his beer. Jean regarded him closely. Was he some kind of serial killer who would knock her unconscious and dismember her in a secluded alley? She didn't think so, but she also didn't think he was particularly stable—he seemed so genuinely convinced about what he had told her. She looked for the cues she used in Dr. Goldstein's office whenever one of the patients arrived "Emotionally Elevated" to decide if they were dangerous or not. He squirmed a little under her inspection. The strange explanation had cost him something, something like admitting a crush. He looked shucked and vulnerable. She didn't really know Iggy all that well, but she believed he posed no danger to her.

"Okay, let's check it out," she finally said.

"Yeah?" He stood, pulling a cigarette from the splayed open pack in front of him, and smiled as he put it to his lips. "You won't be sorry."

Five

Jean closed a little early, without guilt. She didn't want to be late for the bakery in case Iggy was playing some practical joke on her, the newcomer, which—as she thought about it more—seemed to be most plausibly what was going on. Iggy pulled down the gate to Red and Gold, and she padlocked it shut, her fingertips already feeling the sting of the early winter temperature. She really, really needed to get a coat.

"So? Which way?" she asked.

Iggy lit another cigarette and offered her one, too. She shook her head. "Seriously, if this isn't real, I can't be late."

Iggy was more open now, after all of the beers inside. Jean noticed this in everyone she served, how they all became sharper, more readable versions of themselves. He gave her a strange, intense look—stripped of sexual interest, but full of some other, quizzical intensity. Like looking at a pressed botanical sample under glass. "I'm not supposed to do this. You're just so nice, and I really wanted to help you out."

"What do you mean, 'not supposed to'?"

"It's all supposed to be, like, hush–hush, man."

"Look, if you're having qualms, I can just take the train to the bakery. It's not a big deal." Jean was mostly relieved to have a loophole out of the prank, but couldn't deny her slight dis-appointment over missing a potentially extraordinary experi-ence, no matter how unlikely. She also thought that if Iggy didn't make up his mind soon, she was going to be late.

"No, no, no—I'm not having qualms, man." Iggy's gaze darted up and down the empty street. "This way." He led her around the corner to a neon-lit twenty-four-hour diner in be-tween a laundromat and a closed Chinese restaurant. He held the door open for her and Jean allowed herself a moment of re-lief in the surprisingly bustling, humid dining room. Her fro-zen fingers relaxed at her sides as she took in the strange crowd hunched over plates of fries and cups of coffee. Most of them were the types she expected to see out and about in the middle of the night, but some weren't. An elderly couple sat opposite one another, their hands clutched across the table. They looked alike—almost like siblings, but Jean couldn't tell if it was just their matching hairstyles and similar clothes.

Another woman caught her eye at a table in a corner—slightly beyond middle age in a shoulder-padded jacket with an intense perm, the kind you saw sometimes in a rural Pennsylvania gro-cery store, but almost never in the East Village.

"Wow, they're really busy," Jean said.

"Yeah," Iggy replied, chewing on a fingernail. "You want anything?"

Jean shook her head, not sure what she was supposed to say. Iggy nodded toward the bathrooms and she followed close be-hind. He stood in the corridor in front of a door marked with a chipped cherry-red Employees Only sign.

"Stay close to me, okay?"

"Okay."

"Actually, maybe you should hold my hand," he murmured.

"Really?" Jean infused her tone with a stab of humor.

"Not like that, God."

"Ouch," she replied.

He laughed and reached for her, weaving their fingers together. He closed his eyes and pushed open the Employees Only door. Jean didn't have time to be surprised or to ask anything else. Iggy clicked the door shut behind them, and when the door closed, something changed. The dim pressed in all around her as they walked no more than five steps forward. The darkness had a weight, heavy, almost like walking in a swimming pool. It wasn't unpleasant. Jean's heart raced the way it used to when she ran sprints—that bursting, leaping feeling burned through her.

One moment they were in that bright hallway that smelled of burnt oil and the next minute they were in a cramped, smoky supply closet. Piles of paper and a small safe were lined up on an empty shelf. The other shelves that surrounded them were crowded with cleaning products and toilet paper. Jean gasped and covered her mouth with her free hand. Her breath stuttered in her lungs.

"What was that?"

"Shortcut," Iggy replied with a wide, satisfied smile.

"No, really, what the hell just happened?" Jean's once cold hands were sweaty and trembling.

"Honestly, I'm not really sure how it works, but here. See for yourself." Iggy opened the door from the makeshift office onto a hallway almost identical to the diner's they had just left. But, in the new hallway there was a long crowded line by the bathrooms. A girl leaning against the wall smirked at Jean and Iggy as they emerged from the closet hand in hand.

"Couldn't wait, huh?"

Iggy lifted his shoulders in a charming shrug and Jean blushed.

They squeezed past the rest of the line and Jean saw that they were in another bar—this one much busier than Red and Gold. The White Stripes pounded out of the speakers, and Jean was sure she could smell a fog machine, even if she couldn't see any fog.

"Do you feel okay?" Iggy asked.

"Define okay." Jean leaned against him, staggering under the strangeness of what they'd just done.

Iggy laughed. "I mean physically okay—like you don't have a headache or are going to pass out, or puke or anything like that?"

Jean shook her head. "Why? Will I?"

"I don't know. Treats everybody a little differently. Do you want a drink? You might actually have time for one before work." He pulled his phone out of his back pocket to check the time.

"What?" Jean felt dizzy. Maybe she *would* pass out—or maybe it was just the White Stripes and the fog machine.

"You needed to get to the bakery, right? It's across the street."

"What?" Jean put her palm to her forehead to check for a fever.

"I know, right? This is some really wild shit, man," Iggy said. Glee rippled across his face as he drew her toward the bar, their hands still attached. Jean drifted after him, sifting through each of the memories that preceded this moment—the diner, the closet, the dark walk, the office, the bathroom line, the fog machine, this. The moments didn't seem to flow sequentially. Instead, they were spliced together, blurred and incongruous.

"Ig, you didn't," the woman behind the bar accused. Jean looked up, startled, like a person just pinched. It was Claire, Iggy's actress friend from the night before.

"What? I'm helping Jean out," he said, appearing genuinely stung.

"You can't keep doing this to impress girls," Claire said, her voice sharp.

"I'm not! Jean's not impressed at all—look at her!"

Jean untwisted her fingers from Iggy's and held on to the edge of the bar, afraid she might fall, but also afraid the bar might disappear. It was a consuming vertiginous feeling; she kept her eyes on Claire's face, waiting for it to dissolve in front of her.

"Jesus Christ." Claire rolled her eyes and pushed a glass of water in front of Jean. "Here, drink that really fast. You'll feel better in a second."

Jean stared at the water, and the way her hand looped around it. The glass felt solid beneath her fingers, and as she drank, the ice clinked against her teeth. All of it was real if she was real. The water felt painfully cold going down her throat, but Claire was right—she did feel better.

"I have to go to work. Right?" Jean looked over at Iggy, a little dizzy.

"Do you want me to walk you over?" Iggy asked, setting another glass of water in front of her.

"No, I think I'll be okay. What just happened?"

"You seem fine to me. Just try not to think about it too much." Iggy smiled kindly.

Claire snorted. "What, you're a doctor now, Ignacio?" Claire leveled an intense stare at Jean. "Be careful tonight."

"Don't scare her, man." Iggy gave Jean a hearty slap on the back and turned her toward the door. "You sure you don't want me to walk you?"

Jean shook her head and wandered toward the exit and the doorman slumped against the wall. He nodded at her as she pushed her way out, dazed, into the street. The bakery gate was unlocked. She opened it halfway, with a rusty shudder, and ducked underneath.

Inside the lights blazed bright and Mary J. Blige played in the café's expensive sound system. Lu's face shone, too, as she took in Jean's arrival. "Well, well, well! You're early—nice."

"Yeah," Jean said slowly, unwinding her scarf from her throat.

She washed her hands and watched the water run over her skin, blurring the outline of her body. Had she dreamed that strange transit? Had she hallucinated the heaviness of the air inside of that closet—had she hallucinated the diner? She held a dripping hand up to her face, examining it closely; was she having an incredibly vivid dream?

"Hey," Lu said. "You alright?"

Jean shook her head and clenched her hands into fists to control their trembling. "Yeah, I'm fine. Just a weird night at the bar."

Lu looked up with a sympathetic nod. "Do you want a coffee?"

"Sure, thanks." She pressed her lips into a tight smile and tied on a clean apron.

"You know, this kind of work can be a shock," Lu said carefully. She set a paper cup beside Jean and then cracked a parade of eggs into the belly of the kitchen's giant mixer. "Especially if you're changing careers." She flicked an empty shell into the garbage beside her.

"Career is a very generous word." Jean weighed out flour from an enormous tub in the storage room.

"What about your last job?" Lu had to raise her voice over the insistent motor of the mixer.

Jean snorted. "Just because I worked in an office for a famous doctor doesn't mean I had a career. I've basically just been fucking around and trying to keep myself alive." A familiar hitch of failure bloomed in her chest. Sometimes the life she had been given felt like a waste. The only time she'd ever made a move was out of fear—a contortion, not a thoughtful step forward. Jean felt temporarily electrocuted by this slipped admission— what was she doing, sharing personal revelations with someone who was, essentially, a stranger? It was wildly unlike her.

"Famous how?" Lu hollered over the mixer.

"What?"

"You said the doctor was famous—I'm just curious. How does a psychiatrist get famous? Like Dr. Drew or something?"

Jean paused, not sure how to answer. She wasn't sure if she could answer at all, worried that her every thought would pour onto the floor like spilled batter if she opened her mouth. In her prime, Dr. Goldstein was the most respected and sought-after family therapist in the city. Everyone thought she would retire when she began to lose her sight, but she kept working. People came from all over the world to see her, just for an hour. She still treated patients regularly, with great care. Jean had been hired to help with her practice, to read to her, and type her dictated notes. Dr. Goldstein had voice-recording software on her ancient desktop, but didn't like the inconsistent results. Too many technical terms confused the machine, she said.

"She kind of invented therapy where the whole family is in sessions together."

"Huh. Seems like a weird thing to have to invent. People didn't already do that?"

"Not when Dr. Goldstein was starting out." Jean shrugged and took a long sip from the mercifully warm cup beside her. "That was, like, sixty years ago. What about you? Have you always wanted to be a chef?" she asked quickly, hoping Lu would take the hint and change the subject.

Lu switched the mixer off, so that Jean's last few words hung there, too loud, in the stainless steel kitchen. "I don't know about *chef*." Lu's cheeks pinked a little—the flattery had absolutely been deliberate, and Jean was pleased to see that it had produced the desired result. It was the oldest trick in the book; if you wanted somebody to stop asking about you, just ask about them. A subtle compliment thrown in only sped things along.

"I was in the military when I was really young. It's an easy jump from the service to kitchens."

"Oh yeah?" Jean turned a spotlight of genuine interest on this new piece of information about her co-worker and boss. "What was that like, being in the military?"

"Wow." Lu laughed. "Exactly what you might think. Being a woman in those places, well, it's exactly what you might think." Lu's voice grew tighter, the repetition of phrase almost like a talisman against further explanation. Jean felt a twist of guilt about provoking any bad feeling in Lu; Jean didn't like prodding anyone in this way.

"I can see what drew you to working in a kitchen," Jean said, trying to redirect their conversation onto a softer track. "It's nice to focus."

"Exactly." Lu sighed. "If you mess up, it's easy to know why. And it's easy to fix. Usually."

"That must be so comforting." Jean nodded, slowly sieving the flour she had measured into the mixer, watching it drift into the golden pool of beaten eggs.

"I'm really glad Omar brought you in," Lu said kindly.

"Me too."

"And I'm really glad you've been on time so I don't have to fire you!" Lu said with a giggle. "I mean, especially with your old job out of the picture."

"What do you mean?"

"I called that doctor again to get your reference and nobody picked up. Maybe she really did retire to Puerto Rico or something," Lu said with a shrug.

"Yeah, maybe," Jean said, her smile watery and her nerves shot. She wondered what sacrifice she had made to be on time, and if she had made a huge mistake quitting her old job.

Six

Jean woke the next day late in the afternoon. Standing up was nearly impossible—all of the muscles in her body were clenched. Even her eyebrows were sore. She lay there for a minute, kneading the backs of her legs. It hurt to reach down. She wondered if she was getting sick. When Jean finally sat upright, she was overwhelmed by a ringing in her ears. She swallowed hard, but there was no evidence of a scratchy throat, nor was there the telltale sting in her eyes that presaged all of her life's fevers.

Jean reached for her phone and wondered if she should call Iggy; maybe their adventure the night before was taking some delayed physical toll. She felt an uncharacteristic eagerness to talk to him about the shortcuts at work later. She could barely lift the slight weight of her phone to eye level. The tiny screen revealed several missed calls from the same number, and a lone voicemail.

When she played it, there was a sickening lag before the caller spoke—she began with a thick gasp for air. "Jean, I'm sorry to call like this. It's Myra, Myra Goldstein. I don't know exactly how to phrase it, especially in a message like this, but can you please call me back at this number? Please?" Dr. Goldstein's voice broke like an egg, revealing an improbably desperate center. "It's very, very important, Jean." The call clicked off, abruptly, even though it seemed like Dr. Goldstein was still trying to speak.

Jean felt a nauseating lurch, like missing a step and falling down a flight of stairs. She redialed the number, but Dr. Goldstein didn't answer—the phone only rang and rang. Jean tried again and this time it picked up immediately, answered by an error message telling her the number was no longer in service. She called the office and was greeted by the sound of her own voice asking her to leave a message. "Hello, you've reached the office of Dr. Myra Goldstein. Please leave a message and someone will get back to you as soon as possible. If this is a medical emergency, please hang up and dial 911 or go to the nearest emergency room." Jean wondered, momentarily, if she *should* hang up and call 911—Dr. Goldstein had sounded genuinely distressed. But then she wondered what she would tell the operator. She realized how long it had been since she heard the beep in her message, so she hung up and called again.

"Hi, Dr. Goldstein and Arpita. It's Jean." She waited a moment, not sure what to say—maybe there was no cause for worry. Maybe she had just imagined the alarm in Dr. Goldstein's voice. "Just checking in to see how things are going for you both. I'm available for most of this afternoon—you can call me back really anytime before four thirty. Okay, speak to you soon."

She staggered to the shower, hoping the hot water would help her wake up, and saw that there wasn't much afternoon left. Jean showered quickly and made herself a coffee and scrambled eggs in her bathrobe. She salted the eggs so aggressively that her lips tingled when she ate. She felt immediately better after eating—

even her muscles became more limber and getting dressed wasn't the torture it had seemed a few minutes before. She examined her body in the mirror on the dresser. Something seemed off about the way she was standing. She lifted her shoulders up to her ears and then shrugged them back down again dramatically. Maybe she'd just slept badly and had to reset all of the bones in her body to feel normal again.

She combed through her wet hair with her fingers and put on some eyeliner using one of the ancient sticks she had in a drawer from an old Halloween costume. She couldn't explain it, but she had an irresistible urge to look not quite like herself, to align her slightly shifted exterior with her slightly shifted interior. She shoved a hat down onto her damp head and an anticipatory shiver at the cold outside rocked through her. She put on another sweater. Jean wrapped herself in her jacket and scarf and forced herself out into the wind that sliced through her carefully layered clothing.

Her face was numb by the time she pushed open the door at Red and Gold. Something felt off the minute she stepped inside. First of all, Iggy wasn't there. Instead, Omar greeted her with a half-hearted wave.

"Hey," she said, rubbing her hands together. Her gloves from the pharmacy had long since disappeared. "Where's Iggy?"

Omar shrugged. "No idea. He just didn't come in. I got a call when the liquor delivery showed up this afternoon and the gate was still down. You think you can take it from here? I have to go to my other job."

"I guess?" Jean knew she couldn't take it from there. She was still finding her legs behind the bar, and still reeling from the symptoms of the not-flu that she had felt upon waking. There was no way she'd be able to keep up with the volume of any kind of rush. "Can anybody else come in? Can that other girl—Ingrid?" Ingrid was a mysterious name on the schedule. It belonged to a girl who was always calling in for someone to cover for her because she had an audition, or a shoot, or was at the emergency room with a friend, or at the humane society with a litter of abandoned kittens.

"I called her, but she didn't pick up. You know Ingrid."

"Yeah," she said, even though she hadn't met Ingrid once.

"Okay cool." Omar shrugged on his jacket and sped past her before she could ask anything else.

"Wait, is the drawer counted?" she called after him.

"Uh-huh." The door slammed shut behind him.

Jean got to work, hauling ice and beers from the basement walk-in. As she filled the dishwashing sink, she fought back cowardly thoughts like leaving a note that the pipes had burst and then hiding out in the basement until it was time to close. But she needed the money, so she prepared herself for what she knew would be awful. The inevitability of her inadequacy to meet the challenge of a tsunami of orders loomed, suffocating. But Jean had endured other, much more awful things. She could endure this, too. Jean closed her eyes, hunting for a quiet moment to bolster herself. But instead of the flash of calm she expected, Jean saw herself on the living room floor at her parents' house. The too-vacuumed carpet scraped against her cheek where its filaments had lost their fuzz. Her parents argued, so close she could touch their legs.

"It was never supposed to be her." Jean's mother's voice was harsh, like a burned thing. "My baby—it was never supposed to be her. And you." Her mother's voice cracked into a sob. "It was never supposed to be you." In a blink, it was over. The tactile reality of the memory terrified her, so Jean did what she always did when something terrified her. She fled, this time, into her work.

By 7:00 p.m., Jean was drowning. A new band with the guys from Jonathan Fire*Eater was opening at the venue around the corner, but the show was running late. Their fans had packed Red and Gold, directing all of their fury and impatience at

Jean. One of them—a skinny kid with a mass of curly hair and a too-tight T-shirt spattered with stars and emblazoned with ALISON'S SWEET 16 WAS OUT OF THIS WORLD—was so disgusted that he spat on the floor in her direction. The faller-downer gave her a sleepy, sympathetic smile that nearly put her over the edge into tears. She made one drink at a time, but it was like bailing water out of a boat with a sewing thimble. Each order landed like an insult, plucked at her nerves, and eroded her dignity. Someone put a Sum 41 album on repeat on the juke-box to be cute. Jean was too frayed to remember the jukebox override button. Her hands stung with minuscule cuts from all of the bottle caps she had too hastily removed from their tops, and she was running out of glasses. The faller-downer mourn-fully pushed a few empties in her direction.

A lean man in all denim, his face weary and grooved with age, pushed through the crowd. He ducked under the pass and stood next to Jean. "Um, excuse me!" she shouted. "Sir, you can't do that!" Jean was shocked by the panic in her voice.

"No, no, no," the man said, holding his hands up meekly as though to defend his face from a punch. "Omar sent me over to help out."

Jean's body flooded with relief. Thank God! Thank Omar! Thank this withered angel who was suddenly picking up orders from the other side of the bar with the speed of a much younger man. Jean barely had time to observe him—she only saw that he was close to the age her parents would have been, and that he had the quiet, safe energy of a sweet old horse. The orders came and came; the music continued to be terrible. When a group of girls started dancing on the booths, Omar's emergency friend gently dispersed them, all apologetic smiles, and returned to the bar within the time it took her to fix another round of shots for the sashed and glittering bachelorettes in the back who had overtaken the pool table.

Right on cue, like the countdown to New Year's Eve, the

crowd disintegrated when the band they were waiting for slunk onstage at the venue down the street. Jean had never been so desperately glad as she was to see all of those fans go.

She filled a glass with Sprite and gulped it down, desperate for hydration and the hit it would give her blood sugar. Omar's friend nodded at her kindly.

"These nights can be tough, especially when you're in the weeds on your own."

"Oh my God," Jean said, bracing the side of her waist like she had in the days when she used to run. "You saved me. I would've actually died if you hadn't shown up. Like my brain would have liquefied and started coming out of my ears, and I would just have been no more."

"Nah, you would've figured something out." He waved her down. She noticed, now, upon examining him more closely, that he was watching her, too. He had seen more than most people would have in her moment of weakness, when her guard was down. There was an unmistakable, practiced empathy etched around her savior's eyes.

"I'm Jean," she said, trying to sound friendly and calm through her relief, to put him at greater ease.

"I know," he said. "Alan." He placed a hand on his chest and tapped his fingers there as though counting out the beat to the song blaring above them.

"How do you know Omar?"

"I work at the pet store next door to his uncle's restaurant. He's a sweet kid."

"A pet store? That sounds like a nice job."

"It is." He nodded. "The Woof-n-Wag on Avenue A."

"Oh yeah. I've walked by it. How come you're so good at this?"

"It's like riding a bike. I bartended for years. But you know, the hours. Plus, I got sober, so I was looking for something different."

Jean nodded and made another four vodka sodas for a cluster of stragglers who had gone from dancing in their booth to
weeping in each other's arms.

"Are you new?" Alan asked.

"Oh, yeah—I'm sure it was pretty obvious. I started a couple
of weeks ago."

"No, I mean, are you new to the city?"

"What?" Jean felt an odd shock, again that strange fissure in
her demeanor, a tiny crack revealing who she really was. Alan
was really looking—she felt seen and didn't like it. "Oh, no, I
mean…" She paused and took a steadying breath to clear the
tinge of annoyance from her voice. She didn't want Alan to
know that he'd struck a soft, vulnerable place. "I've lived here
for years. But in a different way—maybe that's what you're picking up on?" she supplied.

"What kind of different way?" Jean's gratitude for Alan was
swiftly evaporating with each prying question.

"I used to be a nine-to-fiver. It's a big change."

Alan smiled at a couple of boys in thick-rimmed glasses who
stared closely at him and whispered to one other as they waited
for their change. He pushed his thinning gray bangs out of his
eyes and cleared his throat. "That is a night and day situation.
Literally." Jean could see him deciding not to press her about
it, and she knew it was because her discomfort was obvious as
a siren. She was grateful—again!—to this friend of Omar's but
also irritated with herself. She was disappointed that she had lost
control of her story.

"I should probably get going," he said, motioning around the
now-thin crowd. None of these people would be drinking too
much more, and Jean could handle the smaller, later rush alone.

"Oh, of course," she replied, entirely relieved that this perceptive new acquaintance would soon disappear from her life
completely. "Let me give you some cash," she said, reaching for
the pile where the tips lay pooled in a jagged, disorganized heap.

"You know what? Don't worry about it," he said, waving her away.

"No, no, no, I absolutely insist. You saved my bacon—it's the least I can do."

"No really, it's okay. I might go around the corner and try to catch some of this show. What do you think?"

Jean shrugged, trying to smile. "Have fun?"

"Great meeting you, Jean."

"It was great meeting you, too. And thanks again."

"Think nothing of it." He drifted out of the bar as benignly as a bit of dandelion fluff, trailed by the trio of heavily spectacled patrons he had just served.

As her shift drew to a close, Jean suppressed all memory of Alan and how he had made her feel. By the time she locked up, it was as though he had never set foot inside Red and Gold. She was so tired, so desperate to just go home and go to bed, but Lu was waiting for her at the bakery. Jean wasn't sure she could go through the shortcut alone so she climbed into a cab instead, scolding herself silently for the expense.

No one heard from Iggy in the days that followed. The bar hummed with low-grade scandal, and the rest of the staff patched together a schedule, which meant more shifts for Jean. A great deal of unease swirled around her promotion. It seemed wrong for someone to just disappear, but in this nocturnal world, it evidently happened all the time. None of her other co-workers were worried—when she asked Mitch about it, he just seemed annoyed.

"Jean Jeanie, maybe this is something you never had to deal with at your nine-to-five, bless your sweet little heart, but in this line of work it's all part of the landscape. Somebody's boyfriend gets a job in Toronto, so they move to Canada. Somebody's band goes on tour, so they leave. Somebody gets a gallery show in Paris, so they take off for the continent. Shit, even steady-as-houses

Omar went to Lebanon to visit his grandma for a whole summer without telling anybody." Mitch stroked his newly grown-out moustache.

"Safe as houses."

"What?"

"It's safe as houses," Jean corrected.

"Whatever it is, it happens. It's nothing to worry about." Mitch's reassurances were all strange to Jean, who came from a very different place—these sudden lurches in life direction made her ordered mind pulse with anxiety, but the contrast in and existence of this scale of possibility also thrilled her. "If you're that torn up about it, go to his show on Sunday. If he isn't there, I bet somebody will know where he went."

"Yeah, you're right. I promised him I'd go anyway."

"Then go, Jean Jeanie. What's stopping you?"

Seven

On Sunday, Jean struggled to leave her apartment for Iggy's show. She wasn't eager to bump into Luke again—and she most definitely would, since it was his band, too—but she wanted to dispel the dread she felt around Iggy's sudden vanishing. Getting a glimpse of him onstage, in sound body, would be all she needed to dissolve the sense that something nefarious had kept him from Red and Gold.

Her laundry was done, her healthy dinner made at home and eaten, her polite chitchat with Molly and Christine on a rare weekend at home exchanged. She checked NY1 for the temperature and, seeing it was the coldest night of the month so far, put on yet another sweater before she took off. The band was playing at a bar within walking distance of the bakery. The sandwich board out on the sidewalk advertised six bands. Each name on the list was sillier than the last. Jean couldn't remember which one was Iggy's—she hoped she hadn't missed it already.

The exhausted-looking bouncer checked her ID and waved her through into the mostly empty bar. It was split into two dank rooms; the first looked a lot like Red and Gold, and the second, through a narrowing hallway that also held the bathrooms, was the room with the stage. Jean followed the sound of feedback and a smattering of tepid applause to the second room, and, when she didn't see anyone she recognized, she settled in at the near-empty bar.

"Hi," she said, when a man slunk over to take her order. He had the same bloated, disheveled look as Mitch, but without the veneer of friendliness. "Can I just get a ginger ale?" He frowned and pushed a glass toward her. "Can you tell me how many bands have gone on already?"

"They're the first," he said; even his voice sounded sour.

"Thanks." She set an unnecessarily extravagant tip on the bar between them and drank her soda impatiently. A couple on a first or second date played foosball in the corner, high on the success of their apparent match. Jean stretched her calves against the rung of her barstool, more grateful than ever to be alone. Every time she watched a person contort themself to fit into the life of another, her stomach turned. There was something so painfully tender about that very first part—a thing she had begun to witness with terrifying regularity at Red and Gold. She almost couldn't watch sometimes.

Jean decided she would wait until the next band went on, and then go home. She was tired—Iggy's absence had created more work for her, and her body was still adjusting to the constant standing. She forced a yawn, trying to rid herself of the persistent ringing in her ears. If it was an infection, she'd probably need to go to the doctor for antibiotics—a visit which she absolutely could not afford. She allowed herself a swell of regret over losing her insurance from Dr. Goldstein's office, and then wondered if maybe Dr. Goldstein could call a prescription into the pharmacy for her if she got really desperate. She pulled her phone out of her jacket pocket and checked to see if there were any missed calls from either Arpita or Dr. Goldstein. But no one had called and that brought a familiar wave of relief. Jean enjoyed these flat, quiet spaces, periods where probably no one remembered she existed. There was something so soothing about it, like disappearing into a long run in the days before her injury. For the first time, though, Jean wondered if it also wasn't very sad.

She swallowed back the thought and nodded to the surly barman for another ginger ale. He swapped out her empty glass for a full one and lingered in front of her. "You got a friend playing tonight?" His voice tumbled out in a rough monotone.

"Yeah. I don't remember the name of the band, though." She shrugged.

"Who's your friend?"

"Iggy," she said, pausing when she realized she didn't actually know Iggy's last name.

"Oh sure." The bartender nodded and smiled, his face transformed like a flipped coin. "The Cases of the Baskervilles."

"Right," she said, grateful for the supplied information. "Right." She toasted him with her refilled ginger ale.

"Have you seen them play before?"

"Nope. First time."

"How do you know Ig?"

"We work together at Red and Gold."

"Cool." The bartender pointed up at the ceiling and she looked up at the rusting tile there before realizing he was telling her to wait a second. She looked down, trying to disguise her embarrassment as a nod. He went over to get another round for the second dates. Jean caught a glimpse of her face in the mirror behind the bar and saw that it was too late, that she had turned entirely scarlet. Her blushes had always been bad. The doorman let in a wave of customers, all together, all laughing, and Jean hunched into her jacket a bit more tightly. At this point in her life, Jean was an expert at disappearing into the background.

Which was why the tap on her shoulder came as such a shock. "Hey, it's Jean, right?"

Jean turned and set the back of her hand against her cheek to disguise her flush. "What? Oh hey, yes." She turned to find Claire, Iggy's actress friend, settling onto the barstool beside her. Claire's overplucked eyebrows were drawn down on her forehead like two dashes of Morse code.

"I'm really glad you're here," Claire said, waving at the bartender, like you would wave to a neighbor. "I was wondering if you've heard anything from Ig at all."

Jean's stomach pitched. She knew she was about to set foot upon a terrain of interaction she was not prepared for. She thought the night would be easy, a peel and stick kind of solution to her vague concern. Claire's expression dashed her hopes for the evening.

"I haven't seen him at all, actually. He hasn't shown up for any of his shifts at the bar. So I guess he's fired? I don't know. I came tonight because I wanted to make sure everything was okay. I figured he wouldn't miss this…"

Claire shook her head. "That stupid fuck," she said.

"Did something happen?" Jean inched her barstool away from Claire—the other woman's explosive energy was unmistakable.

"You tell me," Claire said, stabbing a finger toward her.

"I'm sorry?" Jean squinted, confused.

"The last time I saw him was when he came through that shortcut with *you*," Claire accused.

"What?"

"What do you mean, what? *What happened when you guys went through?*"

"I have no idea! I can't stop thinking about it—I have no idea what happened. Or if it happened at all."

Claire's face softened. Another tap on her shoulder startled

Jean in the other direction. "Oh man, look who's here!" Luke stood too close, his mouth open, exhaling recently-taken-shot breath into her face.

"Hi," she said, trying to duck away. She was trapped between Luke and Claire, unsure of how to extricate herself, physically or theoretically.

"I'm so glad you came." Luke slung a sloppy arm around her shoulders, nuzzling in close.

"We were just about to use the ladies'," Claire said, standing up and making room for Jean to slip out of Luke's enthusiastic grip. "Come on." Claire waved her outside instead and unwrapped a fresh pack of cigarettes. She didn't offer one to Jean. Jean was relieved to be outside. Very little prevented her from just turning around, walking home, and forgetting everything about the night, about Iggy, and about the shortcut.

"Listen," Claire began. "I know all of this is new to you, whatever that means, but you're not some oblivious hayseed."

"Thank you?" Jean wrapped her scarf more tightly around her throat.

"Hey, Lucy Liu, can I bum one of those?" A drunken stranger lurched toward Claire, pointing at her cigarette. "I'll give you a dollar."

"Fuck off," Claire said, turning away from the street. Her gaze fell squarely on Jean. "I didn't mean to be so confrontational in there." Claire exhaled a stream of smoke toward the sky. "I'm just worried about my friend." She lowered her head and glared at her feet on the sidewalk. "I didn't think he would be so careless."

"What do you mean, careless?" Jean asked.

Claire gave her a hard stare. "Do you want to go for a walk? I think we really need to talk."

Claire pushed past the clots of smokers who spilled out of bars lining the busy street. Taxis stopped in inconvenient places, breathing in and belching out more groups of people onto the sidewalk. Everyone was loud; everyone had somewhere to go. It made a nice, sedate stroll and chat nearly impossible. Claire gave her head an irritated little shake.

"Here." Claire drew closer and looped the crooks of their elbows together. "Let's walk over to the park." She led the way, and Jean bobbed along with her as they flowed down Delancey Street through snarls of sloppily locked bikes and bodies in varying degrees of motion and direction.

The park was dark. The streetlights bled faintly through the canopy of branches and the little square was thick with shadows. They found a vacant bench in a section of concrete and half-frozen shrubs.

Claire sat down with a creaky sigh. "I know this is weird, and I didn't want to get into a whole thing in front of other people."

Jean sat beside her and nodded. The distance between them was the size of a full backpack.

"I've been worried about Iggy for a while. We're friends from high school; did you know?"

Jean shook her head.

"Yeah, we moved up here at the same time and lived together at first." Claire took in Jean's expression. "As roommates," she clarified, slashing her hand through the air between them. "Ig wasn't doing too well there for a while, but it's probably not my place to share that. Anyway, in the last year or two he seemed a lot better. Joining all of these bands, going to somebody's practice pretty much every day. It helped keep him busy. And he really seemed to be straightening out. I was proud of him."

"Sure," Jean said.

"I didn't mean to snap at you earlier. It's only because I feel guilty, for being the one who told him about the shortcuts. But how could I not tell him? I had to—it was exciting, you know what I mean? I almost needed to tell him because I could hardly believe it myself."

"Yeah, that's right where I am. How did you find out about

all this, if you don't mind my asking?" Jean couldn't swallow the questions down. Now that they were speaking openly about it, she couldn't stop herself from pushing ahead.

Claire paused and looked down at the space of empty bench between them. "A friend," she said, flashing Jean a half smile. "Actually, your friend and mine—Luke."

All of Jean's muscles clenched, wanting desperately to sever herself from this tangle of friends she was suddenly somehow a part of. She spoke to her body gently, silently, as she had learned to do over the years—*this isn't dangerous; we are okay.* "Friends is a stretch," she said, trying to stay kind.

"I knew him from class—we were in the same program. He was showing off, you know how it is. Luke had this party at one of his dad's apartments in Gramercy."

Jean's face cracked open with surprise.

"Yeah, it's like that." Claire nodded and ran a hand over her smooth, dark hair. "Luke's family is stupid rich. His dad is some pharmaceutical nightmare. Anyway, Luke gets high and tells me about the shortcuts. He says they've been around since the seventies, and I totally, absolutely did not believe him."

"They?" Jean asked. "You mean there's more than one?"

"There's definitely more than one, but I don't want to get ahead of myself here. So, Luke told me exactly where the closest one was, and, full disclosure, I was pretty high at this point, too, and went to check it out. I called Ig, freaking out, like you need to see this—I need another person to come over here and tell me if this is real or if I'm just really high. You know?"

Jean nodded. She understood the need for confirmation; it galloped through her body at that very moment.

"I took Ig through, and neither of us honestly believed what happened. It took days, I mean *days*, for me to get my head around it. I showed Iggy because I needed, like, the corroboration, and maybe that's really why I feel guilty. Because it was a selfish thing to do." Claire's voice broke, like she was already crying, and Jean braced herself for Claire's emotions to spill out between them on that bench.

"No, that's not being selfish," Jean said, trying desperately to staunch the flow of feeling. "It's normal when something extraordinary happens to you to want to share that experience with someone else. It isn't only about corroboration."

"You think?" Claire's nose ran, and she sniffed.

"Sure." Jean nodded, trying to keep her tone as calm and reassuring as possible, despite the scrum of rats forming at the foot of the garbage can across from them.

"Well, when I showed Iggy, his reaction surprised me. He wasn't scared at all—it was like telling a kid their new school is actually a Six Flags. He's been using them a lot. Like a lot, a lot. He says it opens him up creatively. I guess for a musician looking for inspiration, it's kind of a miracle." She narrowed her eyes and met Jean's gaze meaningfully. "These shortcuts were becoming a habit—like multiple times a day—and I think that's maybe why he's gone missing."

Jean glanced away quickly; Claire's gaze was too intense. "You think he's really missing?"

"Nobody's seen him—not his bands, not his roommates, not his co-workers." She ticked them all off on her fingertips one by one. "At first I thought maybe he disappeared with a girl somewhere, or started using again, or both, but even at his most irresponsible, Iggy never disappeared for this long. Ever."

"Did you call his family?"

Claire pursed her lips. "Yeah, they haven't heard from him—but they're not as worried as they should be. They never are," she muttered.

"What do you think happened?" Jean asked carefully.

"I keep imagining the worst things." Claire's voice flickered. "I don't think these shortcuts are good for you, you know, physically. You probably felt something after you went through, right?"

"I felt like I was getting sick—is that what it was?"

Claire lit another cigarette, this time offering one to Jean. Jean declined, and Claire shrugged, inhaling deeply. "Yeah, that's one of the side effects."

"Side effects?" Jean knew she didn't sound as horrified as she felt. What had she done? "What kind of side effects?"

"Headaches, getting dizzy. Throwing up. Sometimes my joints hurt. I don't think the human body is really good at going through time like that," Claire went on.

"Through time?"

"Space, time, whatever." Claire made an impatient repetitive roll of the wrist. "Every time I go through, I feel a little worse." She frowned down at her nails.

"Why do you keep doing it?"

"Are you serious?" Claire laughed. "Have you ever been curious about anything? Not all of us need like a superspiffy way to get to work. Some of us are actually interested in the mysteries of the universe. Are you even a person if you're not?"

Jean turned her face away from Claire, toward the pack of rats. She felt her face grow hot. This was another terrible thing—a thing she hated about herself—when she got something wrong, she got it so wrong.

"Hey," Claire said softly. "I wasn't trying to make you feel bad."

"No, it's okay. What about the rest of your friends? What about Luke? Shouldn't he feel responsible, too?"

"I mean, he probably should, but he doesn't. Not really. No, the responsibility is all mine," Claire insisted.

"Maybe it's mine, too. If I was the last person to go through with him, like you said."

"Well, what do we do now?" Claire stamped out the cigarette with a theatrical twist of her ankle.

"Maybe we should go look for him," Jean said, growing unexpectedly angrier. The swell of emotion was unusual for her, but she explained it away easily—of course she would be emotional if she felt responsible for the disappearance of another person.

"What do you mean?" Claire asked, wiping her eyes with the back of her hand.

"I mean, we can just go back to the diner. We can search the shortcut, right?"

"That's the problem." Claire worried her bottom lip with her teeth. "There are so many shortcuts."

Jean's stomach dropped. A cluster of skateboarding kids thundered past, scattering the rats. Jean drew her feet up onto the bench and rested her chin on her knees. "How many?" She was surprised by the volume of her voice. She had to get herself under control.

"I don't know," Claire said, deliberately lowering her voice. "Lots."

"Lots like ten or lots like thousands?" Jean couldn't believe what she was asking.

"Not thousands," Claire said, quickly shaking her head. "I don't know—maybe it could be. I don't really know exactly how many there are. It's like, the more you use, the more you find."

"How many have you found?" Jean asked.

"Like, twenty-ish?"

"Twenty!"

"Shh…"

"What about Iggy? Did he know about all twenty?"

"Oh yeah, definitely. I mean, he probably knew more. Knows more."

"Do they all fit together, like lead to one another?"

"Honestly, I'm not sure. Some do and some don't. I was still trying to figure it all out before Ig disappeared."

"Do you think he got, like, stuck?"

Claire began to weep, messy and all of a sudden. "I hope not."

Jean was chilled. How would a human body survive a suspension in those strange, dense passageways, for multiple days and nights?

"Well, let's start with the ones you know about. Maybe we'll find him passed out in a closet somewhere."

"Here's hoping," Claire said, as she gazed up at the murky, light-polluted city sky. "Alright. Let's go."

"What, like now?"

"Yes, now."

Eight

Jean and Claire walked through the park, past the improbable physics of tightly parked cars, past the streets filled with bars and Sunday night patrons trying to squeeze out the very last of what the weekend offered. Jean wanted to start at the diner, since that was a shortcut all three of them knew—it was a common denominator. Claire headed straight toward the bathrooms and Employees Only door. Jean grabbed the edge of Claire's coat, a spike of alarm holding her in the entryway. "Wait a second," she said. "Can we sit down and make more of a plan?" Jean's panic startled her, like a mugger in the dark.

Claire's eyes flashed with tears, but she nodded. They sat down in a booth next to the window. Jean wanted to be as far away from the other customers as she could, but it was impossible. The diner was as busy that night as it had been when Iggy brought her. A paunchy middle-aged waiter slapped down two menus and water for them both with an efficiency Jean admired. "Something to drink?" he asked them.

"May I have a coffee, please?" Jean asked.

"Me too, thanks." Claire unwrapped herself from her navy peacoat and pressed the palms of her hands against her eye sockets, desperate, like she was trying to hold them in.

"Okay," Jean said, scooting the silverware and neatly rolled napkin off her paper placemat. She pulled a pen from her canvas bag and wrote DINER at the top. Jean stared down at her neat handwriting and willed the same order into her racing thoughts.

Claire clasped her hands together and set them on the table. "So, we're going to make a list?"

"Yes, we're going to make a list, and then we're going to make a strategy—repeatable actions we can execute at, or in, I don't know how you'd say it, each shortcut."

"Wow, you have a real energy here," Claire said carefully. Jean's face reddened yet again. "No, I don't mean like in a bad way. Like, very impressive, yes, we need to be organized." She straightened herself in the booth, correcting her posture. "Okay, so, let's make a list. Which one did you use in here?"

"There's more than one?" Jean's eyes grew so wide they stung.

"There's the one by the bathroom, and there's one in the kitchen. Through the walk-in."

Jean's brain glowed with shock. "You mean all these people who work here know? How many people know about these things?"

Claire shrugged. "Who knows?"

"And how is this, like, not common knowledge? I don't get it."

Claire gave her a careful stare; it was full of assessment, and even a kind of interest. "You'll see. When we go through more, you'll see."

"Huh?"

"Besides, if I had told you, or if Ig had told you, but you hadn't gone through yourself, would you have believed it?"

"Here you go, ladies." The waiter deposited their coffees. "Anything to eat?"

"Could I get just a pancake?" Claire asked.

"One pancake, you got it. How about for you, miss?" he asked Jean.

Jean mentally calculated the contents of her wallet. Claire noted her pause and said, "This is on me, Jean."

"Are you sure?"

"Definitely. My brother helps with my rent—he's a Realtor and does really well. So everything I make at the bar is like, you know, pocket money."

"A grilled cheese, please." Jean looked away, ashamed by her reduced circumstances, but very hungry, nevertheless.

Claire tipped a sugar packet into her coffee and stirred. "I'm glad you're here—it feels good not to be doing this alone."

Jean had the realization that she also felt better, not being in that diner alone. She sharply elbowed the thought aside. "Okay, let's just make the list."

By the time Jean had eaten her grilled cheese, Claire finished writing out the locations she'd used before. She added a few more shortcuts she suspected but had never seen firsthand, and boxed them in with a wavy, penned line.

"Alright, so what are we going to do? Just go through them? And then what? Go back?"

Claire shook her head. "No, definitely not. You can't go back and forth. You have to keep moving forward, like on and on in a chain. But be prepared; it takes a toll on you. Like, physically." Jean shivered under Claire's words. Jean didn't want to think about these additional strikes against her body, which had already endured so much.

"It's not a bad plan. If Iggy is stuck, he'll be on the way through, right?"

Claire nodded slowly.

"What do you think is the best way to look for him? I barely remember what it was like. Like were my eyes even open?" Jean shook her head.

"I know what you mean. I don't think you can trust your eyes in there, you know? I think we just have to call out, as loud as we can, when we're going through."

"And what if he answers us?"

"If he answers us, we follow his voice, grab him, and then pull him through the rest of the way with us."

"Is it more dangerous with more people? Should you or I go alone?"

"No, no, no, no," Claire said, adamantly bouncing her knee under the table. "No fucking way, dude. The more people you have, the safer you are. Two is always better than one, and three is even better."

"Okay," Jean said. "That makes me feel a little better."

The waiter cleared their plates, then cleared his throat. "You ladies traveling tonight?"

"That's right," Claire said, her hands folded in a neat clasp.

"Make sure you keep an eye on the time," he warned, setting the check in front of Claire.

"Thanks, we will." Claire nodded and he walked away with a smile.

"What was that? About the time?" Jean asked, leaning forward.

"Oh, Ig didn't tell you? You can't go through when it's daylight. You aren't supposed to go through too early or too late in the night."

"What? Why? That makes no sense."

Claire shrugged. "None of this really makes sense." She laid down a folded-up twenty-dollar bill extracted from the cellophane slip over her cigarette pack.

"Do you think that's what Iggy did?"

"I sure hope not." Claire's expression faded.

"What happens if you do?"

"I've never done it and I don't know anybody who has, but it can't be good if it's pretty much the only thing you get warned about. I'm going out for one last smoke and then we'll go. Sorry—I just need to steady my nerves."

Jean nodded and stood to wash her hands in the bathroom. The water drizzled slowly from the tap, much too cold. She looked at her face in the mirror and stared into her eyes. She looked awake, but couldn't shake the heavy, tacky sensation that this was all a dream. It was too surreal, too terrible, too exciting, all at the same time.

Jean opened the door to find Claire studying their slapdash map scrawled onto the placemat. Claire had drawn arrows from the entrances and exits that were closest together—if they were quick, they could do all of this in a single night. At least, Jean hoped they could. She didn't have much free time for a search like this. Especially if she had to go back to work the next day and the search could only be done at night.

"Ready?" Claire asked.

"Ready." They linked hands, their fingers twisting together, and stepped through the Employees Only door.

Jean screamed her voice raw for Iggy. So did Claire. The air had that eerie density Jean remembered from her first time there. Her heart flew in that same euphoric way. She tried to keep her eyes open and to focus on something, anything, distinctive, but all she saw was shadow. There were no other human figures near them, just a dense, gray darkness that moved like the ocean. She clutched Claire's hand, her own growing sweaty with nerves. "Iggy!" she yelled one last time before bumping into the door that let them out in the storage closet of the bar across the street from her bakery. The bar, she realized, where Claire worked. They stood there for a long, hopeful moment, waiting for some sign of Iggy. But, the longer they waited, standing still like that, the dizzier Jean became. Finally, she was the one to push the door open, to disgorge them back into the city.

Jean discovered she was sweating—the places where her shirt and layers of sweater pressed into her armpits were soaked through. She wrinkled her nose.

"You okay?" Claire asked, setting a palm on Jean's shoulder— Jean was unsure whether the hand was there to steady her, or Claire, or settle them both.

"I don't know." Jean winced. "I feel weird."

Claire nodded. "Give it a minute. You want to sit down?" She led her over to a low shelf and they perched on the dusty plywood side by side. Claire rubbed her back gently, and Jean froze under the tender contact. Claire swiftly removed her arm. "I'm going to get you a Coke. That'll help. But then we should keep going."

Jean nodded, aware that she was out of breath. She drew in a lungful of air, held it for seven seconds, and then blew it out. It was a technique she had picked up from Dr. Goldstein. It had always worked for Jean, no matter what. And it seemed to be working now, she noted with relief, as her vision focused, and her breathing grew more even.

Claire burst through the closet door and a wave of music followed her. "Here," Claire said, handing her a glass of soda. "It's busy out there."

"Sundays are weird," Jean said, taking a long sip of the sweet, cold drink. She shivered, and suddenly found herself back on the floor of her parents' house, her body still small, her parents still shouting.

"I'm sorry, okay? I'm sorry that you're such a fucking failure," her father said. A heavy thing clumped on the ground beside her. An upended ashtray; she could tell by the smell. Dropped or thrown, she couldn't tell.

"I should never have let you talk me into moving out here. I feel like I'm dying!"

"What are you, fucking Zsa Zsa Gabor? You told me you hated living in the city."

"The only thing I hate is you!"

Jean blinked, back in the closet, still catching her breath. She pinched the bridge of her nose until it hurt.

"How are you doing?" Claire held her gaze and took the glass back and drank, too.

"I think I'm okay. Should we go? How far is the next one?"

"Not too far. A little walk will probably be good for you. It's overwhelming if you aren't used to it."

Jean bundled herself back up and found that she was gripping Claire's hand through the bar, being led like a babysitting charge. Claire nodded a goodbye to the bartenders and the doorman, and soon they were back out on the sidewalk. Jean glanced up and down the street—she squinted into the blur of lights and could almost make out the bar where Iggy's band had played without him.

"I can't believe we were just here," she said. "Sort of. How long have you been working at that bar?"

"A couple years, off and on. I've done a bunch of weird part-time things. You kind of have to when you're going to auditions all the time."

"But that's good, right? That you're going to auditions a lot? It must mean you're a good actress."

Claire shrugged. "I'm okay, but the thing that's really fucked-up is that it doesn't really matter how good you are. It's all based on how you look. At least for the auditions I get. It's so demoralizing. I can't even begin to explain what it's like to be in a room filled with people who look almost exactly like you."

"Whoa."

"Yeah, whoa—come on." Claire pulled her along. Jean put her other, unheld hand in her jacket pocket, ducked her head against the wind, and followed Claire a few blocks away to a record store, still open, painted black inside and out. A laconic androgynous kid—too thin, too pale—manned the register, which also appeared to be a coffee bar.

"Hey, Carlos," Claire said, waving her free hand at the clerk.

He nodded to them. "You here to shop or are you all going through?" His voice was heavy with a southern accent, like a ladle dipped into a dish of syrup.

"We're going through."

Carlos looked at his phone. "You're okay on time, I guess." He stepped around the counter and unhooked a keychain from his belt loop. He shuffled toward a back door and unlocked it, revealing a darkened stairway. He motioned them forward. "Smell you later."

Claire squeezed her hand and started down the staircase. It was narrow—barely wide enough for both of them on each step, but they continued, descending side by side. Jean braced herself against the wall. "So," Claire said, her voice a little too loud. "There's a landing at the bottom where the shop's basement is, but we're not going to stop there. We're going to just keep walking. You'll feel it. Start calling for Iggy then, okay?"

Jean nodded. They passed the basement landing and the staircase narrowed even more. The stairwell contracted around them, and Jean's hand against the wall grew useless as she soon had the sensation of falling, almost being pulled down through a vacuum. "Iggy!" she called. Claire's voice seemed far away, even though her body felt close. Jean alighted on the other side with a stumble—almost like exiting an escalator.

Her eyes burned with light. The smell was strange—not the musty basement of the record store, or the stale alcohol scent of a bar. It smelled like paint, and a light was glaring right into Jean's face. She sneezed.

"Bless you," said Claire, pulling her out of the beam of light. As Jean's eyes adjusted, she discovered that she was in a theater— a small, black box theater—in the middle of a performance. Jean's alarm ebbed when she noticed that they were backstage;

a harried stagehand pushed her aside, farther into the wings, with the flat of his hand, as though it were a broom and he was sweeping her out of sight.

"Sorry!" Claire whispered. "I thought you guys were between shows!" The stagehand rolled his eyes at them and pointed down another dusty hallway. Jean and Claire moved deeper into the backstage belly of the theater, past a row of folding tables cluttered with empty coffee cups, and stacks of leotards, to the exit. Claire heaved the fire exit door open and they were back out onto the street.

The door slammed behind them and the sound was like a switch, flicking Jean back into her parents' house. This time, the arguing came from the TV and a neatly coiffed bickering couple at a restaurant. Jean was still small, swallowed in the arms of her sobbing mother, surrounded by her familiar scent of Oil of Olay. "I'm so sorry, Jeanie." Her mother rocked her, but the rocking wasn't comforting, it was frenzied, almost violent. "You know I love you, don't you?"

Jean tripped over a lip of uneven sidewalk and shook herself back into the present, back with Claire.

"Did you hear Ig?" Claire asked.

"I didn't." Jean stamped her feet, reminding her body that it was back on earth.

"I'm getting worried. This isn't working." Claire's voice thickened.

Jean reached out and, before she could stop herself, pulled Claire into a hug. She was half horrified and half thrilled by the ease with which she had initiated the casual intimacy. "Listen, we don't know it isn't working. We've only gone through two. From a statistics perspective, we were never going to find him this early on."

"Yeah, okay, you're right." Claire looked up at her. "How are you feeling?"

Jean checked in with her body and felt surprisingly normal. "I think I feel fine—is that weird?"

Claire shrugged. "All of this is weird. Maybe you're getting used to it—like acclimating—more quickly than most people."

"Maybe. Where are we?" Jean looked around, for a familiar landmark.

"West Village. I actually just went to an audition over here. 'Asian prostitute #2.'" Claire snorted with disgust. "Didn't get it."

"That sounds really hard, all of that rejection."

"You have no idea," Claire said bitterly. "I don't know why I do it to myself. It's just, when it works, I fucking love it. Anyway."

"Right." Jean drew the creased placemat out of her pocket. "Now where?"

The next location was in an NYU building—a basement ceramics studio. The shortcut opened through a broken old kiln and spat them out uptown. They went through four more—at a deli on the Upper East Side, a movie concession stand in Kips Bay, a filthy Dunkin' Donuts bathroom in the Financial District, and a gilded Indian restaurant in Murray Hill. Iggy wasn't in any of the cuts, and Jean could barely walk she was so doubled over with nausea. Even Claire looked roughed up.

"It's after four—too late to go through any more tonight," Claire said. "But we need to check the rest of them." Claire's posture had collapsed, as though someone had struck her square in the chest.

"I don't have off until next Sunday night," Jean said, her voice dipping into familiar, apologetic territory.

"Do you think you can switch shifts with someone and try again tomorrow? I'm just worried that the longer he's stuck, the worse his chances are of getting unstuck. If you can't do it, I'll just go myself."

Jean's throat started to close up when she imagined Claire going through the rest of the shortcuts alone. She didn't know why her sudden allegiance with Claire produced so much fondness—she barely knew the girl. "I'll try to find someone to cover my shift tomorrow."

"Do you want to come home with me?" Claire reddened. "Not like that—I just think that you aren't going to feel so well."

Jean considered Claire's offer, feeling an unexpected thrill at the thought. "Oh, thanks, but I'll be okay. My roommates will be worried if I don't come home."

"As long as you're not by yourself. Here, hand me your phone. I'll give you my number. If you feel sick, or just want company, or if you find somebody to cover your shift, call me."

"I will."

They looked at each other for a minute—Jean wondered if Claire would try to invite her home again, and she half hoped not, half prayed that she would.

"How are you getting back?" Claire asked.

"I'll probably walk. I really don't want to throw up on the train."

"Fair," Claire said and smiled. "Hold on one second." Claire disappeared into a deli and emerged with a baby-pink vitamin water. "Here, take this. Drink it while you walk. It'll help."

"Thank you," Jean said, taking the drink and feeling more moved than she expected. Her eyes felt hot.

"Hey." Claire looked at her. "This was a weird night. This was some weird shit to do with somebody you barely know. Thanks for coming with me."

Jean looked down. "Don't thank me—I'm worried about Iggy, too. I couldn't not."

"Sure you could. You very easily could have bailed. Thank you." Claire gave her a little wave and walked toward the train.

Jean stood under the very last slice of night and drank her gift.

That night Jean dreamed about her parents. They were in a church pew, all three of them. The cedar and mothball smell loomed stronger in her dream than it had in real life. Jean had dreaded visits to church—its interior felt like a broken bone. Her parents, miserable, flanked her, one on either side. It was the way they had always stood together, presenting a united front at school functions, in photographs, and always, at church. Her father's lanky stance was so recognizable in her own that it made her flinch.

Her mother, dishwater blond with that terrible perm, had been what people called striking before she got so tired. By the time Jean knew her, her mother was exhausted. All three of them had matching hollows beneath their eyes. They looked like the before shots in ads for vitality restoring supplements. Jean hadn't kept any pictures, so she couldn't be sure if what her subconscious remembered was accurate, but the images it conjured were close enough. Were bad enough. In the dream, her parents turned to face her, both hitching inward as though powered by the grim mechanics of some terrible music box.

Neither of them spoke, but both of their mouths were open, in matching black gapes. Pencil-wide lines of blood ran from the corners of their mouths, the way they had when Jean had last seen their bodies, side by side on the medical examiner's table. For closure, which everybody thought she needed. But Jean hadn't found closure in that moment, only an awful wondering why they were so close together. In life, they had rarely been close enough to touch.

She woke consumed by a violent thirst. Her pelvis and right leg throbbed, as though reminding her how thoroughly her body had been pulverized those many years ago in the accident. When she had been the only one to survive. She had been so lucky. What a poor, lucky thing, people had said. It was no wonder to anyone why she had fled the town that contained that medical examiner's office, the hospital room where she had spent the better part of a year waiting for her bones to knit back together, the road on which her family had been smashed apart, and the glowing realization that the thing that had released her from a sad life was also horribly sad.

Nine

This time Jean woke to the trill of her phone. As soon as it quieted, she reached for it. Her muscles contracted in a familiar riot of pain. She pulled in her knees and did some hamstring stretches from her running days. While she waited for the muscle tissue to give, she listened to her messages on speaker.

"Hi, Jean," a young woman's voice began, grave. "So, it's Arpita again? Sorry for this strange message, and sorry for calling you last night, too, but I didn't know what else to do. And it feels wrong not to do anything?"

Jean put a cool palm to her closed eyelids to ease a throb of pain. Nobody had called her last night—she was certain. She'd been checking the time on her phone before every shortcut she and Claire took.

"Dr. Goldstein's son fired me, so technically it's none of my business, but somebody should do something. I think maybe you could call the city, or I could, for somebody to come out and investigate? If you ask me, it's some kind of elder abuse—I don't know how else to describe it. This is my cell phone number; call me back when you can, please."

Jean sat up and cringed. She wondered whether the tinny compressed sound was garbled or if she'd heard what she thought she'd heard. She redialed Arpita's number, but it went straight to voicemail. She called Dr. Goldstein's office, but didn't leave another message. Instead, she dialed through to the answering service—reserved for special cases and emergencies. This was nothing if not a special case, Jean thought.

"Dr. Goldstein's answering service," a woman's voice answered.

"Hi, is this Donna?" Jean asked.

"Yes, is it—is this Jean Smith?"

"Hi, Donna, yes it's me—how've you been?"

"It's so good to hear your voice, honey! I was just thinking about you the other day." Jean was struck by that hot sticky reminder of what it felt like to be remembered fondly. So complicated, but also, she acknowledged, comforting.

"I'm glad you're back in the picture," Donna continued. "Sounds like some funny business is going on over there."

"That's what Arpita said."

"Hmm, yeah, you know she left, right?"

"She told me she was fired."

"What? That's not what Mr. Goldstein said."

"You mean Dr. Goldstein's son?"

"That's the one." Donna's voice dipped into a lower, more personal register. "Listen, I don't mind telling you that I don't like the way that man speaks to me."

"I don't understand." Jean closed her eyes against an insistent, woozy wave. "Donna, why are you talking to him at all? What's going on with Dr. Goldstein?"

"This is what I'm saying, honey—anytime I put anybody through to her, I get him. At first, I figured it was temporary, like maybe she was having some health problems and that he was just helping out with her referrals."

"But…"

"Well, I sure don't think that anymore."

"Can you put my message through?"

"What? You want me to put a message through from *you*?"

"I can't get a hold of her, and I just want to make sure she's alright."

"You're a good girl, Jean," Donna said kindly. "I'll put it through, but I can't guarantee she'll call you back. Like I said, I give *him* all her messages. The son. You sure you want him to call you?"

"I'm sure," Jean said. "Thank you." She hung up and got dressed for work. She texted Omar about covering for her, but he couldn't do it since he was already covering for Iggy. Mitch was already working, so she couldn't ask him. She texted the mysterious Ingrid, but Ingrid never responded. Jean pulled on a clean pair of socks and was struck with a great idea.

She brushed her teeth, admiring her elegant solution. Her phone buzzed and rattled on the porcelain edge of the sink. She spat and answered the call.

"Is this Jean Smith?" a masculine voice with a sharp, New York accent asked.

"Yes?"

"Well?"

"I'm sorry?" She wiped the toothpaste from her mouth and inspected her skin in the bathroom mirror.

"You called my mother's answering service. They said it was urgent." The voice was laced with an aggressive, accusatory energy.

"Oh, yes—hello!" Jean tapped into the rehearsed, bright tone she had perfected during her years managing Dr. Goldstein's schedule. "This is Jean. I used to work with Dr. Goldstein. Is this Jeffrey?"

"This is Mr. Goldstein."

"Right, yes, Mr. Goldstein. I called because I wanted to check in on your mother. We've been playing phone tag for a while, and I wanted to pin her down for a quick chat."

"So you called the answering service for a 'quick chat'?" He oozed contempt through the invisible line that connected them. "Can I ask why you didn't wait for my mother to call you back? Don't you think that's a little hysterical? What makes you think you have the right to bypass patients with real emergencies to tie up this line?"

Jean grew angry. "Well, I spoke with Arpita, her new assistant, and she seemed concerned. So, when I couldn't reach your mother through the regular channels, I thought I'd try this."

"Arpita," he scoffed. "Where'd you find her, I'd like to know?"

"Dr. Goldstein hired Arpita—she was overqualified for the job, actually. Way more qualified than I was," she joked, trying to deescalate the phone call.

"That I believe."

Jean sucked her minty teeth and stared sternly into the mirror at her reflection, imagining Jeffrey's sagging pasty face in place of her own. She could barely remember him in person— her imagined image was a composite of the framed photographs perched across Dr. Goldstein's office. She took a deep breath that she hoped he could hear.

"Is your mother there?"

"You left my mother's employment, so I have no idea why you have such an urgent need to speak with her."

"I want to check in, as a courtesy."

"Well, sweetheart, as a courtesy, I'd suggest you patiently await her response through the 'regular channels' as you say. Don't call this line again. It's for emergencies only." The phone went dead.

Jean gently unclenched her jaw. She shook her head at her

reflection—her face gravely disapproving. She checked the caller ID, but it was a blocked number: neither Dr. Goldstein's office nor her home phone number. Strange. Maybe on another morning, if she could get up early enough, she would take her old route to work and check the office. Maybe she'd catch Dr. Goldstein—hopefully without Jeffrey—there.

Jean combed her fingers through her hair and scooped a few twenties out of the box on her dresser where she kept her tips. She stood by the door for too long, staring out the single narrow window in the living room. The bare tree branches at her eye level wavered in the wind. She wondered if the old Eastern European mother who had visited the apartment had caught herself staring out the same window. Another good reason to go to Dr. Goldstein's office would be to see if she'd left her winter coat there. Jean held her fingers down on the wad of sweatshirt and sweater she'd layered and pulled her denim jacket on. She buttoned it up with difficulty over her yarn-bloated torso.

Jean grabbed a hat and went out, locking the door carefully. *In a home invasion, locks don't really do shit, Jeanie, but you have to use them.* She stood frozen in the hallway and forced herself to breathe. Her father's voice rang out in her mind with icy clarity. She was stunned that even after a decade, these ghosts of her past could flare to life so easily. Jean waited in the hallway, grateful to be alone, until her body remembered where it was— that it was safe.

The Woof-n-Wag was empty except for a striped ginger cat stretched out in a rectangular patch of sun beside a glossy cardboard cutout of a golden retriever. "Hello?" Jean pulled off her hat in the tiny, aggressively heated shop.

"I'll be with you in one second," a voice called from the back room.

Jean scanned the dusty shelves, lined mostly with pet food and squeaky toys.

"Oh, hi, Jean." Alan, Omar's friend and her co-worker for a night, emerged from behind the counter. His wiry Mick Jagger body and thinning '70s haircut were set off by an incongruous blue work smock emblazoned with the Woof-n-Wag logo—two cartoon dogs high-fiving. "Can I help you find something?"

"Actually, I stopped by to see you. I wanted to give you your tips from when you helped out." She handed over the curl of bills and put her hands back into her jacket pockets so he wouldn't try to give the money back.

"That's real nice of you," he said.

She stood there, swaying like a tree outside in the bluster, oddly calmed by the heat in the shop. "You okay?" he asked.

"What? Oh yeah, just warming up. Sorry."

"Don't apologize. You just look a little shell-shocked." He reached out as though to high-five her, just like the dogs on his smock, but his hand fell limp against his side.

"Yeah, I had kind of a weird night last night. Which is also why I'm here." She stepped her feet together like a person about to get measured at the doctor's office. "I really appreciate your help the other day—I truly would not have survived."

"Nah." Alan moved a rubber mouse that had been abandoned by some browsing customer back onto the hook where it belonged, next to a row of other startled-looking rodents. "You would've been fine."

"That's very generous." She looked into a corner of the room thick with dust, searching for the best way to ask her favor. "I was hoping you might be willing to help out again tonight. If you could cover me for a few hours, I'd be eternally grateful. Plus, you'd be working with Omar, so you'd know somebody."

"Oh, I don't know, Jean," he said. "It's not really what I do, you know? That was an extreme circumstance."

"If I could ask someone else, I would, but you're the only one who can help me out. I have—" She hesitated for a moment, not wanting to share Iggy's improbably desperate business with a stranger. But Alan seemed safe in a way she couldn't quite explain. "I have a friend in crisis," she finally finished.

"Well, in that case, I guess I can't say no."

Jean's smile stung the corners of her mouth. The unexpected kindness twisted into her. "I owe you one," she said, restraining her emotion to normal, socially acceptable levels.

"Nah, don't worry about it." Alan waved her away. "I'll go over when I close up here. Is five okay?"

"That's perfect, thank you."

Jean couldn't help but feel suspicious when things were going her way. She knew balance was governed by gravity, an unforgivable force, and that any goodness she enjoyed would inevitably be met with an equal and opposite impact. So, she didn't enjoy it too much—just a brief bask, warming her hands at a friendly hearth—and braced herself for the next hit.

She ran across the street and ate a slice of pizza. The tiny pizzeria was empty except for her and the cook folding a stack of boxes for the dinner rush. Jean had adjusted to these strange mealtimes; her body had even begun to expect them. The body could always be relied upon, even after years of conditioning toward some other, different way—she could count on her body to make the right demands. One of the greatest lessons Jean had learned from the physical disaster she had endured was that if she listened to it, her body wouldn't let her down.

She called Claire from the cozy orange glow of the pizzeria, her feet perched on the ledge of the storefront window.

"I found someone to cover for me at the bar," she said.

"That's amazing!" Claire said. "How are you feeling today?"

"I feel okay." Jean shifted her shoulders back and forth and realized that the soreness had disappeared. Her nausea was completely gone, too.

"Wow—I mean, good. It took me a few weeks before going

through felt normal at all. Can you meet me at work? I'm off in an hour. It'll be after dark."

"Sure." Jean thought about bringing pizza for Claire but decided against it. Their friendship was already growing more rapidly than she was comfortable with—it didn't need more reinforcement through a thoughtful surprise pizza. Jean had grown used to suppressing the kindnesses that would endear her to acquaintances and colleagues. She admired and protected the clean lines that ordered her solitude. Traversing the shortcuts with Claire was building an intimacy that Jean didn't quite understand how to navigate or dismantle. She wasn't sure how to be careful here.

Jean decided to walk to Claire's bar to settle her thoughts. To kill some time, she headed west across Houston Street, past the herds of Christmas shopping tourists in Soho. Jean had a secret fondness for the tourists—leaning over litters of imitation handbags arranged lovingly on blankets on the sidewalk—as she crossed into Chinatown. Jean liked how the wandering groups were always dressed the same, like packs of obscure sports teams. The tourists thinned and she moved on.

Jean reassured herself that her burgeoning friendship with Claire would end as soon as Iggy was found, and her conscience could rest. She tucked herself away from the wind in the doorway of a vacant storefront and checked her phone for a message from Dr. Goldstein. She didn't like the way that story—a story that should have been evolving away from her—tugged at her attention.

No one had called, but she realized that she was running late to meet Claire. She had walked too far west. Jean looked up, searching for the closest subway stop. The street looked maddeningly familiar in the purple light of dusk. She rounded the corner of an alley that abutted a wall-sized photo of a Realtor's beaming head and discovered the back door to the theater she and Claire had exited the night before. Taking the theater's shortcut back would be the fastest, easiest way to meet Claire on time. Jean pushed at the door, delighted when it gave.

"Hello?" she called. A fluorescent light shone at the end of the hall. Jean discovered the cluttered dressing room in even worse shape than the night before. A lone woman—a little older than Jean—scooped drifts of used Kleenex into a garbage bag. "Excuse me?" Jean said.

The woman gasped and clapped a hand over her heart. "My God, you scared the shit out of me."

"I'm sorry," Jean said. "I'm looking—" She struggled to find the right way to ask her question. "I'm looking for the way through in here?"

The woman stared at her; a cold sore burned on her top lip. "Isn't it a little too early for that? I thought you all just came out of there—I didn't realize you could go in."

"It's after sunset." Jean shrugged like a person who knew these things.

"Okay, I'm not your mom." An image of Jean's mom, alive and whole, skated through her mind. Her throat stung at the disturbingly vivid remembrance of her mother's dark-lashed hazel eyes and out-of-date perm. Jean swallowed back the burning and willed her mother away. The woman led her toward the stage, dragging the half-empty garbage bag behind her like a macabre train. "There," she said, pointing at a curtain in the wings.

"Thanks," Jean said, waving her goodbye with a diluted salute. She pushed the curtain aside and stepped through the gap.

It was the first time Jean had cut through alone. She was so accustomed to being pulled along, that she was surprised for a moment that she wasn't moving. The shock of air density compressed her lungs, but she pushed forward, calling for Iggy a few times out of habit. This particular passage seemed more clogged than the ones she'd taken with Claire—like her feet were shuffling through a bank of cold, wet leaves. It was harder to move alone. She wondered if her difficulty of movement had something to do with traveling so early in the evening. Before she could wonder any longer, she was compressed out—like pastry cream through a bag—into another dark, hot room.

Jean cast her gaze about for the stairs at the bottom of the record store, but all she saw was the gentle slope of a concrete ramp leading to another emergency exit door. Jean felt the usual dread of being faced with an emergency exit. Like so many other doors in the city, opening it could mean sounding an alarm and ensuing mayhem, or it could mean nothing at all. Jean pushed the door open and the alarm tripped, screeching and wailing in an unfamiliar tempo.

Jean discovered that she wasn't in the record store at all; she was in a movie theater—a rapidly emptying movie theater. The patrons seemed legitimately panicked. There was none of the lackadaisical response to the alarm she was accustomed to, where people thought it was probably nothing, and were generally almost always right. These people were screaming.

The crowd's panic cracked the suppressed contents of Jean's mind. Her car accident roared out like a leashed beast, poisoning an entire decade of curated calm. Jean's brain convinced her that she was a teenager again, bleeding on the side of the road. Terror steamed through her, and all she could do was hold still.

There was something wrong, not only with the crowd's outsize reaction to the screeching alarm, but with the colors that flashed by her. A swirl of muted autumn tones and synthetic fabrics in unfamiliar cuts surrounded her—and hair—so much hair. The fleeing audience looked like extras in a movie. Had she wandered onto a film set and into some chaotic scene in a movie that would come out in two years? Jean turned and glanced at the screen. A young, bearded Richard Dreyfuss peered down on them as large as a dinosaur, the ocean bobbing around him, massive. She had seen this movie before—it had to be some retrospective, she rationalized.

A woman raced into her, catching Jean's side with her shoulder. The woman's familiar hazel eyes caught Jean's and Jean couldn't breathe. The woman's perm suddenly didn't look so out-of-date in this movie theater playing *Jaws*. "I'm so sorry," the woman said, before she turned and ran again.

Jean staggered to the wall, completely immobilized by the teeming strangeness. The woman had looked exactly like her mother—or maybe she hadn't. Maybe Jean's eyes saw what they wanted to see. Or what they thought she wanted to see. Where was the record store basement? She edged closer to the emergency door and slipped back the way she came, tumbling back through the shortcut—then running, pressing herself through. She shivered under the gleam of sweat developing on her skin. She thought she was running, but she was really just engaged in an aggressive shuffle. Jean's heart thrashed out that euphoric runner's high within the safety of her rib cage. As she pressed forward, she reminded herself she was alright—her body was intact, was still moving. Her heart was still beating.

The swath of curtains backstage at the tiny West Village theater trapped her like a fly on a glue strip. She emerged into a silent semicircle of meditating actors in various states of costume. They appeared not to notice her, and she ran—this time at full speed—through the hallway, past the dressing room and onto the street. Her phone was hot in her pocket. She was very late for Claire; she texted her apologies, and jogged to the train station, feeling nothing, not even the temperature, not even the dart of her old injury, only the urgency that underscored her panic.

Ten

Claire was smoking outside of the bar, her stylish belted wool coat already on. "Hey," she said, her voice edged with disappointment.

"I'm sorry," Jean said. "Something weird happened. With the shortcuts."

"Shh," Claire said, motioning her down the street. "Talk and walk."

"I took that one that we used last night. I was worried about being late, and I thought if I could take that one in the theater back to the record store I could be here faster."

"You went the *other way*?" Claire froze on the sidewalk, and a girl in a faux fur jacket bumped into her. "I'm sorry," Claire said to the scowling girl as she stepped to the side, pulling Jean with her. "You're only supposed to go one way!"

"I didn't know that!" Jean was surprised by the vehemence in her voice. How was she supposed to know? Nobody told her anything about how it all worked—it wasn't like there was some manual she had shirked reading.

"Dude! They only go one way! Didn't Iggy tell you that? Didn't I tell you that?" She rolled her eyes up to the night sky and took one last drag of her cigarette. She exhaled with a little frustrated hop. "That was not smart, Jean."

"I'm *sorry!*" Jean was about thirty seconds away from crying, her least favorite feeling. Worse than actually breaking down was convincing herself that she could still stop it from coming.

Claire threw her cigarette onto the street in a violent arc.

"Well, you're okay and that's all that matters," Claire said sharply.

"I don't understand. Why can't you go both ways?" Jean asked, discreetly swiping at her runny nose with the back of her hand.

"I mean, you *can*. Clearly, since you just did." Claire nodded to the left. "Here, let's go this way. I really want to get through the rest of our list tonight." Claire took off toward the subway stop at East Broadway. They passed two couples dressed for a costume party; one as Axl Rose and Slash, and the other as Boston Celtics. Slash tossed his glossy wigged head as though anticipating their acknowledgment. Claire rushed past them.

"What do you mean? How do you know which way is forward, or the right way?"

"The 'right' way is the way people go through, I don't know! I always figured it was like a one-way street. It only goes in one direction."

"What happens if you go the wrong way?"

"I mean, you tell me! I've never gone the wrong way." Claire's raised voice was muted beneath the rush of traffic cramming itself onto the bridge. "Sorry," she muttered, and raced down the subway steps. "I shouldn't yell."

"It took me to a movie theater. It was strange, like being in a movie theater in a movie."

"What do you mean?"

"It was an old movie, and the people looked old."

"Like an AARP situation?"

"No, like old-timey. Like they were the people in the old movie who climbed down out of the screen."

Claire shook her head and clicked her way through the turnstile. "I'm confused. The people came out of the movie?"

"No, no," Jean said, pausing on the platform. A mysterious blast of hot air warmed her through. "Not like that. Honestly, I don't even know. Maybe I just had a panic attack or something. Maybe I wasn't there at all, and I was still in the theater. The other theater."

"What?" A commuter drooped on a nearby bench, flanked by bulging plastic Duane Reade bags.

"You know what—never mind. I think I'm just out of it from going through so many times yesterday."

Claire patted her back, soothing, and this time Jean didn't shrug her off. An arriving train on the opposite track thundered through, barely slowing; its empty belly glowed. Jean let the sound wash through her, and pulled herself together. "Listen, let's just stay calm," Claire said. "We have one goal, here. Let's just focus on that. Promise you won't use the shortcuts without me again, okay?"

"Alright." Jean nodded, and an Asian grandfather on a nearby bench with two small kids on either side of him broke into song.

"We have to stick together, you know?"

Jean nodded, stumbling into a seat on the next uptown train. Jean watched her reflection in the darkened window across the car and saw her face soften as she relaxed into the space beside Claire.

"Something else happened," she began, her mouth and her thoughts blooming open almost involuntarily. "Another reason I was a little out of sorts. I saw a person who looked like my mom. She died a long time ago, and I guess it just hit me in a weird way." Jean was shocked, too late to clap a hand over her mouth.

"I'm so sorry, Jean."

"We didn't have the best relationship." Jean watched her mouth move in her reflection but couldn't keep it closed. "But she was my mom, you know?"

"Moms are hard. You know I'm adopted, right?" Claire picked at a chip of nail polish on her thumb. "My parents are super Christian and super white. My mom never really figured out how to parent me. Which, honestly, was probably for the best. We don't really talk anymore."

"I'm sorry, too, Claire."

"It's okay. My brother and I are pretty close now. It's good that we're working together—you can always count on people who know how to take care of themselves." Claire shot her a faint smile.

Jean was so stunned that she could barely answer—she had never spoken about her parents to anyone since she moved to New York. Jean couldn't begin to untie the complex knots in her feelings, so she veered away instead, pursuing more neutral questions. "How come there are so many more shortcuts downtown?"

"They're all over—I just know about more downtown ones since that's where I've been looking," Claire said. "But you know, once you find one, there's always another one."

"How do you keep finding them? Or how did Iggy find so many more without you?"

Claire shrugged. "You meet people, you know. Like, enthusiasts." Her glance cut into Jean like a blade. "It's not all fun. A lot of dark stuff can happen. It's addictive, going through. You feel it, right?"

Jean nodded, recalling the runner's high she'd experienced taking the cuts.

"Well, that feeling while you're going through, it gets stronger, feels better, the longer you do it. Which is why I should've kept a closer eye on Ig." Claire rubbed at her cheeks and forehead like a person washing her face over a bathroom sink.

"You guys are close."

"He's like family."

"We'll find him." Jean reached to give Claire a pat on the shoulder, but thought better of it and pressed her hands together in her lap. She stared at Claire in the darkened window that pooled across from them. Claire was small—Jean loomed even sitting beside her. Jean's nose was sharp; Claire's nose was delicate, a sculptor's pinch of clay. All of Jean's features seemed large compared to Claire's. Jean admired the way Claire's blunt dark bob roughed up the edges of her delicate face. Jean wondered if she could grow her hair out into one of those *Amelie* haircuts, too, but decided it would look ridiculous. Her enormous head didn't need a frame like that.

The train lurched to a stop on the Upper East Side. They climbed up the subway steps and followed the edge of Central Park. The girls huddled close, their bodies seamed together, better to block the wind. The leaves still on the branches rattled overhead as a group of kids accompanied by nannies raced by on scooters. Two matching, coatless children in karate uniforms ran past, clipping Jean as they fled.

"We're almost there," Claire said, turning down onto a gently sloped path. The park was filled with shadows, none of them menacing. It was a clear night and Jean always felt a little dizzy when the beauty of the city aligned in such a cinematic way. They paused beneath a vaulted brick arch. The cars on the street hummed overhead.

"Right here," Claire whispered. "Try to be discreet."

"Right where?"

Claire pushed Jean lightly between the shoulder blades and steered her toward a closed ticket booth for Central Park's small zoo.

Claire stared down at the door handle. "Shit, it's locked." She stamped her foot on the path.

"Is there another way to get in?" Jean asked.

Claire shook her head. "They usually leave it open."

Jean glanced down at the lock, a single cylinder embedded in the spherical knob. A fairly old one. She withdrew her keys and flicked open the awl on her tiny Swiss Army knife. She twisted gently, as though trying to remove the stamen of a flower without disturbing a single petal. The lock gave beneath her fingers with a fluid, satisfying click. As she turned it open, she knew it would continue to function perfectly once they were gone. She motioned Claire through the door and twisted the little metal tab back to its locked position when she shut the door behind them. The booth smelled like feet and cash, and Jean was keenly aware of how closely she was crowded in with Claire.

"Whoa, Jean, that was a very sexy thing to do."

Jean flushed. "Thank you," she replied, flustered.

"How did you do that?"

"My dad was a locksmith." The information leapt out of her involuntarily, painfully, like a handful of vomited up bolts.

"Is he retired now?"

"No, he, uh, passed away." Jean frowned at the way her personal disclosures were beginning to accumulate.

"Both of your parents are gone? Oh, I'm so sorry," Claire said.

Jean shook her head. "It's not your fault." The rare times she had this conversation, she answered the same way. *It's not your fault.* People usually stopped there. Most people didn't press, no matter how curious they were. She was relieved to discover that Claire was one of those well-mannered, tactful people who didn't say another word about it.

"Over here," Claire said. "You might want to hold your breath. This one starts off kind of weird."

A fissure of thrill prickled through Jean's body. She couldn't overlook the physicality of her anticipation—it felt good. Jean hadn't been on a long run in nearly ten years, and churning through a shortcut was the closest she'd ever felt to the private triumph of her body's fulfilled potential. No wonder Claire had said the shortcuts were addictive. She held her breath and followed Claire through a narrow gap in the wall that looked like a construction mistake.

The passage glimmered, like it was filled with water. Jean's hair floated around her head, and she could feel the pressure of the shortcut against her scalp. Claire's hand was slippery and foreign in her own—like a contracting, gelatinous sea creature. She didn't open her mouth to call for Iggy, but Claire did. Jean heard the other girl's voice wobble under the force of the passage and shuffled her feet against the ground to remind herself that she wasn't actually swimming.

They stumbled into the darkness of a closed lingerie shop on Orchard Street. A hanging display of a stuffed bra and girdle swung and hit Jean in the face. Instead of laughing, Claire looked crestfallen. "I really thought we'd find him in there. This was Iggy's favorite one."

"Hey, don't get discouraged," Jean said, rubbing at her bonked eye. "We still have a few more shots." Jean, while eager to find Iggy, secretly hoped that she and Claire would have more time on their strange but exhilarating adventure.

"We have four. We have four more shots," Claire said.

"Well, we'll take those four and then talk about what to do next if they don't work out. That's all we can do, right?"

"Right." Claire sniffed. "You can be very reassuring. How did you learn that?"

"My old job, probably. I used to work in a therapist's office. You see a lot of weird stuff in there." Again, Jean experienced that involuntary unfurling, like she was some mollusk being pried open on the deck of a boat. It was uncomfortable, but a soft pulse of relief flickered within the discomfort.

"Yeah, I bet. It's actually not the weirdest transition—therapist's office to bar." Claire led them through another emergency door— this one, thankfully, without an alarm—into the mostly vacant

Monday night stretch of underwear row on Orchard Street. "Is it? That different?"

"It's extremely different." Jean considered her words, not wanting to give more away than she had to. But she couldn't have stopped herself from talking if she tried—the compulsion was that strong. "My old job was quieter—I barely saw anybody for longer than five minutes at a time. Except my boss."

"Why did you leave? Was your boss hard to work with?"

"She was..." Jean wasn't sure of the truth herself. She only knew that she had started feeling so close to Dr. Goldstein that she couldn't ignore it anymore. But that wasn't something you could say to an acquaintance who just wanted a normal answer. Especially if you wanted that acquaintance to like you. "She was really good at her job."

"How do you know that? I'm assuming you didn't see her, like, for therapy, right? Since that would be unethical and everything. I assume."

"No, I didn't see her, but I watched her all the time. Not just with her patients but with other people. Like the doorman and the plumber and her neighbors and strangers. She was a good person. Really good at listening."

"Did she die, too?"

"What?" Jean paused as though she'd been struck. "No." Jean couldn't control her tone and that frightened her. It had to be these shortcuts.

"Sorry, it sounded very final. The way you were talking about her."

"No, she's still alive. Still working. People come from all over the world to see her. I did a lot of organizing and scheduling and things like that. Kind of the opposite of the spontaneity of the bar. But mostly I just watched her and watched the people who came in to see her. You have to make sure they're going to behave the way you expect a person to behave. People snap sometimes. Not a lot, but it happens. Watching people, that's the only thing that's really the same about working for her and at the bar."

Jean stumbled, a little hungover from all of the emotional sharing. She forced herself to stay quiet, and Claire was immersed in her own thoughts, too, as they walked farther downtown. Jean watched her feet closely, but her shoes weren't striking the sidewalk anymore; instead they shuffled in dew-slicked grass. Jean was jolted out of the city night and dropped into a rural Pennsylvania afternoon. "It's like nobody hears me." Her mother walked ahead with another woman. Jean didn't know the woman, but she moved like a teacher, tired but attentive. "Living with Bob and Jean—it's like living with strangers, you know? Like I've never met them. Like God pulled me out of the life I was supposed to have and put me in that house. It doesn't feel right. It never has." Jean's tiny heart stopped. She felt the words like kicks to the abdomen. Her child's body hurt. Jean registered the same pain in her adult body and snapped back into place beside Claire. She rubbed her stomach in the place that had hurt so hard.

The next three shortcuts were disappointingly empty of Iggy. The first—through a refrigerated storeroom of a CVS in the Financial District—revealed a couple of employees getting it on; the second, through the laundry loading dock of a Day's Inn, revealed a cooing flock of birds; and the third, another restaurant bathroom, yielded nothing more than a stomach-turning floral room spray that made Jean gag.

"This doesn't look good, Jean." Claire massaged the side of her neck wearily. "All these no's are starting to feel like my audition history," she muttered.

Jean's head pounded. "We have one more. We'll go through and if he's not there, we'll make another plan."

Claire nodded. "I hate this one. It is, *by far,* the absolute worst one, and I don't think Iggy would ever use it."

"But we can't rule it out."

"No, we can't. How are you feeling?"

"Awful. But it's only eleven, and I have to get back to work after this."

"Oh no, you won't make it."

"Sure I will."

"No, this last one is rough. I mean it is *very* unpleasant, going through. I saved it for last for a reason."

"What do you mean?"

"You'll see." Claire walked on in the dark, her shadow blinking under the streetlights.

Eleven

The last shortcut was through the back door of a glass-boxed luxury car showroom. Maseratis and Hummers crammed in close on the gleaming marble floor. A saleswoman in a cocktail dress approached them and her impossibly white teeth shone under the lights. Usher blared in the background. "Hi there," she said, in a heavy Russian accent. "How can I help you ladies?"

"We're just going through," Claire said. The shape of the woman's mouth didn't change, but her smile wobbled from a seductive curve to a stiff, involuntary grin. "Of course. Well, I'm sure you know where to go."

"Sure do, thanks!" Claire said, a little too brightly, compensating for the woman's sudden grimness. "Don't look so worried," she said to Jean quietly, taking her hand as she had done before launching them both down each of the previous cuts. "It's not pretty, but it works."

"Anything special I should do? Hold my breath?"

Claire gave her a sympathetic look. "Just hold on." Claire gave her fingers a squeeze and opened a door to a silver Mercedes C-Class crowded against the back wall.

There was no lead-up to this shortcut; it slurped them up like a giant, greedy mouth. It was uncomfortable, compressive, and also inexpressibly gooey, like being sucked back into the birth canal. Jean had a hard time remaining calm. Her body thrashed against the space, her heartbeat painful in the exertion of its own interior violence. Jean had had many panic attacks in her short life, so she knew what to expect. Part of her strategy with the attacks was the talking herself down: *this isn't actually dangerous; it's only a trick of the mind.* She tried this now, except she was lying, and her body knew it. Claire's voice called out for Iggy, high and wild as Jean's erratic heart rate. Jean could barely move. Perhaps the same had happened to Iggy and he stood here, somewhere, frozen, just like her.

Claire yanked her forward until they both lurched out of that vortex of terror into a night game of softball at a park coiled beside the East River. They had emerged from a maintenance shed, and the scent of mulch as well as the metallic tang of blood overwhelmed Jean. She crouched in the artificial grass, close enough to the game to be one of the outfielders. Claire dropped to the ground beside her. "He wasn't there," she said, quiet.

Jean collapsed forward onto her hands and knees, unable to prevent the irresistible shove of gravity, and fell further, onto her stomach. She rolled over and looked at Claire. The short, synthetic grass itched her cheek. "We'll make another plan." The grass smelled like piss. Jean sat up slowly, trying not to vomit.

Claire shook her head. "I can't believe he's gone, because of me."

"You don't know that. He has to be somewhere out here." She lifted her arm and drew a hovering arc in the space between them.

Claire covered her face with her hands. "What if he's dead?"

Jean paused. She wanted to say something kind or comforting, but instead she said, "You should call someone."

"Who am I going to call? Iggy's *family*?"

"No, I mean, you should call someone for you. A friend."

Claire shook her head, stood, and staggered away, leaving Jean on the ground in a confused heap. Jean tried to sit up but discovered she was no longer on the city park's turf. She was kneeling on the concrete terrace of a low apartment building, the cement scratching the skin where her Strawberry Shortcake nightgown rode up. Her father was passed out in the car in the lot below. His box of tools was splayed open before her and she selected carefully from it, testing the lock at her eye level. An impatient landlord in his pajamas stood smoking beside her. "Hurry the fuck up, kid," he said, banging on the door as she worked.

Jean's fingers were cold and slow in the night air. She flinched away from his anger and tried to work. When the lock gave, she knew she'd done a clumsy job. It was ruined—the landlord would have to replace it, but she didn't tell him that. "About fucking time." He stamped his cigarette out and shoved the door open, stepping over Jean where she sat, cross-legged, packing up the tools.

"Holy shit!" The landlord lurched back through the door, holding his T-shirt over his nose. Jean shuddered as the unmistakable odor of decay hit her in a gruesome wave. She knew she shouldn't—a scent like that meant bad news—but she looked through the doorway.

A woman covered in blood and flies lay askew on the floor. Jean turned just in time to vomit away from the landlord's bare feet and the box of her father's priceless tools.

"What the hell, get out of here, kid!" The landlord moved to close the door against the smell, against the sight. Jean knew she had to go but she also knew she couldn't leave without the money for the job.

"It's fifty dollars?" Her voice hung, uncertain, in the air.

The smack of ball on glove eventually snapped her out of it, and she rolled herself up slowly. Dizziness crashed against the insides of her skull. She pulled her phone from her jacket pocket. It was already after 1:00 a.m. Jean stood up and wobbled to her shift at the bakery.

That night, they made cinnamon rolls. Not regular ones— Lu's special ones, with cardamom and dulce de leche. Lu was nervous because the next day the rolls would debut on the restaurant's dessert menu. Her last riff on French pastries had not been well received, and the owner of the café and the chef at the restaurant had given her a stern warning. Jean couldn't imagine anyone giving Lu a warning of any kind.

She could almost see Lu's nervous energy snap in the air, like the static sparks in a load of laundry fresh from the dryer. Jean knew when a person crackled like this, they could be dangerous. And, while she didn't fear a physical confrontation from Lu, she still kept her head down and her mouth shut. Nas's *Illmatic*, a heavily rotated favorite of Lu's, bled through the speakers. Jean weighed out bowls of spices for the filling, but the numbers on the digital scale blurred before her eyes. Maybe using the cuts one after the other had temporarily affected her vision. Maybe she just needed glasses. All of Jean's squinting intensified her headache so much that her ears stung. She didn't want to say anything, but the pain compelled her. "Do we have any Tylenol here?" Her voice sounded nervous and abrasive.

"What?" Lu asked sharply, rolling out a thin sheet of dough across the worktable.

"Tylenol?"

"First aid kit. On the shelf where they keep the cups and lids and shit." Jean stared at Lu's hands, pressing and pulling the dough. It made her blood run cold; it looked so much like skin.

"Yes?" Lu prompted, acknowledging herself watched.

"Nothing, sorry." Jean poured herself another coffee. Her

body was angry. She closed her eyes, making promises to do better later. Jean fumbled with the plastic first aid kit, and it fell to the floor, shattering medical supplies across the ground. She heard Lu shout just before her vision blurred into one giant dark spot. Jean knew what it was to faint—she knew it was happening now. She gripped the counter and broke her fall to the Italian ceramic floor before her mind went truly dark.

The sound of a slap, skin on skin, brought her back to the café floor. Lu's furious face loomed over her. "Are you serious? You're fainting on me right now? *Today?*" Jean realized Lu was slapping her face indiscriminately, just covering her cheeks and forehead and the bridge of her nose with tiny smacks. Jean forced her eyes open.

"Oh, thank God. What happened? Are you okay? I didn't know if I should call an ambulance or what, but I figured you didn't have insurance, so I just waited."

"Yeah, I don't have insurance" were the first words out of Jean's mouth. "I'm fine, though."

"What happened?" Lu regarded her closely.

"I have no idea."

"Are you sick? Dehydrated? Did you eat tonight?"

Jean shook her head where it rested on Lu's folded legs. It felt like a massive, elaborate design of dominoes was thunderously collapsing inside of her body.

"You're a real dummy, you know that?" Lu sounded more relieved than angry, and that made Jean feel a little better. "I know you don't have a lot of time between your shifts, but you've got to take care of yourself. Here." She gently shifted Jean up and rested her back against the base of the counter. Jean's sight line revealed a flurry of straw wrappers underneath that the porter had missed. Lu disappeared but Jean could hear her behind the bank of shelves, moving amid a clatter of plastic bins opening and closing. The kiss and smack of a refrigerator door punctuated her work. She rounded the corner, and all Jean could see were her pants and dusty kitchen clogs.

"Here." Lu handed down a sandwich on a plate—one of the good plates, not from the café but from the restaurant.

Jean took a bite and felt a little better. The bracing salt of olive paste and creamy cheese on the warm bread they had just made would make anyone feel better. She still felt a little nauseated and off, but ate the sandwich, hoping it would recalibrate her system— or at least get her through the last hour of her shift. She handed up the empty plate to Lu, who had stayed there, standing over her.

"You still don't look so good."

"My eyes hurt," Jean confessed. She tipped her head up so that she could see Lu's face.

It was drawn with concern. "Do you need to go home?"

Jean shook her head. "Of course not—I'll be fine. Let me just drink some more water and wash my hands."

Lu helped her up and held her at the elbow like she was somebody's old grandmother shuffling down the church aisle to take Communion. "I'm really okay," Jean said, as she dried her hands.

Back at the workbench, Jean took over rolling out the dough while Lu mixed the precise spice measurements.

"Should I put nuts in this?" Lu stirred the bronze powder together, frowning.

"I would say yes, but people have allergies. You have to think about that." Jean was relieved that the conversation was settling into familiar, easy territory.

"Can I ask you something else?"

"Sure." Jean smiled, or at least thought she smiled, over the landscape of flattened dough.

"What's really going on with you?"

Jean froze, panicked.

"Is it drugs?"

"Oh my God!" Jean exclaimed, an involuntary indignation rising up behind her ribs.

"Well? Is it?" Lu looked only into the bowl, not at her.

"No, it isn't *drugs*." The rolling pin in Jean's hands clattered to the floor.

"You sure you don't want to come clean? Now would be the time."

"It's nothing! I'm completely fine," Jean said, trying to control her response.

"If it's not drugs, what is it? It's definitely something. Are you pregnant? People faint when they're pregnant. My Auntie Fatima passed out all the time when she was pregnant with Omar."

"*No!* Jesus." Jean scrubbed her hands across her face and through her hair.

"Well? It's something, Jean. And while it may not be my personal business, it's definitely my professional business if you're passing out at work."

Jean closed her eyes tight, willing away the question, willing away Lu entirely.

"As much as I wish I could be delicate here, I absolutely do not have the time. What's going on?"

"It's going to sound totally absurd," Jean began, but swiftly clamped her mouth shut. She was desperate to keep the information contained, buried inside her body, but her body wouldn't hold it. Her body pushed the information out; it emerged with the inescapable velocity of a bulb buried in the earth. "There are these shortcuts, all over the city."

"No, no, no." Lu groaned, throwing down the whisk she had been using to combine the different sugars. "You've got to be fucking kidding me. Not you, Jean! Not you, too." She shook her head, and her posture collapsed.

"What? You know about the shortcuts?" Jean asked, incredulous. "Does Omar know?"

"Do you think I was born yesterday? And no, Omar doesn't know and he better not find out about them from you." Lu flung her whisk into the sink. "These fucking cinnamon rolls are not going to happen tonight, are they?" Lu paced the perimeter of the kitchen, dead silent, while Jean told her about Iggy and all that she and Claire had done to recover him.

"That was really fucking stupid, Jean. You know that, right?"

"I felt responsible," Jean said, looking down at the hand-painted tile beneath her feet. "Since I went through with him right before he disappeared. I don't want that on my conscience."

"Listen," Lu said, finally pausing in front of her. "Your conscience is one thing. I can't tell you anything about that—but your actual human life—*your health*—that is something I can tell you about. These shortcuts aren't free, no matter what anybody tells you. They take it out of you. I mean physically. You can probably tell! You're not stupid."

Jean stared down at her hands and couldn't answer.

"That's right, you're passing out at work! And forget what it does to your health—your friend Iggy? Do you really think he's the first person to disappear like that?"

"What?" Jean looked up sharply.

"You really think this is something new, that he's the first person this happened to?" Lu shook her head, her mouth set in a disgusted, fed-up line.

"What are you saying?"

"I'm saying a lot of people disappear thanks to this bullshit. *I* lost someone to this bullshit." Lu ran the water in the sink steaming hot over the flour-encrusted dishes.

"Oh, Lu, I'm so sorry."

"Someone I loved a lot. My friend Steph—she was like a sister to me. She lived in my building and we grew up together, you know? She was smart, too." Lu squirted an aggressive amount of detergent into the sink. The tang of lemons lifted in the air. "She got, I don't know, obsessed with these things. Like she couldn't talk or think about anything else. And then one day she was gone. Those fucking things ate her alive."

"What happened to her?"

"Jean, if I knew what happened to her, I'd be a lot happier."

"Look, I'm sorry—I know this is inappropriate and that I'm being incredibly unprofessional, but I need to do the right thing. You don't have to tell me anything, but maybe you know somebody who'd talk to me about this? I don't know what to do, and neither does Claire. I can't just let a person vanish without…"

"Without what?" Lu asked sharply.

"Without doing everything I can."

Lu turned abruptly to face her. Her eyes burned through Jean. "I am telling you, *everything you can* is not enough. It won't ever be enough. Now pull yourself together and help me make these cinnamon rolls."

They did finish the cinnamon rolls and Jean left her shift feeling jittery and obscenely awake. The events of the night jabbed at her like a thousand insistent fingers, and no matter how many times she rolled and shifted in her bed, she couldn't find comfort. Everything was open and unresolved; she couldn't stop thinking.

She reached for her phone to check the time. It was nearly 7:30 a.m. Maybe, since she was already awake, she should make that visit to Dr. Goldstein's office. Replays of the uncomfortable conversations with Donna and Jeffrey punctuated her sleepless thoughts. She hadn't texted Claire about her conversation with Lu over the shortcuts, but she knew that she should.

Jean dressed quickly, hoping to get out of the apartment before Molly and Christine woke up, but realized her mistake once she was back out on the frigid sidewalk. The office would be closed till 10:00 a.m. She'd have to kill an hour or so before going uptown. Jean walked to the diner, the one that held the first shortcut she had ever taken, for breakfast. She ordered a coffee and a plate of pancakes, her appetite fully restored. The diner was mostly empty—the only customers there were people like her: people on their way to or from work. There was no hint of mischief anywhere among the polished chrome fixtures or weary faces of the few people keeping to themselves over their meals. The only volume aside from the sounds of the kitchen came from a table where a very young mother nursed a baby and spoon-fed cottage cheese to a babbling toddler.

She left a pile of cash for the thin-lipped, exhausted waiter, and stood to use the bathroom. In the hallway she paused to consider the Employees Only door. The knob didn't turn under her hand. She was compelled, for a minute, to pick the lock and go through again, just one more time, to check for Iggy. She couldn't help but think this particular shortcut was significant, that he was there, stranded, because of her. It couldn't be a co-incidence that he disappeared right after he revealed this par-ticular shortcut to *her*. If Jean knew the body didn't lie, she also knew there was no such thing as a coincidence. A coincidence was just another word for connection. But she resisted the com-pulsion to check; it was morning, after all. She didn't want to make any more stupid mistakes.

She took the train to Central Park West, relaxing in the post–rush hour silence of the mostly filled seats. The energy inside the subway car was cotton candy soft, filled with peo-ple who had been asleep only minutes ago. Jean loved noticing this softness—a rare, precious thing in such a big, difficult city. Whenever she could find it, it felt like a great secret.

This commute was muscle memory—the transfer, the exit, the turn around the corner of sidewalk, and then the park, gleaming up ahead. She headed toward the two matching tow-ers where Dr. Goldstein lived and worked. The street entrance to Dr. Goldstein's office was still locked. The office was on the ground floor of the first tower, and her apartment was on the forty-fourth. The towers shone shell pink in the thin early morning sun, and Jean squinted against their brilliance as she entered the first one. She rounded a marble corner toward the service entrance to Dr. Goldstein's office.

Jean had never returned the office key. Dr. Goldstein never

demanded it back, and Jean couldn't quite part with it—it was a memento of her time there that made the rest of her keys look less lonely on their little silver hoop. She withdrew her keychain from her jacket pocket and unlocked the door. Jean was certain Dr. Goldstein wouldn't mind her having access to the office. At least, Jean told herself that to settle her qualms over the technicality of breaking and entering a place where people's medical records were stored. The lock turned beneath her fingers and Jean gasped at what waited for her inside. Her winter coat, encased in a dry cleaner's plastic wrap, hung on the back of the door.

A pervading odor of mold swelled out at her and turned Jean's stomach. She held her breath and pulled her scarf up over her nose and mouth. She flicked on the lights and walked into her little office, the offshoot of Dr. Goldstein's larger plush one.

The office was unrecognizable. Banks of filing cabinets were yanked away from the walls and crowded the middle of the room. Her old desk chair lay on its side on the floor like a stroke victim. Jean's heart raced. She was frozen by the disarray. Could Jeffrey have done this? Jean cast back in her memory for any other possible culprits—maybe a former patient?

Jean unlocked the bolt that connected her old office to Dr. Goldstein's. She expected to see the familiar clean carpets, Dr. Goldstein's tasteful arrangement of furniture designed to accommodate all types of families in all types of distress, the black-and-white prints of photographed canyons and mountain ranges surrounding them on the walls.

Instead, Jean saw more of the same chaos. Some of the furniture was missing and a few of the carpets were rolled back. The scent of mold was strongest in Dr. Goldstein's office. Her heavy walnut desk was scarred with strange, small markings. The closer Jean looked at them, the more sinister they grew. Like a grim Magic Eye poster, coalescing into a desperate 3D image she couldn't quite determine; she only knew it was there. Jean pressed her fingers against her throat to check her pulse. It was another trick she had learned over the years, to ground herself when she began to feel the gallop of panic.

All of Dr. Goldstein's knickknacks and photographs were gone, with one strange exception. The photograph of Jeffrey, the one Jean had recalled while speaking to him on the phone. It sat on the ruined empty desk, in the place where Dr. Goldstein's massive computer monitor had once stood. The photograph was old, from Jeffrey's graduate school graduation ceremony. He stood beside his mother—she was in heels and their faces were at the same height. Dr. Goldstein's neat gray bob swayed pleasantly around her smiling face, and her glasses were those overlarge wire-framed pairs people wore in the '80s. Jeffrey looked uncomfortable, like his clothes didn't fit quite right, but also shy. Jean had always thought it was a sweet picture, but when she picked it up to examine it more closely, she saw a hard set to Jeffrey's mouth that transformed his face from uncomfortable to enraged. Once she saw it, she couldn't unsee it. She was careful to put the frame back exactly as it was. She switched off the lights, seized her coat, and locked the door behind her.

The sidewalk outside was crowded by a tour group. They formed a colossal, seductive swirl. It would be so easy, Jean thought, to dissolve among them. Nobody would fault her for minding her own business and turning around. But Jean's body insisted, like it was holding her in place. Even if she could just go home, she knew she shouldn't.

She was caught in a temporary scrum of men in nearly identical suits. One of them caught her eyes in a lurid gaze. She grimaced through them and realized she was already walking toward the residential entrance of Dr. Goldstein's apartment building. Jean didn't feel right spinning through the revolving front door. The girl reflected back at her in the mirrored lobby looked unfamiliar and sallow.

"Oh no, is that Jean?" Marcus was the weekday doorman

in Dr. Goldstein's residential building. His friendliness was rococo—almost overwhelming in its cheer and bonhomie.

"Hey, Marcus. Just stopping by to check in on Dr. Goldstein."

Marcus came around the lobby's reception desk and embraced her in the kind of hug given at holiday parties. "It's good to see you! How come you didn't stop by sooner?"

"I've been working a lot—at my new job."

"Right, right, of course." Marcus nodded gravely. "Do you want a coffee? Come sit with me a second."

Jean paused, but, after a moment, nodded. It would be good to talk to Marcus, to catch up. He was observant and would know if something strange was going on with Dr. Goldstein.

"Cover for me a second. I'll be right back."

Jean sat back in the ergonomic rolling desk chair and was suddenly overtaken by weariness. A white-blond woman in a heavy burgundy wool coat took her dog out. Jean tried to smile as though she was supposed to be there, but it didn't matter; the woman barely registered her presence.

Marcus held the side door open for her as he reentered the building; the little dog refused to use the revolving door. "You take care, Snips," he said, with a nod at the dog. Marcus's hands were full of wares from the coffee cart in front of the building. "You want a bagel? I got an extra one just in case." He tenderly set down a fat, warm cream cheese bagel in front of her, and she was so touched, she opened it and started to eat, even though she had only just had her breakfast. Or dinner. Or whatever it was.

"Thanks, Marcus—this is really kind of you."

"Don't thank me. This is our little reunion! And here's your coffee." Marcus punched open the tiny plastic tab for her as though she were his child or his lover. Her eyes filled with tears. "Oh no, Jean, no." Marcus shook his head. "This reunion is a happy one. How you been?"

"I've been working a lot," Jean began. "I guess I'm just stressed. How are you? How's everything here?" She took a large bite of the bagel and chewed theatrically to fend off any follow-up questions about her emotional state. Marcus had only ever seen her at her most professional.

"Well, *I'm* fine."

"That's good," Jean said, smiling over the rim of her paper coffee cup. "How does Dr. Goldstein seem to you?"

"Ah," Marcus nodded. "Right. I haven't seen the girl who took over for you lately, Arpita?"

"Yes, Arpita. She called me actually, saying she was worried. Which, honestly, is why I'm here."

"Arpita is a nice girl," Marcus said, his face like a diplomat's. He unfolded the foil from his egg and cheese sandwich.

"But?" Jean said.

"There's no but!" Marcus held his hands up like a stand-up comic.

"There's a but; I can tell." Jean took a sip.

"It's a small but. Very small."

"Okay?" Jean held her cup in both hands and felt truly warm for the first time in forty-eight hours.

"Arpita is a nice girl, but she's not you. This was just a job for her, you could tell. I always thought Dr. Goldstein looked at you like a daughter, you know?"

Jean froze. She could no longer suppress the dangerous surge of feeling that word released—*daughter.* It was just a word, but when it was used to describe her, Jean was overcome with wild sadness. An endearing term, eternally raw, one that she had strived to insulate herself from. But of course that's how Dr. Goldstein had seen her. Of course that was really why she quit. Jean had never imagined that anyone else could see it, but there it had been, as obvious as a new haircut.

"Is Dr. Goldstein okay?" Jean asked slowly. She barely recognized her own voice. It sounded low and rough.

Marcus bent his head over the desk, over the open guest book for visitors, and Jean spotted a dark drop of liquid that stained the collar of his uniform jacket. "Listen, I'm not supposed to see anything, except when I am, you know?"

Jean nodded. They were so close there was barely a fist's breadth between them.

"I don't like what I'm not supposed to be seeing with Dr. Goldstein."

"You mean with her son?"

Marcus nodded.

"Do you think…" Jean rested her coffee cup on the desk; it suddenly felt too heavy to hold. "Do you think he's hurting her?"

"Yes." The bitterness in Marcus's voice burned in her ears.

"Why do you think that? Have you seen something?"

Marcus glanced at the elevators, all quiet in their silent, engraved row. "I know he's taking advantage. He talks to her like she's an animal. I always liked Dr. Goldstein. She was a really friendly person. But now, she doesn't say a word to me. Even if she's alone."

"Does *he* ever talk to you?"

"He's never said a word to me. Not even hello, not even a wave. Something's not right with him."

"Should I go up? Are they there?"

"I haven't seen them all week. I'll tell you what. You still have your key?"

Jean shook her head. "Not to her apartment—just to the office next door."

"How about I give you her mail? If I let you up, I'll have to explain it—which I don't know if I should. But if you ask me to let you up there, I will. I really will, Jean, because I trust you and it would be the right thing to do."

"I don't want you to lose your job, Marcus."

"Right now, I'm just talking to an old friend. I'm not going to lose anything. But you should know nobody's checked that mailbox in a couple of weeks."

Jean raised her eyebrows.

"That's right. I got a whole pile of mail in the back. Let's finish our breakfast here and then I'll leave the box for you in the mailroom. You're still on her authorized list to pick up mail and any deliveries. She never took you off."

"Has she had any deliveries?" Jean asked, leaning in even closer.

"Some furniture, big things like that. Not regular deliveries. Not even groceries." Marcus pursed his lips.

"What else? Marcus, you can tell me."

"She's had a lot of visitors. At first, I thought it was family since her son was visiting, but these people who are coming to see her? These people are not family."

"Are they Jeffrey's friends?"

"These people don't look too friendly."

Jean took a deep breath and finished the last of her coffee. "Thanks for telling me all of this."

Marcus shrugged. "Like I said, I always liked Dr. Goldstein. I don't think anybody should be treated the way she's being treated."

"Should I call the police? If it's elder abuse, maybe I should do that?"

"I can't tell you what to do. I don't know what he's doing to her—if it's physical or mental or whatnot, I can't say. I can only give you her mail."

Jean nodded, her nostrils suddenly filled with the scent of artificial cinnamon. She felt a creeping, prickling feeling behind her ears, like when her hair had been long and she tied a ponytail too tight. It was an eerie sensation—a feeling of being watched.

"I have all of it packed up. I'll go put it in the mailroom. I don't want the cameras picking up anything special. It's just between us."

"Of course."

Marcus told her all about his son's soccer team and she told him about making pastries at the café, but not the bar. She wasn't sure why. Mostly it was because she didn't want Marcus to worry about her. Jean wanted to be the same reliable girl in his eyes that she had always been—the kind of girl you would entrust a box of personal documents with. Not the kind of girl who was hungover thanks to her unorthodox experiments with space and time. Not the kind of girl with co-workers who disappeared.

Jean and Marcus hugged, and she gave him her email address in case his son needed help studying for the SATs. She knew he would never reach out, but felt like she needed to contribute to the exchange. Jean went to the mailroom and nostalgia shuddered through her. She had come to this mailroom thousands of times. She tried to remember what it was like to be that aimless, quiet person. A person who was steady and sensible. A person who had never heard of the shortcuts.

The sight of her name scrawled in Sharpie on the side of a cardboard file box nearly tipped her over the sharp edge of her feelings. Jean hadn't thought about Marcus once for all of the weeks she'd been away. Here, a person she had seen every day— many times a day—was swallowed up somewhere in her mind. But Marcus had thought of her.

Jean lifted the box into her arms. She left through the service door and stumbled, finally feeling the hours of missed sleep. She thought she heard a gasp from somewhere behind her. She turned but saw no one.

Twelve

Jean was desperate to be home. She was desperate to be off her feet. Jean had never been so tempted to hail a taxi or to scry out another shortcut. Instead, she carried the box with her dry-cleaned coat folded on top down into the subway, ferried it through both of her transfers, and trod it up the three flights of stairs to her mercifully empty apartment. She couldn't shake the feeling that someone had followed her. Maybe it was just another symptom from all of her recent shortcut use.

It was nearly noon, and Molly and Christine were gone for the day. Jean dropped the box and pulled off all her clothes. She let the shower wash away the night that had felt like twenty nights, drank a glass of water, lowered her blinds, and went to bed.

Jean woke up just in time to get dressed before leaving for her shift at Red and Gold. She snatched up all of her abandoned clothes and the box full of mail, and packed everything into her room, away from the eyes of her roommates. The apartment smelled like garlic in a hot pan, and Jean's stomach grumbled. She turned on the tap and reached for her toothbrush. As the mint foamed in her mouth she combed her hair down and away from her face with her free hand, inspecting her appearance. In the dark bar, nobody would notice how unkempt she was. Compared to Mitch, she would look positively polished. A small smile from her lips bounced back at her in the mirror. Jean spat into the sink and scraped the smile away as she remembered everything Marcus told her about Jeffrey and his "friends."

She opened the bathroom door and yelped. Molly was waiting just outside, holding a fragrant mug of tea and wearing an open, empathetic expression.

"Oh my God! Molly! You scared me." Jean let out a relieved little sigh.

"I'm sorry. I just wanted to make sure I caught you before you left for work. Your new schedule is bananas." Molly's curly red hair was twisted up off her freckly neck with a plastic butterfly clip.

"Oh yeah. It's definitely been an adjustment. Is everything okay? You got the cash I left for rent and bills and everything, right?"

"Oh absolutely," Molly said, nodding vigorously. "I just wanted to check in with you. We haven't seen you in so long." Christine joined them, holding a greasy wooden spoon aloft and away from her clothes.

"Hey, Jean," Christine said. "Long time no see." She motioned to Molly to give her a sip from the mug. Jean averted her eyes from the domestic intimacy.

"Yeah, it's just this new, flipped, like, night schedule."

"How are you doing? Is it going okay?" Molly asked, regarding her with a pensive squint. "I saw that you found your coat! That's great." Molly pointed to the hook by the door where Jean's parka nestled beside the other jackets and scarves. Jean's heart stuttered—she didn't remember peeling the coat out of its plastic wrap and putting it where it belonged.

Jean shook her head. "Everything's fine!" She heard the tightly strung brightness in her voice, but it was too late to do anything about it. She rushed toward the door and jammed her feet into her boots. "My new job is actually really interesting. I'm loving the work in the kitchen. It's so creative," she embellished. "I really feel like I hit on a hidden talent, you know?"

Molly nodded again; this time the tightness around her mouth eased a little. "That's great. Listen, I know you've always said no in the past, but I wanted to reach out about Thanksgiving one more time."

"Oh, right." Jean looped her scarf around her face. She could still smell the mildew from Dr. Goldstein's office.

"I just don't want you to be alone." Molly's forehead bunched in concern.

"I'm not going to be alone," Jean replied, a little too loudly. "I'm doing a thing with my new co-workers at the bakery. You know, at the restaurant," she lied.

"That sounds really fun," Christine said, her voice kind. "See, babe? She's doing great." Molly gave them both the same tight smile.

"If you're sure," she said.

"Oh I am. But thanks for looking out for me." Jean paused and looked Molly in the eye, the same way she would have with one of Dr. Goldstein's patients who had a billing issue and felt frustrated. "It means a lot. I'm sorry I haven't been around as much, but I am doing great. It's just the schedule that's weird."

Molly nodded. "Okay. Let's plan something for your next day off so we can catch up."

"Sounds good," Jean said, knowing with great relief it would never happen. "Well, I better go."

"Jean, aren't you going to put on your coat?" Molly asked.

Jean managed a weak laugh. "Wow, yeah. It's been so long

since I've had it." She shrugged on the dark gray parka and zipped it up, bracing herself in anticipation of another whiff of mildew. But all she could smell was the smoky, buttery fragrance of movie theater popcorn. "Weird," she whispered, half to Molly and Christine and half to herself. "I'll see you guys later."

Red and Gold was humming. There must have been some holiday because the college kids were all out. Every table was occupied, and Mitch was in the weeds. A scrum of youths made cutting comments about Mitch's speed and attention, and her usually jovial co-worker looked more worn-out than she'd ever seen him. Jean quickly shed her coat and joined him behind the bar.

"Nice to have you back," Mitch grumbled.

"Hey." She nodded hello and took an order for four vodka sodas. "What's going on in here tonight?"

"Fall break. These kids have off for Thanksgiving."

"Already?"

"They get a lot of time off, these students." Mitch shot a disapproving glare at a trio of boys in matching haircuts and varying degrees of skinny ties. "That's all you," he said, glancing in their direction.

Jean cracked open three PBRs and shuffled them forward.

"Can you make some change for me?" A tall girl wearing a necktie as a belt winked at her. Jean smiled and made the change.

"How was it working with Alan last night?" she asked Mitch.

"The best. I love that beautiful man. Do you think he'd take any of Iggy's shifts?"

"Probably not. He has another job. Do you really think Iggy just took off for good?"

"Sure, sure," Mitch said, smiling at a girl and an older woman who was obviously her mother. "Why? You worried?"

"I don't know. Yes?"

"Jean Jeanie, with the hidden depths! I'd never guess you were such a softie—I'm sure he's fine."

Jean furrowed her brow and considered mentioning the short-cuts to him. A bizarre jukebox transition—"Teenage Dirtbag" to "Suffragette City"—distracted her.

The rest of the shift passed in a kaleidoscopic blur. Jean made hundreds of vodka sodas, but then—inexplicably—hundreds of cosmos, a drink she had never made before that night. The mother and daughter ordered appletinis, and Jean had no idea what to do, but Mitch seemed happy to take over for her. There was a minor lull when the venue next door opened, but the crowd remained unusually constant.

In a small break where everyone had been served and nobody needed anything, Mitch leaned into flirting with the mother in the mother-daughter pair. "Jean!" Mitch called. "Come take a shot with us. It's on the lovely Phyllis, here!"

Jean shook her head, smiling. "That's very generous."

"I insist, really," Phyllis said, her voice pitched too high. Mitch lined up four bright blue shots and Jean took one. She had to leave for the bakery in about an hour, and she figured the shot would give her the morale boost she needed to get from one job to the next. She cringed at the prospect of showing up for Lu late, especially after what happened the night before, and considered the cost of a taxi.

"It wasn't that bad, was it?" Mitch asked, slapping her on the back.

Jean smiled and relaxed her face. "No, it was great. Thanks so much, Phyllis." Jean reached her hand over the bar and shook Phyllis's hand formally, as though they were meeting at a wedding reception. "Mitch, do you mind if I leave a little early? I can't be late to the bakery."

"The bakery! My, my, you are an industrious girl," Phyllis slurred.

"So true, Phyllis," Mitch said with a wink. Phyllis junior

giggled beside her mother. "Excuse us a minute, would you ladies?" He shot them a roguish smile.

"Listen," he said, washing a batch of dishes. "Normally I would be like, have at it. But today is out of control. No predictions coming true this weekend, you know what I mean? We could get slammed ten minutes before closing, and while I love you, I need you here. Is that okay?"

"Yeah, sure. No problem."

"Good, because I'm trying to get Phyllis to take me back to her hotel tonight."

"TMI, Mitch."

"What? I love hotel breakfast."

Jean made a wave of closing time margaritas for a group of work colleagues whose happy hour had gone off the rails. Joy Division droned on endlessly thanks to a melancholy fan in a bolo tie bogarting the jukebox. Jean willed the time to pass quickly; she was already getting tired. Her big morning uptown had worn her out. Something about contorting herself into her old life—getting on those same trains, being who she used to be for Marcus, even setting foot in the office—it all reminded her she wasn't the same person who quit those many weeks ago.

Mitch finally pulled down the gate and she turned up the lights, singeing her eyes. Jean started counting out the drawer while Mitch counted the tips. "We did good tonight, Jean Jeanie," he said, whistling the chorus to David Bowie's song.

"That's a relief." She sighed.

"Why? Things getting tight? It's the holidays, I get it."

"Things are always tight."

"What're you doing for them? For the holidays?"

"What do you mean?" Jean asked, suspicious.

"Thanksgiving, for example." Mitch gestured with a flourish, like a magician producing a coin from some unsuspecting person's ear.

"Oh my God! Why is everyone suddenly obsessed with Thanksgiving?" Jean's anger corkscrewed out into the empty bar. She hated these kinds of questions; she hated that Mitch hadn't let her leave early; she hated jolly Phyllis and her jolly daughter.

"Whoa, whoa, whoa. Easy there, tiger. Wow, who knew cool as a cucumber Jeanie had a temper on her?"

"Sorry," Jean muttered, counting the last of the five-dollar bills.

"No, I'm sorry. It's none of my business. I just assumed you had some loving familial arms to run to and that would require a plane ticket. Holiday travel adds up. I'm going to see my sister in Nashville for Christmas."

"That's nice."

"Yeah, she has two little boys, and my parents will probably make it out there, too. Maybe…"

"What?"

"If you don't have any plans…"

"I don't."

"Maybe you'll want to cover some of my shifts that week?"

"I'd be happy to, but since we mostly work together, that's not going to really help much."

"Fucking Iggy, man. Leaving us in the lurch right at the holidays. Like Scrooge fucking McDuck."

A bolt of guilt lanced Jean clean through. "I'm sure whatever happened, he couldn't help it."

Mitch scrutinized her through narrowed eyes. "Yeah, sure he couldn't."

"Look," Jean said, pocketing her tips. "Whatever I can do to help. I'll be here. But now I have to go or else I'll be late!"

Jean jogged the few blocks to the train. Whenever she moved her body like this, she had to fight it to stay slow and moderate. Her body always wanted to run. Nervous energy pinged through her muscles. Nothing would feel better than to stretch her limbs and heart as far as they could go, to sweat out all of the harsh strangeness that had accumulated inside of her. But Jean was smart. She knew what would happen to her if she allowed her body to take what it wanted. She would be trapped in bed for days, recuperating for an indefinite amount of time, missing work, missing everything. It was better if she stayed on an even keel. *Look what happened to you when you strayed from your lane,* she scolded herself, thinking of Iggy and the mess with the shortcuts that she had gotten caught up in.

Jean shook her head firmly and walked down the subway steps carefully, like a sensible person. A train rumbled away on the opposite track. Jean stood, leaning out over the well of tracks, beyond the yellow line that had inspired such fear in her when she first arrived in the city. She squinted into the dark and willed the train to come. She checked the time on her phone again—she was going to be really late. It was so late, even a taxi wouldn't save her.

"Okay," she said out loud. A slouching woman sitting on the bench next to her suddenly sat up. Jean turned around, and really ran this time. She ran up the steps and she ran through the empty streets, dodging cyclists and veering out of the way of taxis peeling up and down the avenue. She ran until she was at the diner, and she had never felt more dangerous.

The diner was as busy as it had been that first night she came in with Iggy. Busier, even. She composed herself while she twisted through the legs hanging out in the aisle and the sustained hustle of the waiters and busboys. A woman caught her eye; her gaze was like a needle in a record's groove—sharp and hunting. Jean felt a twinge of recognition; the woman looked familiar. She was older, stylish; her light hair curled around her shoulders. She sat in a booth alone in a neat dark wool coat. Jean smoothed her hair back, her temples misty with sweat. The woman was probably at Red and Gold earlier. Jean squinted to get a better look. She might have been with one of Iggy's friends at Transmission. Jean was getting too suspicious. Maybe it was another side effect of the shortcuts.

Jean quickened her pace and kept her eyes on the floor as she passed the woman in the booth. She shouldered open the Employees Only door with a familiarity that startled her—it seemed sinister that she now knew the weight of the wood and the action of the hinge. She pushed past the unease and walked through the passage, holding her breath. Maybe if she didn't inhale whatever existed in that murk, it wouldn't affect her so much.

On the other side, she felt more affected than ever. Jean staggered through her dizziness toward the opening into the bar basement. The lights were still dim, and the music was still loud. Claire's familiar figure shone from behind the bar, haloed by the lit shelf of spirits behind her. Jean was careful not to be seen as she slid through the crowd toward the exit. The doorman nodded at her with recognition and Jean felt a burst of panic. She tried to look normal and unassuming and smiled on her way out. Outside, a town car sped past her with its windows down blaring Outkast's "Hey Ya!"

Jean's fingers and toes tingled and she was swept into the pew of her old Pennsylvania church, stuffy with heat. Her body burned and itched—it was right before she got the chicken pox. Jean remembered the pink wool Sunday dress from that winter. She shifted and wiggled between her parents. "Bob, can you just take her outside? This is so embarrassing," her mother whispered over her head.

"Fine." Her father was cranky. Jean knew it was because he would rather be sleeping. It was what he'd screamed at her mother that morning over the cold scrambled eggs she couldn't stomach. They stood outside next to the car. "What's your problem?" he asked, chewing on a thumbnail. "Why do you keep making that sound?"

"My throat hurts," Jean told him as she scratched her arms through the itchy woolen sleeves. "Can I get my coat?"

"Can you quit whining for one fucking second?"

"Excuse me." An older lady stood on the steps of the church, holding Jean's faded plum jacket.

"Oh, thanks, Mrs. Rollins."

"It's no trouble. Your daughter doesn't look very well." Her eyes narrowed with disapproval.

"She's perfectly fine, aren't you, Jeanie?" He slapped her on the back a little too hard. Jean jolted under the force of it and nodded quietly. "Thanks for your concern, but we're A-OK."

"If you say so. God bless you both."

Her father snorted once Mrs. Rollins was back inside. "That nosy bitch can't mind her business for one goddamn minute. I fucking hate that your mother drags us here. Let her get a ride home with Mrs. Rollins. Me and you have other business, right, Jeanie?" He drove them to the liquor store parking lot, where Jean sweated through the steep climb of her fever in the back seat, her dress soaked through by the time her father began to snore in the driver's seat.

Jean felt herself back on the street, but the remnants of fever— that exhaustion and thirst—still clawed at her throat. She ducked under the gate for her next shift, and thought she saw the blond woman in the wool coat again. She shook her head. There were lots of blond women in wool coats in New York City.

Jean kept herself on her feet for the whole shift at the bakery, and even suggested adding more lemon zest to a pastry crème. She could tell that Lu was pleased with her. Lu was in a good mood all night. Jean had begun to collect Lu's tells the way she had Dr. Goldstein's. When Dr. Goldstein was in a bad mood, she always asked Jean for more water. Jean would get up to re-fill her glass, even if it was still mostly full. When Lu was in a good mood, they listened to Boyz II Men. All night. The hap-pier Lu was, the louder the music. Jean stood over the worktable, painstakingly grating the additional zest, the bald lemons lined up like shorn carcasses after a hunt.

"So," Lu said, turning down the volume so Jean knew she was serious. "You take my advice and leave that shit alone?"

Jean felt another throb of guilt. She decided the least dangerous thing to do would be to tell the truth.

"No."

Lu's voice grew brittle. "And why is that?"

"I don't know," Jean confessed. She lost her grip on the microplane and zested the tips of her knuckles. In the spark of that slipup, she resolved to stop using the shortcuts. Lu was right. She knew nothing good could come of it.

Lu turned the music off after that, and Jean zested on early into the morning. Her mind wandered to Dr. Goldstein and her son, hunting for a solution. She homed in on Jeffrey Goldstein and imagined a heart attack in the dead of night: a collapse no one would see or hear or meddle with. No kind passerby or medical intervention would scoop the life back into his body. He would be gone, and Dr. Goldstein's old life would resume.

Jean imagined his funeral—poorly attended, Dr. Goldstein sniffling in a smart black suit. Her eyes were sad but clear. Jean imagined another her, another Arpita, reassembling Dr. Goldstein's practice. Moving the furniture back where it belonged, a tactful letter—sometimes a letter that would turn into a sympathetic phone call—to all of her old patients. There was no way Dr. Goldstein was seeing patients in that office.

She and Lu silently parted ways on the sidewalk after letting in the morning baristas. Jean's fingers grew stiff with the cold, even inside her pockets. Still, she couldn't quite go home. She walked in the direction of her apartment instead of taking the train or the bus. The day broke reluctantly around her. It was going to be overcast; maybe it would even snow. The streets were empty in the neighborhoods between home and work. A few intrepid runners glided by, but none of them spared her a glance.

As she crossed the park, she was conscious of a stopped figure—someone was definitely watching her. She wrapped her fingers around her phone—the plastic seam where the factory had put the two halves of it together pinched the heel of her hand.

"Hey," the figure shouted, moving toward her.

Jean kept her head down, wondering if she would have time to call for help in the moments it would take for the figure to close the space between them. She desperately searched the perimeter of the park for another morning runner. If it came down to it, she reminded herself, she, too, could run. To save her life, she could always run.

The figure drew nearer, the outline of their body menacing against the bare tree branches. Jean braced herself against the ground, preparing to take off the way she once had at her high school track meets.

"Jean?" She paused, her heart thundering in the meat of her tongue. The figure jogged forward though the gloom, and as it drew closer, it coalesced into a familiar one: Alan. Jean's muscles relaxed. She closed her eyes, utterly relieved.

"Alan, hey," she said. "I thought you were some murderous stalker."

"Oh man, sorry about that." Alan inclined his head toward her in a sheepish bow.

"No worries—just glad it's you." Jean tried to temper her fluster by faking a cough.

"Where are you headed?"

"Finished my shift at the bakery. Heading home, I guess."

"Ah, right, the bakery. Sometimes it's hard to go straight home, isn't it?" Alan asked the question so softly it was like holding out the back of a hand to an animal.

Jean nodded, further relieved to feel understood in this small way.

"I'm actually on my way in to work. You want to come with me? We can get doughnuts."

"Sure, that would be great. But no doughnuts for me. I've been tasting caramel all night."

"Poor you," Alan said. His smile was worn but charming—Jean could almost see how handsome he had once been.

"Come on." He nodded for her to follow him. The morning grew lighter and grayer, but the humidity softened the temperature a little. Jean noticed that Alan was just as poorly dressed for winter as she had been. A cracked leather jacket and wool cap were his only protection against the weather.

"You don't have a winter coat?" Jean observed.

"I don't really need one." He shrugged. "My routes are pretty predictable and pretty short," he said, holding the door open to a coffee shop down the block from the pet store. The gates of most of the bars and restaurants were down, even though the sound of music still bled from underneath a few of them.

The girl behind the counter yawned. "Good morning," she said.

"Two coffees?" Alan asked and Jean nodded. "Can I get one of those doughnuts? The chocolate one."

The pastry case was still steamy from the hardworking percolator sitting right behind it. "You want something?" the sleepy girl asked Jean.

"Can I have a bagel?"

Alan paid, then Jean paid—the girl's eyelids drooped. "Just give me a second," she said.

Jean started to feel sleepy herself; the temperature inside of the coffee shop was as soothing as a warm bath.

"Here." The girl handed over their breakfasts, but her movements were off, as though their hands belonged to the characters in her dream.

"Thank you," Jean said wryly.

"Ah don't give Margot a hard time. She does her best," Alan said, leading her back out onto the sidewalk. "Here, can you hold this?" He handed her his coffee and unlocked the Woof-n-Wag.

"You're very generous, you know that? And patient." Jean took a sip of her coffee. "You'd actually make a great therapist."

"You think?" He held the door open for her.

"I know. Not everybody can do it. But you could."

Alan shrugged good-naturedly. "Kind of missed the boat, I guess."

The store was fully decorated for Christmas. All of the windows were festooned with silver tinsel. "You guys skip Thanksgiving around here, huh?" Jean said.

"The owner thinks the Christmassy stuff makes people spend more money." Alan switched on the neon Woof-n-Wag sign in the front window—a hot pink outline of the two high-fiving dogs.

"Does it?"

"Definitely." Alan disappeared in the back and reemerged in his bright blue work smock. He turned on the stereo—a top 40s station heavy on the Christmas tune rotation.

"Is the music part of the holiday purchase strategy?" Jean asked, over a cheery version of "Here Comes Santa Claus."

"Sure is." Alan set his coffee and doughnut down on the counter and motioned Jean over. They ate and drank in the fluorescent light of the store. The concentrated odor of synthetic fruit permeated the air, but Jean quickly grew used to it.

"Mitch was talking about you last night," she said, wiping the cream cheese from her face.

"Who's Mitch?" Alan asked.

"Ouch! Poor Mitch. He's very memorable. The guy who worked with you and Omar when you covered for me at Red and Gold."

"Oh right. What did he say?"

"All nice things. He wants you to take Iggy's shifts."

"Who's Iggy?"

Jean looked down and felt suddenly light-headed. "He used to work with us."

"That's very flattering, but I really don't work in bars anymore. Like I said, when you're old and sober, it's a special occasion thing. What happened to Iggy? He quit?"

"Not exactly." Jean hesitated.

"Is this something you want to talk about? I can't tell." Alan's voice was gentle. "I can usually tell."

"Actually, yeah. I think I do want to talk about it." Jean was surprised by her frankness. "He disappeared."

Alan winced. "Is he okay?"

"I don't know." Jean fiddled with the plastic tab of her coffee cup lid. "I think it's my fault."

"What do you mean?" Alan leaned back, the portrait of gentle. "Did you do something to hurt him? Like, romantically?"

"No, no, no." Jean shook her head. "Nothing like that. He disappeared after he showed me something he probably shouldn't have."

Alan drew his brows together and leaned forward, folding his hands like a newscaster, really showing his age in the gesture. "What was it? Are you in trouble?"

Jean was again visited by that foreign compulsion, as though the words had tiny legs of their own. "Shortcuts. He showed me a shortcut. Do you know what that is?" She was stunned by her involuntary disclosure.

"I think so. Unfortunately." Alan looked very gray—his face drained of color—as though he were the subject of an old photograph. "Oh, Jean. I thought you meant drugs. Honestly, I wish you had meant drugs," Alan muttered.

"Alan, you're scaring me."

Alan rested his chin in his hands as though his neck couldn't support the weight of his skull. "I'm sorry," he said, "but those shortcuts are incredibly dangerous."

"I think Iggy might be stuck in one."

"Yeah," Alan said with a harsh half laugh. "I bet he is. Please, Jean, *please* promise me you won't use them again."

"I won't," Jean replied urgently. "Believe me, I've had enough. But, Alan, you've got to tell me if you know where I could find him. I feel so guilty that I can't help."

Alan exhaled for a long time and tucked his hands into the pockets of his smock. "I really shouldn't talk about this." He closed his eyes.

"I won't tell anyone," she promised.

"Of course you will," he said, underscoring the sentiment with another grim laugh. "It's how this works. Once you start talking about them, you can't really stop. I bet you've noticed that, right?"

Jean was chilled by the accuracy of what Alan had said.

"If I tell you, you have to promise me you won't go through again, that you won't even go near another one—okay?"

"Okay," she agreed, holding her breath.

"Please don't lie to me, Jean. The way you feel guilty about your friend? I would feel a thousand times guiltier if something happened to you. Because I know better."

"Nobody knows better," Jean said, shaking her head. "No matter how old people get, nobody ever knows better."

Alan let out an incredulous laugh. "Wow. Okay." He took a deep breath and stared at a crooked cat poster on the opposite wall. "You *can* get stuck, but not on the way in. You get stuck once you're already there, all the way through."

"What do you mean?"

Alan regarded her gravely. His serious expression was intensely at odds with his cartoon work smock. "How much do you actually know about this?"

"Not much, apparently?"

Alan sighed. "Okay, this is not going to be easy. Okay." He closed his eyes.

"Alan, you're making me nervous."

"You should be nervous." Alan opened his eyes. "Alright. Let me start from the beginning. The first time I did a shortcut it was fourth of July, in 1973."

"1973?" Jean's eyes were wide with shock.

Alan nodded, and dropped his chin so that he wasn't looking at her, or his hands, or anything at all. Jean felt the cruelty of what she had asked of Alan; recalling this was an act of pain. "I was at Max's Kansas City to see the Dolls and I was high as shit. Which is why I thought—well, I don't really know what I thought. I was with a friend, this girl Rose, who always seemed to know everybody anywhere we went. You know that kind of person?"

Jean nodded, even though, really, she didn't.

"Rose made it like a game. Like a harmless game." His eyes snapped up to her, watery and fierce. "Except it's not a game, and it's not harmless."

Jean nodded him forward, desperate to hear the rest.

"We went through the one in the Union Square subway station, and as I mentioned, I was high as shit. I barely knew what was going on, except we came out in Central Park somewhere. And Rose was just laughing—like I said, like it was a game. I took it again, a lot after that. Sometimes with Rose, sometimes with other people. Always the same way, always like a fucking game. I'll never forgive myself for that." He looked at Jean in the eye again. "I'll never forgive myself for misunderstanding what I did."

"What did you do?" Jean whispered.

"I did exactly what you and your friend were doing. Screwed around until it started to get dark. I mean really dark."

"Dark how?"

"Physically dark, mentally dark. Feeling like I'd had the shit kicked out of me every morning, even worse than usual. If I hadn't been strung out all the time, I probably would've noticed sooner, but…" Alan shrugged. "You know what I mean, I'm sure."

Jean nodded, this time grimacing.

"It's not healthy for your body or your brain. I started losing track of time. Worse than usual, I mean." He let out a grim laugh. "I was in a band back then and just wouldn't show up when I was supposed to. I fucked up a lot. My memory still isn't the same. There are names I can't remember, places I'd need a map to find. I keep my world small, so I always know where I'm going."

Jean shuddered before she could stop herself.

Alan looked at her carefully, almost fondly. "It sounds awful because it is awful, Jean."

"What about my friend—you said you think he's stuck. Where exactly?"

Alan paced the perimeter of the shop, straightening the displays as he went along, going about his business so thoroughly Jean thought he had forgotten about her. She felt a little foolish all of a sudden, just sitting there over her cream cheese bagel.

"It's a crime, I think, that you don't know what you've been doing," he said, finally. Alan's voice was terribly soft—the effort to control his tone was palpable. "That's the thing about the shortcuts. They seem casual and fun, but really they're a nightmare. They're a fucking human rights violation." He paused, holding a rubber squeaky toy shaped like a tomato. "Did anybody tell you what happens when you go through the wrong way? I mean, the opposite way?"

"Sort of." Jean clamped down the confession bursting in her throat.

"Sort of," Alan repeated in a whisper, gazing up at the stained Styrofoam-tiled drop ceiling. "Jean." He set the tomato on the counter beside her coffee cup. "If you go the other way, you go back in time. That's how and where people get stuck."

"What?" Jean laughed a little; her face felt numb.

"The first rule is never fucking ever go the wrong way. Because once you go that way, there's basically no chance of coming out."

"What?" Jean whispered.

"If your friend disappeared using a shortcut the wrong way, then he's gone. He could be gone twenty days in the past or twenty years. There's no way to know."

Jean stared at the plastic red tomato, its overt cheer an offense to all of her senses. "But like, do you think he's okay? Like alive?"

"Probably, yes."

"How do you know, Alan? How do you even know that's what happened?"

"Because I did it, and I wish I never fucking had." Alan gripped the sides of his throat like a person trying to escape the grip of deep water. "I can't talk about it, and I'm sorry about that." He took a long, deep breath. "I wish I could tell you everything, but it's one of my hard lines. I don't look back over that line. I can't."

"I'm really sorry I brought all of this up." Jean boiled with guilt. She saw how much it had cost him, to tell her everything he had.

"If it keeps you out of those cuts, all of this dredging was worth it. If I can keep you from losing your life to this nightmare, then I can handle a little discomfort. You're a good kid, Jean. But I think you need to forget about your friend. Hope for the best. Maybe he paid attention in school and is placing some good bets."

Jean shook her head. "I still don't understand any of this."

Alan put a hand on her shoulder like a dad in an afterschool special. "You aren't supposed to understand any of this. None of it is actually supposed to be happening."

"Then what do I do? Nothing?" Jean felt her throat swell closed with emotion.

"You go on with your life, and you stay away from those

shortcuts. And you tell anybody else who will listen to stay away from the shortcuts, too."

"Thanks, Alan."

"It's okay. We've got to look out for each other, a couple of loners like us."

Jean smiled into her coffee.

"What are you doing for Thanksgiving?" he asked, placing the tomato back on a shelf behind the register.

"Oh my God! Can everybody stop it about Thanksgiving already? Why is everyone so in love with a holiday that celebrates mass genocide in which they are all mostly complicit?"

"Ah, so it's like that."

"What's like that?"

Alan smiled, the first real smile he'd cracked all morning. "Being young can be really hard."

"Wow, Alan, that is a very patronizing thing to say." Jean wiped her runny nose and straightened a dusty pyramid of canned dog food, mainly so she had a reason to turn away and collect herself.

"Listen." Alan met her on the other side of the pyramid and turned the inward-facing labels out. "If you don't feel like being alone, you can come sit with me here."

"Here?" Jean looked around at all of the twinkly cotton faux snowdrifts.

"Yeah, here. It's actually kind of the perfect place to spend the holidays."

Before Jean could stop herself, she realized she was laughing— and so was Alan.

"Okay, yeah thanks," she said, wiping her eyes with the back of her hand. "I'll think about it."

Thirteen

Jean's apartment was freezing. The window in Christine and Molly's room was open. It was strange, so unlike Molly or Christine, two of the most responsible roommates on earth, to overlook something like that before they left for the day. Jean hesitated on the threshold, loath to enter a personal space like this, particularly without permission. She knew this irrational fear came from her childhood—from tiptoeing around her parents and their constant arguing. But Molly and Christine weren't her parents; she didn't have to worry about her parents ever again. So, she went through to shut and lock the window.

Jean knew she should feel more tired, but maybe it was all of the extra coffees or the revelations Alan had shared that had her circulatory system humming like a freight truck on the highway. Jean opened the medicine cabinet and swallowed a few of Molly's Excedrin to beat back the fierce headache prying its way into her skull. In her room, the box filled with Dr. Goldstein's mail grabbed her attention.

Jean eyed it warily. She was filled with dread at the thought of sifting through the letters, of discovering what was really going on with her old boss. She was scared to find something terrible, and worried that if she did, she might not know what to do about it. Jean's hands trembled as she reached for the lid. It was ridiculous to be so afraid of a cardboard box.

She set the box on the pink marble coffee table Molly had inherited from her grandma Peg, who had downsized to an assisted living facility the year before. The box looked so at home atop it that Jean was even more reluctant to open it and disturb the tableau. Jean shook her head. She would pull herself together and open the box and stop being a baby. It was probably mostly junk mail.

Jean lifted the lid and gazed inside at the contents. She clicked into mail-sorting work mode easily. After all, she had done the exact same thing, daily, for years at her desk in Dr. Goldstein's office. There were glossy postcards hawking faster internet and industrial cleaning services, and a few journals Dr. Goldstein subscribed to. Jean piled everything in the recycling bin that wasn't expressly personal or interesting. The utility bills she set aside helplessly; she would have to find a way to get them to Dr. Goldstein.

When everything had been sorted, there were only two pieces of mail that caught her eye. The first was a plain white envelope addressed in a nearly illegible scrawl. The stamp—a gloomy cartoon Garfield—lounged in the corner. The other was an oversized pastel blue greeting card envelope that did not contain its matching card. The envelope flopped in her hands, drooping around the irregularly folded piece of paper jammed inside.

Jean slit open the pastel blue envelope and unfolded the sheet of paper inside. The text was streaked through with white, and the heading was formal—the way they probably taught students in decades-old home ec classes how to type a business letter. It was dated two weeks earlier. Even the day of the week was spelled out in all of its majesty: Thursday. The sender's name was familiar—a name that Jean had invoiced hundreds of times over the years. Alice Berkowitz had been seeing Dr. Goldstein with her ex-husband and their two adult children for as long as Jean had worked at the office. She got the sense that the family had been coming to see Dr. Goldstein since the adult children were actual children. There was an air of ease and comfort, as though Dr. Goldstein had been a kind aunt they dropped in on once a week. They always accepted Jean's previsit offers of coffee and tea. Dr. Goldstein even kept a cinnamon tea on hand for Erin, the daughter; nobody else ever drank it.

Dear Dr. Goldstein,

It is with a heavy heart that I sit to write this. Lou and the kids and I all came to the same conclusion after our session last month. We are all very worried about you. You really don't seem like yourself. It was painful for all four of us. Particularly your son's disruption.

At first, I kept canceling and rescheduling our next appointment, hopeful that this was a blip. But I know now that we must cease treatment with you. It's easy to forget that we have been in a professional relationship all of these years, and I am so grateful for your help with everything and keeping us a close family unit even through the divorce. I've always said you were a magician. I only wish I could return the favor and help you through what must be a very troubling time.

Seeing you the way you were at our last appointment was so difficult. I know you are a professional woman, but please, if I can ever help, know that I would be happy to. Lou or I would do anything for you.

But, unfortunately, per the contract we signed with you in April of 1987, I am writing to you to terminate our treatment. This was

*certainly not a decision made by choice, but by necessity, to pre-
serve the integrity of our family. You of all people know just how
precious and hard-won that integrity has been for us. I wish you
only the best, and if you ever find yourself in a different situation,
we would be happy to work with you again.*

Yours,
Alice Berkowitz

Jean held the letter like a blade, careful not to touch the
edges. In all of her years, Dr. Goldstein was the one to dis-
continue treatment, because her patients had gotten better. If
anything, the inverse was more regular—new families were
always trying to get appointments. Anytime her old boss was
quoted in a national publication, or interviewed for a segment
on the news, the requests came pouring in. And, almost always, Jean—along with Dr. Goldstein—declined these requests.
Only a very few times had Dr. Goldstein been so intrigued or
moved by a family's story that she took them on or offered to
travel to consult. She wondered what Jeffrey could have done
that was so off-putting, and she wondered what had grown so
wrong with Dr. Goldstein.

Jean opened her laptop and logged in to her old admin email
account. A raft of boldfaced new messages loomed out at her,
and Jean quickly looked away. She wasn't going to get distracted.
She would reach out to Alice Berkowitz and that was all. That
was plenty.

She clicked open a fresh window and located Alice's email
address. Her hands hovered over the keys as she considered the
best way to begin. She thought informality might be a positive contrast to the strangled, semifaded note of cancelation she
had just opened. This was what Jean was best at, after all—it
was what made her such a good assistant to Dr. Goldstein. She
could always predict what people wanted to hear. And Jean
could tell Alice was desperate for some warmth and familiarity.

She closed her eyes and let her mind fill with goodwill; a trick Dr. Goldstein had taught her right at the beginning. Channel what you want to feel.

Hi Ms. Berkowitz,

I hope you still remember me—I was Dr. Goldstein's last assistant. I have such fond memories of you and your family coming into the office and hope you are all well and thriving. After Dr. Goldstein's new assistant left the practice, I've been helping out with the mail. I couldn't help but notice your genuine concern for Dr. Goldstein in the last letter you sent. Would you be willing to speak with me about it whenever you have the time? I'm sure you are very busy, but I, too, am having some concerns about Dr. Goldstein and just want to make sure I have all of the information before getting any agencies or authorities involved. Please find my cell phone number below and call me if and when you have some time.
   I hope Erin is still drinking lots of cinnamon tea!

Yours truly,
Jean Smith

She closed her computer and opened her phone to discover absolutely nothing except the late morning hour. If Jean didn't go to sleep now, she'd be dead on her feet at Red and Gold that night. She rubbed her hands over her face and ran them through her hair. Grease and grimy buildup slipped over her fingers, and she shuddered, certain she wouldn't have time to sleep and take a shower.

Jean tidied up the living room and folded down the cardboard box. She tucked it away with the other recycling, so that all traces of Dr. Goldstein's mail had vanished—all traces except that strange envelope with the Garfield stamp. Jean decided to save it for later. Her hands were already full with Alice and Alan and Iggy and Claire. If somebody else needed her help and attention, they would just have to wait until she slept off the rest of her headache. The Excedrin had only pushed it back so far.

Jean ran herself a glass of water, tossed the Garfield envelope on the floor beside her unmade bed, and inserted herself into the sheets that desperately needed washing. She pushed her face into the pillow and fell into a sleep that could only be described as a colossal kindness to her overextended body.

Her shift at Red and Gold that night was a swamp. It was busy, again, thanks to the school holiday. Every customer who approached her seemed frantic, almost dangerous. She didn't realize she was flinching while serving them until Omar said something.

"Holidays getting to you, huh?"

"Something like that."

"Well, keep it outside, okay? We're all splitting tips here."

"Sorry," she said, looking down into the river of cranberry juice filling the glass in her hands. The girl who ordered it had lavishly overshared about her looming urinary tract infection.

Jean did her best to force herself into robotic territory. She knew how to let her body take over this way—the only problem was, she was still sort of new. Her body was still learning this work behind the bar, and she kept slipping, making careless mistakes that took twice as long to fix. She could feel Omar's irritation on her like lamplight. It wasn't long before she was wincing away from him, too. The only mercy was that the night skipped forward, and her shift felt shortened by the endless parade of orders. Jean went to the bathroom while Omar counted the drawer. She stared herself down in the scratched and tagged mirror. Her image was barely visible through the murky scrawl. Jean looked herself in the eye and swore, no matter how late she might be, that she wouldn't go through another shortcut.

In the dim light of the closing bar, Jean saw a figure who wasn't supposed to be there, a girl in the shape of a customer, sitting down with her face expectantly tilted up waiting for her drink. It was Claire.

"Friend of yours," Omar said, with an accusing point of his chin at Claire. "You probably want to go," he said, in the same tone a prosecutor would list a defendant's crimes.

"I can stay—at least until I leave for my shift with Lu."

"Okay, wash these dishes and talk to your friend. I'll finish closing up."

"Thanks, Omar. Sorry I was so off tonight," Jean muttered.

Omar shrugged and shook his head. Jean gave him a wide berth and settled in behind the sink in front of Claire.

"What the hell?" Claire asked, her voice falsely cheerful. "Why haven't you called me? What's going on with you, Jean?"

Jean washed the glasses; her chapped hands burned in the hot chemical solution. She didn't want to answer. She wished that Claire was some imagined ghost Claire, an apparition who required no answers or actual attention. She was so, so tired. Claire snapped her fingers in Jean's face.

"Seriously, Jean! What the hell?" Her snaps were a rude metronome, syncopating each word.

Jean felt her way up along the slope of her anger. She climbed the feeling like a mountain. Jean never let fury overtake her; she was surprised that it hurt and felt good at the same time.

"Don't talk to me like that." Jean's voice was gratifyingly icy.

Claire sat up and straightened her casual slouch over the bar, putting more space between them.

"What the hell yourself—how dare you come into my place of work and talk shit like that? I think you should leave. We're closed," Jean continued. Her voice, while not too loud, still took up the whole room. Jean was astonished. If she had known letting herself feel furious would be like flying, she would have tried it earlier.

Claire remained silent, blinking into the dim light. She slipped off the barstool with a series of backward looks at Jean and fumbled at the door to let herself out.

Jean felt Omar's eyes on her again, different. "Why don't you get going?"

Jean nodded, still feeling the thrill of her fury without the hangover of the embarrassment. She hailed a profligate taxi— too cold and too angry to spare any prayers that the train would arrive in time for her to not be late.

Her phone buzzed in her pocket, and a row of messages from Claire unspooled in her palm: an apologetic but insistently questioning scroll. Jean punched the phone dark and got out of the cab, her anger still swirling in her body like snow.

"Hi, Jean," Lu greeted her cautiously.

"Hi." Jean washed her hands and tied on a clean apron. Lu turned Salt-N-Pepa's "None of Your Business" down, sensing Jean's elevated mood.

"Turn it up," Jean said, and got to work.

Fourteen

The next day dawned with regret. Jean knew she would have to call Claire back but put it off, taking an extralong shower and lingering over her cornflakes. Jean refilled the bowl long after she was full, just to keep herself from starting something she was not quite ready to begin. Her phone sat on the mint-green kitchen table beside her, where her coffee cup should be. It buzzed awake and skittered across the tabletop.

"Hello?" Jean answered it, guilty and cautious.

"Hi, is that Jean?" A woman's tremulous voice echoed on the other side.

"Yes?"

"This is Alice Berkowitz. You asked me to call you?"

Jean fell heavily back in her chair. The cornflakes wobbled in her bowl.

"Oh yes, Ms. Berkowitz. Hi. How are you?"

"We're fine. Very good, actually. I don't know if you heard, but Erin got engaged and it looks like we're going to have a wedding this spring."

"That's such great news—I hadn't heard that. Congratulations to all of you."

"Thank you. You know, I'm glad you got in touch. I've been really worried about Myra. I know you left a little while ago, but I think you might have been the only one holding that place together."

Jean's vision swam. "Oh, I don't know about that."

"You're too humble, Jean."

"Well, thank you so much for calling me back. Like I said, I was helping out with some of the mail and when I saw your letter, I just—I wanted to get in touch."

"Right." Alice lit a cigarette on the other end; Jean could tell by the flick of a lighter.

"You've been seeing Dr. Goldstein for so long. I mean, you must have seen her through some hard times over the years—after her sister passed away and all of that. I was just wondering what about this hard time made you stop treatment?"

"I'll be honest with you, Jean, we're actually all doing very well. Thanks in most part to Myra. We probably should've stopped coming in a long time ago. Maybe I kept manufacturing little problems so we could all keep going. Because I like her, you know?"

"I know." Everyone liked Dr. Goldstein. She was adept at striking the correct balance of stern but warm—the same way you'd know how much pressure to apply to open a jar without breaking it.

"And then that son of hers starts sitting in—don't even get me started on what a mess that was." The paper on Alice's cigarette crackled through the line.

"I'm sorry, what? Jeffrey *sat in*? During your appointment?"

"That's right."

Jean's brow creased almost painfully. "I'm sorry, I'm so confused."

"You and me both."

"How did she explain it? His presence?"

"She didn't explain it. *He* did! He said that he was his mother's caregiver now, and that he needed to be there in case she had a health issue during the session."

"What? And Dr. Goldstein was okay with that?"

Alice paused. "I have to tell you, Jean, she seemed a little out to lunch, if you know what I mean. Medicated."

"Oh."

"I was too shocked to say anything at first, and you know, it's hard to tell when somebody is sick like that. I was thinking my God, is it cancer? Is it MS? You just don't know. I think we all felt caught off guard, but we didn't want to be rude, so we just went ahead."

"If you don't mind my asking, how did the session go? I mean, how different was it from your sessions in the past?"

"It was apples and oranges, honey. Apples and oranges."

"So, he only sat in that one time?"

"Yes, just that one time."

"How did she seem before that, in the sessions you had with her after I left? Did she seem sick?"

"Not at all. But you never know with these kinds of things, right? And if her son is there to take care of her because she's really sick, then shame on me for thinking anything else."

"What else are you thinking, Ms. Berkowitz?"

"To be honest, I think that son is a creepy little asshole who is doping up his aging mother so he can steal from her. But I hope I'm wrong!" Alice tacked on cheerfully.

"I hope so, too," Jean whispered.

"You have a good heart, Jean. Let me know if there's ever anything I can do for Myra. You have my number now, right?"

"Right."

"Well, you take care. And happy Thanksgiving!"

"Happy Thanksgiving."

Jean was uneasy, leaning over her cereal for the better part of an hour as she considered what Alice had said. Dr. Goldstein could be sick—that might have been the kernel at the heart of her last voicemail to Jean. It might also have accounted for the unexpected questions that had been the catalyst for Jean's resignation. Jean put her head down on the table, compressed by guilty thoughts. Dr. Goldstein was not her employer or her grandmother or even her neighbor. Jean's intervention would be inappropriate. Right or wrong, she had drawn an unmistakable line between herself and Dr. Goldstein when she quit. And yet, there was a single, Garfield-bearing link to her old boss and it was sitting on the floor by her bed.

Jean reached for the note. She decided she would let the slip of paper inside tip the scale; if it was some innocuous correspondence, she would let go of her suspicions around Dr. Goldstein and Jeffrey. If the envelope contained something troubling, well, she would try to help. The envelope felt hot in her hands.

Inside, Jean discovered a rectangle of folded lined yellow paper hastily torn from a legal pad. The handwriting was a dense, crowded cursive. Jean skipped to the end for the identity of the sender: Tony. There was only one Tony, outside of Dr. Goldstein's patients, who ever called the office. It was Dr. Esposito, her former boss's research partner and colleague of decades. Dr. Esposito's story was a sad one. He had developed a rapidly progressing form of dementia and had to close his practice. His family relocated him to an assisted living facility in a matter of months. Jean only knew about it because so many of Dr. Esposito's patients were referred to Dr. Goldstein's office. It had all happened during her last weeks in the office.

Myra,

We haven't spoken in months. Jeffrey said you didn't want me to call any longer, and at first I was a fool and believed him. I miss you terribly, and don't know how to manage these thoughts and regrets without you. As every day passes, I feel the enormity of what we did as a physical pain. The same way you and I tore into the natural order of the world, I feel every one of my very cells turn to chaos. I can't bear this burden alone. I am suffering, dying multiple times a day. It's as though every morning I get up, step out into the street, and walk into oncoming traffic. Please call me, even if you won't see me—I need to hear your voice. I hope you get this. I didn't know how else to reach you.

Love,
Tony.

Jean choked on her coffee—had Dr. Goldstein and Dr. Esposito been lovers? Or had they killed someone? Dr. Esposito's guilt steamed off the page. Jean's thoughts galloped with potential scenarios—maybe Dr. Esposito was Jeffrey's real father? Anything, it seemed, could be possible.

Jean took a deep breath and held it until her chest and throat burned. The only question she had to answer was whether the note held the door open for her, to continue investigating what was going on with Dr. Goldstein. She read it through one more time with the same squeamishness she would've felt accidentally walking in on Dr. Goldstein in the bathroom. Whatever plagued Dr. Esposito, a smoke signal for danger wafted up from his letter. This was not a love note, Jean concluded. It was a cry for help. She opened her laptop and searched for Dr. Esposito's contact information, but found nothing. Jean decided to look up Dr. Esposito when she went into her shift at the bakery that night—she knew exactly where Lu stacked the bloated phone books in the storeroom.

When her phone rang, she was surprised it was already in her hand to answer.

"Jean? It's Claire."

A collision of feelings jammed Jean's throat closed, making it difficult to speak. "Mm-hmm" was all she could manage.

"Listen, I'm sorry about last night. I've been thinking about it, and what I did was not okay. I shouldn't have come in like that. I was just really upset."

"I know," Jean managed.

"Can we talk?"

"We're talking now."

"No, I mean, like in person."

"I guess so?"

"Great." Claire sighed with relief. "Do you want to meet up for dinner tonight? Or are you working?"

"I'm working, but not at the bar. Just at the bakery. Today I have to be there at midnight. We're making a wedding cake. Special order."

"Wow, okay. Let's meet at eight—at Iacapo. It's near the bakery, right? Some of my friends work there; it's really nice. Have you been?"

"Not yet." Iacapo was the restaurant next door, the sister to the café. "Sure, that works."

"Thanks for agreeing to this, Jean. There's something really important I want to tell you. I'll see you tonight."

"Yeah," Jean replied. "See you tonight."

Jean pushed aside the heavy curtain separating the harsh weather from the restaurant's tiny, chic vestibule. A trim host in a stern pair of glasses stood, waiting, and startled her with his nearness.

"Welcome to Iacapo," the host said, his voice as welcoming as a parking ticket.

"Hi, I'm Jean. I'm meeting my friend—I think she's already here?"

"Your friend's name, please?" The host hovered a fingertip over the clipboard resting on his forearm.

"Claire?" Jean paused, realizing that she didn't know Claire's last name. She hoped the host wouldn't ask for it.

"Oh, you're *Claire's* friend." His face cracked open with delight. "Come with me." He turned and waved at her to follow. The clipboard dangled from his swinging arm, smacking against the side of his leg. Interpol played as he settled her in at the mostly full bar. "Hey, Carlos—it's Claire's friend. Take care of her, alright?"

Jean recognized the bartender immediately as the kid working in the hybrid record–coffee shop where she and Claire had used the shortcut in the basement. He looked like a figure out of her high school history textbook, illustrating life during the California gold rush. The old-fashioned cut of his shirt and uniform suspenders gave his already-severe features a new sharpness. Jean smiled nervously. "Hi."

"Hi." Carlos stared at her with an intensity she thought probably helped him get a lot of tips at this job. He set a menu in front of her. "You want a drink?" His southern accent added depth to his costumey appearance.

"Sure. Anything."

Carlos glugged a generous pour of amber wine into the glass at her place setting. "This is one of our natural bottles. You'd have to sell your mother for a case of this. If you don't like it, I'll get you something else. I just really love giving this shit away. Give me one second." He moved to the other end of the bar to fold a woman's napkin—she had gone outside for a cigarette. Jean took a sip and watched the neat, disciplined movements of his hands. The wine tasted like flowers and sun.

"So, what do you think?" he asked, returning to where she sat.

"I like it. It tastes like summer. You know," Jean continued, feeling the wine already warming her through thanks to her cavernously empty stomach, "I actually work here, too. Well, next door, at the bakery."

"Oh really? No way." Carlos topped up her glass.

Jean pointed to the little boxed-in section of the menu with the desserts. "I made these cannoli last night. Well, this morning."

"Small world," Carlos said, giving her a strange look.

"Yeah, it really is, isn't it?" Jean had the eerie sensation of being turned inside out, like a sweater.

"Hi, Jean—hey, Carlos," Claire said, pushing herself into the seat between Jean and the couple beside her who were sharing a magazine. Claire folded Jean into a hug and Jean didn't resist; if anything, she leaned into it. Claire smelled like outside, like she'd been walking for a long time. She leaned over the bar and gave Carlos a Continental double peck. "Can I just get a beer?"

"Of course." Carlos looked at each of them carefully, as though he were memorizing their features for a police sketch he was going to have to dictate later.

"Thanks for meeting me," Claire said, turning all of her attention on Jean, effectively dispatching Carlos back to work, separating him from their conversation. This pleased Jean, but she wasn't sure exactly why. "I feel terrible about how pushy I got last night. I was rude and that was inexcusable. I'd had a really bad audition earlier and was feeling cranky on top of everything else, but whatever, that's not the point. I really need to talk to you. To tell you something. This thing with Iggy is eating me alive. I know it's not your problem, but we've already searched so much together, and when you said you felt responsible, I don't know. I felt like it connected us in this somehow. Do you know what I mean?" Claire reached out toward Jean's throat, plucking a fallen leaf from the dried floral arrangement hanging from the ceiling that had lodged on her collar.

"I do feel responsible," Jean said. "And I'm sorry I got so

angry. I wasn't really mad at you. I'm angry about all of this." She turned her body away and looked down at her menu.

Claire rested the flat of her hand on Jean's back. "I get it. This is all so intense. It's a lot to take in."

"You have no idea," Jean muttered, the sentence pouring out of her mouth more vicious than she intended. Claire drew her hand back into her lap.

"Here you go," Carlos said, returning with Claire's drink.

"Thanks, babe," Claire said with a wink.

"Did you tell her?" Carlos said, his gaze fixed significantly on Claire's face.

"Almost." Claire turned her body toward Jean.

Carlos shook his head. "She deserves to know. She made the cannoli, for God's sake," Carlos said, stabbing at the menu on the counter. "If you know what I mean."

Jean finished her wine in one enormous gulp. "Okay, what the fuck is going on here, you guys?"

"Yes, Claire—what?" Carlos said innocently.

Claire shook her head, her hair obscuring her features. "No, listen, it's okay. We're going to talk about it. Okay?"

"Hmm," Carlos said.

"Can we have two of the Bolognese pastas?" Claire turned to Jean. "Wait, is that okay? Are you a vegetarian?"

"No, that's fine."

"You're going to love it. It's the best thing I've ever eaten. The food here is amazing, but you probably already know that since you kind of work here." A nervous giggle punctuated Claire's rapidly strung together thoughts.

"Claire," Jean said, staring her directly in the eye.

"Right. Well, it's a weird thing. I just want to preface everything I'm saying here with This Is a Weird Thing. I actually know who you are."

Jean tilted her head, sizing Claire up the way she would any patient in Dr. Goldstein's office. She narrowed her eyes, squinting to check the size of Claire's pupils.

"I mean, obviously, I know who you are *now*, but I knew who you were even before I met you. We all did."

"What? Who all did?"

"Me, Iggy, obviously. Luke. I mean everybody who was there that night at Transmission." Claire ticked the names off on her fingers as she spoke. "Even Carlos." She nodded at where he stood shaking a cocktail glumly at the end of the bar. "We all knew who you were, and we were honestly trying not to scare you."

"What are you talking about? I'm not anybody."

Claire covered the hand resting beside Jean's empty glass with both of her own in an ardent, almost aggressive gesture. "Jean, you are literally the only person we give a shit about right now. Nobody wanted to be obvious about it, especially at first. I mean, you didn't even know. It was actually really charming." Claire shook her head, smiling. "At first it seemed just fun—like we were fans, but then when Iggy disappeared..."

"Fans? What are you talking about?"

"Okay." Claire lifted her gaze to the ceiling. Jean followed it for a moment, wondering if maybe the punch line to this joke was hidden in the elaborate trompe l'oeil mural of birds and sky painted there. "Alright." Claire motioned Carlos over for a refill on her drink.

"Did you tell her?" Carlos raised his eyebrows.

"Not exactly," Claire muttered.

"We knew that you worked with Dr. Goldstein for a long time," Carlos said simply, refilling her wineglass.

"So? Everybody who knows me knows that." Jean took another long sip, wanting to wipe away the bizarre fog of uncertainty building inside of her.

"But most people don't know—and you didn't know either—

that the shortcuts exist *because of* Dr. Goldstein." Claire's voice was careful, gentle.

"What are you talking about?" Jean's voice wavered, underscored by a nervous laugh.

Carlos leaned forward, conspiratorial. "Dr. Goldstein opened the first one in 1970. I can't believe you didn't know," he said, with a marveling shake of his head.

Jean felt stung in a way she hadn't experienced since being left out of everything as a middle schooler. "What do you mean, opened one? It's not like a fucking Ziploc bag." Jean pushed away from the bar, and stood up, unsteady on her feet but unable to sit there any longer. The shock of the secrecy left her feeling profoundly wounded—by Claire, by Iggy, even by Dr. Goldstein. Jean let the feeling wash through her.

She turned to Claire and held her gaze. "I don't get it—why didn't you tell me before?"

"It was embarrassing—you don't even want to know how embarrassing."

"Actually, I do."

"Luke hired an investigator, to see if your Dr. Goldstein was the same one who, you know, started everything."

"What? You had someone *following* me?"

"No, no, not exactly. It really didn't seem like a big deal. Luke's dad has this lady on retainer. She was just confirming what we already thought." Claire reached out to her, but Jean stepped back abruptly, knocking into the person sitting on her other side—another parent-child duo out together for the holiday weekend. "I'm so sorry, sir," Jean said, turning away from the bewildered suburban dad and mortified-looking son, away from the bar, away from Claire.

"I need to go outside." Jean pushed through the packed restaurant, barely sparing a glance for the people she bumped into along the way. She shoved past the line of people standing on the cobblestone street outside making hopeful eye contact with the host. She steadied herself against a motorcycle veiled in a black tarp. She smelled the jasmine in Claire's perfume before she heard her voice.

"Wait," Jean said. "Please, just give me a minute." She didn't want to hear what Claire had to say. She wanted to let herself feel the betrayal, to process it in a new way. It hurt, but she couldn't deny that it felt like she was growing.

"Look, I'm sorry. I know how fucked-up this is. Really, seriously, I do." Claire spoke and Jean kept her eyes on the motorcycle's black tarp. "But I think your old boss may be the only person who can find Iggy, and we need to go talk to her."

Jean laughed and held a hand up as though keeping back a dangerous animal. "You really have to do better than that. Start again."

"Okay," Claire said, taking a step forward.

"No, no, no—stay there, but keep talking." Jean set both hands on her lower back the way she used to collapse onto herself after a sprint. She closed her eyes against the dark, the cold air sharp on her chapped eyelids.

"Okay, well, like Carlos said, the shortcuts exist because of your old boss."

"Yeah, start there. What does that mean?"

"Carlos knows more about the history than I do, but I guess it means that in the sixties your boss and this other guy, Anthony Esposito—"

"Wait, Dr. Esposito?" Jean's eyes flickered open.

"Yeah? You know him, too?" Claire's voice rose to an involuntary peak of surprise.

"Just keep going, please." Jean turned around, trying to temporarily corral all of her thoughts.

"Well, the two of them were working with an experimental pharmaceutical. I guess in their therapy sessions everybody was supposed to take it before they talked—since it's all family therapy, right?"

Jean nodded, oblivious of whether Claire could see her affirmation or not.

"Well, everybody would take it before the session and the medication would open them up, in a way. It was supposed to bring more compassion, or whatever, to the conversations. The drug was supposed to get you in other people's heads. And it did such a good job that it basically made these invisible little tunnels from one person's mind to another's. I think it fucked a lot of people up. I mean, this was all trials—they definitely kept it quiet when it didn't work. I don't know, maybe it did work, but wasn't worth the side effects, you know?"

"No, I honestly don't know." Jean composed herself by degrees, gently, like pleating a sheet of paper into a fan.

"Right, I'm sorry. Anyway, in the trials with Goldstein and Esposito, I guess the tunnels got wider and bigger the more doses they gave—they had to do a certain number of doses with the same families. I think the study was just five families, but there might have been another couple, I'm not sure. Anyway, the weird thing was that when the families were together and had a fight, or an intense emotional experience, the space around them would tunnel in. Or out. I'm not sure."

"How do you know all this?"

"Luke. His dad is basically the owner of Selestron, the company that made the drug. Luke overheard a lot about it growing up, and he got obsessed with it. We all went to college together in the city and it was this weird hobby of ours to find them."

"This is too much! Just wait a second. What was that name again? Of the company?"

"Selestron—did your boss ever talk about it?"

"Wait, wait." Jean put her hand up as though erasing the parts of the conversation she didn't like. "What happened to the families? The five families? What happened to them?"

"Who knows?" Claire shrugged.

"Jesus Christ." Jean rubbed her face and squatted down onto

the sidewalk, like a person overcome, a woman about to succumb to an undignified sidewalk vomit. She looked up at Claire from her position on the concrete. "And you were all hanging out with me because of my old *job*? That is extremely creepy."

"I'm sorry," Claire said, taking a step toward her, then thinking better of it and stepping back.

"What were you trying to get from me, exactly?"

"We weren't trying to get anything. We were curious about you. Like I said, we were more fans than anything."

"And what, you thought I was going to bring you to meet Dr. Goldstein, like she was Britney Spears or something?"

"What? No, not at all. Nothing like that." Claire shook her head vehemently and the tone of her voice swerved in the air. "We just wanted to meet you."

"Well, clearly if you thought you were getting any inside information you were all pretty disappointed. Apparently, I'm oblivious to everything."

"Don't say that." Claire crouched beside Jean. "I'm really glad I met you. We all are. And if you never wanted to see any of us again, I would absolutely get it. But the thing is, Jean, I need your help to find Iggy. When you said you were responsible before, I kind of thought you already knew?"

"But I didn't know!"

"No, I realize that now. And I'm not saying you *are* responsible for any of this, like, generally. Jean. Jean, look at me."

Jean met her eyes briefly before she dropped them back down to a matted nest of massacred McDonald's containers.

"I need your help. You're the only one who can help me find Iggy."

"And how do I do that? Take you to see Dr. Goldstein? I can't even get in to see her myself. Besides, Iggy might be so gone there's nothing we can do about it. Do you have any idea how far away he even is?"

"Wait, what do you mean?" Claire stood abruptly from her

crouch. "I thought you didn't know anything about the short-cuts." Claire's voice flickered from soft to accusing.

"I think I might actually know where he is. But not because of Dr. Goldstein; because of this guy, Alan." A realization dawned on Jean in that instant: she was important. She was important to Iggy, to Alan, to Claire, to Dr. Goldstein. Jean allowed herself to feel the possibility that she could fix this.

"Alan?"

"Can we go inside—I'm freezing." Jean uncurled herself from the compact denim stone she had become on the sidewalk and stood to her full height.

Fifteen

Inside, the restaurant was more crowded than ever—the temperature and humidity reminded Jean of her fourth grade field trip to the Pittsburgh Zoo and its climate-controlled rainforest room. She felt the same foreign shock she'd felt as a nine-year-old, her senses jolting at the contrast. Jean and Claire found their empty seats; their chairs were so crowded together they were touching. Jean carefully maneuvered herself in after Claire.

"I just need to ask. How did she keep it from you? Dr. Goldstein?"

"We weren't close like that. And I don't think she had much to do with the shortcuts after the initial study."

"Are you sure about that?" Claire gave her a strange look.

"I mean, obviously, no! I'm not sure about anything."

"Hey," Carlos said accusingly, pushing their refilled glasses forward. "I didn't know if you two were coming back." He looked at Claire. "How did she take it?"

"Fine," Jean said acidly.

"Cool. Two mafaldine Bolognese," Carlos announced, setting the dishes before them with a practiced flourish.

"Thanks," Claire said, with a businesslike smile. Jean was suddenly ravenous; the pasta was beautiful, all golden and shining. Jean spooled the lacy noodles into her mouth, grateful for every bite after so many drinks on an empty stomach. Jean felt more like herself when she was finished, fully aware of Claire's eyes on her while she ate.

Jean pressed her napkin to her lips.

"Well?" Claire asked.

"I'm pretty sure Iggy isn't stuck in any of the cuts."

"Okay," Claire said. "Then where do you think he is?"

"This is the part I don't really understand. You warned me before, about not going through the other way—remember? Do you know what happens when you do that?"

Claire's face grew scarlet in the dim light. "Not really. It's just something I've always heard. That it kind of fucks you up forever. I figured it was like when people tell you not to have sex on ecstasy. Better not do it and find out. Going through one way is enough for me."

"Well, maybe not for Iggy. You said he was reckless with the shortcuts, right?"

"More reckless than the rest of us. But Iggy is like that with everything. Always pushing anything as far as it goes. He says it's for his creative process."

"Do you think he went the wrong way on purpose?"

"Maybe? If he thought it would help him write a better song or inspire him or some shit like that."

Carlos approached them with another bottle and Jean flattened her hand across the top of her glass. "I have to work tonight."

"I don't," Claire said. She pulled Jean's glass toward her plate and motioned for Carlos to pour on.

Jean drank deeply from her water glass, the ice long since melted.

"So, do *you* know more about what happens when you go the wrong way?" Claire's tone was bent harshly by the extra drink.

"I think so, and I think it might mean we won't be seeing Iggy again. Although I'm pretty sure, if what I think happened actually happened, he's alive and probably doing okay." Jean took a deep breath. "When you go the wrong way, you go into the wrong time."

"What do you mean, the wrong time?"

"I'm not a hundred percent sure, but I think back in time? Somewhere between when you said Dr. Goldstein and Dr. Esposito opened the first one and yesterday. Or, I guess, the day before he went the wrong way."

"Well, shit."

"Pretty much." Jean toasted her with the slightly warm water. "I have to go to work."

"Wait, you mean that's it? What can we do?"

"I don't think there's anything we can do, unless we want to get stuck, too. And honestly, there's no knowing which way he went in, where he got stranded, or anything else even vaguely relevant."

"How can you be *so cold*?" Claire shivered as though Jean herself were a draft seeping through a window.

"I'm not cold." Jean felt the accusation like a slap. "I'm just realistic. Right now, if Iggy's friends and family miss him and are worried—you're the only one who can reassure them and tell them he's okay."

"And what exactly am I supposed to say, *Jean*?" The extra drink had sharpened Claire into an unpleasant dinner companion.

"I don't know! Tell them what you want. And think about it—if Iggy went back in time and remembered literally anything about, I don't know, sports or history or whatever, he could go to Vegas, place a bunch of bets, and be a millionaire. That's not a bad way to end a bizarre story." Jean hoped she made it seem like she was finished and had washed her hands of Claire and Iggy and the shortcuts entirely. Jean wasn't a good actress, but she hoped she was good enough in that moment to freeze Claire's search so that she could begin her own.

Jean shifted her weight off the stool. She needed to walk, to clear her head and to clear the alcohol from her blood. She had to be at work in an hour and wanted to do a good job; she still felt vaguely guilty about her last shift with Lu. She would give it her all tonight.

Jean squared her shoulders and stood up straight. She reached out and gripped Claire's shoulder like a cowboy in a movie about to kiss the ingenue. She was shot through with a little thrill at feeling so unlike herself. "If you want to do the right thing, stop using the shortcuts. Forget about them, please. They're bad for you—bad for your brain, for your health, for everything." Jean wasn't sure if this was true, but it seemed right to echo Alan's urgency. "Just live your actual life, okay?" She didn't wait for Claire to answer; she turned around and walked out into the night, hoping Iggy really was okay, counting his stacks of money at a table in Vegas.

The temperature had dropped below freezing. With an hour to kill before her shift, Jean welcomed a long bracing walk. She needed to snap out of it, to sober up after the free wine, a gift that seemed sinister in retrospect. They had been trying to pry her open, to dig more, as far as she would let them. Jean was anxious to talk to Dr. Esposito, especially after learning what she had about the shortcuts' origins.

Jean's head was so hot, not even the icy gale force wind could set her right. She checked her phone. Her fingers were frozen together into an unwieldy mitten hand. She turned back, hoping that when she got to work her fingers would be mobile enough to do the delicate piping work Lu had warned her about.

The bakery was louder than Jean was used to. The raucous full house next door beat like a giant's heart on the other side of the wall.

"It's weird being here so early," Jean said, shrugging out of her parka.

Lu waved from where she sat, like a customer, at one of the chic pale wood tables. "And you're even a little earlier than you needed to be."

"I know." Jean slid into the chair across from her and looked down at the sheet of drawing paper beneath Lu's hands. "We're making that? Are you sure?" Jean leaned in to inspect the drawing more closely. It was a sketch of a four-tiered cake, tinted a bright turquoise all over. Tiny white blossoms and scrolls of icing cascaded down the sides. The effect was beautiful, but not restrained.

"We're gonna try," Lu said, with a wavering smile.

"I mean, full disclosure here, I've never made anything like that. If you were secretly hoping I went to art school or something, I'm going to really disappoint you there. The lowest grade I ever got in school was actually in art."

"Shit, I thought you might have some special moves I didn't know about." Lu's smile widened.

"I have no special moves, Lu. Not even one." Jean felt a pang in the truth of that declaration.

"That's okay, because I actually have a couple in my back pocket. Come on."

Jean slipped into the rhythm of her newly familiar partnership with Lu. The choreography of their nights involved Jean weighing out and sifting the ingredients, while Lu supervised the eggs, butter, consistency, really everything else. They mixed the cake batters one at a time, and Lu let Jean take over an entire layer—lemon.

"I can't believe you're trusting me with this." Jean's hands

shook as she zested and squeezed the juice from a pile of lemons as large as a lapdog. "It's someone's wedding!"

Lu shrugged. "If you fuck up, there are three other layers."
She put a hand on Jean's shoulder. "But you won't fuck up."

"Thanks." Jean smiled, surprised to feel proud and sort of
happy. "So," Jean continued, riding the unexpectedly playful
wave that swept through their shift. "Have you ever been married?"

Lu paused where she rolled out the fondant; her palms were
already stained a shocking mint green. "Actually, yes."

"What?" Jean turned toward Lu and away from the enormous bowl of eggs she was beating to a silk. "Are you serious?"

"I am." Lu crossed her heart, though a small smile pulled at
her mouth. "I'm telling you, it's the military! They make everyone get married. Good for morale and everything. Plus, my
parents." She rolled her eyes. "He was also Lebanese."

"Was your husband in the army, too?"

"Ex-husband, and yeah. He was a good guy. Very friendly.
His new wife sends me a card every year. They're in Virginia
somewhere. They have kids—like, a lot of kids."

"Wow. The road not taken."

"Please, that road was never on my map. What about you?"
Lu raised her eyebrows meaningfully.

"I've always been very single."

"How single is that?"

"No secret ex-husbands, that's for sure."

"My ex-husband isn't secret—you just didn't ask. Marriage is
no joke, though. Are your parents still together?"

Jean paused, slowing her mixing gradually. "My parents are
dead, actually. Car accident." She had never confessed the loss
of her parents so smoothly or easily before. Jean waited for the
guilt to flood her, but it didn't come. She wasn't torn through
with the kinds of feelings she had pushed down for the last decade. Aside from the obvious guilt of making it out of the car

when they didn't, she had always been overwhelmed by the more complex shame of not loving them enough, of being miserable in their quiet, sad home. But Jean didn't feel that shame as she set the whisk back in motion. Jean finally understood that it was okay that she was okay. That she deserved to be okay, even. Jean was surprised but relieved, that the revelation surfaced with such ease.

"Oh, Jean, I'm so sorry," Lu said.

"It's alright. It was a long time ago." Jean hoped she made it sound like they had died when she was a baby, like they had slipped out of the world without being known to her at all. She didn't want Lu to feel sorry for her.

"Hey," Jean said, while Lu trained her attention back onto the texture of her buttercream and let the fondant rest. "Can I take a quick break? I think I need a coffee."

"Sure. As long as you make me one, too."

Jean put a new filter in the coffee maker and scooped in a few extra heaps of fragrant grounds to give the pot a kick that she desperately needed. Was it because she was tired, or was it because she was still a little drunk that she had confessed so easily to Lu? A tiny, uncomfortable poke somewhere behind her ribs reminded her of the several times she had run her body and mind through the shortcuts in the last week. If the origins of the cuts were to make people more open to one another, it made sense that it might affect Jean the same way. She frowned at the hissing percolator.

She scanned the shelves where Lu kept all of her notes and a few reference cookbooks. Jean pulled down a phone book and found the number to Dr. Esposito's medical practice. His retirement had been so recent, Jean was sure the office would have a forwarding address, or at the very least, the name of another practice for any patients who might be calling. The address was in Chelsea; she remembered that from the times Dr. Goldstein asked her to messenger documents or little gifts to her colleague. Jean punched the number into her phone and saved it. She would try the office tomorrow; it might take some time, but she would find him.

Jean walked the coffees back into the kitchen. The scent of her lemon cakes filled the room, and she felt a glow of pride.

"Here you go," she said, handing Lu the extra coffee.

"Listen, Jean, I was thinking." Lu set the cup down as she swirled a layer of buttercream across the first of her three tiers; this one was German chocolate. "If you aren't doing anything for Thanksgiving tomorrow, you should come over to my aunt's. Omar will be there. We'd love to have you."

Jean anticipated the familiar panic any invitation to a family function brought on, but it didn't come. She remained neutral. Steady. She took a long sip of coffee. "That's really nice of you, but I actually already have plans."

"Oh yeah? With who?" Lu narrowed her eyes over the rim of her coffee cup, eternally sharp, never missing a thing.

"With my friend Alan," Jean laughed, trying to convey indignation. "What? I do!"

"Alan? Is this like a gentleman caller?"

"What? Ew, no." Jean wrinkled her nose and felt a little guilty about how unappealing Alan as a romantic prospect struck her.

"Okay, if you say so. Take your cakes out of the oven. They're done—I can smell it."

Jean and Lu worked late into the night, but Jean left before the sun was up. They didn't have to make the usual pastries since the next day was Thanksgiving and the café and restaurant were both closed. The cake turned out even better than the drawing. Jean couldn't believe that she and Lu had created something so magnificent and enormous in a single night. It almost made sense that the beautiful thing they created would disappear in a single night, too, swallowed down the throats of hundreds of celebrating people. And when Lu pressed an extra hundred-dollar bill into her hand on the way out, she believed it was well deserved.

The bars were still open as Jean made her way home, and Thanksgiving Eve was swarming. Jean knew what time it was without having to check her phone—3:15 a.m.; she'd bet ten years of her life on it. The noise was at the most frantic it could get—full-on squeals and fights—before people started to get tired and maudlin. Jean liked the anonymity in the noise. It was easy to disappear when everyone was drunk or high or danced out enough to believe that they were the center of the world.

"Hey, it's Jean!" A figure bounded toward her, gangly and unwelcome. Jean put her hands up as though she were being attacked. "Whoa, whoa, whoa," the figure said. "It's me—Luke. The guy you went home with and never called back."

"Excuse me?" Jean straightened to her full height, a feat that left her towering over the figure that had seemed so large but was mostly shadow.

"What? You seriously don't remember me?" In the harsh light of the passing taxi headlights Luke was nearly unrecognizable. He had none of the enthusiastic charm she remembered from the night they met.

"Of course I remember you. You just look a little different." Jean grimaced, remembering that this entirely too-forward person had seen her naked.

"Well, I sure remember you," he said, reaching for her, mimicking the tone of a 1940s leading man. Jean dodged his attempted embrace.

"I think it's better if you keep your distance." She was happy with how harshly she delivered the command.

"Why would you say that?" Luke put a hand over his heart as though he were staunching a stab wound.

"I just had dinner with your friend Claire?" she said meaningfully.

"You just had dinner? Just now?" He staggered toward her.

"No, earlier. She told me everything. About Iggy, and you and your friends and your whole…Scooby-Doo situation."

"Scooby-Doo?" He paused, midstagger. "Oh, the investigator. I feel bad about that, I really do. About keeping you in the dark—about all of that. We were all just *so fascinated*, you know? The shortcuts were all we could talk about. I mean, what a secret to obsess over! And really Claire was the one who thought you might have bonus information about everything. We should've told you we knew. Iggy should've told you."

"*You* should have told me." Jean crossed her arms over her chest and glared down at him, hoping she looked as stern as she felt.

"You're absolutely right to be mad at me. I'm a *dick*. Seriously." He was contrite, entreating. "But I really like you!" He laughed, the same way a person might laugh if you offered them a novelty stick of gum that blew up in their face. "Come on. Please come in and have a drink with me. I'm buying—you can't say no. It'll break my heart."

"I'm really tired. I've been at work."

He took her by the hand in an unfamiliar, gallant, old-fashioned gesture. "You work too hard, Jean."

Jean stared at the place their hands touched. "What are you doing?" She nodded with her chin where he gripped her fingers. "They teach you that in finishing school?" His gaze turned fleetingly sour before he blinded her with a delighted smile.

"Claire shouldn't have told you about all that."

"You all have too many secrets," Jean said, extracting her hand.

"Yeah, we do." He nodded gravely and his face finally looked familiar to her. Jean couldn't explain the rush of relief she felt at reconciling this Luke with the Luke she had gone home with. "You really should call me, Jean, if you want to know more. There's a lot more to know. *A lot*." The familiar expression vanished in an instant, like a sleight of hand.

Jean shook her head. The only thing she really knew was that she wanted to flee, to get off the street, into her apartment, and into her own bed. "Bye, Luke."

"I'll see you around," he said, watching her pick her way down the sidewalk around stalled couples and groups of people slouched over their phones.

"I doubt it," she called. She disappeared from his view and got swallowed up in the night, just like anybody else.

Sixteen

The morning of Thanksgiving broke sunny and mild. Jean woke up earlier than she meant to, thanks in no small part to the stun of light streaming through her bedroom window. The apartment was quiet—Molly and Christine were long gone, surely wrapping puff pastry around different cheeses in one of their ancestral kitchens.

Jean made her bed, made her coffee, and made the call to Dr. Esposito's old office number, even though she was sure no one would be there on the holiday. If they were there at all.

The message she received was curt, even a little aggressive. A man's voice bit off every word like a ravenous diner. "Dr. Esposito is no longer seeing patients. Current patients should call New York Hospital for more information. If this is an emergency, call 911." Jean was only certain about one thing: the voice was not Dr. Esposito's, whose accent had been unmistakably thickened by a childhood spent in Queens. The voice she heard was familiar, though she could not place it. Like a voice-over actor whose commercials had played in the background of her life.

Jean called the main information number at New York Hospital. While she waited on hold, she began to clean the refrigerator. She set her phone on the counter, the tinny instrumental version of Garbage's "Special" only vaguely audible as she inspected the viability of a package of celery at the bottom of the crisper.

"New York Hospital. Hello?"

Jean fumbled for the phone and dropped the celery. "Yes, hi, how are you—I'm looking for Dr. Anthony Esposito's forwarding information. I just called the office and the message told me to call here to reach him."

"One moment. Anthony Esposito, you said? Are you a patient? All of his patients are going to Schermeranz."

Jean hesitated. "Yes," she lied, her voice too upbeat. "I'm a patient."

"Date of birth?"

"11/05/55." She didn't know why, but her mother's birth date rose to the top of her memory. One of Dr. Goldstein's patients had had the exact same birthday, and it pierced Jean's mood anytime she sent an invoice or called in a prescription refill.

"Last name?"

"O'Neil."

"Sharon?"

"Yes, that's right." Jean felt blurred in two, as though she really was Sharon O'Neil and herself at the same time.

"Alright, Sharon, you got a pen?"

"Yes, go ahead." Jean took down the number, and she noticed that her handwriting looked strange, distorted, as though she'd been writing with her left hand.

"Happy Thanksgiving."

"You too," Jean said, buttoning the call off. Recalling her mother's birthday undeniably unsettled her, but she let herself feel the strangeness instead of pushing it away. Jean carefully put the number she'd written down into her phone, thinking about how odd it was that so many of the same numbers could carry such different meanings.

Her mother's last birthday had been a nightmare, the kind of thing that would shake any normal person out of a sound sleep. Her mother turned thirty-nine—she would never be older than that. Every year on her birthday, Jean's mother went to the cemetery. Her mother was a devout person, and she seemed to think these visits were owed in some spiritual balance sheet. Every year, Jean went with her. On her mother's last year, they made the usual rounds. What surprised Jean most, on every one of these annual visits, was how much shorter and less impressive the tombstones became as, every year, she grew taller. She remembered coming to the cemetery when the gravestones towered over her, all except the small ones topped with lounging angels that marked the bodies of children.

It was not a romantic or haunting cemetery in an ivy-covered churchyard. The chain-link fence that ringed the cemetery was littered with signs about not smoking, restrictions on the types of flowers to be left and planted there, and what hours were relegated for active burials. Jean and her mother always visited the same graves: her mother's parents, who shared a tombstone, and her mother's grandmother's—the only black monument in the rows of gray and white. Every year her mother would point to the headstone on her parents' grave where her own name and birth date—11/5/55—loomed. "That's where I'll go, Jean. Don't forget it, okay? Don't let them try and put me next to your father." And every year Jean would nod, not sure if this was the kind of thing other parents talked about with their young children. Maybe they did.

Her mother stood on the ground, hovering over her dead parents for a long time. Sometimes she cried, sometimes she just looked into the distance, disappearing from Jean entirely. The last time they went, she didn't cry. Before they left, they made the obligatory stop at her great-grandmother's grave to wipe off the dust and debris that had gathered on the stone. On her mother's—and Jean's—last visit to the polished black headstone, her mother said something unexpected.

"Maybe they all did the best they could. What do I know?" She shrugged and lit a cigarette, crouched at the foot of the grave, pulling dead weeds from the base and wiping away a clot of dried grass caught in a corner. "I wonder if you'll ever think that about me." Jean's mother finished her cigarette slowly, stubbing it out in the dirt. She left it protruding from the earth like some carcinogenic crocus.

It was the last thing she ever left anywhere.

Jean had been in the back seat, which, everyone said, had saved her life. Jean didn't tell anyone about her parents' voices in the car—the way they lashed out at each other. She didn't tell anyone about her father's backhand into her mother's face, about the blood that ran there before the smash of metal and windshield. She didn't tell anyone about her mother's hands on the wheel, the way she tried to peel it away from her father. She only nodded and looked down, agreeing how lucky she had been.

That Thanksgiving—only weeks after the accident—had been a nightmare, too. Jean wished it could have been another day, any other day. Not a day she was forced to reckon with her gratitude by every nurse, doctor, well-meaning classmate's mother, newscaster, parade correspondent, neighbor, and radio DJ. Yes, she was grateful to be alive, but she was also grateful to be the only one who had survived. The thought was vicious and intensely her own, something that she could never shake or forget, always feeling that current beneath the person she grew into—that she had to be bad to be grateful for a thing like that. No matter how much she studied and learned, and no matter how many years she spent in Dr. Goldstein's office, she could never disabuse herself of the notion that she was, at heart, bad.

Jean had perfected the art of ignoring this revelation. She had mostly scrubbed her life of reminders of her parents and her life before coming to New York. She owned no pictures or mementos; the house—and all of its contents—that her parents had been renting was seized to pay their debts. Her track coach, Mrs. Altamore, mercifully took her in until she turned eighteen. She jammed Jean in with her large extended family with efficiency and cheer. Jean sometimes thought of her old coach, and the debt of gratitude she would owe her for the rest of her life—but Jean never called or wrote to her. And Jean had the ubiquitous pleasure of a name so common that she was eternally hard to find.

She had no physical items to mark the memories of her parents and those darkest days of her childhood, but the dates would always come. She expected that saying her mother's birth date aloud would open another painful gap. But this time, it felt different. Jean didn't feel frozen by her guilt and shame. This time, she wondered if her mother really had done the best she could. Jean wondered if she herself had done the best she could, too, to survive such a thing on her own.

In these complicated moments, she missed running the most— that hot, clarifying rush, bringing with it a blissful amnesia of anything that had happened even a minute before. She wiped every plastic surface inside of the empty refrigerator in her apartment until her lungs burned from the bleach spray. Jean confidently rearranged the contents of the fridge. Molly and Christine would be delighted to have all of that room for the leftovers they would certainly heft back from Long Island.

Jean knew she needed to leave the apartment. She was stunned by the realization that this might be the first Thanksgiving she didn't want to be alone. She double-checked the lights and locks, always so self-conscious about being a careless roommate in her haste. Once she was outside, she walked quickly, the wind at her back, pushing her down First Avenue with its invisible hand.

Jean opened the door to the Woof-n-Wag, thinking maybe she should have knocked. A sleigh bell jangled cheerfully overhead, and Alan looked up from where he sat behind the counter. His face flashed with irritability and then relief.

"Hi, Jean," he said without standing up or waving. "I'm so glad you came."

"Really?" She walked into the shop, checking the corners for any sign of lurking customers, but found it empty. Jean pulled off her hat and set it on the counter, running her cold fingers through her hair and pressing them against her scalp to warm them up.

"Really." Alan smiled. "Hang on a second." He disappeared in the back and reemerged with another stool, the kind that belonged in someone's kitchen at a breakfast bar.

"Thanks." Jean sat cautiously, noting its wobbling legs.

"I didn't think you were going to come."

"Me neither, honestly. I'm not great with days like this."

Alan pursed his lips and nodded in commiseration. "So, what should we do? You want to help me with inventory?"

Jean smiled. "I would actually love to."

In the storeroom Jean and Alan took turns counting boxes, crates, and bags. One person counted while the other scrawled their reports onto a xeroxed spreadsheet taped to the wall.

"So, why do you hate Thanksgiving so much?" Alan asked, as cautious and gentle as Dr. Goldstein might be with a skittish patient. "Is it a family thing?"

"Sort of. It's a lack of family thing. My parents died around this time."

Alan's face went slack. "Oh no, I'm so sorry."

She shook her head. "It's not your fault. It was an accident; we were all in the car together. But it's more than just losing them—it's feeling a kind of release with their death? I was almost seventeen, basically counting the days until I could leave home." Jean felt hot as the declaration burned through her lips and teeth. "You must think I'm a real asshole, but they were so unhappy. Really, more unhappy than I think I could even understand. My dad had anger problems. Bad ones, and my mom never would've left him because she didn't believe in divorce. I'm sorry, I don't know why I just said all that." She burned with the incredulity of confessing, once again. She could feel Alan's attention trained carefully on her face.

"I don't think you're an asshole, Jean. Everything is more complicated than it looks. Always." He paused and cleared his throat. "You know, I was in an accident, too, once."

Jean's heart swelled with gratitude, improbably and drastically, like the cartoon Grinch's. "What happened?"

Alan shook his head, a small smile on his lips. "It was nothing like what you went through. It was a bowling accident."

"What?" Jean laughed, startled.

"Hey! It's not funny!" he said, his face mock serious. "Nobody died, except my career."

"Oh no," Jean said, her voice soft with apology. "Will you tell me what happened?"

"It's a long story. Well, longish."

Jean made a show of looking out into the empty store, and Alan nodded, his smile growing wider. "Yeah, yeah, yeah. Okay, where to start. I was in this band, a long time ago. In another life."

"What band was it?"

"You ever heard of The Throwaways?"

Jean's eyes grew wide. "Alan. You were in The Throwaways?" Jean knew The Throwaways by reputation mostly—many of her fellow students had worshipped at their iconic 1970s New York City band altar.

"Yeah, I was. I played guitar. Played being the key word here. Past tense."

"What happened?"

Alan shook his head. "It was more stupid than you could ever imagine."

"I don't know, Alan," Jean said, folding a Post-it into an origami swan. "I can imagine some pretty stupid things."

Alan nodded and looked around the empty store, as though hunting for the best way in. "The first thing to know is that in my youth, I was a fucking idiot."

Jean snorted and folded on.

"I mean, everyone is, I know that, but I was a fucking idiot *deluxe*, you know what I mean? I did whatever I wanted, without really thinking about it. I was a junkie, but you already know that. I only cared about myself, honestly. I loved music, but all The Throwaways stuff came so easy. Like one day, we were practicing in my cousin Hazel's basement and the next day we were opening for David Bowie. There was no real struggle. I didn't know how good I had it until I didn't have it anymore."

Alan ran a hand through his thinning, mousy hair. Jean looked at him closely, trying to pin down an age. She was never good at that kind of thing; his slim build made him look younger than he likely was.

"I've told this story a million times, but it never gets easier, you know?"

"I know," Jean replied softly.

"Okay, well, it was after we played a show in Detroit. It was at the Fisher Theater, very fancy, even for us. In those days, you can imagine what I was like. Maybe. Actually, I kind of hope you can't imagine what I was like. Anyway, we went out with some people after the show, and the girls we were with wanted to go bowling."

"Sure," said Jean.

"One of these girls was actually some kind of bowling ringer. I mean she was really good. I don't remember much about that night, but I remember one of these girls was like the Shaq of bowling. She had her own bowling ball in the trunk of her car, like, ready to go! We were all mostly screwing around, especially me." He looked into Jean's eyes gravely. "I've never been a very good bowler. Anyway, I was not all there." He tapped at his temple. "I wasn't all there, and I wasn't paying attention—and my hand got crushed in the ball return thingy."

Jean winced away from the swan's paper wings, imagining the impact and the visceral crush of bones and tendons.

"Yeah, it was even worse than you think because I was wearing a bunch of rings. You know what happens when you're wearing rings and your hand gets crushed?"

Jean shook her head, her eyes nearly closed in a squint of dismay. Alan made a slicing motion across his throat with an accompanying, highly evocative sound effect. "Your tendons get *sliced*."

Jean covered her mouth like a carsick person might.

Alan nodded. "Yeah, it was as bad and disgusting as it sounds. I had a bunch of surgeries in the beginning, but nothing brought back my mobility, you know?" He held his hand in the air between them, a visual aid. Fluid, raised scars, whitened with time, coursed across the fingers and palm, and Alan pointed to one of the shorter ones. "This one was from the last surgery. The fifth one. This was a long time ago, and I'm sure now the technology is better or whatever, but now I'm broke. I can't afford any more hand surgeries. I had to pay out of pocket for the last one. The Throwaways didn't exactly have Blue Cross Blue Shield."

"I'm so sorry, Alan," Jean said, still staring at his sinewy, scarred hand, as though it were some hypnotist's watch. She could almost see the timeline of the glamorous past he left behind and the lucrative future that had escaped him winding around the remnants of his injury. "Does it still hurt? Can you play at all anymore?"

"Nope, kid, I can't play anymore. Not a chord, not a note." He stood up and cleared away the colorful sheaf of papers they had pulled out for cross-referencing the inventory. "So, did all of that talk about smashed bones and dangling tendons make you hungry? Should we order pizza or Chinese? What do you think is the least Thanksgiving-y?"

Jean shrugged. "Pizza? Fewest food groups."

Alan nodded sagely. "Good idea. A plain-ass pizza, not a single topping, in deference to the antiholiday spirit." Jean smiled in response.

Their pizza was ready quickly. There was no delivery person on that night because of the holiday, so Jean offered to run around the corner and pick it up. She and Alan pooled their cash and she left it all on the pizza counter with one of the most comfortable "Happy Thanksgiving" wishes she had ever doled out.

Back inside the warm, dog treat–scented Woof-n-Wag, Jean settled in at the counter beside Alan. They ate directly out of the box while The Clash swelled in company around them.

"You know what I think, Jean?"

"What?"

"I think neither of us will ever leave New York." Alan cracked open a can of Coke he brought out from the back and offered it to her.

"Really? How come?" Jean accepted it and took a bracing sip.

"Because this city is a great place to be left alone."

They clinked their pizza crusts to that, and Jean finished the best Thanksgiving dinner she'd ever had.

Seventeen

For the first time in a long time, Jean woke up without a single ache in her body. Not even the persistent twinge that usually camped out in her hip socket in cold weather. The winter light was bright, and the morning was already well on its way to becoming afternoon. She had slept hard. After dinner with Alan, she walked home and read a copy of *The Da Vinci Code* that Molly had left under a scented candle to catch wax drips. She must have stayed up reading later than she thought. Her phone said it was already 10:30.

She cleared her throat, anxious to get through to Dr. Esposito, and dialed the number for Dr. Schermeranz that she had saved the day before. The phone rang a long time. Jean was about to hang up when someone answered. It sounded like a young teenager or a child. "Sup?"

"Hello? I'm looking for Dr. Schermeranz?"

"Grandpa!" the voice called directly into her ear, followed

by the unmistakable clatter of phone on floor. Jean wasn't sure if she should call back or wait.

A static fumble and then an assured "This is Dr. Schermeranz."

"Hello? Dr. Schermeranz?" Jean didn't trust her own voice, wondering if she sounded as young as the person who had just dropped the phone.

"Yes. That's what I just said, isn't it?"

"Right, yes. I got your number because I was looking for Dr. Esposito."

"Ah, of course. Poor old Tony. What can I do for you? Are you looking for a referral? I'm retired now, but after his unfortunate last year, I offered to consult with any of his former patients and point them in the direction of a good practitioner. I'd be more than glad to help you."

"Oh, really? That's great." Jean fumbled for a pen and paper, rolling out of bed and into the kitchen to search, self-conscious about her state of undress on a professional call. "I'm actually not a patient; I'm a—an acquaintance, I guess you could say. I used to work for Dr. Myra Goldstein and have been in touch with Dr. Esposito over the years. I just wanted to check in with him. After I'd heard he was sick."

"Well, that's certainly kind of you." Dr. Schermeranz's voice pinged with suspicion. "What did you say your name was again?"

"Jean. Jean Smith."

"Well, Jean, Dr. Esposito is in a nursing home on Staten Island, and he isn't seeing visitors."

"Oh, I'm so sorry to hear that. I had no idea he was so poorly."

"Well, that's how things go, I'm afraid. The mortal coil will insist on the customary shuffle."

"Right, of course. Would you be able to tell me the name of the nursing home? I'd love to send a card at least; Dr. Esposito was always very kind to me." All lies—Dr. Esposito treated Jean like some indentured servant who came with the office. At best, he ignored her. At worst, he made demands that were humiliating and half-heartedly lecherous.

"Ah, I see." Dr. Schermeranz's tone leaned into gossipy, knowing territory. He must have assumed that Jean had succumbed to his colleague's amorous efforts at some point. "Well, I suppose it wouldn't do any harm to tell you that he's at St. Damian's. I don't know how lucid he is now, but I'm sure a kind word from an *old friend* like yourself would be welcome."

Jean rolled her eyes. "Thank you so much. I really appreciate your taking the time." She hung up with a rushed "Happy Holidays!" She called 411, a luxury she chided herself for, and waited to be connected to St. Damian's. The phone rang and rang, but Jean didn't hang up because she refused to pay for 411 twice.

"St. Damian's," a lightly accented voice answered.

"Yes, hi, I was calling to see when visiting hours are."

"Visiting hours are anytime you want them to be, young lady."

"Oh, that's great. What's the best way to get there?"

"Well, once you get over the Verrazzano, get in the right lane…"

"Oh, sorry, I meant what train should I take?"

"Train? You don't have a car?"

"I don't." Jean's heart sank under the weight of a new obstacle.

"I guess you could take a ferry and then the bus and then walk from the bus. Or take a cab?"

It was a very expensive suggestion.

"You know what? I'll ask a friend to give me a ride."

"That's probably for the best." Jean could hear the rustle of the woman nodding on the other end. "Which of our residents are you coming in to see?"

"Anthony Esposito."

"Tony? Well, fair warning, he's not much for visitors."

"Thanks for the heads-up. I'll be over as soon as I can." It wasn't a lie. Jean was flooded with an urgency to find Dr. Esposito, to wring any information she could from his disintegrating mind before it was too late. But her problem was a vehicular one. She didn't have a car, and she didn't know anybody with a car. Not even Molly or Christine knew anybody with a car, which was the bane of their Long Island Visiting Enthusiasts' existence. Jean dressed for work and considered all of her potential car-lending leads.

Working at Red and Gold that night felt like working in a sandstorm. Mitch was in a terrible mood. He was rude to the customers and curt with Jean and Omar. No matter how fast Jean tried to be, more orders, more insults, more stinging problems flew in her face. There were no faux smoke breaks that night. Omar turned cranky, too, so it was like working, alone, in a sandstorm. By the time they caught their first break thanks to the Yeah Yeah Yeahs playing next door, even Jean's generally easy mood had begun to turn.

She slugged back a glass of Coke with no ice. "What is going *on* tonight?" she asked. "Mitch, are you okay?"

Mitch looked at her with the expression of a high school principal—exhausted and helpless. "Bad day" was all he said.

Omar rolled his eyes.

"What?" Mitch said, all confrontation. "I had a bad day." He emphasized each word but spoke through clenched teeth. "I'll be back in a minute." He thundered away, careless of his body and bumping into people on the way out.

"Seriously," Jean said, giving Omar a direct look. "What is going on?"

"Mitch has a gamb-a-ling prob-lem," Omar said in a soft singsong. "Pretty sure he just lost big. I think that was why he couldn't make it to his sister's for the holiday."

"Oh." Jean wasn't sure what she expected to hear, but it wasn't that. "That's a shame, but come the fuck on."

"Exactly."

Jean made a few rounds collecting glasses and cans in the slightly emptied bar while Omar fielded drink orders. A body loomed behind her, and she tensed as a hand reached for her shoulder.

"Listen," said Mitch. "I'm really sorry, Jean. I shouldn't have spoken to you and Omar like that. What's going on is only going on with me. I apologize." He took a deep breath. "I'm going to turn it around."

"That's great," Jean said, handing him the plastic bin filled with dishes. "I'm going to the bathroom."

When Jean returned, he was a new Mitch—back to his regular, jovial self. Jean envied people who could flip their emotions, in either direction, like fickle gymnasts. Her survival as a child and young person had always relied upon her ability to sustain the emotional equivalent of a pond's surface in deep winter: silent, opaque, so frozen you could drive a truck onto it. She desperately hoped it wasn't too late to change that.

Omar gave her a cautious look when Mitch started juggling limes for the amusement of a pack of girls just barely hatched out of their teens. "I'm getting whiplash," Jean said, as they looked on and the girls laughed.

"Yeah, he's like this sometimes. You okay?" Omar asked.

"Sure!" Jean was suddenly terrified her face had betrayed something she couldn't take back. "Are *you* okay?" She turned her full attention on Omar and he seemed just as startled.

"Yeah, I'm okay."

"Everybody's okay!" Mitch announced to the assemblage of girls wearing an array of LIVESTRONG bracelets.

"Hey, Omar," Jean said, as they began to pick through the bins Mitch had collected, throwing out the garbage lodged between the dishes. "Do you have a car?"

Omar laughed, with the same enthusiasm as the juggling spectators. "Definitely not."

"Do you know anybody who does?"

"You know who has a car, Jean Jeanie?" Mitch paused, tossing a lime to each of his admirers. "Your friend. That girl who used to come in for Iggy. The Asian girl."

"Claire?" Jean frowned as she considered the complications of looping Claire back into her plans.

"That's the one. She drove us to Great Escape one time."

"Huh." Jean ran out the rest of her shift and pondered the best way to frame her request. At the very least, Jean figured Claire owed her a favor.

Jean called Claire on her way to the bakery. She was certain that since Claire was at work she wouldn't pick up. A hopeful flare burned in Jean's chest when she realized that borrowing Claire's car might all be arranged in voicemail messages. She nearly dropped the phone when Claire answered.

"Jean?"

"Hi, yes. I thought you'd be at work."

"I traded shifts. Wow, I honestly didn't expect to hear from you again."

"Oh."

"Look, I just want to say how sorry I am about—"

"Listen, let's move on. I really don't want to talk about it." That, at least, was the truth. "I'm calling because I need a favor." Jean paused at the lip of the subway stairs, leprous with old gum. "I need a car for this weekend—on Sunday. Mitch said you had a car, and not to put too fine a point on it, but I feel like you kind of owe me one?"

Claire barked a nervous laugh down the line. "I mean, yeah, I definitely owe you one." Jean wanted to dislike Claire more, wanted to be angrier, but an insistent flow of forgiving thoughts coursed through her. "Sunday you said? This Sunday?"

"Yeah. The earlier the better." The arriving train rumbled beneath her feet. "I'm actually late for work. I need to get on the train."

"Okay. Go, go, go. Meet me on Sunday at that coffee shop on Avenue A, the one on the north corner of the park. Is nine a.m. okay?"

"Yeah, that works."

"See you soon—and, Jean? I'm really glad you called."

On Sunday, Jean waited at the coffee shop where she and Alan had stopped for breakfast. Jean wasn't sure what kind of small talk Claire would expect; maybe she would simply hand off the keys. Jean's stomach lurched at the thought of sitting with Claire at one of the tiny, sticky tables. She really wasn't sure where she wanted the friendship to go.

Claire was ten minutes late. She sat down in a flurry of apologies and left her coat on.

"It's so cold!" She rubbed her hands together briskly.

"Didn't you drive here?" Jean asked, suddenly suspicious.

"Not exactly."

"Wait, so I can't borrow your car?"

"Technically, I don't have a car," Claire admitted, her eyes on her hands.

"What? What about Great Escape?" Jean leaned forward, incredulous.

"It was Luke's car, actually," Claire said.

"Luke?"

"Yeah. Rich kids always have a car." She shook her head. "Even though most of them can't even drive." Claire removed the plastic lid from her chai latte and blew across its foamy surface.

"Wait, I'm confused. Are you lending me Luke's car?"

"Sort of…" Claire overmixed her drink with a little wooden stirrer, an obvious attempt to mask her sheepishness. "I mean, that was the plan, but when I mentioned to Luke that I was lending the car to a friend, he asked which friend, and I told him you—" Claire winced "—which maybe in retrospect I shouldn't have, and now he's insisting on driving."

"Didn't you say he can't drive? I need to go to Staten Island, not just a couple of blocks," Jean said.

"He has a license." Claire shrugged. "And he's insisting. He said he would drive you anywhere." Jean wrapped her arms around herself. Claire watched her closely. "I'm sorry—I really didn't expect him to react this way, but hey, he's outside and ready to go. You don't even have to be nice to him. I think he'd actually prefer that." Claire smiled into her chai.

"Okay." Jean ran her hands through her hair and slumped forward. "I guess it's fine as long as you come, too?"

"Of course, Jean. Whatever you need. I'm so sorry about everything. I wouldn't blame you if you never forgive me."

"It's not about forgiveness, it's about getting to Staten Island," Jean muttered down at the loved-linked initials carved into the tabletop.

Luke waited outside by the car, his face carefully blank. "Hey there, Jean," he said, turning toward her as though Claire was invisible. He looked particularly miniature standing in front of a parked delivery van. "I'm really sorry about the other night. I'm glad you decided to call."

"But I didn't call." Jean spoke to him slowly, the way you would over a bad phone connection.

"Right, I just mean I'm glad we have another chance to get this right."

"I'm not trying to get anything right." She motioned back and forth between them. "I just need a ride, man."

"Right, of course." Luke moved in so close that his nose almost touched Jean's shoulder. "Where are we going again? Jersey?"

"Staten Island," Jean said, pinching the bridge of her nose and readying herself for a disaster.

Luke's brand-new Acura was already dinged on the passenger side, and the scrape of missing paint looked so painfully shorn that it made Jean wince. Luke opened the passenger door for her, but she slipped around him and climbed into the back. Thanks to her accident, Jean wasn't great in cars. It was one of the reasons she had moved to New York. The rare times she rode in a taxi or a bus felt so different from entering a car like this, a car that was headed toward a highway, across a bridge, under the helm of somebody who couldn't really drive. She was a bad passenger, but an excellent driver, due to Mrs. Altamore's insistence upon defensive driving courses for all of the teenagers in her household.

As soon as Luke turned the key in the ignition the car flooded with New Order. It was turned up so loud that it made her teeth hurt. Jean handed the printed-out MapQuest directions to St. Damian's up to Claire. She tried to settle back into the camel-colored leather interior and pretend she was somewhere else. The Acura lurched to a stop at a light on Houston Street.

"Do you know how to get to the Verrazzano?" Claire shouted.

"What?" Luke shouted back. "Are you talking to me?"

"Do you know how to get to the Verrazzano Bridge?"

"I don't think so." Luke shook his head, glancing in the rearview mirror and trying to make furtive eye contact with Jean. Jean closed her eyes and pretended to be asleep.

Claire snapped her fingers at the windshield. "It's green, come on. Make a left here."

Eventually, Claire turned down the music so that her directions could be heard. Jean rested her head against the window and watched the city slide by. Luke was a terrible driver. He lurched into other lanes without signaling and nearly rearended a Jeep with a Baby on Board sign suction cupped to its back window. It was early on a weekend; Jean wondered how long her errand would take and what the traffic would be like on the way home. She wondered if maybe she should ask to drive back.

"You're the worst driver," Claire said.

"I am not!" Luke replied indignantly, looking around the interior of the car as though for witnesses to vouch for him. "I just need some practice. My parents like me having a car, in case there's an emergency." He shrugged, not even having the decency to look embarrassed about having such caring parents with so much disposable income.

"What are we doing in Staten Island, Jean?" Claire asked, turning around in her seat. "Or are you not going to tell us? You don't have to," she added quickly.

Jean pointed at Claire, like bingo! She closed her eyes again, feeling the sun flash warm across her body even as her cheek grew cold against the glass.

"Don't you love how mysterious she is?" Luke said.

Once they were on Staten Island, Luke's torrid driving quieted. Even a child in a driver's ed class could navigate these roads, Jean thought, finally relaxing. She hoped her joints wouldn't be sore from where she had been tensing.

A low row of pale houses lined the street across from where St. Damian's loomed. It was a midcentury mint-green institution that looked even more severe against the bare tree branches that slapped at its sides in the wind.

"Yikes, Jean," Claire said, lifting her eyebrows in mock horror.

"What's going on in there?" Luke asked.

"Lobotomies for sure," Claire said drily.

"I'm just going in to visit a friend. You guys can wait here." Jean really hoped Luke would stay in the car.

"Yeah no," Claire said, with a humorless laugh. "We're not going to let you go in there by yourself. Right?"

"Right," Luke said, switching the car off. Jean didn't feel like arguing. If they were going to find out, they might as well find out in real time.

The three young people entered the building along with an

icy breeze. A few limp holiday decorations swung as the door closed behind them. An electric menorah missing all of its flame-shaped bulbs sat on the unmanned front desk.

"Is there, like, a bell?" Luke asked. He shuffled around the linoleum lobby. "Hello?" he called out.

"I'll be right with you." A light-skinned middle-aged woman in a pair of lavender scrubs came out to meet them. Her hands were filled with tiny loose bulbs for the menorah. Jean watched her, transfixed, as she screwed them in one by one, like setting teeth into a pair of dentures. "How can I help you?" she asked. Her voice strobed with a soft Caribbean accent.

"Hi. I think maybe we spoke on the phone?" Jean said. "I'm here to visit a resident."

"Well, welcome to St. Damian's. Who are you here to see?" Jean watched her twist in another bulb.

"Tony Esposito," Jean said. Luke gasped behind her, and she felt Claire go completely still.

"Oh, Tony, yes. I remember you. He's in room eleven. First floor—down the hall. We had to move him where we could keep a closer eye on him."

"Thanks," Jean said.

"Kids, be careful, okay? Guests are not always Tony's cup of tea." The woman screwed in another bulb and Jean, Claire, and Luke walked single file down the painted concrete hallway to room eleven. The door was slightly ajar and had a sheet of paper with Dr. Esposito's name on it taped to the front.

Jean knocked. "Hello?" she called. There was no sound from within, but a pungent odor of mothballs wafted out. She looked at Claire and Luke, a quick, nervous glance for each of them. Before either could say a word, she pushed the door wide and stepped through. Jean wasn't sure what she was expecting, but Dr. Esposito looked exactly like himself. His beard and mustache were neatly trimmed, and his thick gray hair, while a little longer than she remembered, looked clean and combed.

He was not some pale, languishing, skeletal figure in a hospital gown. In fact, he appeared to be in better physical health than Jean had ever seen him.

"Well, well," he said, sitting up a little and folding his newspaper into a neat square. "That's not Jean Smith, is it?"

"It is," Jean said, approaching the tidily made bed. "Hi."

"Please, have a seat." Dr. Esposito removed his glasses and motioned for her to sit at the edge of the bed. Jean sat, but just barely, feeling a little squeamish about sitting on the bed of a person she had known strictly in a professional capacity. Her thighs burned from doing more squatting than sitting. Dr. Esposito took no notice of Claire or Luke, training his intent gaze fully on Jean.

"How are you feeling?" she asked.

"How am I feeling?" He laughed bitterly. "I feel fine. Did you think I'd be anything less than fine?" His tone was layered with irritation.

Jean tried to wipe her face of expression, the way she'd seen Dr. Goldstein do whenever she interacted with a patient. She had no idea what to do or say, and thought it would be wise to provide a blank space for Dr. Esposito to tell the story he wanted to tell. "Honestly, I wasn't sure what to expect when I heard you were in a place like this." Jean vacuumed all inflection from her voice and waited for him to answer. He did seem fine, but then, Jean knew better than anyone how fine a person could seem.

"Really?" He raised a single, skeptical eyebrow. "I appreciate you taking the time to find me. How is Myra doing? I thought she might come herself, but I'm grateful that she thought enough of me to send anyone, even you."

A pulse of anger beat through her, but she was able to curb it. "Dr. Goldstein didn't send me. I quit a while ago." Jean leaned forward, settling herself more firmly on the mattress. She wished they were alone. "I actually wanted to come speak to you because I'm worried about her."

Dr. Esposito's expressive brows lurched low on his forehead. "About Myra? What do you mean?"

"I haven't been able to get in touch with her. Every time I've tried to call or visit, her son, Jeffrey, has…intercepted me."

"I know his name! You don't have to remind me. I still have all my faculties." He smacked his folded newspaper on top of the worn blanket with surprising force.

"Yes, of course, sorry."

"Don't apologize! I don't have time for apologies anymore. What are you trying to say, Jean? Just spit it out."

"I think something's really wrong. At first, I thought it might be elder abuse, or another…domestic thing like that, but I think it's something…more."

Dr. Esposito raised his eyes to the Styrofoam ceiling tiles. "Of course it's something more, you idiotic creature."

Jean sat back and let the insult land squarely. "I'm not sure what you expect me to know," she said.

Dr. Esposito grumbled. "It's like putting out a house fire with a watering can, trying to explain this to someone."

"Why don't you start with the note you sent Dr. Goldstein. About your regrets?" Jean said, lodging her voice into its coldest register. She heard a shocked inhale in the doorway behind her, but she didn't know and didn't care which of her travel companions it came from.

Dr. Esposito looked up at her sharply. "There you go. That's where you should have started." Jean nodded at him to go on. "How much do you know?" His eyes narrowed.

"I know about the shortcuts."

"The shortcuts? Is that what you call them?" He sounded grimly amused.

"Does it matter what I call them?"

"No. What matters is that they exist. And they exist because of our work, Myra's and mine, with Selestron. Ah, so you know that much, too."

Jean nodded.

"Well, did you know that it was Selestron that put me in here, to keep me quiet? They didn't want me talking about any of it because they're in the throes of a brand-new spin-off project using our studies. So here I am, on their dime."

"What? No, that can't be true," Luke interjected, stepping forward and fully entering the room.

"And who's this?" Dr. Esposito asked. "Your young man, Jean?"

"He wishes," Claire muttered.

"I'm Luke Van Cleven."

Dr. Esposito released a bitter laugh. "Well, thank your father for me, for setting me up in such grand accommodations." He swept his arms wide and cast his gaze about the room.

"What?" Jean looked straight at Luke, the first time she'd looked directly at him all day.

Luke looked at the ground, awash with shame. "My father, well, Selestron is his company. Our company, I guess." A memory, something Claire had mentioned, tingled in the back of Jean's mind.

An oversized Styrofoam cup filled with ice chips—a familiar relic from Jean's hospital days—sailed past her head and connected squarely with Luke's face. Dr. Esposito turned a look on her that barely concealed his fury. "Interesting friends you have, Jean."

Jean held up her hands and bobbled them like shaking heads. "No, no, no, Dr. Esposito. We are not friends. I can assure you."

Luke wiped his face with his sleeve. "Listen, I don't know who put you in here, but if it really was somebody at Selestron, your best bet at getting out of here is me."

Dr. Esposito folded his hands in his lap. "I suppose I'm all ears then."

"We have a problem." Claire stepped inside and closed the door behind her as she spoke. "And if you help us, maybe Luke's dad will help you."

"Jesus, Claire!" Jean reeled. "This isn't some back room in Little Italy."

"Isn't it?" Claire asked. Her eyes narrowed. "I won't say that I'm not honored to meet you, Dr. Esposito," she added. "It's just that we don't have time for charm or even tact. I need to know if you're going to help us or not."

"Going to help you or not with what?" Dr. Esposito massaged his temples wearily.

"Our friend is missing. He went through one of the shortcuts and now he's missing." Claire moved closer until she was standing at the head of the bed, like a priest giving last rites.

"There isn't much I can do to help you there."

"Can we just rewind for one minute?" Jean leaned back against the foot of the bed with an exasperated sigh. "You all might know everything about Luke's dad's company and what he did with Dr. Esposito and Dr. Goldstein, but I don't. I'm worried about Dr. Goldstein, too, and I don't think it can be a coincidence, can it? That you're in here, Dr. Esposito, and that Jeffrey has apparently taken his mother hostage, at the exact same time."

"A very astute observation, Jean." Dr. Esposito's voice lilted with sarcasm.

"Well? Would you mind elaborating?"

"Let's see. I can only take you so far, and then perhaps your young friends here can fill you in once I've reached the limits of my knowledge."

Jean nodded at him to continue while an insistent beep sounded outside in the hall.

"Myra and I were thriving in our family therapy practices— Myra has always been the trailblazer of ideas, and generally she's always right. But this time, I wish I hadn't been so easy to convince." Dr. Esposito's voice cracked with irritation. "I'm sure you already know, Jean, but Myra had been experimenting quite heavily with psychedelics." Jean's eyes widened. It had never occurred to her that kindly, ancient Dr. Goldstein even knew what psychedelics were. "Myra believed there were great therapeutic benefits to using these mind-expanding drugs in a clinical setting. Particularly with entire families as a unit. You can imagine how this was received, particularly when there were children involved. Myra was expressly convinced that every member of the family, even the children, needed to participate in a new era of medically influenced treatment."

Jean nodded, trying to camouflage her shock.

"Unfortunately, I knew someone at Selestron. Not your father," he said, turning to address Luke, "but someone like him." His voice grew cold. "It was the mistake of my life."

"You knew Barry," Luke said, perching on the windowsill.

"Yes. Barry." Dr. Esposito spat the name out like a knocked-out tooth. "Myra and Barry got on like a house on fire. I was really quite jealous for a time. The drug—they called it Empathin, their private joke. It never got an official name, I don't think. We never got that far. Because the study involved children, the FDA wouldn't touch it, so we decided to set up our own clinical trials, using our own patients. Myra and I were already running perfectly calibrated clinics for this very specific experiment. Night clinics. We had to schedule all of the sessions in the evenings—the closer the patient grew to sleep, the more open they became. We dosed the patients, let them doze off, and then woke them for these really phenomenal, breakthrough sessions—I mean so productive, my God—while they were still half-asleep."

"Is that why you can only go through the shortcuts at night?" Jean asked.

"You can go through anytime you like," Dr. Esposito said. "It's a much easier process—the transitions, if you will, are more manageable—at night. Working with the Empathin during the day wasn't ideal but not impossible. At first, it seemed to be going well. Even my jealousy seemed worth the results. People were making progress at remarkable speeds, accomplishing results in three sessions that would normally take thirty years."

"That sounds impressive," Jean said, encouragingly.

"It was. Very impressive. Until the earthquake."

Jean did a double take.

"I'm sorry, did you say earthquake?" Claire asked.

"Ah, you see!" Dr. Esposito said with a triumphant point in Claire's direction. "She doesn't know everything, does she? Do you?" he asked Luke.

Luke shook his head.

"I'm not surprised your father has kept this part to himself."

"What happened?" Jean asked.

"In the second week of the trial, we had a massive earthquake—a bone rattling, off the charts earthquake. But nobody felt it except the people in my office and in Myra's, and the people we had already begun treating with Empathin."

"An earthquake?" Jean said.

"It wasn't an earthquake, obviously. It was something more profound and more terrible. I believe that it was a tear in time and space."

"I don't get it. How did it happen, like physically?" Jean asked.

"Nobody really knows. It just happened! Selestron commissioned a panel of physicists to investigate, but I never saw the results. I would give my right arm to see those reports. The best I could come up with was that some magnetic frequency in the brain on Empathin somehow affected the laws of physics. Myra hypothesized that the variety of brains involved led to multiple openings."

"There's a shortcut for every person who participated in the trial?" Jean asked.

"It's just an informal theory." Dr. Esposito shrugged. "We never confirmed it."

"That's kind of what I'd heard," Luke said, staring at the floor.

"How many people participated?" Jean persisted.

"Including the children? Forty-six in all. Twelve under eighteen."

"Do you think that makes sense, Claire?"

"I don't know. I told you the ones I know about."

"Do you think Iggy found all forty-six?" Luke asked.

"I don't know." Claire's eyes boiled with emotion. She leaned against the window, and the sky looked flat and cold beside her heated face.

"Wait," Jean said, turning to Dr. Esposito. "Do you have a shortcut? Did you take the Empathin?"

He shook his head. "I didn't. But Myra did."

"Of course she did." Jean chewed on her thumbnail.

"Does the type of shortcut depend on, or I don't know, mimic, some characteristic of the person who was treated?" Jean asked.

Dr. Esposito's face compressed in thought. "It's not impossible, if the neurological activity was the source of the force. No two brains are the same. But I wasn't privy to the whole report. I suppose young Master Selestron over there would know more than I."

"I didn't know any of that," Luke said, shaking his head. "But I do know Selestron didn't end up destroying the Empathin. They just canceled the trials and kept it quiet. They've been messing with the formulas since before I was born."

"What are they trying to do?" Jean asked, aghast.

"Who knows? My dad doesn't say much about it."

"I'm so confused—why did Selestron put you in here, all of a sudden? I imagine they made you and Dr. Goldstein sign NDAs or whatever," Jean said.

"Of course. And everyone else who participated in the trials. There were generous financial settlements all around, not that

Selestron couldn't afford it. But I suspect they're reviving some component used to make the Empathin, and they don't want me voicing any objections."

"Something is up." Jean crossed her arms and stood up, staring hard at Luke.

"Yeah, no shit," Claire muttered.

"Luke, can you get any of the physicists' reports for Dr. Esposito to look at? I wouldn't know where to begin to understand any of this, and I doubt you or Claire would either. But something is going on, and we need to figure it out. They put Dr. Esposito in here for a reason; we need to know what they're planning."

"I'm still here and sentient, despite what my admitting orders may state," Dr. Esposito snipped, but an undeniable gleam of anticipation shone from his eyes. "I would certainly have a look."

"Yeah, maybe I could get a copy of the old report, but I doubt I can get anything on what they've been working on recently. I'll try."

"Would that be helpful, do you think?" Jean turned to Dr. Esposito. "Maybe we could get a better idea of what's going on and why they put you in here?"

"I would be interested to read it, but I'm not sure how helpful it would be. My money is on a much more nefarious plan that I'm certain even young Master Selestron isn't privy to."

"Please stop calling me that," Luke begged.

"Well, we can have a starting point at least," Jean said, pacing.

"But none of this helps us find Iggy!" Claire said. She spun around and looked Luke dead in the eye.

"You have to let it go," Luke said. "Iggy's gone. There's no way to find him. We're in over our heads here. Even Dr. Esposito, the Heisenberg of this whole operation, wouldn't know where to find him."

"I'm flattered, but just barely," Dr. Esposito said. "Who is Iggy?"

"He's a friend. My new co-worker, actually. He's the one who disappeared using one of the shortcuts. We think he might have gone the wrong way and been stranded there."

"What was that?" Dr. Esposito leaned forward, his abandoned newspaper crunching at his waist.

"Our friend, he was a shortcut enthusiast," Jean began.

Claire interrupted in a quick hot burst. "He used so many of them. All the time. He thought they made him more creative— he's a musician, you know? An 'artist.' I know you're only supposed to go one way, but I think Iggy reversed his paths. Like, entered through the exit when he shouldn't have. Jean thinks he got stuck in some wrong time."

"And why, Jean, would you think that?" Dr. Esposito said, soft and terrible.

"Because somebody told me that might happen. And, I also might have done it myself one time. By accident." She looked down at her clasped hands. The familiar feeling of bracing for imminent punishment gripped her entirely.

"Excuse me, you what?" Luke said, surging forward.

"Like I said, it was an accident." Jean's eyes caught Dr. Esposito's intent gaze.

"Hmm. And yet here you are, to tell the tale," he said. "Interesting."

"Interesting how?" Claire asked.

"Just that your friend got stuck, but you seem to be with us, unharmed."

"That's a matter of luck, though, isn't it?" Jean asked.

"Is it?" Dr. Esposito asked, cleaning the lenses of his glasses on the thin institutional blanket.

"I'm not sure what you're trying to say here, Dr. Esposito." Jean's hands were fisted tight enough that she could feel the bite of her fingernails.

"I'm suggesting that you might have a special ability here, Jean. If we ever need to use it." Dr. Esposito's tone was suspiciously careful. Jean could sense his excitement glowing through every word.

"With all due respect, Dr. Esposito, I get the feeling that you're not telling us everything," Luke said.

"Oh, I'm not. But only because I have the very beginnings of an idea. If you bring me that report, young Master Selestron, it might speed things along."

"What about Dr. Goldstein?" Jean asked.

"What about her?" Dr. Esposito wasn't cruel: only neutral. He spoke to her like he would answer a patient.

"Well, can we help her?" Jean prompted.

"I think we can certainly try. And the idea I have would help everyone. Maybe—" he turned to Claire "—even your missing friend."

Claire nodded and paced back to the door. "Let's get a move on, then. Luke, you have some calls to make." She locked gazes with Jean and raised her eyebrows, clearly offering her a few extra moments with Dr. Esposito alone. Jean nodded, accepting them. "We'll see you in the car. Come on." She spoke to Luke the way a person might to a dawdling dog pulling on its leash.

Jean took Claire's spot by the window and watched the decaying flag across the street strain against the wind. "Is there anything I could bring you? Or send you? I didn't know," she said, turning toward Dr. Esposito sitting neatly in his bed.

"Of course you didn't know, Jean." He shook his head. "And I don't want anything—I just want to be released from this place."

"Can't imagine why," Jean said with a smile. "Great view."

"Ha. Yes. Just please hurry your friend along. If anything comes of this idea, we'll have to execute it quickly."

Jean nodded and wrapped her scarf around her face. "Does that phone work?" she asked, pointing to the lump of beige rotary on the nightstand.

"What do you think?" Dr. Esposito said.

"Okay, then I'll come to you. Take care of yourself, Dr. Esposito."

"You too, Jean. You too."

Eighteen

The wind snapped at Jean across the parking lot. A watery swell of The Flaming Lips was turned all the way up, and Jean could hear it through the car's closed windows. Luke cut the music as soon as she opened the door.

"Holy shit, Jean! Dr. Anthony fucking Esposito! Why didn't you tell us?" he shouted.

Jean grimaced, considering the long ride home, and buckled her seatbelt.

"Yeah, Jean, Dr. Esposito is a big deal," Claire said, turning in her seat and offering Jean an open pack of snowy Parliament Lights. "Why didn't you tell us who you were seeing? Where we were going? And he thinks he can help Iggy! *That* is a big fucking deal." She grinned and Jean felt involuntarily warmed. Luke reversed out of the parking lot, nearly hitting a groggily moving cat.

"I guess it was good you guys were there," Jean said wearily.

"Yeah, you think?" Luke turned his body entirely toward her. The car swerved a little into the next lane, and the cars around them blared their horns. Jean clenched her jaw to keep her teeth from chattering.

"Luke, my God, keep your eyes on the road!" Claire said, smacking his arm with her free hand. The other ashed her cigarette out of the cracked window. Luke turned the music back up with a triumphant little tap on the dashboard. Jean squeezed her eyes shut tight and pretended to sleep, half praying that they would crash just so she could get it over with and stop anticipating the worst.

Luke dropped her off in front of her building, and Jean thanked them with a little wave. Luke rolled the driver's side window down. "Jean, you should give me your number. So I can let you know what I find out."

"Sure," Jean said, still trying to sustain the fiction that she was normal, easy breezy and not retraumatized by Luke's wild driving. "Just get it from Claire, okay?"

Claire leaned over. "You sure you don't want to come have dinner with us? Young Master Selestron is paying."

"Shut up," Luke muttered.

"I'm having dinner with my roommates," Jean lied.

"Oh. Want me to text you if we go out later?" Claire asked.

"No, that's okay. I'm pretty tired."

"If you say so." Claire shrugged.

"Oh, we're definitely going to text her later," Luke said, as he buzzed the window back up into place.

Jean collapsed into bed and fell into a hard sleep—there was no putting up a fight of any kind. Jean was grateful the sleep was a heavy one because in the morning she awoke to a slew of missed calls and texts, all from Luke. Jean closed her eyes and went back to sleep.

★ ★ ★

"Jean? Finally," Luke said, when she returned his call Monday afternoon.

"Hi, yeah, I had kind of a busy morning. What's going on?"

"Well, first, I found that report that Dr. Esposito wanted."

"Wow, that was fast." Jean poured herself the rest of the cold coffee from the pot and put it in the microwave.

"It was pretty easy to find, actually," Luke said, his smugness coming through the phone. "My parents are in Saint Moritz so the apartment is empty. Marisol knows where everything is, it's incredible."

"That's great." Jean burned her fingers as she extracted the too-hot cup.

"Listen to this." The crunch of shuffling paper scraped over the line. "'While we detected no physiological change in the subjects' neurological systems, the measurement of magnetic fields surrounding each subject altered dramatically from what is generally compatible with life.' And then there's a bunch of formulas here and shit."

"Wow—that sounds…promising."

"Yeah, it's all pretty technical stuff," Luke said proudly.

"I'm sure it'll be really helpful for Dr. Esposito."

"For *sure*," he said enthusiastically. "So, should we take this over today, or…"

"I have to be at work in an hour." Jean sagged with relief, never more grateful for her job. She needed a little space to organize herself before she got back into that room with Dr. Esposito or into that car with Luke and Claire.

"Oh right." Luke's voice dipped with disappointment. "I forgot about that. Can we go tomorrow?"

"Sure—let's go in the morning. I'll text Claire." Claire absolutely had to be there. Jean didn't want Luke thinking this was some kind of distorted date. "I actually have to go, Luke. Nice work!" she added, she hoped, encouragingly.

"Thanks—" Jean hung up before he could say anything else.

Snow pelted Jean on her walk to Red and Gold. These were not soft, benevolent, movie set flakes; this snow was a thousand pellet guns raining ice down upon her from the sky. She was gripped by crankiness.

Omar was cranky, too. They each took a shot hoping it would buoy their spirits, but the alcohol only made them crankier. Jean kept slamming her fingers in the lowboy's sticky sliding door. Fortunately, the weather kept most potential customers away, so the only people they subjected their foul moods to were each other and the few regulars who came in to numb themselves to things more powerful than the cranky moods of those who served them.

"It's a full moon tonight or some shit," Omar said.

"Really?"

"Who knows. Hey, did you ever hear from Iggy?" He dropped the newly filled napkin dispenser and the paper squares scattered and stuck all over the filthy mats behind the bar. "Fuck," he muttered.

Jean crouched to help him pick them up. "No. I know his friend Claire is really worried."

"That's too bad. He was a good guy."

"He's not *dead*," Jean said, filled to the brim with a sudden, irrational fury. "It's bad luck to talk like that." Jean threw a clutch of ruined napkins into the garbage and wiped her hands on the front of her jeans.

"I didn't know you were so superstitious." Omar eyed her from the sink, where he stood washing his hands.

"I'm not." Jean crossed her arms over her chest. "Why would you say that?"

"I misspoke, okay? God." They looked toward the opening

door and its accompanying gust of icy wind with matching relief and annoyance. If nothing else, a few customers could distract and unite them until the end of their shift.

"Hey." It was Luke. He looked at them warily, from one to the other.

"Hey, man, what can I get you?" Jean stepped back, grateful to let Omar take over. She pretended that Luke was a random stranger, just another body through the door. Luke watched her while he ordered from Omar.

Jean moved to the other end of the bar to refill one of the regulars. "On me," she said, with a tight smile.

"I heard you all are taking a little road trip tomorrow," Omar said, an eyebrow raised, when Jean sauntered back as casually as she could.

Jean shot Luke a look. "That's the plan. You never know with this weather, though. Might have to cancel."

"Okay," said Omar. "I'll leave you and your friend alone to work it out. Watch out," he said directly to Luke. "Full moon."

"Is that, like, a period thing?" Luke asked.

"What is wrong with you?" Jean whispered harshly.

"What?" Luke looked mystified.

"Try to be discreet! I mean, come on." She rolled her eyes. This is what happened when you grew up with a silver spoon in your mouth, she thought. You just said and did whatever you wanted. Jean knew that her frustration was outsize and temporary, but that didn't make it any less real.

"I didn't say anything really—just that we were going to Staten Island tomorrow. Omar's not a bad guy."

"No. *Omar* isn't," Jean said meaningfully, shocked at her own cruelty.

"I don't get it. You seem mad." Luke bolted back half of the Rheingold he had ordered. Jean stared openly, completely flummoxed.

"I just think this is something we need to keep to ourselves," she said.

"I'm only trying to help." Luke sulked and finished up his beer.

Jean replaced it with a fresh one. "I'm sorry. You're right. Just, please, let's not literally shout this from the rooftops."

Luke flung a jewel-green file folder on top of the bar. "You probably don't want to talk about this then."

"Is that the report?"

"Uh-huh." Luke dug around in his jacket pockets.

Jean closed her eyes, trying to beat back her bad mood. "Why would you bring that here? Shouldn't you keep it in a safe place?"

"It's with me—safest place there is." Luke extracted a cigarette from the pack he had located. His hands were small and delicate—much more beautiful than hers. "Care to join me?"

"No thanks—I have to help Omar with something."

"I'll be right back." Luke winked and left to smoke. The folder remained abandoned on the sticky bar top. Jean's fingers itched to open it, but she clenched her hands into fists and resisted. The small act of control restored her to some semblance of composure.

Omar spoke just behind her, so close that it made her jump. "So, is that like, your prenup, Jean?"

She turned to face him, trying not to smile. "That's just mean, Omar."

"If Kevin McCallister was coming after me, you bet I'd be a lot sweeter than you."

"Sick," Jean said, wincing.

"Watch out, Jean." Omar's voice turned serious. "That dude isn't going to leave you alone. He's not right in the head." He tapped at his temple.

Luke drank Rheingold after Rheingold. Jean kept an eye on the green folder as she worked and he grew drunker. She wondered if she should slip it into her bag, where it would be safer. At a certain point in the night, Luke was drawn away to the pool table by a couple of girls who had peeled off from a larger group. Luke kept looking over at her despite his drunken attempt at flirting with the girls. Their friends were loud, making the bar seem fuller than it was. Patti Smith wailed overhead, and Jean checked the clock behind the bar.

"Do you think I can take off a little early?"

"Jean," Omar grumbled. "You can't do this every shift."

"I know, I know, but getting to the bakery is going to be extra shitty tonight. This weather!" Jean pointed to the fogged-up front windows. "I'll owe you one. Seriously."

"At this point you owe me a fucking kidney. Ugh, fine." Omar shook his head and Jean crouched down behind the bar for her coat and bag. When she stood up, she was overtaken by a wave of unhappiness. Her bad mood, the weather, and Luke's surprise appearance all Frankensteined into a great wedge of gloom. What was she even doing with her life, working jobs she didn't really care about to live in a city that was almost viral in its drive to defeat a person? What would it be like, she wondered, to try to be happy?

She adjusted the hat on her head and lifted the green folder. "Thanks again, Omar."

"Yeah, yeah," Omar said, all disapproval.

A hand snagged on her elbow as she made her way to the door—Luke, again. "Where are you going?" he asked, his features a perplexed jumble.

"I have to get to my other job."

"Your other job?" He squinted at her through the haze of Rheingolds.

"At the bakery. I really have to go, sorry." She shook her arm, trying to dislodge him. He was slight, but surprisingly strong.

"Can I come with you?"

"Why don't you hang out here?"

"I'd rather come with you."

"I have to leave now or else I'm going to be fired."

"Let me get my coat." Luke met her by the door, at no point aware that the folder was missing. Any moral qualms she'd felt about taking it evaporated.

"Shit, it's cold." Luke shivered in his navy wool pea coat. They passed a storefront littered with neon signs. He huddled closer, and no matter how quickly she tried to walk, he kept pace with her. Jean plunged down the subway steps with relief, and Luke weaved a little behind her, swaying alarmingly to one side. Jean felt a temporary swell of panic at the thought that he would fall and hurt himself, and she would have to wait until an ambulance came. Or even worse, that she would have to go to the hospital with him. Ever since her accident, Jean had done everything in her power to avoid hospitals. She took her vitamins and watched her step. She would rather die than go to another hospital.

As they waited for the train, Luke stood with his toes at the edge of the yellow line. "Jean," he said. "Can I ask you something? I don't know if this is too personal or what."

"You can ask." Jean itched with irritation. At least it distracted her from the cold. "I might not answer you, though."

"Yeah." He looked at his feet thoughtfully. "I get that." He looked from side to side, making sure they were alone on the platform. For a terrifying moment Jean thought he was going to push her onto the tracks. "What was it like, going through the shortcuts the wrong way?"

"What do you mean?"

"What did it *feel* like?" He stumbled too close and Jean took a step back, pretending that she meant to lean against the icy tiled wall.

"It didn't feel like anything—it felt exactly like when you go through normally."

"But not, like, special or better?"

"Not at all."

He mumbled something she didn't hear as the train crashed through and lurched to a stop.

Jean thought, hopefully, that he might just let her get on the train and go his separate way, but when the doors snapped open in front of them, they both got on.

"You do this every night?" he asked. A woman surrounded by plastic shopping bags was the only person in the car with them.

"I do this four nights a week. It's not so bad."

"Do you like working at the bar or the bakery better?"

"I don't know. That's a good question." Luke perked up like a watered plant. "I like them for different reasons and I dislike them for different reasons, you know?"

"Not really. I've actually never had a real job. Isn't that fucked-up?"

"Yeah, it really is." Jean could tell by his reaction that he had conveyed this piece of information exactly the same way many times before, and that most times it had been met with some form of demur.

"Well, not never-never I guess. I had an internship at *Rolling Stone* in college, but that was about it."

"Did you like working there?"

"Hell yeah, but I don't think I was a very good intern, you know?" His smile was guileless and easy.

"I can imagine."

"You're mean, you know that?"

"Nah," she said with a shrug. "You don't know what mean is." She meant it lightly, but the truth broke through her tone. She'd had a front row seat to mean for her entire childhood; Jean hoped to never see anyone talk to another person the way her parents had spoken to each other. Luckily, Luke was dulled by the alcohol and didn't seem to notice.

"How come you didn't call me, Jean? After you went home with me?"

Jean's face grew hot. "Oh, you know. I'm not great with that stuff."

"What? Love?"

"Sure, yeah. Love." She rolled her eyes. A girl with unevenly lined eyes sat down across from them, her earbuds snaking into her zipped-up purse. "Oh shit, this is my stop!" Jean leapt up and ran out just in time, leaving Luke on the train.

Jean hurried to work, in a swirl of guilt and relief. She was right on time and thrilled that Luke wasn't there escorting her to the door like a midcentury teen on a date. She didn't want any of this to follow her into the bakery.

"Your boyfriend called," Lu said, as Jean shucked her jacket and dropped her bag.

"What?"

"He just called here looking for you."

"What? Now? And he's not my boyfriend."

"Said he lost you on the train. He was kind of frantic." Lu pressed her lips together and raised her eyebrows sky-high with glee.

Jean groaned. "Are you serious? Do you think he'll try to come here?"

"He sure seemed like he might."

"Ugh." Jean took out her phone and sent Luke a pointed I'll-see-you-tomorrow text and tied on her apron.

"What's going on with him?" Lu simmered a fragrant syrup in a large pan on the stove.

"Nothing. What's in that?"

"Rosemary and anise. Don't try to distract me. Who is he?"

"He's nobody."

Lu clucked like a kid in the schoolyard. "Poor guy. You're a heartbreaker, Jean."

"I am, definitely—" Jean paused to crack and separate an egg over an enormous copper bowl "—not that." She felt Lu's gaze intensify with every egg she cracked. "What?"

"You're making me nervous. Just do one at a time. If you get a speck of yolk in there it fucks up the whole meringue."

"I remember," Jean said sharply.

"You just seem a little reckless tonight. You know where the ramekins are."

"Fine." Jean huffed to the shelf and plucked two from the stack of clean dishes that towered there.

"What is up with you? Something happened with that boyfriend, didn't it?"

"Jesus Christ, he's not my boyfriend! I've literally never had nor ever wanted a boyfriend."

"Really? A ladies' lady?"

"How is this any of your business, Lu? Aren't you my employer?"

"Not technically—I just thought I might know somebody for you, that's all."

"Thanks, but no thanks. I could not be any less interested in a relationship. I'm not great with people." Even in her emotional disorder, Jean felt the now-familiar spark of surprise, that she could even talk about this with Lu.

"I have to disagree with you there—you are great with people."

"Do you seriously think that?" Jean turned, incredulous.

"Oh yeah, definitely. I like you and I don't like anybody. Same with Omar. You have boys following you to work in the middle of the night. All of these signs point to Great With People."

Jean gave Lu a tight smile. "Maybe what I meant is that I'm not great at getting close with people."

"What, you don't think we're close? Half the shit I say to you I wouldn't say to my own mother." Lu crossed her arms, comically confrontational.

"Huh." Jean paused to turn on the mixer. "I guess we are."

Jean waved away a cloud of confectioner's sugar kicked up by the beaters and thought about what Lu had said. She *did* feel close to Lu, but in an unexpected, easy way. Jean had always believed that getting close to another person—or allowing them to get close to you—was a difficult, even painful process.

But, standing in that kitchen in the middle of the night, Jean realized that getting close to another person could be so natural that you didn't even know it was happening, like a subtle change in the weather. For the rest of her shift, Jean couldn't stop smiling.

Nineteen

The cars crammed in around them on the BQE. An accident ahead had stalled their progress. With the early start, the sunlight streaming through the windows, and Luke's car's superior heating system, Jean didn't have to pretend to doze off. She had slept for only an hour or so before her alarm hauled her out of bed toward Staten Island and Dr. Esposito. Jean's bag pillowed her head, and she was hotly aware of the emerald green folder inside. Luke kept the stereo at a sleep-friendly level, probably because of his hangover. He had grimaced hello but didn't say much to her. Claire chattered about her co-worker's rat infestation. "Their cereal boxes were all chewed up and they thought it was mice but then they *saw* one. In the middle of the *day*, which apparently means there are like, thousands of rats living in her apartment." But, when she noticed how tired Jean was, she fell quiet and left her alone.

"I don't know. Something's going on with her, don't you

think?" Claire's voice seeped through Jean's sleep-congested head—only ten percent alert.

"Something. Definitely."

"I can't believe she took us to see Esposito like it was nothing."

"Mm-hmm," Luke murmured.

Claire lowered her voice a little. "I mean, you guys are—" She paused, giving her words a semilascivious inflection. "Close."

"Hardly. You're probably closer at this point."

"You think?"

"For sure."

A siren blared by and Jean tensed awake; her body never forgot that sound.

"Oh hi, you're up. You want this? We drove through a Dunkin' Donuts while you were sleeping. So exotic, right? Drive-throughs in Staten Island!" Claire handed back an enormous Styrofoam cup of coffee.

"Thanks," Jean said. She sat up and tucked herself more firmly and correctly behind her seatbelt. She adjusted the lap belt before opening the plastic tab on the coffee lid. She noticed Claire watching her meticulous seatbelt ritual. Jean was surprised by how unselfconscious she was about it.

St. Damian's glided up on their left like a derelict Soviet cruise ship. An ambulance was parked outside, its lights flashing silently, back doors gaping open.

"Did you get some rest?" Claire asked.

"Yeah, thanks," Jean answered absently, mesmerized by the lights. Claire followed her gaze.

"I hope everything's okay." Jean knew that Claire meant Dr. Esposito, and she hoped so, too.

An EMT leaned against the reception desk and scrawled across the clipboard in her hands. The woman who had met them at reception on their first visit rushed back out to the desk and signed the clipboard. The EMT's partner wheeled an unconscious old woman on a gurney out into the lobby. The sheet meant to cover her had been kicked off and was balled up at her feet, half dragging on the floor. Luke picked up the trailing fabric and rested it carefully on the woman's shins. The EMT with the clipboard gave him a sharp look.

"Oh, hi, kids," the receptionist said. "You're back. Give me just a second here. Got to get Lois squared away."

Claire, Luke, and Jean watched the EMTs bundle Lois outside and into the ambulance. The receptionist spoke to them, but her voice was silent through the glass. The flicker of red light from the siren sent a chill down Jean's spine.

"Should we just go on back?" Luke said, walking into the hallway lined with closed residents' doors.

"Yeah, she looks busy." Claire motioned them forward and they moved together, involuntarily coordinating their movements through the narrow hall. Luke knocked at Dr. Esposito's door. They looked at one another, waiting. When there was no answer, Claire pushed the door open. Dr. Esposito's bed was empty, but crisply made.

"Hello again," Dr. Esposito said, entering the room behind them.

Luke gasped. "Whoa, where were you?"

"Shower." Dr. Esposito shook his head. "After seven decades of life, you essentially end up back in a college dormitory. Please come in."

Jean looked at the coffee in her hand and wilted a little. They should've brought something for him. If she hadn't been so tired that morning, she would've suggested it.

"Here you go," Claire said, handing over the waxed paper bag. "We brought you some doughnuts." Jean smiled at her thoughtfulness.

"Oh, thank you." Dr. Esposito placed the bag on the radiator with distaste.

"And we brought you this." Jean fished in her bag for the green folder. Dr. Esposito grabbed it and flipped it open. He moved to the window and shoved the blinds aside to let in more light. Jean watched his mind eagerly snag onto the contents of the report. His expression was familiar, one that Jean recognized and remembered flickering across Dr. Goldstein's face. She suddenly felt so sad that she turned away and faced the corner, focusing intently on the seam where the painted concrete walls met.

"So, does that help at all?" Luke asked. "I tried reading it myself, but honestly I got pretty tripped up once I saw the equations."

Dr. Esposito held up his hand. "Please, give me a minute."

Luke fiddled with the string to call for help, flicking it back and forth against the wall in a tiny, futile game of tetherball. Jean's coffee had gone cold, but she drank it down, even the granular sugary sludge at the bottom.

"You okay, Jean?" Claire asked softly.

"I'm fine." Jean couldn't muster a smile but tried to raise her eyebrows encouragingly.

"You sure you don't want to talk about anything?"

"I'm just really tired, okay?" Jean didn't suppress the irritation in her voice, hoping it would deter Claire from asking her anything else. She wasn't ready to talk about Dr. Goldstein, especially not with Claire.

"Well, this is not at all what I was expecting," Dr. Esposito said finally, interrupting them.

"Oh," Luke said, fingering the pull string dejectedly.

"It's much more detailed than I could have imagined."

"Oh," Luke repeated, breaking into a radiant smile.

"Of course, I'll need more time with this, but I think, just on an initial perusal, my idea may very well be a success." Dr. Esposito scratched at his damp scalp.

"Can you tell us more about it now?" Claire asked.

Dr. Esposito paced across the small room to where Jean stood in the corner. He looked at her closely as he spoke. "I want to undo the damage that Myra and I did."

"Okay," Claire said, following them into the corner. Dr. Esposito took Jean by the arm like they were a nineteenth-century couple at a ball and crossed the room with her.

"I need you to be fully on board, Jean. If you refuse to do this, I wouldn't blame you." He paused in front of the window and considered her expression closely. "It's a huge risk, and you are a very young person. I understand if you don't want to give any of that up."

"What do you mean?" Jean asked, awkwardly holding her cup around his arm.

Dr. Esposito gently pulled the cup from her hand and placed it on the radiator beside the abandoned bag of doughnuts. He took her hands in his, in an almost uncomfortably romantic gesture—as though he were about to propose. Jean regarded their four hands warily.

"I want to *completely undo* what we did."

"Yes, you said that," Claire said, closing in on their intimate pose with Luke at her heels.

"I want to heal the damage Myra and I inflicted." He nodded toward the green folder. "I want to seal the rifts our patients made in space and time."

"Okay," Jean said slowly, looking at Claire and Luke for reassurance but not long enough to make full eye contact with either of them.

"I need you to go back and show this to Myra." Dr. Esposito nodded at the folder again.

"You want Jean to take the report to her old boss? But won't her son be suspicious?" Luke asked.

"No. I want Jean to go back to 1970, when Myra first started all of this."

"What?" Claire said. "But isn't that dangerous?"

"It's extremely dangerous," Dr. Esposito said. "Which is why if Jean doesn't want to do it, I would understand."

"If she doesn't want to do it, then what?" Luke asked.

"Then I'll do it myself, though I doubt I'll be successful." Dr. Esposito turned to look at Luke as he spoke.

"Wait, wait, wait—why can't I just do it? Or Claire? Or anybody else who's used the cuts?" Luke asked.

"Because Jean is the only one who has gone in the wrong way and come back out unharmed," Dr. Esposito said.

"Of course I'll do it," Jean said quickly. "But I'm not the only one who's gone the wrong way and made it back. I know someone else who has." Jean dropped Dr. Esposito's hands.

"And they're okay, too? I'm confused—I thought it was impossible. Can this person go with you? To help out?" Claire squinted as she spoke, as though working out a complicated math problem.

"No, he's not okay. Which is why I'd never ask him to come with me. He can tell me, though, exactly where to go."

Luke banged his hands against the steering wheel along with every word while driving. "Alan fucking Grudge, Jean!" He turned to face her in the back seat; she clenched her jaw as the car wobbled from his erratic movements.

"If Iggy were here, he'd be dying." Claire sighed. "The Throwaways are, like, his favorite band."

"Seriously, are you friends with every notable geezer in New York?" He turned back to face the road and Jean relaxed.

"Alan isn't that old."

"Alan!" He turned to Claire. "Are you hearing this? My God." He turned back to Jean. "Should I be jealous?"

"Ugh," said Claire with an eye roll. "Please don't embarrass us in front of Alan Grudge, Lucas."

"Sorry I'm not as cool and collected as you two."

"You can just wait in the car," Jean said.

"So, you'll bring her but not me?" Luke parallel parked across from the Woof-n-Wag.

"Actually, you both should probably wait in the car. I don't want him to get worried—he's a little skittish," she added quickly. Jean ran across the street before either of them could unbuckle their seatbelts. Alan was ringing up a customer, an older man holding a fluffy white dog.

"Let me know if she likes it. If not, we'll give you a refund," Alan said as he packed a row of impossibly small tins of dog food into a paper bag. He nodded at Jean. "I'll be right with you."

Jean waited by the door until the man and dog left, lingering, held in place by her indecision over where to begin.

"What's up, Jean?" Alan asked.

Jean stared at the floor.

"You need something?"

She looked up and met his gaze. Alan's features were limned with concern, but his expression was open and pleasant. "So, you aren't going to like this," she began. "But please just listen."

"Okay," he said gently. "Don't look so worried. You can always come to me if you need something. Unless it's money." He made an apologetic face. "There I can't help you."

"Well, I don't technically need anything. It's more just that I want to get your opinion on something."

"Just ask me, Jean."

"Okay." She clasped her hands like a woman giving a presentation in a TV drama. "It's about the shortcuts. Please don't say anything until I'm done." She held up a hand for his silence. "And please don't say anything about this to anyone else. I found out this week that my old boss was responsible for opening up the shortcuts to begin with. Partially responsible. Her research partner feels a lot of regret about it all and thinks he found a way to close them up for good. *But*, it would mean that I have to go through the wrong way, back to 1970, and tell them not to do the experiment. I have to go through the first shortcut, or I guess, technically, the place the first shortcut spits you out. I have to go through the *first* shortcut the wrong way."

"What? Why do *you* need to do it?"

"Because I've done it before, and I was okay? And I know everything about her—my old boss. So, when she sees me— that is, if she sees me—I can prove to her that this is real and I'm not some scammer or whatever trying to bullshit her. It's not really a big deal if you think about it. All I have to do is get in and get out."

"Jesus, Jean." Alan shook his head and gave her a hard look.

"I know." Jean winced.

"What do you want from me?"

"Accuracy. I need to go through the right shortcut—the first one. Well, I mean, the earliest one."

"What?" Alan's eyebrows were squeezed tight, like a kid in a spelling bee. "Why don't you ask your old boss, or her old part- ner? Don't they know?"

Jean shook her head. "They don't. They know about the first one—in Chelsea—but they don't know where it goes. I think the shortcuts got away from them more quickly than they could have imagined. Alan—" she took a step closer and he met her eyes "—you know more about the shortcuts than anyone I know. You understand what they can do to people, what they can take."

"Exactly," he said sharply. "Which is why you shouldn't get in the middle of whatever this is. Let them find somebody else. You're a good kid, and you've been through enough."

His pity stung—she hated it. A fresh bolt of angry resolve pushed her forward. "Look, if we do this right, the world is a better place. Isn't it?" She didn't wait for him to answer. "I'm going to do it. It'll be harder if you don't help me, but I'm going to do it."

Alan released a disapproving growl and disappeared into the back room. Jean turned to leave, but then, suddenly, he re- emerged. "Alright," he said. "I'll help you."

Claire, Luke, and Jean huddled around the leash display at the back of the store, waiting for Alan to finish his shift.

"Did you ever have a dog, growing up?" Claire asked.

"I did—Major. He was such a good boy. A black Lab," Luke said with a sigh. "Did you?" he asked Claire.

Claire shook her head. "We only ever had cats. I'm still a total cat person. What about you, Jean?"

"What? No." She wished Alan would hurry up and close.

Alan emerged from the back room in his jean jacket, transformed from a guy in an awkward smock to a guy you would notice in a restaurant. "Alright, you three," he said. Jean felt a jolt of distaste at being lumped in with Claire and Luke like that. It felt like an insult that Alan didn't see her as someone apart from them.

They filed out of the Woof-n-Wag like obedient schoolchildren on a field trip. It was dark and cold outside of the decorative cheer of the shop. Jean didn't like to admit it, not even to herself, but she was excited about using a shortcut again. She found herself missing that disheveled thrill, the feeling that her heart had been jumping on a tiny trampoline in her chest. Jean tried to tamp down her anticipation and keep it clinical. She was not doing a great job.

"Mr. Grudge?" Luke asked. "Where are we going?"

"Soho," Alan replied. They followed him south where the streets grew brighter with holiday cheer. Christmas lights hung in the trees and window displays burst with canned spray snow. The shop windows grew more tasteful the farther south they walked. The canned frost turned to gold leaves and real holly, where shops sold candles and soap that cost almost as much as Jean's rent.

Alan paused in front of a bustling department store: Bloomingdale's.

"What, here?" Claire asked.

Alan nodded, looking at Jean as he spoke. "It's the first wrong way. I'll show you where it is, but nobody's going through it right now, okay?" He turned to face Claire and Luke for confirmation.

"Yeah, of course. You don't need to worry about us, Mr. Grudge," Luke said, hands raised like a caught thief.

The interior of the store was overly bright after their walk down Houston Street through the dusk. A woman knocked into Alan, her arms filled with clothes clinging to their clear plastic hangers.

He led them to the back of the store, to a row of fitting rooms. "It's through there." He pointed at the last cubicle, its door handle marked by a red OCCUPIED sphere. They clustered around the door as a line of women waiting to try on clothes eyed them with open-mouthed indignation.

"I guess some people think they don't need to wait," the bottle blonde next in line said pointedly.

"We're maintenance, ma'am," Alan said smoothly.

"Well, good. Whoever's in that one has been in there forever."

Alan knocked on the closed door. "Just a second," a voice responded. Alan's eyes grew wide, legitimately surprised that a person could be inside. Claire tilted her head and knocked again.

"Just a second, I said!" The door rattled open and a dark-skinned girl with impossibly symmetrical bone structure emerged. She wore one of the holiday-colored sweaters on the display mannequins in the store. The affixed name tag read JOYCE.

"Jo?" Claire said, her voice a little too high.

"Yes?" Joyce's tone shifted to mild with superhuman speed.

"Don't you remember me? From Denise Cho's acting class? It's Claire."

"Oh right," she answered, sliding by them coolly and turning her attention to the indignant blond woman in line. She unlocked another fitting room toward the front and ushered her in. "Let me know if you need any other sizes, ma'am."

"It's about time," the woman muttered. Joyce turned and shone a smile at the four of them before she briskly walked away.

Jean and Luke stared at one another, while Alan opened the door to investigate the fitting room Joyce had just vacated. Claire stayed close on the saleswoman's heels. "Jo," she said, chasing her through the store. "Joyce!"

"What's going on?" Luke asked.

"I have no idea." Jean shook her head.

"What do we do?" Luke said.

"You can bring this to me in a 12," the blond woman said, popping her head out of the door of the dressing room. She tossed a peacock blue cocktail dress at Luke's head.

"You got it, lady," Luke said, winking at her.

Jean took in the rising anger in the growing dressing room line. "Let's go check on Alan," she said, pulling Luke back to the last stall.

Alan stood in the middle of what looked like any other dressing room. The tiny cubicle was mirrored and identical lines of hooks were drilled into the other two walls. Alan was so tall his head nearly brushed the drop ceiling. "Close the door," he said to Luke. "Lock it." Luke hung the blue dress neatly on the wall and locked the door behind them. Alan popped the center Styrofoam ceiling tile out of place and a welcome blast of cold air flooded the tiny room that was rapidly overheating with the three of their bodies crammed in.

"You think you can get in there, Jean?"

Jean peered inside of the dark cavern overhead. "Yeah. I'll probably need a ladder or something."

"Plan ahead, then." Alan replaced the tile.

"Have you gone through this one?" Luke asked.

"I've come out through this one," Alan said, meaningfully, looking only at Jean.

"I'll be careful, Alan. I'll be okay."

"I hope so."

A sharp rap on the door interrupted them. "Guys, you should come out here." Claire and Joyce stood on the other side of the door; Claire was flushed with excitement.

"Everyone," Claire said. "This is Jo."

"Hi, Jo." Luke attempted a handshake, the kind of handshake you had to be born adjacent to a boardroom to reproduce. Jo shook it, suspicious, pulling her meticulously braided hair over one shoulder.

"Jo," Claire continued, a little menacing, "is an old friend in the business."

"What business?" Alan asked.

"Show business." Claire grinned. "Apparently Jo is very familiar with the shortcuts."

"Can we please talk about this somewhere more private? I don't want to lose my job." It was Jo's turn to be menacing.

"Why don't you tell them you have terrible diarrhea and have to leave right now?" Claire urged.

"Can you just meet me upstairs by the home goods? It's usually pretty quiet up there." Jo looked around nervously and locked the door to the shortcut cubicle.

"Excuse me!" The blond woman stood with her hands on her hips, a gold-sequined minidress at odds with the athletic socks on her feet. "Where is my size 12?"

Twenty

Claire picked up a set of overpriced coasters and examined the geometric pattern etched into their faces. They had been waiting on Jo for a while. "It's interesting. How there are coaster people and people who don't have coasters. I bet you were a coaster family." She pointed at Luke.

He shrugged. "Were you?"

"Of course, but not fancy like these." Claire waved the pack of coasters like a flag. "What about you, Jean?"

"We were definitely not a coaster family." Normally, she would have sealed herself up against such a question, deliberately, as though tightly lacing a boot. But now, sharing with the others felt good, like stretching before a long run.

Alan gave her an odd look. "We weren't either," he said.

"It's pretty convenient, that you know someone who can help us out," Jean said to Claire pointedly.

"I promise you, it's just a coincidence," Claire muttered. "I hoped I would never see that girl again. She's a backstabbing viper."

"I've never really believed in coincidences," Alan said, studying Claire as though seeing her for the first time.

"There's no such thing as coincidence—only connections," Jean agreed.

"Well, the next time your friend from acting class spreads vicious rumors about you to every casting director in the city, we can have a measured debate on equal footing about the existence of coincidence. I promise you, I did not plan this, but if it helps us in the long run, who cares?" Claire crossed her arms over her chest, stung.

"Alright, you all really need to leave." Jo paced toward them across the empty mezzanine.

"We aren't leaving until you talk to us." Claire sat down on the edge of a raised display dais. "This is Luke, Jean, and Alan, and we're going to need to use that dressing room. Privately."

Jo looked toward the heavens. "Look, I don't know what you all are into, and frankly that's none of my business, but that dressing room is off-limits."

"Surely you can make an exception," Luke said good-naturedly, like a person for whom many exceptions had been made.

"You owe me one, Jo." Claire looked at her, eyebrows raised meaningfully.

"I already apologized!" Jo replied, indignant. "What else do you want me to do?"

"Let us use the dressing room one night next week. Make sure nobody interrupts us. That's literally it. Okay? Sound good?"

"If you leave right now and I never see any of you again afterward, sure."

"Sounds good," Jean said. "Please put your number in." She handed across her phone.

"I don't want her calling me," Jo said, nodding toward Claire, as she prodded her phone number into Jean's contacts.

"No problem. Thanks, Jo. We'll be in touch." Jean forced a polite smile.

"Yeah, I'm sure you will."

The next morning, Alan insisted on coming with them to St. Damian's, and Jean was grateful for his presence in the car.

"So, Alan, Mr. Grudge," Luke said from the driver's seat. "What was it like? Being in The Throwaways?"

"Ew, Luke—stop!" Claire smacked his arm and he ran over a pothole, sending all of Jean's muscles into a painful, collective grip.

Alan noticed and took her hand like a TV nurse. Jean looked at their hands on the burnished leather upholstery of the middle seat and felt a warm kick in her chest. "To be honest, kid, I don't remember a whole hell of a lot."

The receptionist at St. Damian's was markedly less sunny when they arrived. "You're here to see your uncle again, right?" she said, giving Jean a significant look.

"Yes?" Jean said, her brow compressed while she tried to do the communication calculus.

"Absolutely," Claire cut in brightly. "Jean is here to see her uncle Tony."

"That's what I thought," the receptionist said, jabbing a finger at the ledger. "Please don't forget to sign in, Miss Esposito. We've had a lot of traffic through here just now, especially because of Lois's incident."

"Of course," Jean said, printing J. Esposito onto the page.

"I'd suggest keeping your visit with your uncle on the shorter side." The receptionist looked sternly at the door behind them. "He's had quite a few visitors since yesterday."

"I see. Thank you for letting me know."

The receptionist nodded them through.

"Oh," Luke said, pausing at the mouth of the hallway. "How is that lady doing? The one the ambulance came for?"

"Ah." The receptionist cast her gaze down to the cracked linoleum tile. "Lois didn't make it, I'm afraid."

"Oh no." Luke's face fell. "That's terrible."

"It is." She nodded. "Like I said, we had a lot going on here last night with the medical examiner's office coming to investigate and all. But you should go and enjoy your time with Tony. And like I said, it's better if you keep it short."

Dr. Esposito sat on the radiator by the window, huddled under a blanket. He leapt to his feet when the door opened. The blanket was draped over his shoulders like a child playing dress-up. "We have to make this quick," he said, reaching for Jean as they all crowded into his room. "Who's this?" he asked, casting a suspicious glance toward his newest visitor.

"Alan." He placed a hand on his chest.

Dr. Esposito narrowed his eyes at Jean.

"My friend," she clarified.

Dr. Esposito pulled the emerald green folder from the folds of the blanket. "Take this—hide it. Now." Dr. Esposito's eyes were wide and frightened.

"Dr. Esposito, are you okay?" Jean asked, taking the folder and tucking it into her bag. He pushed it deeper into her tote.

"Don't let them see it. Do you have anything else in there you can throw over it, so they won't be able to tell?"

"So who won't be able to tell?" Claire asked.

"*Selestron,*" Dr. Esposito hissed.

"What?" Jean asked.

"They came to see me." He chewed at his ragged cuticles. "Did you hear me? Hide it!"

"I am, I am," Jean soothed, making a show of tucking her scarf over the folder's edge.

"Listen, Jean," Dr. Esposito continued. "You can't come back here. I don't want them following you, too. Did you find it? The right opening?"

"We did—at least I think we did. I mean there's no way to actually know until I try it."

"It's the earliest one I can remember," Alan said.

"If that's true, if there's any possibility it's the right one, you need to go through immediately."

"Immediately?" Alan's voice crackled with alarm.

Dr. Esposito nodded so rapidly his glasses trembled toward the tip of his nose. "This is a very unorthodox idea, Jean. But we *cannot fail*. If you had any idea what Selestron is up to—" He shook his head, and his glasses tracked the other way. "This is a long shot, I know that, and we have to do anything that will improve our odds. I've included my notes in this file, but that's all I can do."

"Sure, yes, I'll try right away."

"If it doesn't work, you'll just have to try another way in. But whatever you do, you can't come back here. Selestron is getting even more suspicious, and it's a miracle they didn't find the folder when they were here last night. Thank God I was paranoid enough to hide it in Lois's room."

"What do you mean, last night?" Luke interrupted.

"Some very threatening gentlemen came to see me last night."

"What? Like hired goons or something?" Luke laughed a little.

"Exactly like that, Master Selestron," Dr. Esposito said, poisonously.

"Come on, Luke," Claire muttered.

"I didn't send them!"

"Listen!" Dr. Esposito raised his voice. "They could be coming back right now, so please just listen. Jean." His eyes glowed with strange intent and Jean wondered if maybe Dr. Esposito really was in the paranoid clutches of dementia and not with them in the real world. "Before you go through, I think you should take some Empathin. Just one dose. To make sure you get back all the way."

"Are you sure?" Jean asked. "Won't it just make me open a new shortcut?"

Dr. Esposito shook his head vehemently. "I've been working with the physicists' calculations and going through all of their data. If you take it just as you go through, it'll transport you more—" He cleared his throat. "Cleanly. I suspect it will keep your body, and especially your brain, intact."

"Christ," said Alan, turning his back to the rest of them.

"Okay." She nodded. "Where do I get it? Is it like a pill?"

"It was a spray. A bit like Windex, actually, in odor and appearance. I'm not sure how it looks now, or if we can even find the original formula. That would be up to Master Selestron."

"*Please* stop calling me that."

"Can she go through without it?" Claire asked.

"She can." Dr. Esposito nodded slowly. "But I think taking the Empathin would ensure she can come *back*."

"Well, then I'll have to find some," Luke said. "Since Jean is saving our asses."

"And the asses of the entire world," Dr. Esposito said, so gravely, Jean couldn't help the laughter ripening in her throat. "Go, please, now, all of you. Don't get Hyacinth in trouble, or anyone else here. They've been kind to me, all things considered."

"Will you be alright, Dr. Esposito?" Jean asked, clasping his elbow, the closest she could bring herself to hugging him.

"If you're successful, Jean, we'll all be alright. I'll never have been here. If this goes right, you'll be able to find me in my office, leading my normal life."

"Well, I hope that's where I'll see you next."

"So do I, Jean. And thank you for taking this risk."

★ ★ ★

Alan paused at the receptionist's desk on their way out. "Miss Esposito, just one last thing," he said. "Maybe you should take a look and see who exactly dropped in on your uncle last night."

"Oh, good idea." Jean hummed with embarrassment for not thinking of something so basic.

"Be my guest." The receptionist opened the ledger and ran her finger down the row of inked names. She stopped to tap on a narrow rectangle, filled out in capital letters. "This gentleman has been in more than once."

They crowded around the book, leaning in to squint out the name.

"Son of a bitch," Luke said. "That's my dad." They turned to stare at him, even the receptionist. Luke didn't meet anyone's eyes. "Well, that should make this easier and harder," he said. Luke walked ahead, dazed. He stood beside the car but didn't unlock it.

"Luke!" Claire snapped the locked door handle.

"Oh right," he said.

"Want me to drive?" Jean asked, leaning toward him hopefully but keeping her distance.

"Sure," he said, patting his jacket pockets down for his keys. "Here."

Jean unlocked the car and sat in the driver's seat. Luke got in beside her. Claire and Alan shifted in the back seat while Jean adjusted the mirrors and buckled herself in with care. She twisted the radio's knob to silent and took a deep breath. She turned the key in the ignition and the car moved forward smoothly beneath her hands on the steering wheel. Jean imagined that she and the car were one creature, and that all of the strength and ease of the vehicle also belonged to her.

"So, Luke, you ready to talk about this?" Claire asked, shifting forward in her seat. "Buddy?" She tapped his shoulder when he didn't answer.

"Yeah, I think so. Just trying to get my head around it. My dad is supposed to be in Zurich. But that was definitely his handwriting."

"I think we can safely assume he's here, then, right? And not in Zurich?" Claire prompted.

"It just seems weird that he would lie about that. To me." Luke stared through the windshield, his features perplexed. "And like, where is he staying? He's not at home. I mean, I was just there looking for that report and the place was all closed up. Even Marisol was leaving to visit her brother. My mom is definitely in Switzerland. I called her there this morning. At the hotel they always stay at."

"Jean," Alan said. "What did you think of what the doctor said, about taking the Empathin? Is that something you want to do?"

"I mean, I'll do it. I think *want* is a little beyond how I feel about it, but I'll do it." Jean stared intently at the dashed lines on the road in front of her. "I trust Dr. Esposito and if he thinks it's our best chance—my best chance—I'll do it."

"You really trust him—really?" Alan said.

"I've known him a lot longer than I've known any of you." Jean realized, too late, that her words cast an uncomfortable silence over the car.

Claire was the first to speak. "If you trust him, that's good enough for me. Luke, your dad's company has to have some extra Empathin, right? Like in a freezer or storage or whatever? I have no idea how this works."

"Honestly, me neither," Luke said.

"Are you friendly with anyone your dad works with? Doesn't he have a secretary or something?" Claire said.

"He has an assistant, yeah. But she hates me."

"Anybody else?" Claire asked, bouncing her knee and sending a tremor through the entire car. "Why don't we just go over there, to your parents'?" Claire suggested. "If your dad's staying somewhere else, we can look around a little."

"What if my dad *is* there?"

"Then you're just hanging out with some friends, right? Showing off your palatial ancestral home," Claire concluded with a cheerful pat on the back of Jean's seat. She jolted a little behind the wheel.

Luke sighed. "Fine, let's go."

Jean drove like she was in a dream, following Luke's directions to her old boss's neighborhood, to the tower that mirrored Dr. Goldstein's. He directed her to the building's garage—a garage she had walked by thousands of times. Luke waved to the attendant and ushered them to the entrance of Dr. Goldstein's building's other half. It wasn't that strange, Jean told herself with a tiny shake. A lot of moneyed people lived in these buildings. This kind of property belonged to a certain type of person, and it made sense that Dr. Goldstein and Luke's parents were the same kind of person.

"Hey, Felipe," Luke said, nodding at the doorman.

"Hi, Luke—how you been?"

"Pretty good."

"You having a party?"

Luke laughed, easily, naturally, like a person who had a lot of experience with happiness. "Just hanging out." They glided down the hall toward the elevators, surrounded by marble, probably from the same quarry as the marble in Dr. Goldstein's tower. Jean eyed the engraved brass that crowned the elevator doors— the same plump-faced Greeks lounged above.

"Are you okay, Jean?" Claire asked.

She nodded weakly. "Am I awake? I'm having some serious déjà vu."

"It's all that going through," Alan said, a disapproving downturn to his mouth. "It's not good for you."

"Well, it'll all be over soon. Right?" Claire jabbed the elevator call button.

"Right," Jean said. The elevator doors yawned open, and Jean was carried inside by the bodies of her companions. She went limp and let them courier her down the eerily familiar rose-carpeted hallway to Luke's family apartment—the reversed number, 2021, of Dr. Goldstein's.

Luke turned his key in the lock and Jean anticipated a replica of Dr. Goldstein's home, down to the floral settee and ebony credenza in the foyer. But Luke's parents' apartment was like a movie set, filled with midcentury modern furniture and a series of oversized graphic abstract paintings in black, white, and red.

Jean paused in front of one of the paintings, reaching out to kiss the canvas with a fingertip. "Those are real," Claire said. "Mondrian. You're not supposed to touch them. Because of the oils in your skin." Claire moved through the apartment with ease. She flipped on light switches and hung her coat in the hall closet. Luke tapped a code into the keypad by the front door and shuffled ahead. Jean and Alan followed him to the kitchen, still wrapped in their jackets. Alan's gaze snagged on Jean's and they both gave their heads a simultaneous shake.

"Can I get you anything?" Luke asked, leaning into an oversized stainless steel refrigerator. "There's not much in here. Pellegrino? Sancerre? We might have some Pringles... Marisol always keeps Pringles in case I stop by." Claire reappeared around the corner and threw a scarlet tube of chips at Luke's head. He fumbled but made the catch. Alan and Jean watched Luke peel back the foil and set it on the table like a vase filled with flowers. He motioned for them to sit down. Alan and Jean sat side by side while Claire expertly keyed open the wine from the fridge and poured it out into four cut crystal juice glasses. Alan turned his glass upside down before Claire could fill it. Jean sat on her hands.

Claire crossed her legs and leaned back in the chair opposite Jean. She tipped back her drink and downed half of it before refilling her glass. "First things first," she said. "Does your dad have any kind of security system in here?"

Luke scratched at the back of his head. "I mean, like an alarm system, yeah."

"What about cameras or microphones?" She reached for a stack of Pringles.

"I don't know, to be honest. I don't think so."

Alan scanned the corners of the room. "Not in this room, he doesn't." He stood. "You said he has an office here?"

"Yeah, it's this way." Luke pointed for them to follow.

"Jean." Claire held on to her elbow, delaying them as the others went ahead. "Are you and Alan, like, together?"

"Excuse me?" Jean reeled back with surprise.

"You two just seem close, that's all."

"Do we?" Jean felt her face flush. "I guess we are close—I don't know—we're alike. But it's nothing like that. Nothing romantic."

"That's cool. I just wondered." Claire pointed at a closed door. "This room is for Luke's stuffed animals. His stuffed animals had their own apartment—still do! Can you believe it?" She shook her head.

"Looks clear to me!" Alan called down the hall, puncturing their private conversation.

"We should go." Jean nodded in Alan's direction.

"Right," Claire said. "We should." She gave her shoulders a little shake and reached out, resting a palm on Jean's forearm to stall her. "I just want you to know how brave I think you are. I like to think I'd be that brave, but I don't think I would."

"Oh." Jean shrugged, even though her insides felt hot. "Thanks." She hurried after Alan and found Luke already moving different piles of papers around on a sleek walnut dining table repurposed as a desk. A heavy bronze lamp lit the room like a police drama.

"I doubt we'll find any Empathin here—no way would my

dad keep samples of anything in the house. I don't think. But we could find out which facility they're in, if there's any at all. If we're lucky, it'll be in one of the New Jersey ones and not an Alabama one."

"An Alabama one?" Jean asked, hands clasped, not exactly sure where to enter the search. Claire and Alan swirled around her, shuffling and moving things with the care of cat burglars, or people with lots of experience snooping.

"Selestron has offices everywhere." Luke shrugged. "But storage in Alabama is cheap. They have like ten refrigerated warehouses down there. Tuscaloosa."

"We don't have time to go to Tuscaloosa," Claire said, moving a delicate bonsai tree in a jade pot onto the floor.

"So, let's hope it's in Jersey," Alan said. He opened one of the filing cabinets against the wall and strummed through the bristling plastic tabs.

"Hold up." Luke tapped at the sleek gray desktop computer behind his father's desk. "I think I found it. Or something like it. It says Empatrex, not Empathin, but do you think that could still be it? It's in Jersey…"

"It's worth checking out. Should we go?" Claire said.

"Now?" Luke looked up.

"If not now, when?" Alan said. "Come on. We don't have a lot of time." They shuffled the office back to rights and Jean couldn't shake the sense that she was just a part of the room, floating around the rest of them, not quite part of the plan.

"That was quick," Felipe said, when they filed back through the lobby.

"We found another party," Luke said with a sly smile.

"Can I wait in here while you guys get the car? I'm still really cold," Jean lied, and waved them out.

"Having a good one?" Felipe asked. His teeth were enormous and even in his smile.

"Sort of." Jean set her palms on the desk between them and

they both stared down at her hands. "Do you know if Marcus is working tonight? Next door?"

"Marcus? He's usually on today." Felipe displayed a knowing smile.

"Great, thank you."

"You can use the side door here." He pointed to a concealed panel behind the desk. "You know, if he's expecting you."

"Thanks," Jean said with relief. She felt Felipe's curious eyes on her body as she maneuvered around the desk.

He held the door open, and Jean nodded as she stepped through a narrow gap in the gleaming slab of oak. Dr. Goldstein's side was subtly brighter—as though all of the light fixtures had been fitted with higher-watt bulbs.

"Whoa, Jean!" Marcus greeted her. He was standing at the reception area set up on the other side.

"Have fun, you two." Felipe closed the panel and sealed Jean into Dr. Goldstein's tower.

"Hi. I was in the neighborhood." Jean shrugged.

Marcus regarded her with the same kind of attention usually reserved for closed doors to too-full closets. "Is everything okay?"

"Not really." She shook her head. "But I'm working on it."

"Hmm." Marcus squinted at her. "Why don't we sit down over here." He led her to the arranged upholstered chairs where visitors usually waited. "So, what brings you here today," he joked gently.

She pressed her palms into her lap. "I just wanted to check in about Dr. Goldstein. Have you seen her at all? Has she been around?"

"I haven't seen her." Marcus shook his head. "But her son has been through a few times."

"Do you think she's up there?" Both of their gazes shifted to the brightly polished paneled ceiling.

"I hope not," Marcus said. "It's not healthy to be cooped up like that."

"I have to go in a minute." Jean closed her eyes for a long moment; they suddenly felt very dry. "But if you see her—alone—can you let her know where I work? She has my number, but just in case she needs to find me right away, I'm there most nights."

"Sure, of course—here, let me get a pen."

Jean scrawled Red and Gold's address on a tiny pad of paper with a minuscule illustration of the Majestic at the top. "Thank you, Marcus."

"Listen, Dr. Goldstein is a nice lady. Anything I can do to help."

Jean stood up and half hugged him, half shook his hand, achieving a kind of courtly arm clasp.

"Take care of yourself, Jean."

"You too."

Alan waited on the sidewalk in front of the Majestic's double set of revolving glass doors. He looked out of place, leaning against the side of the building. A doorman from another building walked by with three identical dogs and noted him with a very specific kind of nod. Alan waved, trying to convey friendly and innocuous, but it only made him look more like a glamorous praying mantis, totally out of place.

"Hey," Jean said.

"Friend of yours?" Alan raised an eyebrow and nodded toward Dr. Goldstein's lobby.

"Yeah." Jean braced herself against a gust of wind, ducking slightly behind Alan. "Dr. Goldstein's apartment is on this side."

"What?" Alan's eyes widened. "That's weird, Jean. That's really, really weird." He shifted, removing her temporary shelter from the wind.

"It is, right? What do you think it means?"

"It has to mean something—they must know each other. If they worked together all those years ago."

"I don't think Dr. Goldstein worked with Luke's dad. He was probably just a kid then."

"But if it's a family business…"

"Let's ask the family." Jean motioned her chin toward the curb where Luke inched the car closer.

Twenty-One

Back in the car, the city flowed past them in a blur. Jean squeezed her eyes shut as they lurched to a stop at a light near the mouth of the Holland Tunnel.

"So, your great-grandpa started the company," Alan said.

Luke nodded. "Lucas the first."

"Sounds like the French monarchy, for fuck's sake," Claire muttered. Alan had taken Luke's spot, and folded his long limbs into the front seat.

"But he wasn't around when they started the Empathin experiments. Was he?" Jean asked.

"Oh, he was. He lived to be like ninety-eight, but he was a vegetable by then. Drooling into his Ovaltine, you know?"

"So, who was in charge? Your grandpa?"

"Yep, in the seventies it was Lucas the second. Lucas 2.0."

"Is he still…with us?" Alan asked.

"No. He died really suddenly. Caused a lot of drama, actually. Grandpa Lucas left a lot of unfinished business. Heart attack in the eighties. I got to take two weeks off from school for the funeral and everything else."

"What do you mean, everything else?" Jean asked, leaning forward into the wave of heat from the dashboard vents.

"Like I said," Luke continued. "There was a lot of unfinished business. We all had to sign a bunch of shit. We went to like thirty different lawyers' offices."

"Do you think any of that unfinished business had to do with the Empathin?" Claire asked.

"Probably." Luke drove over a pothole and the whole car trembled.

"Did you read anything you signed?" Jean asked.

"What do you think? I was in middle school."

"How likely is it that we'll actually get into this warehouse in Jersey?" Alan asked.

"We'll get in. I don't know how long we can stay. I can definitely bullshit my way through the gate, but after that, I'm not sure."

"What are we saying, about why we're there?" Claire asked. "What's our motivation?"

"That I'm just checking up on things?" Luke turned to speak into the back seat and Jean shuddered as the car swerved. "Dropping by? That I'm taking initiative?"

"What about that you're looking for your dad? Maybe you could say he told you to meet him there," Jean suggested.

"They would know if he was there," Luke said, almost accusing.

"You could say he's on the way," Claire pointed out. "If you don't make a habit of these kinds of drop-ins, I think Jean is right. That makes the most sense. You need a believable excuse."

"Okay." Luke settled his hands firmly on the wheel and rested his gaze intently on the road, responsible driving cues that flooded Jean with relief.

"Guys, I know this is the least of our problems, but I have to be at the bakery by two a.m. I really can't lose this job," Jean said. If she didn't evaporate over the course of her mission, she was still going to have to make rent.

"We'll get you there," Alan said calmly. "Seems like our time in the warehouse is going to be short, no matter what." He regarded the slip of paper in his hands where Luke had copied the address gleaned from his father's computer screen.

Claire reached for the slip of paper. "Young Master Selestron here can do the distracting while we do the looking."

"Seriously, I could not hate that nickname more," Luke said. Jean could see the peevish twist to his mouth in the rearview mirror. "You're lucky I'm a born performer," he muttered.

Jean peered at the abbreviated instructions as Claire held them up to the light of the streetlamps flashing by. It wasn't much, just a list of letters and numbers.

"I wish we knew what this meant," Claire muttered.

"I wish I could help, but I've literally never been here. The only Bayonne I've been to is in France," Luke said with a mild chuckle.

Claire rolled her eyes. "Can you stop showing off for literally sixty seconds?"

"Those letters and numbers will probably make more sense once we're in there," Alan said. "Like building or wing numbers. I've worked in a couple of warehouses in my day." The car fell silent, and Jean was again grateful for Alan's presence.

Bayonne loomed ahead over a forbidding iron bridge. The night sky raced overhead as they passed rows of little LEGO-like houses and a port stacked with shipping containers waiting to be loaded and unloaded. They followed a dark ribbon of road punctured by lampposts until Luke paused at the entrance of a roughly paved driveway.

"This should be it," he said, doubt lifting his voice to a higher register.

"Well, go ahead then," Claire encouraged.

Luke drove up the slope and exhaled once the well-lit warehouse came into view. "You're such a weenie," Claire said, flicking the back of his head. "Pull yourself together." The gate bore an understated plastic sign with Selestron's logo, a seven-pointed star. If you weren't looking for it, Jean noted, you wouldn't see it.

Luke gritted his teeth into a smile as they slowly approached the gate. Luke rolled down his window and waved to the guard. "Hi there," he said.

The guard, a meaty white guy with a frat house haircut, stared down the car. "You kids need to move along," he said, like they were all in on the same joke. "Private property, okay? Find somewhere else to make trouble." He smacked the top of the car twice, and Jean shuddered back at the splat of his hand on the sunroof.

Luke turned and doled out each of them a smug look. He shifted in the driver's seat and reached for the wallet in his back packet. The longer the guard had to wait, the more uncomfortable he became. Luke slowly extracted his license and handed it over with the aloof carelessness expected of an obscenely privileged young man. "Listen," he said, his voice dripping with smarm. "I know you weren't expecting me, so I won't say anything about the very unusual greeting you just gave me. But I'm meeting my dad here tonight, and if you manage to turn around the attitude now, I'll be sure not to mention it to him."

The color drained from the young guard's face, and the pallor of his skin matched the khaki of his uniform shirt. "I'm so sorry," he stammered. "We weren't expecting you." He buzzed the gate open. "I'll call ahead to the front." The phone receiver was already in his hand.

"Thanks so much." Luke squinted, leaning out of the window just slightly to make out the name tag on the guard's shirt. "Brad. As far as my dad is concerned, the gates of Selestron are a bastion of professionalism. You have a good night!"

"Not bad," Claire said as they drove off.

"That could've been so much worse." Luke sighed, collapsing into the breath. "I think him calling ahead is going to help, don't you?" he asked Alan.

"No way to know. Let's just get in there."

Luke parked in the empty lot, awash in the bleachy light of the lamps overhead. They seemed too high up, Jean thought, like the four of them had been shrunk down. She shivered and hoped their smallness would be a strength inside.

"Listen, if we don't find it, we don't find it," Jean said. "I don't want us to get into any real trouble."

"Aw, that's sweet," Luke said, linking his arm through hers.

"I'm going through no matter what," she said, more to herself than to the rest of them.

"We'll find it," Alan said, from where he strode a few paces ahead of them.

The warehouse's lobby was a tiny carpeted, enclosed space. There was barely enough room for all four of them to stand. The middle-aged man behind the desk sat straight as an illustrated child in an outdated textbook. A disemboweled Payday lay hastily discarded in front of him. Brad had most definitely called ahead.

"Mr. Van Cleven—it's so nice to see you here, sir." He spoke pointedly to Alan, as though the other three did not exist. Luke smiled broadly and reached out a hand to give one of those mystifying boardroom shakes.

"Thanks so much," he said, sustaining the shake for an uncomfortably long time. Jean was sure this was another executive handbook trick—another invisible way to wield power over someone—the modern equivalent of a fiery sword. The startled man behind the desk shifted his attention to Luke.

"Can I get you something? Maybe a cup of coffee?"

"That would be great." Luke's smile didn't waver.

"Any chance I could use your restroom?" Claire asked.

"Good idea," Alan put in. "Long ride." He shrugged.

"Sure, why don't you all follow me and I'll show you. Coffees for you, too?" The guard looked around, bewildered.

"You're an angel—I'd love one," Claire said, adding a wink. Jean thought her performance was a little over-the-top and wondered if this was how Claire behaved in her auditions. Claire and Alan followed the guard into the back, their expressions two sides of the same coin.

The guard returned, his hands filled with Styrofoam cups and packets of sugar and minuscule creamer cartons. "Sorry," he said. "I wasn't sure how you take it."

"Thanks so much—" Luke did that smug lean and squint at the guard's name tag. "Leonel. How long have you been with us at Selestron?"

"Four years now—great benefits." Leonel gave a thumbs-up, as though the health insurance package had been selected by Luke personally. "It's good to meet you, sir. I never thought I would get the honor."

Luke waved him off, magnanimously. "Please, save it for my father. He loves that stuff."

Leonel laughed nervously. Jean again experienced the sensation of invisibility, as though all of her cells had dissolved and she was more part of the air than she was part of the plan. "If we'd known you were coming, I'm sure a lot more people would be here. My supervisor at least."

"How do you like him, your supervisor?"

"He's a good guy. Lets us take time off for our kids' birthdays."

"Selestron cares about family—we're a family business after all." Luke swept a hand over his face and shoulders, the parts of his body that could be a sculpture in a manor home somewhere. Jean inwardly panicked. Leonel couldn't possibly be buying this. But, when she turned to look at the other man, he was nodding with enthusiasm.

Alan wandered back into the lobby. "Um, Jean?"

She stood up too fast, black spots clouding her vision.

"I think Claire needs help in the restroom—the *ladies'* room," he said meaningfully, casting an apologetic glance at Leonel.

"Hey, I've got four sisters. I get it," he said with another forced, nervous chuckle.

"Sure—can you show me where it is?" Jean asked, making a show of gathering her bag as though it were brimming with tampons.

Leonel half stood from the chair he had just reoccupied, but Alan gave him a friendly wave. "I got it, man."

Jean followed him out into the darkness, to a hall wide enough to accommodate a forklift. The lights overhead were dim and Jean could barely make out Claire's figure at the end of the hall. "Okay, listen," Claire said, drawing her hands together in a soft clap. "Alan is a genius." She motioned toward him in a yoga teacher's prayer salute. "He found the spot, but it's locked, which, I don't know why we would assume that it *wouldn't* be, but we need you to MacGyver it open. Do you think you can?"

"I'll try."

"Okay, come with me—Alan, you get back there so the guard doesn't get suspicious. You bought us some time, I hope?"

"Sure did. Good luck, you two." Alan waved and left them at the end of the hall.

"Here." Claire took her hand. "It's this way." The wide hall began to narrow, rapidly and unexpectedly, until Jean felt a little short of breath from being so hemmed in. "It's okay, we're almost there." Claire gave her hand a reassuring squeeze. "Alan is like a fucking raccoon—so much stealth in the dark!"

The warren of doors marked in strange codes grew so narrow that they had to pass through a few of the turns sideways. "How often do you think people come in here?"

"Not very—if that mouse shit is any indication." Claire kicked at the floor. She paused at a stainless steel slab the size of a garage door. The outline of a cereal box–sized hatch glimmered in the low light. "This is it. Alan thinks it's a fridge."

Jean placed her palms on the cool steel of the door and felt the slight hum of a compressor in her fingertips. She pressed on the center of the rectangle and it popped open. "Oh no. It's definitely a temperature regulated situation, but I don't know if I can manage the lock. It looks like there's probably a code, too."

"Alan thinks this last part of what Luke wrote down could be a code, so that might help. Right?" Claire brandished the slip of notepaper from the apartment.

"Well, we didn't come all the way here not to try." Jean fished in her bag for her keys, wishing she had some real tools— literally any real tool. "Here, can you hold this?" She passed the canvas tote to Claire, who gripped it in both hands, wide-eyed.

Jean had gone on lots of jobs with her father, particularly when she was too young to be at home alone. If he was awake and sober enough to answer the phone, he would take any job. Customers almost always paid cash, which almost always disappeared before they got home. Sometimes her father would stop by the liquor store that kept the same hours he did. The owner lived upstairs and was always willing to open for him, a good customer, if he banged loud enough. He almost always banged loud enough.

Sometimes, rarely, he would stop at a dusty bar that looked like an overturned shoebox, leaving Jean to sleep in the back booth. Her father didn't like company when he drank—he only visited the bar when the owner of the liquor store wasn't at home. Most of the time, when he was out on a call, he was already slurry and cranky and made Jean do most of the work. She liked it; she liked the way a lock gave beneath her fingers, the way an obstacle disappeared. She liked her father's gratitude. In these moments, when she did what he couldn't, he warmed her with his pride, sometimes too much, and she blistered beneath it, like a sunburn.

Jean examined the topography of the lock before her, out-lining it with a fingertip. It was funny, she thought, how little locks had changed over the years. Trying to solve the best way into this one stunned her with nostalgia. It wasn't a thoughtless pop and pry—this one was a puzzle.

"Do you think you can open it?" Claire said, fidgeting like she really did need a bathroom.

"Maybe. Probably." Jean longed for the little canister her father carried, filled with needles and tiny pitchforks. She grimaced, thinking how messily she would be forced to dismember the lock using only the Swiss Army knife on her keychain. She gently sawed at the first divot with her file until it gave way with an almost imperceptible unclenching. Jean exhaled with relief when an alarm didn't sound. She extracted the tiny tweezers and splayed open the lock, like a dissected frog in a high school biology class, all while Claire loomed over her shoulder. A shiver of pleasure rushed through her when the lock completely gave way with a soft snap. "Okay," she murmured. "We should be able to get in if we can figure out how this door opens. Do you think it rolls up, like a storefront gate?"

Claire wandered to the edge where the door met the concrete wall. "There's definitely a gap here, now. Come look."

A narrow rim of shadow bled from beneath the revealed crack. Jean shoved her fingers inside and pulled but nothing happened. She looked down where the door kissed the floor, but there was no space at all. "Let's push it," Jean said. "You go on that side and we'll lean against it at the same time—like we opened the hatch." They turned to face each other, each with a shoulder to the door.

"Okay, now," Claire said. The door shuddered and popped open, sliding to one side.

"This is like the kitchen cabinets at Luke's dad's apartment," Claire observed.

Jean regarded the door-sized opening. "Seems like overkill for a warehouse door."

"I think it tells you everything you need to know about Selestron," Claire said, walking through.

"What do you mean?" Jean followed, trying to cover Claire's footsteps with her own.

"I mean, they like what they like. Or Luke's dad likes what he likes."

The cube's cavernous interior glowed with a soft blue light. The walls were lined with more stainless steel cases; their faces revealed the interior temperatures in digital blue—the collective readings were the only source of light. "It's like being in a cave of gems, like in *Snow White* or some shit," Claire whispered. "721. Over there." She consulted the rapidly wrinkling piece of paper in her hands. "I mean, there's a keypad. Should I just try it?" She didn't wait for Jean to answer. The entered code produced no sound, only the muted tap of keys. "Do you think it worked?"

Jean considered the handle; it was like the handle on a dishwasher. She pulled it the same way, and it slid open. Jean winced away at the brightly lit interior and its rows of samples hanging in numbered plastic bags. "Does it say anything about these bags?"

Claire shook her head. "The code was the last thing. Should we just take the blue ones?"

"I guess," Jean said. "Here." She motioned for her bag and held it open as Claire shuffled through the samples. "This one is kind of blue?"

"Throw it in." Jean shrugged. "We can take a closer look once we're out of here." Claire tossed in a few more before firmly sealing the refrigerated chamber. "Let's get the fuck out of here."

They restored the door the best they could and raced back to the bathrooms. Jean was overcome by a pressing desire to giggle. "What is even happening?" she asked.

"I don't know! But how ironic is it that now I have to pee?"

"You got to hold it. Who knows how long we've been gone already? Wait a minute—just wait a minute. We can't be out of breath going back in there."

"I can be as out of breath as I want," Claire said. "I'm the one with the Seven Years' War period."

The energy in the lobby had shifted. Luke and Alan still clustered by the desk; there was nowhere else to go. The guard's head was tilted at an almost sheepish angle. He gazed at the desktop as though it wasn't empty. Luke's shoulders had frozen in a tense line as he spoke into the cell phone gripped to his ear. "Dad—Dad, just—can I say something? How was I supposed to know that? I got a message to meet you here!" He gave a convincing, petulant stamp. "Dad! It's fine—I'll just go. I told you, I don't know! It was a text! I thought something happened to you. I was worried honestly, since you guys were supposed to be in Zurich." He gave the guard an eye roll, which went unnoticed since Leonel was still intent on the desk's suspiciously pristine surface. "Yes! I'm leaving now. God! Yeah, I love you, too." He punched a button and killed the call. "Well, false alarm, I guess."

"Is everything okay?" Claire asked carefully, the question like a row of stones in mud.

Luke waved away her concern, but Jean couldn't tell if his ease was performance or genuine. "My dad *didn't* want me to meet him here. It was a prank, he thinks."

"That's weird," Claire said.

"Sorry we wasted your time, Leonel," Luke said, reaching for another handshake.

"It's no problem, sir."

"Thank you so much for letting me use the restroom!" Claire said airily. Jean and Alan quickly pushed their way outside and headed for the car.

"Fuck, fuck, fuck," Luke said, overtaking them and climbing in the car. "Fuck!" He clenched his fists and shook them in the air.

"What?" Claire asked.

"He knows." Luke collapsed and banged his forehead against the steering wheel.

"What do you mean, he knows? What does he know?" Alan asked.

"My dad knows I'm full of shit." The car lurched suddenly in reverse and Jean clutched the grip handle beside her.

"What's he going to do?" Claire's voice was open and curious, not, Jean noticed, fearful.

"He's going to grill me. He'll want to know what the fuck we were doing there."

"What the fuck *you* were doing there," Claire corrected.

"Sorry, honey, but that place is definitely video surveilled." Luke's eyebrows were raised comically high.

"Yeah, but we didn't leave our names. He won't recognize any of us." Claire arranged her arms in a confident cross over her chest.

"You think that's going to stop my dad?" Luke's tone was heavy with condescension. "Really? What do you think that team of private investigators on speed dial is for?" Luke turned almost 180 degrees in his seat to shout at her.

"Jesus, watch the road, kid," Alan said. "We believe you."

"Well, if I do this right, none of that will matter. If I get to her in time, Dr. Goldstein will never work with Selestron, and we'll never have broken in. Right?"

"Oh shit, did you really have to break in? I thought there was a code!" Luke wailed.

"There was a code, but that wasn't all, okay? We did what we had to do. Jean is right. If she goes through and does what she needs to do, then none of this will matter." Claire shot a smile, secret and warm, in Jean's direction.

"That's easy for you to say. You don't know my dad."

"If you're going to be such a baby, just don't go home." Claire shrugged.

"What about my phone? You know he can track it."

"What about it? Just 'lose it.'" Claire's air quotes were delicate despite the edge in her voice.

"Okay." Luke nodded. "You're right. Sorry about that, you guys." He sighed. "My dad is a scary dude."

"I'm sure that's true." Alan reached across to the driver's seat and gave Luke's shoulder a reassuring pat.

"Where to?" Luke asked, settling himself into the upholstery with a series of dramatically deep breaths.

"I have to be at work, remember?" Jean said.

"Yeah, but it's not even ten." Claire pointed at the tiny analog clock embedded in the dashboard.

"You can drop me off at Red and Gold," Jean said. "If Omar's working I should try and help out. I really owe him for all the leaving early. I'll just stay there until I have to be at the bakery."

"Honestly, I could use a drink myself." Luke rolled down the window and shifted in his seat for his cell phone, preparing to launch it outside.

"No! Not here, dumbass." Claire grabbed it out of his hand. "Lose it in the city. That's way less suspicious. You could not be more clueless." She shook her head. "I think I need that drink the most."

Twenty-Two

Luke dropped Alan off in front of his building and Jean promised to call him the next day. Luke found a spot nearby, but banged into the cars in front of and behind them in his mangled attempt to parallel park. They raced for the warmth of the bar, its glimmer visible through the fogged-up windows.

It was busy for a weeknight. Jean thought a show for a bigger band must have just ended next door. Which was why she didn't see Dr. Goldstein at first. Omar and a petite blond girl worked the bar—it was crowded with demand, except for one small bubble where a figure hunched over her drink. Jean noticed the hunch first. Dr. Goldstein had that stoop to her shoulders particular to women of a certain age. Her pristine helmet of silver hair had been replaced by a disheveled head of curls. Jean's heart beat with a protective urge. "You guys go ahead. Find a seat. I need to talk to someone." She drifted apart from her group and approached her former boss slowly. Dr. Goldstein's presence at the bar was so out of place, Jean thought she might be hallucinating. She reached out and touched the woman's lavender sweater–clad shoulder. "Dr. Goldstein?"

Myra Goldstein turned slowly, her face slack with weariness. "Hello, Jean." She lifted her half-empty glass. "I'm not sure if your colleagues are happy to see me. I think I might be scaring the other customers."

Jean slipped in the space beside her, leaning against the bar. "I'm sure that's not true."

"This Manhattan is just terrible," Dr. Goldstein said, stabbing a plastic cocktail stirrer into her glass.

"I'm not surprised." Jean heaved her weight into her elbows, taking the pressure off her throbbing hip, protesting after so much time sitting in the car. "Is everything okay? I mean, are you alright?"

Dr. Goldstein laughed, one of her genuine high-pitched giggles. Jean usually felt a secret smug accomplishment when she was able to elicit that kind of a laugh from Dr. Goldstein, but, in the gloom of Red and Gold after the day she had endured, she was chilled.

"Everything is very much not okay, Jean." Dr. Goldstein tilted her head like a little bird. "But I think you know that, don't you?"

"Yes, I do." Omar gave her a questioning nod from the other side of the bar, but Jean waved him away, not wanting to be disturbed. "Do you want to go somewhere quieter? We have a lot to talk about."

"I think that would be wise. And I'm afraid that I need to trespass on your hospitality rather urgently. I fled the armed guard in my apartment under the guise of a medical emergency, and I don't think returning is an option. Is there any chance I might be able to stay with you?"

Jean was stunned; she felt the same bright fright—of being in the path of some deep emotional connection—that had compelled her to quit her job. "Oh, of course. Um, I have to be at work in a couple of hours…"

"Work in a couple of hours?" Dr. Goldstein's thin, sharp eyebrows arched. "It's so good to be young."

"Let's go to my apartment and get you settled. And then we can talk more in the morning."

Dr. Goldstein's eyelids closed in relief. "That sounds wonderful."

"Just give me a minute. Do you have your coat?"

"In a manner of speaking."

"Alright. I'll be back in one second."

"Go ahead, Jean—I'll meet you outside."

"Are you sure you can make it by yourself?"

"Jean, I made it all the way down here, didn't I?"

"Right, sorry." Jean was never sure how much help to offer Dr. Goldstein when it came to her eyesight. Her old boss always maneuvered easily around the office and in her apartment, but Jean had thought it was because the terrain was familiar. But what did she know? Only Dr. Goldstein knew how well she could see. Jean drifted along the edge of the bar until she caught the blond bartender's attention. "Hi, I'm Jean," she said hastily. "I work here?"

"Of course—Jean! I've heard so much about you. I'm Ingrid." The girl placed a hand over her black silk camisole.

"The famous Ingrid!" Jean said. "It's great to finally meet you. Listen, can you let my friends know that I had to duck out quickly? Or Iggy's friends, I should say?" She pointed over to where Claire and Luke stood in the back of the bar feeding dollars into the jukebox.

"You got it. Oh, and, Jean? That's your…friend?" She inclined her head slightly toward Dr. Goldstein.

"Yeah?"

"She didn't pay—her drink's on you?"

NATALKA BURIAN ———— 270

"Oh, for sure." Jean's face collapsed into confusion. "Tell Omar I'll take care of it on my next shift."

"No problem. You have a great night." Ingrid beamed.

Outside, Dr. Goldstein was on the sidewalk, wrapped in a cashmere blanket. "I would say we should take a cab, but I don't actually have any cash. It's not too far."

"That's alright. My legs still work, thank God. Can I hold your arm?" Dr. Goldstein didn't wait for Jean's reply and leaned heavily against her as Jean directed her north.

"Dr. Goldstein." Jean cleared her throat. "How did you get here? By yourself, I mean. You didn't even bring your cane?"

Dr. Goldstein sighed. "No. I didn't bring anything. All I brought was this blanket." Dr. Goldstein snickered like a teen cutting curfew.

"But how did you find me?"

"Marcus. He's a good boy. He put me in a cab, talked to the driver and everything and told him exactly where to go. I mean, I haven't had a cent in my hands in months. They really put me under lock and key. We have to make sure I pay him back... Marcus. I mean, *I* have to make sure I pay him back," she added carefully. "The taxi driver even walked me into the bar."

"Oh, Dr. Goldstein, I'm so sorry."

"Please." Dr. Goldstein waved dismissively.

"I shouldn't have quit," Jean said softly.

"What could you have done?" Dr. Goldstein patted her hand. A burst of wind knocked into them and Jean veered toward the curb. She felt entirely caught, but she couldn't tell exactly by what. "I appreciate you taking me in."

"It's the least I can do." It wasn't guilt exactly, but a familiar wave of discomfort rushed through her. "I have two roommates," she warned.

"What should we tell them? That I'm your grandma?" Her former boss sounded equally amused and anxious.

"They know who you are."

"Well, that certainly sounds grim," Dr. Goldstein said with a nervous laugh. "But perhaps we'd better not make any formal introductions?"

"What do you mean?"

"At the risk of sounding paranoid, I'd rather remain anonymous if that's alright with you. When your own son essentially sells you as a hostage to a major pharmaceutical company, you tend to up your guard."

"Sure. If that would make you more comfortable."

"It would." Dr. Goldstein nodded so vigorously that Jean could feel the old woman trembling at her side.

"Well, it shouldn't be a problem tonight. I'm sure they've both been asleep for hours. We won't have to explain anything until they come home from work tomorrow. Here it is." Jean paused and wedged her key in the front door lock. "There are a few flights of stairs," she warned.

"Do you want to tell me what happened with Jeffrey?"

"Not tonight, Jean. Please. Tomorrow."

Dr. Goldstein's pace was careful but steady. The old woman's weariness was difficult to watch; Jean had to actively resist hefting her like a bag of laundry. She untied Dr. Goldstein's shoes and tucked the old woman into her bed. "If you need the bathroom while I'm gone, it's the door next to the kitchen. I'm just going to get you a glass of water, okay?"

Dr. Goldstein only nodded. Her lungs strained to catch enough breath after the stair climb.

"Did you bring any of your medication?"

"No," she said, still winded.

"Okay, we'll worry about that tomorrow." By the time Jean returned with the water, Dr. Goldstein was a lightly snoring pile.

"Oh man," Jean said to no one, and then turned to leave for her shift at the bakery. Her body, thankfully, burned with adrenaline. It was amazing, she thought for the millionth time, what the body could endure.

★ ★ ★

Jean woke earlier than usual. She had slept restlessly on the floor by her bed. The chill before the radiator clanked on was so intense that she had to sleep with her hands wedged under her ass to keep them from going numb. She waited twenty minutes after the door slammed behind Christine and Molly— they commuted together every day, even though it made Molly perpetually fifteen minutes early—and finally eased her body up. Her hip ached even worse than she expected. Jean hobbled to the bathroom, switching on the coffee maker on the way. The creased wax bag of sfogliatelle she'd brought home from the bakery yawned open on the counter. A tiny neon Post-it, the kind she had once used to flag her textbooks, was stuck to the countertop. It was penned with a minuscule row of hearts. Jean felt a satisfying tingle of accomplishment as she washed her face and brushed her teeth. She was a great roommate, she thought, as she spat into the sink. She let herself feel happy that she and Molly and Christine had each other.

Jean found Dr. Goldstein sitting at her kitchen table, wrapped in the now-wrinkled cashmere blanket she had brought. Jean set down two cups of coffee and the bag of sfogliatelle in front of her old boss.

"So." Dr. Goldstein gripped Molly's MALE TEARS mug tightly with both hands. "We have a lot to discuss today."

Jean sat down and took a hot sip of coffee. "How are you feeling this morning?" she asked carefully, her voice scratchy from limited sleep.

"I feel fine. How I feel isn't the problem." Dr. Goldstein took a vicious bite out of one of the pastries. "Where should we begin?"

Jean rubbed a hand over her face. "Alright. I think I probably know more than you think I know—should I start there? With what I know?"

"By all means." Dr. Goldstein was irritated. Jean felt a flash of fondness; Dr. Goldstein didn't suffer fools.

"Well, I went to visit Dr. Esposito—"

"You saw Tony? Is he alright?"

"I think so. For now. He told me about the Empathin."

Dr. Goldstein froze. "I see."

"And I broke into a Selestron warehouse last night and took a sample."

Dr. Goldstein choked on her coffee. "What?" She coughed uncontrollably. "Why would you do something like that?"

Jean was suddenly furious. "Because I'm going backward through the shortcuts *you* created, and Dr. Esposito said taking the Empathin before I go through would protect me."

"Shortcuts," Dr. Goldstein murmured and pressed her lips in a disapproving line. "Is that what they're calling them now?"

"That's really the first question you have?" Jean was surprised by the petulant slant in her voice.

"No, of course you're right." Dr. Goldstein offered a contrite tip of her head. "Whose idea is this? Tony's? He's been obsessed with closing them for years."

"And you're not?"

"Obviously I had rather they'd never been opened in the first place, but I didn't really see the harm. Before, at least."

"Are you kidding me? What about the disappearing people? They could all be dead!"

Dr. Goldstein cleared her throat, her voice quaking with discomfort. "Well, I didn't know about that before. Now, well, particularly after my experience over the last several weeks, I am extremely eager to put an end to this. Tony's suggesting that you going through—after taking a dose of the Empathin—will close the gaps?"

"No." Jean shook her head. "I'm going through the first one, backward. Or I guess, technically, the second opening backward, to get to where the first one originated."

Dr. Goldstein shook her head. "You can't be serious, Jean. It doesn't work like that. You can't go through backward."

"I already have." Jean took a sip of her coffee.

"I'm sorry?" It was the first time Jean had seen Dr. Goldstein so perplexed. Her mouth opened, closed, and then opened again. She leaned forward. "What do you mean?"

"I did it a couple of weeks ago." Jean enunciated each word carefully.

"And what happened?" Dr. Goldstein couldn't possibly lean forward any further without climbing over the table.

"Not what I expected." Jean massaged at the tightness in her forehead as she explained. "I went through before. I mean, I went through the right way. A friend from work told me about the shortcuts so that I could get back and forth from my two jobs on time. The shifts are back-to-back. Anyway, he didn't tell me that you couldn't go backward. So, I went the other way, thinking I'd be back near my first job, but actually I was in a movie theater. I guess in another year? Another decade probably. It all sounds so unbelievable."

Dr. Goldstein closed her eyes. "My God. That's what he's trying to do, that miserable son of a bitch."

"What? Who?"

"Lucas Van Cleven."

"What's he trying to do?"

"He's trying to sell immortality." She shook her head, chewing on her pale lip.

"I don't get it."

"He must be trying to buy extra time by going backward through the gaps," Dr. Goldstein murmured.

"What? Like some unholy Disney World ride?"

"I think so." Dr. Goldstein nodded. "I don't know when he discovered that you could return to the past. But he must've known for some time since apparently he's been working on Empatrex for years."

"What's Empatrex?"

"I'm sorry, Jean—I've only learned about most of this myself a few weeks ago. When Mr. Van Cleven colluded with my son to imprison me."

"How did that happen?"

"Lucas and Jeffrey went to the same high school, and apparently, Lucas reached out with a unique opportunity via some alumni message board."

"What was the opportunity?"

"A supermodel's salary to keep me locked up as a twenty-four-hour living reference for this Empatrex project. And now I also suspect trapping me in my apartment ensured that I wouldn't have a change of heart and do any meddling—like Tony has—" she smiled fondly "—to compromise it."

"Are you alright? I mean, physically?" Jean covered the old woman's hand with her own, a little shocked but mainly thrilled by the easy intimacy.

Dr. Goldstein jolted a little, equally startled. "I'm fine, but embarrassed I didn't see this coming. When I met Lucas, Mr. Van Cleven's father, this all seemed much less reckless. Also, we were lovers, so that made things feel more informal."

"Wow, Dr. Goldstein."

"Yes, well, now it makes everything seem very tawdry."

"Wait, what can you tell me about the Empatrex?" Jean held up a crossing guard's palm. "Dr. Esposito only told us about Empathin. Are they not the same thing?"

"Empathin was the drug Tony and I trialed in the 1970s with a select group of patients."

"Right—hold on one second." Jean stood to collect her tote bag hanging by the door. She spilled the bagged samples out onto the table. "I'm not sure which one it is, but I think I have it here. Can you tell me which one I should use?"

"I'm sorry, Jean, but I can't. I can barely see the outline of you."

"Dr. Esposito said it looked like Windex, but it could be any of these. He said I should take it before I go through. I have to go through tonight."

"And, why are you going through tonight?"

"Because I'm going to find you in 1970 and tell you not to do the Empathin trials."

Dr. Goldstein's unrestrained giggle filled the small kitchen. "You can't be serious."

"It was Dr. Esposito's idea." Jean organized the samples in a row indignantly.

"Of course it was." Dr. Goldstein tilted her head back, staring up at the ceiling she could not see. "Alright." She rolled her neck in a smooth, elegant circle, like a dancer. "Suppose you did reach me and were able to convince me you weren't a deeply troubled young woman—which, by the way, poses its own particular challenge. Do you know what we used to do with troubled young women in the 1970s? Even me? I shudder to remember." Dr. Goldstein covered her eyes with her hands. "Just assume for one moment you were able to convince me. What then? If Tony and I don't pursue the trial, why wouldn't someone else?"

"Well," Jean began, her gaze darting from corner to corner of the room as though searching for a good answer from the slowly cracking shell of paint. "You said that you were…close…with the president of Selestron, right? Isn't that worth something?"

"Again, Jean, I must emphasize that it was the 1970s. A much more *casual* era."

"But presumably you had a working relationship with the person, too, right? You had to be a little involved, I would imagine, with the chemists and everything. I think you might be underselling your qualifications here. You may be the only person who could nip this experiment in the bud. Manufacture some side effects, something!"

"What a significant burden to place on one person," Dr. Goldstein said with a wry little smile.

"But you *could* do it, Dr. Goldstein." Jean leaned forward. "You forget—I know exactly how smart you are. I'm sure you could talk Dr. Esposito into going along with literally anything to sabotage the trial."

"Almost certainly," Dr. Goldstein agreed, lifting her coffee to her lips. "I was also having an affair with Barry Winters, Selestron's lead chemist at the time. So that could help."

"Well, there you go."

"Alright, I suppose it's possible. If you can persuade me now, you'll likely be able to persuade me thirty years from now. I guess it's all up to you."

"I'm going to do my best. Dr. Esposito told me to give you a folder that should go a long way in convincing you."

"A folder," Dr. Goldstein said skeptically.

"Yes, a bunch of post-study analyses by these physicists Selestron hired after the Empathin trial. I didn't understand any of it, but Dr. Esposito seems to think that you will and that it'll be disturbing enough to get you to stop. If we had more time, I would try to read it all to you now." Jean paused. "Is there anything I could tell you? You know, some deep dark secret that would convince you that I'm from the future and not an escaped patient from Bellevue?" Jean half joked.

"Hmm." Dr. Goldstein cocked her head so extremely that Jean feared for her delicate, osteoporosis-compromised neck. "You could tell me about Mr. Ruggles McBug."

"Okay?"

"He was my imaginary friend as a child. I told almost no one about him—it would be a good trick, if you need it."

"I'll consider it my parachute." Jean grinned.

Dr. Goldstein folded her hands primly on the kitchen table. "Can I ask you something?"

"Sure." Jean stood to refill her coffee and Dr. Goldstein's.

"Why you?"

"What do you mean?"

"Why are you so determined that you be the one to do this—to compromise your safety, not just your physical safety, but your mental and emotional safety? Why are you so invested in this task?"

Jean stood at the counter with her back turned to her former employer. Something about this half measure of privacy made her feel bolder, like a person with a slightly different brain. Maybe she was a person with a slightly different brain, after all of her time in the shortcuts. It was changing her—in hundreds of subtle ways, it definitely was.

"I guess it's because I'm alone. Or I've felt so alone for such a long time. I used to think I deserved it, but I don't want to feel like that anymore." Jean's voice trembled. "I think I need to do something important. To be part of something important. To feel less alone."

Jean sent out a flurry of texts, and soon Alan and Claire were seated around the kitchen table with Dr. Goldstein. Jean had never had a single guest in the apartment, and now here she was, with three at once. She didn't quite feel like herself—she felt like another Jean, one who had started out the same way, but had experienced a completely different twenty-six years up to that day.

"Jean," Claire snapped, redirecting her attention to the row of samples that had been removed from their bags. "What do you think? This one or this one?" Claire pointed at the Selestron vials on the table.

"I guess I could take both. Or neither." Jean had stared so hard and so long at the samples that she had ceased to notice any difference.

"I don't think you should take both," Alan said. "But I'm not a doctor." He looked pointedly in Dr. Goldstein's direction, who, of course, couldn't see him.

"I wish I could talk to Tony," Dr. Goldstein said, as she tapped her overlong, unkempt fingernails on the tabletop. "I wonder why he thought it would be so important."

"He said it was to protect Jean," Alan said.

"Yes, I understand that, young man." Dr. Goldstein sighed. "But protect what? To protect her how? To prevent cancer-causing mutations in her cells? To keep her bones from disintegrating?"

"Disintegrating bones?" Claire asked, reeling in her seat. "Is that something that actually happens?"

"I don't know!" Dr. Goldstein said. "Tony obviously believes this is important, but I just don't know how or why. What I can tell you is that Empatrex should look quite similar to the Empathin."

"How do you know that?" Claire asked. "And what happens if Jean takes the Empatrex instead of the Empathin?"

"I have no idea what will happen if she takes either, young lady," Dr. Goldstein said. "But I've been spending a great deal of time in the company of some of Selestron's best and brightest in the confines of my apartment, and it is a great thorn in their side that they aren't able to formulate the Empatrex into a capsule or some other more modern delivery system. Apparently, it only holds its properties as a liquid."

Jean took a deep breath. "Okay, then I'm just going to take one before I go in and one after."

"Will that be dangerous, Dr. Goldstein?" Alan asked. "If she takes the Empatrex?"

"Well, it certainly won't be safe!" Dr. Goldstein heaved a frustrated sigh.

"Doesn't matter. It's all the same kind of dangerous. I'm going to do it. I've decided." Jean clenched her hands into fists and was bolstered by a new internal feeling of power. A kind of power that came from making a choice and sticking to it.

"Do you think you'll believe her?" Alan asked, drinking from the paper cup of coffee he'd brought.

"I don't know." Dr. Goldstein pursed her lips.

"We'll find out tonight, I guess." Jean tried to force a measure of cheer into her voice. "And Jo is still on board, right? So that's something in our favor," she said, turning to Claire and waving her phone as though displaying the texts she had exchanged with Jo earlier that morning.

"Yeah. We're not asking for much, that's for sure. All she has to do is unlock the fucking door. She knows she owes me."

"Dr. Goldstein, will you be alright here by yourself?" Jean asked.

"Of course. I'm not the one we should be worried about." She folded her hands on the table neatly and adjusted her posture, like she was in a session with one of her patients.

"Anybody hear from Luke?" Alan asked carefully.

"Not today. He was doing pretty well last night. I think he might've gone home with your co-worker, Jean."

"Omar?"

"No, the blond girl." Claire waved at the air dismissively. "He'll call once he gets a new phone. Which I'm sure will be as soon as he gets up. What do you all want to do until it gets dark?"

They ended up crowded on the futon and watched *White Christmas*. Jean made a few bags of Molly and Christine's artificially buttered microwave popcorn. She was struck again by how foreign it was to complete such a normal hosting exercise. She'd suggested the popcorn only because she'd seen this kind of thing done on TV. The limited breadth of her functionality as a social person had never bothered her before, but now, in the dry, overheated, buttery-smelling apartment, she felt the limitations of her life as keenly as a blade. What she told Dr. Goldstein had been true; Jean didn't want to be alone anymore. All of the guilt and shame she felt surviving her parents didn't make her unworthy of love and friendship. Jean allowed herself to feel warmed by the companionship in her small living room and tried not to cry as Danny Kaye danced across the screen.

"I haven't heard these songs in ages." Dr. Goldstein crunched a handful of popcorn; Jean had never seen her do something so indecorous. "If I recall correctly, Bing Crosby is a little long in the tooth for this role."

"You got that right. It's sick, frankly. Rosemary Clooney would never," Claire said. "Oh, Jean—do you think you should change, to like, get into character? You don't want to look too out of place when you go through. What do you think, Alan?"

"In New York? You could wear a spacesuit and nobody would stop to look at you."

"Even in the seventies?" Claire asked.

"Especially in the seventies," Dr. Goldstein said.

Jean stared through the window at the gradually darkening sky and wondered if she didn't make it through in one piece, if this moment in her living room was the closest to real intimacy she would ever get. The revelation cracked through her so violently that she was forced to stand up, to move, to accommodate the feeling rushing through her body. She didn't want that afternoon to be the last or the only moment of emotional communion she shared with others—she wanted so many more moments. Jean stung with the wanting. "I'll be right back."

When she was safely in the bathroom, Jean considered her body, inventorying its wholeness. She stretched her calves and hamstrings like she used to do before a run. The repetition was soothing. She leaned forward a little further than she should have, pushing her bad hip. Jean liked pressing against the edge of discomfort. It shocked her back into her body, back into her life, whenever she began to feel unmoored.

A soft knock sounded on the door. "One second." She ran the water in the sink and drank from the tap, like she used to do when she was a kid. Jean wondered if everyone was just who they were when they were a kid, or if it was just her. She looked herself in the eyes—the same eyes that had looked back at her from her elementary school–aged face. She hoped she would be the same, or at least recognizable, after what she was about to do.

"Jean?" Alan's voice called through the door. "We should go."

Jean wiped her mouth with the back of her hand. "Yeah, okay. Let's go."

On the downtown bus, Jean texted Molly and Christine to let them know she had a guest—an elderly guest with impaired vision—at the apartment. Please make sure she has what she needs. She's an old family friend who came to me for help. Jean punched her phone off and tucked it into her bag between the samples and the folder that Dr. Esposito had pressed so urgently into her hands.

"What if you get stuck, too?" Claire asked, staring out at the orange sky.

"If I get stuck, I get stuck. I can live in 1970 New York. It wouldn't be a bad life. I have no family or anything here to miss me."

"We would miss you," Claire said firmly. "We would miss you a lot."

Jean was overwhelmed with the impulse to hug Claire, but before she could respond, the bus lurched to their stop on Broadway. They rushed against the flow of people running for their trains and buses and taxis up to the block where Jo waited.

Night had truly fallen, and Jo's figure was clear behind the front window glass. She stood in front of the plastic white display of snowflakes and twinkly pine trees as though she, too, were part of the holiday scene. The Bloomingdale's was nestled in the middle of the block, and a halal cart wrapped in an American flag was parked outside, packing up for the night. Claire waved at Jo and a flicker of motion caught Jean's eye.

Two men—one in a navy suit and one in a trim pinstripe—launched out of a glossy black Suburban idling by the hydrant in front of the store. Jean saw what was happening before the men could get close. She fell back, separating herself from Claire and Alan, and hid behind the cart. She pretended to study the menu, affecting the casual stance of any regular person on her lunch break.

"Guys, I'm so sorry." Luke's voice sliced through the tussle as the suited men easily caught hold of Claire and Alan. Jean's head burned with anger.

"Let go of me, asshole!" Claire shouted, kicking out against the man that held her. Alan had gone completely limp and silent.

"I'm sorry—my dad knew! That girl from last night told him." Luke half descended from the gaping door of the SUV, hanging there like a loose tooth.

"What girl from last night?" Claire asked.

"The one who works with Jean. I used a credit card at the bar. My dad called and told her to hang on to me until this morning, so when I left her place he was there. I told that girl way more than I should have." Luke shook his head sadly.

"You used your credit card *at the bar*? You are such an idiot!" Claire screamed from the back of her throat. "Help!" she yelled. "I am being assaulted!"

"That's enough." A disembodied voice floated out of the car and Luke winced, as though the sound waves were made of pepper spray. "Why don't you invite your friends in, Luke." Luke reluctantly hopped down from the passenger side and got out of the way so the suited men could shove Claire and Alan inside. He looked very small beside his father's hulking employees. Jo watched, open-mouthed, from the window, like some horrified mannequin.

The halal cart operator openly stared, his expression a mixture of annoyance and pity. "I'm closed," he said. "Back tomorrow at ten."

"Right, yeah, sorry." Jean ducked her head and secured her bag more firmly against her ribs. She would go now, sweep past the commotion by the Suburban, and catch Jo while she remained undetected. She had as much right to walk into a department store as any other person after work on a weekday. Jean breathed in the fiction, that she was just some woman, on her way home from work, buying a cardigan to wear to her cousin's baby shower over the weekend. She waved to the food cart operator and walked smoothly down the sidewalk, widening her steps so that she hugged the sides of the buildings rather than the edge of the sidewalk. She was almost certain that Luke had seen her, but he didn't show any sign of recognition. Jean shot a flare of protective thoughts through the tinted glass of the Suburban, and ardently hoped that Claire and Alan would be alright. She pushed down her fear for them, her anger toward Luke, and all of her frustration that the night had taken this turn. She squashed it and made herself feel enormous and strong. She locked gazes with Jo through the glass.

Nobody leapt from the car for her. She brushed a deliberately casual hand through her hair as she opened the door. *I am not nervous about anything—I am just a person who needs a sweater for a baby shower,* she told herself sternly, in the same tone she told herself to do her physical therapy exercises after her accident.

She nodded at Jo, who clamored out from behind the display gracelessly clutching a plaid scarf. "Who the hell were those people?" Jo asked, twisting the scarf in her hands.

"I don't know, but the sooner you get me through the safer you are. Think of this as an acting exercise. If they come in, you're just Joyce, I'm just a person who came in to buy a sweater, and that dressing room is just a dressing room, right?" The tone of her voice was harsh and efficient.

"Yeah." Jo nodded, galvanized by her determination. "Right this way. I'm sure we can find what you're looking for." Her performance was a little stiff, but since they weren't performing for anyone, Jean fractionally relaxed.

"Here." Jo plucked a trio of blouses from a nearby rack. "Let's get you into these." She ushered Jean to the back of the store as a flicker of dark figures swarmed the entrance. Jean hurried, not sure whether they were regular customers or if they worked for Selestron. A few legs poked out beneath the rows of doors, but there was no line. Jo unlocked the tiny room in the back and pushed Jean inside. "You're going to need the step stool. Wait a minute."

Jean closed the door, still clutching the armful of blouses. She submerged her face in the fabric, overwhelmed by the enormity of what she had undertaken. Jean inhaled the citrus room spray–scented polyester and steadied herself. She could do this.

A clatter grew outside of the dressing rooms—low voices flooded the back of the store with urgency. A series of terse knocks and indignant replies rolled through the hall of compact rooms. Jean stood on the little bench built into the side and tried to keep her breathing even and quiet; the buttons from the blouses pressed spherical welts into her skin.

The voices paused outside of her dressing room, and the same knock struck the door. When she didn't answer, the handle crunched against the lock. Jean knew exactly how measly the lock was, how swiftly it could be dispensed with. "Why is this one locked?" a deep voice inquired.

"Pipe burst back there last week," Jo said.

"Floor doesn't look wet."

"We had to replace the carpet. They were worried about the moisture molding the inventory."

"Hmm." The other voice was skeptical. "We're going to need to get in there."

Jo heaved a lavish sigh. "I'll have to get my manager. She has the keys. Right this way." Jean was impressed by Jo's improvisation, but her nervous system was also, simultaneously, in shreds. There was clearly no step stool coming. She looked up at the ceiling tiles, trying to remember exactly which one Alan had removed. She leaned across to the hook on the wall and hung up the blouses, removing the hanger from the laciest one. She poked at the ceiling with the hanger and one of the tiles dislodged fairly easily. She gaped up at the opening, black as the pupil of an eye. Jean was tall, but she wasn't quite tall enough to hoist herself through. She gritted her teeth and tightened her hands into fists. She had been an athlete once—she had to try. She knew better than anyone what a human body could remember.

Twenty-Three

Jean pulled out the Selestron-branded plastic bags; one of the vials inside had started to leak. She twisted off the top and examined the remaining blue fluid. She gulped it down and winced against the bitter, burnt almond taste. She carefully tied the straps of her tote bag closed. Jean could not lose the folder Dr. Esposito had given her, since it was the only real proof she had to offer Dr. Goldstein, a layer of insurance to convince her that Jean was who she said she was.

She looped the straps over her shoulders, like a deflated backpack, and reached up into the gap, feeling for some kind of structural fretwork to grab hold of. She felt something cool and rusty—likely a water pipe or gas line. Jean hoped that, whatever it was, it would support her hanging weight. She tensed all of her muscles at once and leapt, clasping the bar with both hands. It rattled under her fingers, and she prayed that she wasn't going to cause some kind of gas explosion.

Jean closed her eyes and thought about her body, about every fiber of muscle and tissue, about every cell that pulsed so brightly with life—she thought about her strong miraculous body that wouldn't let her die in that car, the body that put itself back together after being literally flattened. She lifted her torso up into the yawning emptiness, buzzed with gratitude and marvel. Jean's palm found a tiny platform—the width of a single hastily sawn two-by-four—wedged beside the pipe. She pulled herself up like a gymnast on the parallel bars and managed to get one foot onto the ledge.

The dim shadows clotted around her, and as her eyes adjusted, Jean was able to make out a series of abandoned objects: a raft of rubber beach balls tied together for a summer window display, a stack of folded newspapers and magazines, a torn neon pink poncho, and a dusty rolled-up sleeping bag. Jean searched for the obvious path into the shortcut, but everything about the space looked strange and amorphous. She craned her neck back, staring up. A pool of darkness swirled several arm lengths above her. An audible disturbance came from beneath her feet, and Jean peered down into the opening to the visible dressing room.

"Excuse me," Jo barked. With her heart racing, Jean gently lowered the tile back into place, just before clocking Jo's upturned face; the expression on it flickered from panic to relief. Voices trembled below, and Jean did her best to step quietly along the beams, looking for some kind of ladder or box to climb on. In the end, she decided the stack of newspapers were her best option, and she made two trips, collecting enough to give her a modest boost. Jean lifted herself on top of the stack and felt a draft, tugging at the ends of her hair. The draft was not friendly—it was vigorous and insistent. She wasn't sure what to do, or how to succumb to the suction of its force. Jean reached her arms up experimentally and felt very silly, like a person in an Abducted by Aliens reenactment.

She could not deny that *something* was pulling at her. She took a deep breath and leapt, launching herself up into the pull. The pile of newspapers and magazines scattered beneath her feet, and for one lacerating moment, Jean was suspended in the vacuum. Until she wasn't. She collapsed onto a dock, her body threshed and limp. The river sloshed below. Jean shivered—it was windy by the water. She scrambled to sit up and checked that her bag was still there, and that everything she needed inside of the bag was there, too.

She braced her palms against the splintery wood of the dock and pushed herself up. Jean swallowed back a wave of nausea, an aftershock from the shortcut, and looked around. Hoboken glittered across the water. A single car rolled by—a dark Cutlass Supreme with its headlights switched off.

She wasn't sure where on the West Side she was, but, as she walked toward the beating center of the city, Chelsea materialized around her. The rusty High Line loomed sinister above, and knots of figures hid in the darkness beneath it. Jean walked quickly, reminding herself not to gawk. She wasn't a tourist—she was there to do a job. The sooner she made her way to the Majestic and Dr. Goldstein, the better. Jean marched across the cobblestone streets toward the bright pulse of Tenth Avenue. She kept her gaze down and ran into a young woman in a chic fur coat. "Sorry," Jean said, holding her hands up, not wanting to draw more attention to herself.

The anonymity of the subway pulled her forward. She couldn't stop now. There was no way to turn around, really. Jean was struck by her inadequacies for the task ahead. She wasn't some spy—she was only Jean. But there was no point feeling sorry for herself now. She squared her shoulders, determined to be bold, determined to press through the city like any other New Yorker. It was who she was after all. She was a New Yorker just like the rest of these people. Just with flatter hair.

She was wedged down the stairs of the 20th Street subway entrance in a waterfall of men in three-piece suits. She flowed along with them, scooping inside of her bag for her metro card before realizing she'd need to get tokens. She froze at the turn-stile and a middle-aged woman wearing a black felt hat hollered, "What is your problem?"

Jean hopped to the side and got in line at the booth, which, mercifully, looked exactly the same. She fished in her bag for her wallet and slipped a twenty into the mouth of the ticket counter.

"Very funny," the clerk said, rolling his eyes.

"I'm sorry?"

"Do you have any American dollars?"

"I don't understand."

"Do you speak English?" The clerk shoved the bill back through the opening between their two worlds. "Sweetheart, you better find a translator or make some friends, because I don't take Monopoly money."

Jean clutched the rejected cash tightly in her palm. "Sorry," she said, her jaw clenched. Andrew Jackson's oversized face stared up at her disapprovingly from the new twenty-dollar bill. Jean ran back up the steps, flustered. She pushed through dozens of protests and unfamiliar scents until she was back out on the street. It was too cold to walk the sixty blocks to Dr. Goldstein's office, so she ran across the street and sank into the other en-trance. Jean gracelessly but quickly hopped the turnstile, suf-fering a disapproving look from another commuter holding a burgundy attaché case. She hoped the train routes were the same. There was no helpful map displayed on the platform, so she couldn't be sure. She didn't have far to go—as long as she got some distance uptown, she could still catch Dr. Goldstein at her office, even if she had to walk the very last part of the way.

The crush of the train felt like a familiar hug. The pack of rush hour transcended all times, and Jean gratefully submerged herself in the anonymity of the overfilled car. She stood shoved between the door and the protruding button-down–covered belly of a man in an open trench coat and a hat. He was so tall

Jean could barely see the top of his throat. She rode the train to 81st Street, grateful that the Museum of Natural History provided an eternal landmark. A flood of high school–aged kids boarded the train and nearly knocked her over with their raucous joy as she fought her way to the exit.

The yellowed light in the station cast everyone in a gentle but sickly tone. A busker played "Crimson and Clover" on a creaky, slightly out of tune violin. The temperature was softer, milder, by the park. It was definitely warmer than it had been in Jean's time. The streets were emptier, too—the people on the sidewalk were furtive and uncertain, darting quickly into their buildings and cars. The cluster of people huddled at the bus stop stood differently, too. Their posture was dramatically closed off, as though without earbuds and phones to fiddle with, they had constructed impenetrable force fields around themselves. The Majestic, at least, looked exactly the same. Lit by the same arrangement of spotlights, its awning was a slightly more vibrant emerald. There was no street entrance to Dr. Goldstein's office, the way there was in her time.

Jean swirled through the revolving doors and approached the desk with all of the confidence she could muster. The doorman was a paunchy middle-aged white man with a pencil lead–gray moustache. HERB, his engraved name tag announced.

"Hello," Jean began, sifting the hysteria out of her smile. "I'm here to see Dr. Goldstein. In Suite 1A."

"Go on back." He waved her through with a meaty hand, a wide wedding band and a heavy signet ring catching the light. "They might be closed up for the day."

"Thank you!" Jean called. Her feet knew exactly where to go—she was so close to her other life. Every footstep felt familiar, like a freckle on her skin, but also entirely unsettling, as though her body knew something drastic was out of place. The echo in the hallway as her shoes tapped against the marble was undeniably eerie. It was absolutely right but absolutely wrong

all at the same time. Like the world knew she was doing something illicit and wanted her to know that it knew.

"Yeah, I get it," Jean muttered as she shouldered the door
open to Suite 1A. The italicized font on the gilded plaque was
the only feature that did not match her recollection. In her time,
Dr. Goldstein's name and credentials were announced in bold
capital letters.

The waiting room was empty. The embroidered mandala on
the carpet was the same, as were the framed Georgia O'Keeffe
prints alternating with expansive photographed desert landscapes.
The only change inside the waiting room was the magazines.
She rang the bell at the desk—the same bell she used to proc-
tor. Even the boxes of tissues were the same bleached, institutional blue gray. "I'll be with you in a second," a voice called.
Jean knew it came from a person at the desk in her old office—
she knew the exact cadence of the sound waves bouncing off
the tiny room.

She studied the little cards of stock with Dr. Goldstein's name
and address—the only difference was the absence of an email
address.

"How can I help you?" An older woman—certainly too old
to be Dr. Goldstein in 1970—emerged creakily from the office. She wore a belted pink dress with a flared pleated skirt,
a look that whirled out incongruously against her immovable,
shellacked hairstyle.

"I was hoping to find Dr. Goldstein?"

"I'm afraid she's gone home for the day." The woman adjusted
her cat's eye glasses.

"Oh." Jean had enough good sense to mime confusion. "She
asked me to meet her here. I'm the babysitter." She did a rough
calculation, and figured the chances were good that Jeffrey was
still of an age when a child needed supervision.

"Ah, such a sweet child." The woman smiled fondly. "Why

don't you go on next door then. I'll call over and let them know to expect you. You know the apartment number?"

Jean nodded, alarmed at how easy it was.

"Your name, dear?"

"Jean Smith."

The woman gave her another long, fond smile. "My sister's name. You go on, Jean—I'll just call Herb and let him know you're going up."

"Thank you so much." Jean walked back to the reception desk. She tried to keep her pace nonchalant and her breathing steady. The only thing she could trust in this too-familiar unfamiliar world was herself.

The lobby had already been strewn with Christmas decorations—all hot metallics and silver and gold stars.

Jean announced herself. "Hello again," she said, keeping her voice light and her wave easy. "I'm here for apartment 1202—Dr. Goldstein."

"Right, right, right…" Herb said, flipping through sheets on a clipboard by the phone. "And she's expecting you?" His eyebrows ascended in disbelief.

"I'm the babysitter."

Herb checked his wristwatch and made a note on the clipboard. "What's the last name, dear? I don't see anyone on Dr. Goldstein's list." The phone trilled between them and Jean smiled.

"Hi there, Irma." Herb beamed. "Why yes she is, she's just here." He winked at Jean. "Jean Smith, righto. Good night to you, too." He hung up and turned a benign smile on Jean. "Go on up, Miss Smith."

"Thank you so much," Jean said. As she waited for the elevator she marveled at the porousness and ease of all of these boundaries. Surely her youth, whiteness, and gender had something to do with it, but a few words from Irma next door and she'd been ushered in. She could've been some disgruntled, violent patient. Or terrorist. Or simply a liar. There had been no ID check or sign in of any kind. The pull of the elevator made her dizzy, a faint echo of the force in the Bloomingdale's ceiling that had brought her there in the first place. Jean pinched her eyelids closed—nearly sick with wonder that a mortal experience could include an elevator ride three decades away.

Jean moved slowly down the hall, careful to keep her balance. She wondered if the blue liquid was taking effect or if the sensations were something else. The path to Luke's apartment drifted across her thoughts in another bleary layer. So many identical but vastly different walks down this hall. She closed her eyes and took a deep breath—if she survived these travels, Jean wondered how she would remember them. She paused in front of Dr. Goldstein's door. The only difference that separated the doorway from her time was the mezuzah that hung in the frame. She rang the bell and waited. A child, Jeffrey, wailed on the other side of the door.

"Yes?"

Jean gasped when the door opened, revealing a woman in her late thirties, her long hair parted neatly down the middle and tied back with a chic printed scarf. Her shift dress was short and flattering, stylish in its shapelessness. The woman was, unmistakably, her former boss. Or rather, future boss. Jean rubbed at her forehead where she felt a nascent headache stirring. "Can I help you?" Dr. Goldstein took a drag from the burning cigarette in her hand.

"Dr. Goldstein?" Jean stammered.

"Yes?" Dr. Goldstein narrowed her eyes, inspecting Jean more closely.

Jean's mind raced for the most plausible way to gain entry into this, the most implausible part, of her journey. "You probably don't remember me," she began. "I'm actually a student at Barnard, and I have a couple of questions for you. Do you mind if I come in? I would never disturb you if it wasn't urgent." Jean placed an earnest palm over her chest. She saw Dr. Goldstein's expression shift—only slightly—from wary to curious.

"The timing is not ideal. As you can see, it's just about my son's bedtime. Isn't it, Jeffrey?" she called into the depths of the apartment. Dr. Goldstein stood firmly in the doorway. "I don't suppose you could come back another time. Or arrange to meet me at my office?"

"I'm afraid not. As I said, it's urgent."

Dr. Goldstein blew a stream of smoke over her shoulder. "Alright then. If it's urgent." Dr. Goldstein held the door wide and Jean slipped through. The apartment was the same, except for Jeffrey's childhood detritus—drawings and toys and shoes scattered about.

"What a beautiful apartment," Jean said, when she realized Dr. Goldstein was watching her.

"Why don't you have a seat while I speak to my son. Can I get you anything to drink?"

"Yes please," Jean said, desperate for any kind of stalling.

"A Manhattan?"

"Why not?" Jean said, half to herself and half in answer.

"I have a pitcher made up in the kitchen. Why don't you fix one for yourself and one for me?" Dr. Goldstein's voice was so similar—the cadence and tone in her request exactly the same as it was when she asked Jean for something in the next century. But still, there was something off about it, something sharp and prohibitive that reminded Jean she couldn't wholly collapse into its familiarity.

The kitchen was laid out in the exact same way—the glassware, while different, was in the same place. The maraschino cherries were in the same spot in the fridge. It was evidence that people didn't change that much over time; maybe there was a real chance that Jean could get through to this woman she knew—or would eventually know—so well. She took a long swallow from her drink, grateful for its ripple of warmth, and set Dr. Goldstein's on the coffee table. Out of habit, she stood up and began straightening up the room—replacing the throw pillows in the formation Dr. Goldstein preferred, clearing a stack of books from the floor back to the shelf, emptying the ashtrays into the garbage closet in the kitchen.

"Oh," Dr. Goldstein exclaimed. "Thank you. You're quite an industrious person, Miss—" She paused on the edge of the question, snapping open a golden Zippo to light a fresh cigarette.

"Smith." Jean sank back onto the neatened sofa, and Dr. Goldstein took a seat in the armchair opposite her.

"It's funny," she said, tilting her head and pointing toward the sofa's pillows with her cigarette. "I would have done that the same way."

"Great minds think alike, I guess." Jean shrugged, smiling in what she hoped was a friendly way.

"I guess." Dr. Goldstein regarded her closely. "So." She reached for her drink and took a sip. "Why don't you tell me a little bit about why you're here." Jean recognized this opening from Dr. Goldstein's intake sessions with a new patient. She wondered if that was why Dr. Goldstein thought she was there— that she was a young woman in urgent need of psychiatric help. Which, truthfully, she kind of was.

Jean twisted her hands in her lap. "You probably don't remember me," she began. "I'm sure you don't. But I'm very familiar with your work, and I think you can help me with something. A project," Jean improvised.

"I see." Dr. Goldstein ashed her cigarette in the dainty mint-green ceramic tray by her elbow. "I'm sorry, Miss Smith, but I'm quite overextended at the moment." She gestured around the room. "As you can see, I'm the single mother of a young child in addition to supervising the care of all of my patients."

"No, no, no, I completely understand that." Jean leaned forward and clasped her hands together. "I'm not looking for an advisor or a mentor or anything. That wasn't where I was going with this…" She looked around the room at the thriving collection of plants in each corner.

"Wow, that is a *beautiful* orchid."

"Thank you." Dr. Goldstein drained her Manhattan. "I'm going to get another and give you some time to work up to asking what you came here to ask."

Jean knew she didn't have much time left, but she was suddenly swept by the impossibility of what she had to do. She spilled the contents of her tote bag onto the sofa cushion beside her as Dr. Goldstein arrived with her fresh drink.

"What's all this?" she asked, gesturing as the discarded innards of Jean's bag.

"Alright. Let me start by saying I know about the work you've been doing with Dr. Esposito and Selestron. On the Empathin." She winced, waiting for Dr. Goldstein's reaction. Her former boss froze, but her face was eerily relaxed as she lowered herself into the other corner of the couch.

"How could you possibly know about that?" she asked, with that head tilt that made Jean itch with worry.

"Dr. Esposito told me."

"Tony?" Dr. Goldstein leaned in, her gaze inflamed by the alcohol, inspecting. "You seem a little young for him. How old are you?"

"That's a complicated question." Jean paused, twisting her fingers together in her lap. "Okay, I don't have a lot of time, so I'm just going to come out with it."

"Young lady, you don't have to worry about *me*." Dr. Goldstein pointed to her shoulder with a coral-polished fingernail. "Tony and I have a very open relationship."

"What?" Jean squeaked. "It's not like that at all. Jesus. Okay." She took a breath so deep it burned in her nostrils. "I know about the Empathin trials because I know how they turned out." She brandished the plastic bag containing the remaining vial in the space between their bodies. Dr. Goldstein delicately plucked the Ziploc from her grip. Jean watched closely as Dr. Goldstein tipped the vial into her palm.

"Where did you get this?" Dr. Goldstein asked, quietly.

"From a Selestron warehouse in New Jersey."

"This shouldn't be in anyone's possession but mine and Tony's."

"Look, Dr. Goldstein. Myra," Jean tried, but shook her head. "Dr. Goldstein. I'm not from here. I live in 2004. The future. And so do you. And so does Dr. Esposito. He sent me back here to make sure you don't go through with the trials because the consequences are horrible, worse than you could possibly imagine."

Dr. Goldstein dipped her head back and laughed. Her satisfying cackle bounced across the room. "Oh my, that's wonderful. From the future?" Her laughter overtook her so thoroughly she had to pause. She put a finger to her lips and then sighed. "Really, this is too delicious. You are a splendid actress, my dear, really. Where did Tony find you?"

"Please," Jean begged. "I'm not an actress!"

"And you look truly frightened! How wonderful." Dr. Goldstein wiped at the corner of her eye with her sleeve. "I have to thank you both. This is the most I've laughed in months. It's hard, you know, with my little boy. It's difficult to be happy when your child isn't happy."

Jean stood up and paced to the faux fireplace and its marble mantel. "Listen. I have some notes there, in my bag. Please take a look. It's all from Dr. Esposito."

"I suppose I'm the one who has to pay you?" she said with a wry smile. "This?" She held up the bright green folder and Jean nodded. "Hand me my glasses, would you? They're up there, on the mantel."

Dr. Goldstein flipped the folder open and scanned the contents with a nervous giggle. Her face contracted with confusion when she turned to the next page. "This is a joke?" she asked Jean, her voice low.

Jean shook her head. Dr. Goldstein extracted the sheets from the folder and arranged them on the coffee table; one of the pieces of the Selestron report caught in a tangle of Jeffrey's failed origami attempts. Dr. Goldstein crossed her arms over her chest firmly.

"You can't expect me to really believe this?"

"Honestly, I have no idea what he put in that folder. But, I can tell you from personal experience that your work with Selestron will literally tear a hole in the world. Multiple holes."

"You didn't read the note Tony included here?"

"What?" Jean shook her head. "No, I—I tried to read the report but...it was a little beyond me."

Dr. Goldstein shook her head. "I'm going to call Tony now."

"You can't! At least not if you want him to confirm or reassure you about any of this. He doesn't know this is going to happen. You'll both know eventually. You'll see it with your own eyes, but by then you won't be able to do anything about it."

"Mommy?" A little boy—Jeffrey—lurched into the room. He looked like a second or maybe third grader.

"Hi, Jeffrey," Jean said, trying out a friendly wave. Confronting someone who was such an evil adult while they were kind of a cute kid was an entirely jarring experience. "I love that origami you made." Jean tried her best to convey a friendly smile.

"Young lady," Dr. Goldstein began.

"Jean. I know you in 2004. I actually know you really well. In fact, you're probably the person I know best in the world. I know how pathetic that sounds, but you have to know I'm not making this up!" Her heart thumped uncomfortably in her chest.

"I think you should go." Dr. Goldstein rose, her movements unsettlingly composed for someone who had downed multiple Manhattans in the last twenty minutes. Jean reached for her glass and slugged it all back, nearly choking on the maraschino she had deposited in the drink with her own hands. Wouldn't that be some irony, she thought, to accidentally kill herself before she was even born. She coughed, gracelessly moving to the kitchen for a glass of water. Dr. Goldstein followed her, holding on to Jeffrey's hand tightly.

Jean knew how comfortable she looked, shuffling the glasses, running the tap for just long enough for the water to grow cold. Dr. Goldstein radiated fear.

"You need to leave," Dr. Goldstein said icily. "Now."

"I can't leave—not until I know you really understand!" Jean's eyes burned with tears.

"If you won't leave, I'm going to call the police."

"Please don't do that," Jean begged, slamming her drained water glass on the counter. "Sorry—I just—I don't feel exactly like myself."

"That's what I'm worried about." Dr. Goldstein's voice was ruthlessly gentle.

"You had an imaginary friend! An imaginary friend named Ruggles McBug." Jean lurched with nausea.

Dr. Goldstein dropped Jeffrey's hand. She moved closer to Jean, her eyes wide. "What did you say?" Dr. Goldstein's voice was terrible, all sharp angles. She had never spoken to Jean that way; she had never spoken to anyone like that in front of Jean, either.

"You told me to tell you this—you told me! How else would I know?" Jean's breath and heart pounded arrhythmically in her body. "How else could I know?" Jean knew she was shouting, but that seemed unimportant. Light-headedness sank her onto the floor. She crouched there, waiting, listening to the tide of Dr. Goldstein's muffled footsteps on the parquet.

The familiar weight of Dr. Goldstein's palm rested on her back. "Would you like a tranquilizer, Jean?"

Jean shook her head.

"Would you like to get up?"

Jean shook her head again. Dr. Goldstein crouched beside her; a wave of her spicy perfume crashed in Jean's nostrils.

"We'll just sit here, then, for a moment." Dr. Goldstein withdrew her hand, but Jean could still feel the warmth of her body beside her and was comforted. "This must all be very overwhelming for you."

"You have no idea."

"I'm sure I don't."

Jean turned her head, staring at Dr. Goldstein's pantyhose-clad feet. "Are you going to stop it? The trial?"

"I'm not sure."

"You're not sure because you don't want to or because I'm too late?"

"Both, probably."

"But, do you believe me? It's really important that you believe me—because then I really passed the baton to you, you know what I mean?"

"I think so."

"So, do you believe me?"

Dr. Goldstein pursed her lips, most of her mauve lipstick worn away. "I think so."

"Okay, that's good," Jean told herself. "Right?" She shook her head, testing her equilibrium. "I have to go back, I think. Being here for too long probably isn't going to be good for me."

"Alright," Dr. Goldstein said, frankly. "I think you should take Tony's note and read it. But not here," she added hastily, nodding toward Jeffrey.

A flare of panic shot through her, and Jean wondered if it was because of Dr. Goldstein's ominous tone or because of the blue fluid she had consumed.

"Okay. Can I ask you something?" Jean stood and reached silently for Dr. Goldstein's elbow to steady herself onto her feet. "I took a dose of Empathin. From a sample I brought."

"Alright," Dr. Goldstein repeated, slowly.

"But I didn't know how much to take, so I kind of drank the whole thing."

"Tony didn't tell you how to take it?" Dr. Goldstein's brow creased as she pointed to the emerald square on the sofa.

"No—things got difficult—more complicated—before I left. Trust me, you really, really want to stop these trials."

Dr. Goldstein regarded her with another piercing look before she spoke again. "It's a spray," she said.

"That's what Dr. Esposito said."

"To get into the back of the nose and throat. You aren't really supposed to *consume* it."

Jean shrugged. "Desperate times. He said it would help me go through, that it would provide some kind of protection."

"Well, please don't *drink* any more of it. Beyond that, I'm not sure how to advise you, only…" Dr. Goldstein retrieved Jean's tote bag and scooped the contents back inside, except for the folder—the folder, Jean was relieved to see, Dr. Goldstein tucked under her arm. She plucked a piece of notepaper from inside, folded it in half, and handed it to Jean. "…to tell you good luck."

Jean glanced at the folded note from Dr. Esposito before shoving it into her jacket pocket. Dr. Goldstein searched the sofa for more of Jean's overturned belongings. "What's this?" She held up Jean's cell phone with a questioning look.

Jean opened and then closed her mouth. "It's a phone."

"No, not really! A *telephone*?" Dr. Goldstein inspected it closely, turning it over in her hands.

"Really—but please, Dr. Goldstein. I really have to go."

"Of course." Dr. Goldstein dropped Jean's phone in the bag like a freshly picked apple. Jean took a deep breath, her heartbeat finally steady, finally recognizable. Dr. Goldstein held out the bag and Jean shrugged it on, like a lady in an old movie putting on a jacket. Dr. Goldstein removed the sample from its plastic envelope and lifted the vial to eye level between them. She pointed at the solution inside with a single extended pinkie finger. "Put a drop on your finger and just coat the inside of your nose. If you want to go a little further, you can put another drop or two inside of your mouth, but make sure it gets to the back of the throat. Alright?"

"Alright." Jean nodded and took the vial. She slipped it gingerly into the front pocket of her jeans. "Thank you."

"Can I ask you something before you go?"

"Of course."

Dr. Goldstein lowered her head, sheepishly avoiding eye contact with Jean. "What is it like, the future?"

"I don't even know how to begin to answer that."

"But it's still there? No nuclear disasters destroying New York City?"

"Oh." Jean sighed. "No, nothing like that."

"But there is something—I can tell just by looking at you." Dr. Goldstein stared at her frankly.

Jean lowered her eyes to avoid Dr. Goldstein's gaze. "I don't think I can really tell you anything." She didn't know what was alright to say—she had seen Marty McFly dissolve in his family photo. Jean decided less was probably more. Less was probably the most responsible thing.

"Right. That makes sense." Dr. Goldstein's lips crimped. "But I'm still there and I'm alright? And so is Tony?"

"Yes." Jean nodded.

"That's a relief."

"But I think you'll both lead happier lives—have easier consciences, I guess is what I mean—if you stop the trial. And stop working with Selestron."

"You've made your position clear, Jean," Dr. Goldstein said with only a hint of an eye roll in her voice. "What about Jeffrey?"

"What about him?"

"Is he alright?" Dr. Goldstein flushed a little beneath an embarrassed fluster. "Is he going to be alright?"

Jean paused, wanting to keep her answer as bland as possible. "He's a fully grown adult when I meet him," she said.

"Very cryptic." Dr. Goldstein smiled.

"Yeah, well, I'm trying not to show my hand here."

Dr. Goldstein nodded. "I guess you'd better be going." She walked Jean toward the door.

"Right." Jean let herself be guided, soothed by the comfort of someone else's confident intention. She paused in the doorway. "Are you going to stop it?"

"I suppose you'll know sooner than I will. Goodbye, Jean—this is the strangest visit I've ever had, or likely ever will receive." Dr. Goldstein shook her hand; everything about her touch, the clasp, the duration, the vector of the shake, was familiar.

"I sure hope so," Jean said, as the door closed firmly behind her.

Twenty-Four

Jean fled the apartment, striding through the eerily empty streets. The lights glowed more yellow than she remembered, and Jean wasn't sure if their hue was due to the bulbs they used in the '70s or her Empathin-disoriented vision. The Museum of Natural History loomed, even more golden, to Jean's eye. She leapt the turnstile with Olympic nonchalance and waited for the train. And waited. And waited. Jean didn't know what time it was—she didn't wear a watch, and her cell phone was useless, frozen in the time she'd leapt through the shortcut. She could barely see a thing in the dim surroundings of the station's ticket booth, but the clock behind the blurred glass was stopped at 2:20. The platform was emptier than she would expect at home. There were no people dressed for dinner or going out, no groups lingering in after-work camaraderie. There were a few delayed commuters, as impatient as she was, and a gaggle of students leaning against the graffiti-scoured tile.

Jean wandered toward the side of the platform where the kids lounged, feeling silently more aligned with them than the drunk man to her left, in a baggy gray suit, surreptitiously tugging at the scarf around his neck, compulsively reassuring himself of its existence.

She put her hands in her coat pockets to warm them and felt the crunch of Dr. Esposito's folded note. Jean withdrew it and unfolded the paper. She squinted down at Dr. Esposito's handwriting, as illegible and pointed as sutures in skin.

Myra,

These reports are real. You have to believe me. Please take this girl seriously; I'm fairly certain that she's the child of patient 39 (we followed all of the patients after the trial concluded and 39 was the only one we observed who was able to conceive). Just look at her closely—you'll see the resemblance I mean. Read pages 14–32 carefully. Only you can stop this. You don't forgive yourself for what we did.

I love you,
Tony.

"We're going to be late," one of the girls on the platform said, shocking Jean out of her reading. She crumpled the note back into her pocket and zipped it closed. Jean wished she still had the green folder so she could read pages 14–32 again. She wished she knew more about patient 39. Could it have been her mother? The woman in the movie theater flashed to the front of her mind. Jean's mother never talked about her life before moving to Pennsylvania. She spoke about it in vague terms of regret and sin, but never offered any specific details about her youth.

Jean pressed against her forehead, as though she were trying to keep her brain inside her head. She wondered if she would ever know. Jean knew her mother had suffered miscarriages before she was born. There were more miscarriages after she was born, too. Jean's mother always wanted more children. Throughout her youth, Jean carried the secret thought that her mother was disappointed by her survival. She never felt like the "miracle baby" the ladies at church talked about; she felt like she was just practice, a rough draft for the child her mother really wanted.

Jean recalled the gaps of silence, when her mother disappeared after another pregnancy disappeared. She wondered if all of that loss and all of that trouble in her mother's body was because of her participation in the Selestron trial. If she hadn't been patient 39, what kind of mother would she have been to Jean?

When the train finally rumbled through, Jean's fingers and toes tingled with cold. She edged a little farther down the platform to be closer to the noisy kids so that she wouldn't have to board a car alone with her thoughts. The car was as freezing as the station had been; the only difference was an eye-watering, sulfurous stink. Someone had slid all of the car's windows open to air out the smell. Jean buried her nose in her scarf, breathing in her own scent from her own time.

The kids and their noise seemed suddenly far away, and something in the malodorous air shifted. A shiver of warning shimmied through her and Jean listened. When her body talked, she always listened. Jean closed her eyes every time the car lurched at a stop. She felt someone watching her and wished she had a book to read or headphones to jam into her ears to better blend into the crowd on the train.

"Twenty-third Street," the driver announced over the staticky PA. Jean waited until the last second to open her eyes and lurch to her feet. The kids from her stop on the Upper West Side were getting off, too, and she shuffled herself into the group, hoping to camouflage herself from whatever eyes or force had her in its sights.

"Watch it," one of the kids said. She was tiny but walked with the rolling gait of a much more curvaceous person. Jean realized too late she had stepped on her heel.

"Sorry," she muttered, skipping past them and fleeing to the exit. She couldn't explain it, but she knew she had to get out, that some danger, specifically for her, lurked within the hollowed ground of the city.

Jean was stunned anew by the gust of cold air that hit her squarely in the chest. At first she thought she had slipped and was falling, but quickly understood that she had been pushed. A larger, taller figure yanked her around the corner by the strap of her bag. He hauled her back, like some forgotten piece of luggage at the airport. The man's pinstripe-suited arm looped around her throat. Jean gasped. No words were available to her. Her throat was swollen closed with panic, and her muscles and bones all locked into one another.

"I'll just take that off your hands." Jean went limp as the figure tugged the bag from her shoulders. She kept her eyes on the ground, but her ears tuned into every tiny sound: the shuffle of her attacker's feet on the pavement, the thud of the bag, a nauseating smack of chewing gum. The figure not holding her wore a suit, too, the same navy suit she'd seen from behind the halal cart in front of the Bloomingdale's in 2004. *The men who worked for Luke's father had followed her through the shortcut.*

"I don't see anything—cell phone, wallet, shit like that, but nothing we're looking for. You think she's the right kid?"

"Listen to yourself! Only the right kid would have a cell phone." Jean knew there could be more of them, and the thought flooded her with panic.

She vaguely thought about crouching down, about making herself smaller and trying to disappear. Before she could act on the impulse, adrenaline—or something larger and more mysterious—took over her and she began to run. She twisted out of the man's hold, leaving her bag in his hands, and Jean ran all out. Her bones twisted and popped in their sockets.

She knew she would be in the most unbearable kind of pain when she stopped, but she also knew she couldn't stop. She had surprised her attackers—they hadn't expected her to run, and they hadn't expected her to run so fast. Jean was out of shape and hadn't trained in a decade, *but the body never forgets,* she thought and smiled through her gritted teeth.

She sped around the corner of 9th Avenue and doubled back down 24th Street. Jean had already lost them in the dark maze of the city, but she couldn't stop running. She sped under the High Line, searching for a crowd to disappear into, and a lone train rumbled overhead like a benediction. The cold air caught the thin glaze of sweat forming on her face and between her shoulder blades. Jean knew that she really should stop—if she didn't, her body might refuse to move altogether. A loose cluster of people radiated from a doorway ahead. Their good cheer lifted off of them onto the street, producing the kind of magnetic pull possible only when everyone is having an unexpectedly good time.

Jean slowed to a jog, relieved to find safety in numbers, and collapsed into the group's energy. She knew she should find the opening by the dock and get back to her time, but the men from Selestron surely would look for her there. She peered around the heads of flowing, voluminous hair, trying to get a glimpse of what they had all come to see inside. A band played on an elevated platform in the back. The song was familiar, if distorted, through an imbalanced and inadequate sound system. Jean squinted at the stage, zeroing in on a figure with familiar posture on the left of the stage. She pressed closer, trying to catch her breath.

Alan stood in formation with his band under a bleed of mauve lights. He was glamorous but gaunt, his movements confident and fluid. Jean couldn't look away from his perfect hands on the guitar; he held the instrument like it had grown out of his arms. His smile was radiant.

"Jean?" She turned, her body prepared to run again. "Jean—
it's me." A lanky young man in a stylish silver suit grabbed her
shoulder.

"Iggy?" His hair was longer and his face looked a little fuller,
but it was unmistakably Iggy.

"Yeah, man—are you seriously here?" He embraced her in
an extravagant hug, and Jean tried to relax into it instead of
clenching up. This was a miracle after all—a good thing. She
convinced her body to loosen just a little before she held him
back at arm's length.

"Are you okay? Oh my God, do you know how worried
everyone's been about you?"

"Everyone?" Iggy raised a sly eyebrow.

"Your friends—Claire, my God, poor Claire has been worried sick."

"Yeah." Iggy scratched the side of his head. "I do feel bad
about Claire. But, Jean, I'm fucking *great*, man." A young
woman, a Brigitte Bardot doppelganger, slid a possessive hand
into Iggy's. "Jean, this is Viv, my girlfriend." Viv gave Jean a
lukewarm smile.

"How do you know Iggy?" she shouted over the music.

"I—we—" Jean turned back toward the stage, trying to get
her thoughts in order.

"Jean's from my hometown, babe," Iggy said with a wink.
"We haven't seen each other in a long time. I kind of took off
on everybody to come here and I think we need a little catch-
up, you know?"

Viv's gaze was rough as a cat's tongue, but once she had taken
the full measure of Jean, she shrugged and lit a cigarette. "See
you in there?"

"Yeah, yeah—hey, give me one of those, will you?" Viv
handed over the pack and nodded at Jean as she disappeared
into the crowd. Iggy lit a cigarette before offering one to Jean.

She shook her head, realizing she was still breathing hard from her run.

"Where do we even start?" she asked.

Iggy bubbled with laughter. "Dude, you have no idea. Here, come in, catch some of the local flavor." He led Jean further into the building to a wide, low hallway hung with mobile-like sculptures.

"What is this?" she asked.

"Who knows?" Iggy shrugged. "Some art opening, I think. But I came for The Throwaways, man. Here, come on." They threaded through the crowd to a crumbling stairwell. Iggy climbed the stairs with the same blurriness Jean had noticed in Dr. Goldstein's hallway—something about his steps didn't quite line up. Jean circumvented a cascade of broken glass and followed him. Jean was breathless after the fifth flight, but they kept climbing, all the way to the top. Iggy held the emergency door for her with unexpected gallantry. "Here," he said with a grin. "Check it out."

The lip of the roof sloped down, and Iggy sat, swinging his legs over the edge. At first she thought he was fanning himself, but Jean realized that he wanted her to sit beside him.

Below where she and Iggy swung their ankles in the cold, the city was blanketed with lights. The howl of Alan's guitar was faint, but still audible. Jean's eyes were held by the Twin Towers, two broken teeth at the tip of the island. "It's really something, isn't it? To see them being built like that?" Iggy shook his head.

"It's weird—sometimes I forget about them. Not what happened, but about the actual buildings."

"I love seeing the city like this, remembering what I remember on top of it." He sighed happily. "But fuck, Jean, how did you get here? Not that it isn't great to see you."

"I was looking for you."

"Bullshit." Iggy carefully tamped out his cigarette on the ledge beside his hip.

"I mean, sort of—that's how I got so involved. In a way." Jean added it hastily, not sure how straightforward to be with Iggy. "It's a long story, honestly, and I don't have a lot of time, but basically I came here to try to close the shortcuts."

"Why would you want to close them?" Iggy was open, incredulous.

"Another really long story, but mostly because capitalism is evil and because of the potential collapse of space and time." Jean had been aiming for glib but missed her mark by a mile.

"Well, shit. Sounds like a couple of good reasons."

Jean looked closely at her former co-worker. He was genuinely relaxed, at ease in a way she had never seen. All of his forced, almost frenetic, friendliness was gone, and whatever remained was peaceful and natural. "You seem really okay."

"I'm better than okay. I fucking love it here. This is the dream." Iggy turned to her and gripped her arm. "I'm filling in for Sylvain Sylvain, man! From the New York Dolls! This is my actual life." He shook his head. "I know how lucky I am, but shit, how? Why?"

Jean shrugged, smiling. "I was going to ask if you wanted to come back with me."

"Fuck no!" Iggy lurched back as though burned by the suggestion. "I mean, no offense, man, but absolutely not."

"You won't miss anybody or be missed? What about your friends and family?"

"They'll live. My life could really be something here."

"Your life could be something at home," Jean tried, weakly, one last time.

"No thanks, Jean."

"What if I close the shortcuts and you—you know—something happens…"

"You mean, what if I disappear like Michael J. Fox?" He laughed.

"It's not funny!" Jean smacked his arm but had to suppress a smile. "It's your life!"

"Yes, it is my life, and I want to stay here. What if I don't disappear? What if I get to keep doing what I'm doing?"

"I had to ask. You do seem great. You make staying look good, Iggy."

"You could stay, too, Jean." Iggy's mouth curved in a smile. And Jean really wondered if she could. She allowed the fantasy to unspool for a minute, but realized with a jolt that she would miss too much about 2004—Claire, Alan, Lu, even her roommates. She would miss all of the people.

She shook her head. "No, I have to go. Some guys from Selestron are chasing me." Jean stood slowly.

"Some who from what?" Iggy stood beside her, steadying her.

"Long story, but I really do have to go." Jean felt for the vial lodged in her pocket, grateful that she'd been forgetful and hadn't returned it to her bag. Iggy pulled her into another embrace, and this time she accepted and absorbed it—she felt relaxed and at peace, just like Iggy, as she stared out at the old city one last time.

"You should at least stay for the rest of The Throwaways' set. It's a once-in-a-lifetime opportunity, Jean."

"I wish I could." She sighed. "But I need to get back to where I belong."

Jean hadn't expected to see Iggy, and, she thought guiltily, if she expected to find him, she had always thought he'd be desperate, languishing on the street. It felt so good to be wrong. Jean wanted to enjoy her final walk on the sidewalks, sidewalks that she would walk across decades later. She knew it had to be significant, that she was meant to bring something back, a new understanding of time or human nature.

But Jean didn't understand anything about those things. If anything, she understood them a lot less. She did, however, understand something important about herself. Jean finally believed that she could build something new, that she didn't have to be trapped in a half-life after her accident. And she knew, if she made it back to her time, that she would make all of the choices that added up to a full life. She wondered if being a tiny egg in the body of patient 39 had somehow set her up for failure. Maybe she had needed to go through all of those shortcuts to undo that genetic damage. Or maybe not. Maybe Jean would have figured it out on her own.

The thought of her newly discovered power warmed her in the cold chill coming off the river. It was comforting to know the world was so big, that her human experience could be so wide and so strange. She paced the dock, inexplicably hesitant to get back. Voices argued in the distance and the dark water lapped below. Jean felt a flicker on one side, like the blades of a fan directed particularly toward her. Even though she couldn't see it, she was sure it was the world's first shortcut. She thought about the first person who stood in this spot, the person who burst it open while the Empathin pulsed in their human body.

Jean knew that she was just another human body—but she would be the last, a neat bookend. She opened the vial and dosed herself the way Dr. Goldstein had instructed. Her nostrils and throat stung with the scent and taste of decaying oranges. Jean emptied the vial in the river, hoping she wasn't doing any more damage. She leaned into the breeze on the dock and walked through.

Twenty-Five

Jean emerged from the shortcut in Chelsea into the dark crawl space above the Bloomingdale's dressing rooms. The silence around her was punctured by a siren nearby, but the store was quiet. She pulled away the ceiling tile and noted the darkness below. She dropped down into the tiny space with care. She had nothing with her—no keys, no phone. Her bag was still, presumably, in 1970.

Jean warily opened the fitting room door. A faint red glow from the emergency exit signs lit the closed store. If nothing else, Jean was reassured by her solitude. No menacing employees from Selestron sprang out from behind the anoraks to grab her. She wandered the store, looking for clues about what might have happened. Jean wasn't sure what her success would be like in this world, inside of the shuttered Bloomingdale's.

She walked behind the registers, hoping for some clue, at least about the time, but they were cold and dark. The tiny digital screen on the phone beside the registers read 2:00. Jean knew she was locked inside and didn't want to trip an alarm, but wondered if she could call someone to let her out. Unfortunately, Jo's number, along with everyone else's, was trapped in her cell phone. The only number she knew by heart was Dr. Goldstein's office line; nobody would be there at this hour.

Jean wandered to the plate glass window and watched a lone man walking a dog across the street. The store's hours were etched into the door—she could find a place to sleep until the Bloomingdale's opened and then she could walk home. Hopefully, her apartment was still in the same place and hopefully Molly and Christine would be there to buzz her in. She hoped there was still a Molly and Christine.

Jean climbed the stairs to the housewares section and made herself a nest of decorative throw pillows on the ground. Her body, desperate for rest, succumbed to sleep quickly. Jean's dreams, though, were much less straightforward. She dreamed of her apartment. Of an old claw-foot bathtub in the living room. Jean's heart thudded in her chest and the taste of oranges lingered in the back of her throat. The apartment smelled wrong—like roasted potatoes and paint. It was still dark; no microwave or oven clock lit the room. Jean turned around still braced on the tub, searching for her room or the bathroom, but neither was where she had left it.

A young woman slept sitting up in a chair in the corner, her face smooth and relaxed, her long hair braided back. Jean jolted with instant recognition—it was the old woman who had rung her buzzer back when she had first quit her job with Dr. Goldstein. The shape of the sleeping girl's face blurred and twisted into the same pale, powdery face Jean escorted into her apartment.

She lurched toward the door, naked of the extra bolts and locks from her time. The knob was familiar under her hand—the same exact one she turned every day to enter and exit—only smoother. Jean turned it, but couldn't push the door open. It was as if some great force of suction held it closed.

Jean turned back toward the woman in the chair only to find that the apartment had been replaced by her parents' house. She could tell it was winter. The bright white of fresh snow in the moonlight reflected in through the curtained windows. Her parents sat silent on the sofa, but she was still standing.

"It's okay, Jeanie," her mother said. "You have nothing to worry about."

"Get some rest. Tomorrow is a big day."

Jean knew they had probably spoken those words to her before, probably on the eve of a track meet, but their inflection was different. It was eerily peaceful. Jean's dream legs carried her through her old house into her old room and under the covers of her childhood bed. She swallowed hard and was hit with another wave of bitter citrus, and before she knew what was happening, Jean woke to a virtuosic litany of swears.

Sunlight poured through the storefront windows, and Jean carefully sat up in the pile of printed throw pillows. She was desperately thirsty and wanted to go home, but wasn't sure if she should announce herself now or sneak out as a customer later.

Her bladder insisted on announcing now, despite the foul mood of whoever was on the opening shift. Jean carefully replaced the pillows and zipped up her jacket. She gingerly made her way down the stairs, still out of sorts from all of her strange dreams. A clatter sounded from the dressing room followed by more swearing. Jean wondered if there was an employee bathroom she could sneak into somewhere.

"Holy shit! How did you get in here?"

Jean spun around, finding herself eye to eye with a familiar face.

"Jo?" she asked.

"Yes?" Jo shook her head, her expression wavering between aggressive and fearful. Jean realized there was a high probability

Jo wouldn't know who she was in this new 2004. She hoped, ardently, that Jo didn't know who she was.

"It's just, your name tag." Jean motioned to her own chest where a name tag would be pinned.

"Oh, right." Jo sighed. "You scared the shit out of me."

"Yeah, I'm so sorry. I work next door and was accidentally locked in—I tried to find a way out and ended up in here."

"You ended up in *here*?"

"Wild night, you know?" Jean widened her eyes meaningfully.

"Okay?"

"I'm so glad you're here. I really need to get home or else I'll be late for class," Jean riffed. "But before I go, can I use your bathroom?"

Jo let her out onto the street and locked the door firmly behind her. Jean walked down the avenue, searching for signs of change. She was relieved and disappointed all at the same time to see that everything looked exactly the same. Jean's breath steamed in the air. She lifted the hood of her parka against the wind and walked to her apartment. It took a few blocks, but Jean was shocked fully awake by the absence of pain in her body. After her run the night before, she should have been entirely immobile. She rolled her bad ankle and poked experimentally at the hip that ached almost constantly. Jean felt nothing, only the clear, bright glow of good health.

Her street was the same, too—brand-new signage for the dumpling place across the street was the only difference. She leaned away from the wind in the alcove of her front door and buzzed the apartment. An answering buzz startled her. She pushed experimentally, doubtful that the door would open, certain that she was imagining things, but the handle gave beneath her fingers. Jean stood in the vestibule, incredulous. Had the super finally fixed the buzzers? Molly and Christine would be thrilled. She climbed the steps to her door, again noting the buttery ease in her joints.

Something looked different about the front door—the COME BACK WITH A WARRANT welcome mat was missing. She wondered if it was even her apartment anymore. Jean was overwhelmed with an urge to knock, but before she could, the door swung open.

"Hey! There you are—you're going to be late! Big day today." Claire held the door open with one hand and texted on her phone with the other. "Where were you? I bet a walk was good for those pre-performance jitters. But you really should've brought your phone. To keep track of the time at least!"

Jean moved slowly and stepped inside.

"Here, I made you some coffee. It's on the counter." She waved toward the kitchen, her eyes still on her phone.

"Thank you?" Jean reached for the coffee and wondered if she was still asleep. The apartment was bright and hot and quiet, except for an occasional hiss from the radiator. "What time is it? Where are Molly and Christine?"

Claire snapped her gaze from her phone to Jean. "They're in Larchmont, Jean. Where their new house is."

"What?"

"Hurry up and drink that because I think you're going to need more than one cup today."

"What?"

"Wow, Jean, just hurry up. It's already almost ten! You have to be at Dr. Goldstein's in an hour."

"What?"

"Oh my God." Claire rolled her eyes and set down her phone. "Sometimes I can't tell when you're joking. How are you feeling about today? Confident, I hope?"

"I guess so?" Jean was relieved to see Claire, to recognize Claire and be recognized, but she couldn't shake the feeling of slipping. Like she was skating across a frozen pond with no skates. Her apartment and her conversation with Claire, all of it felt right, but she couldn't quite get her footing. A blurred recollection of a housewarming party in Larchmont with Christine's and Molly's beaming faces swam up in her mind.

"We went to their housewarming, in Larchmont," Jean confirmed, staring into her half-full cup of coffee.

"What? Of course we did. I still can't believe you talked me into helping Lu and Steph make a multicourse dinner in that giant suburban kitchen. What does that have to do with your thing today?"

"I'm not sure. Where's my phone?"

"Plugged in next to the toaster, like always." Claire stood and reached over to feel Jean's forehead with her palm. "You don't feel warm."

"I'm fine," Jean said with what she hoped was a reassuring smile. "I just had some weird dreams." She picked up her phone and found a couple of text messages from Alan waiting for her. I'm really nervous. Can we meet a few minutes early?

Jean squeezed her eyes shut and a dim recollection along the lines of Molly and Christine's housewarming prickled in her mind. Sure, she texted back. See you there ten of.

"I hung the outfit we picked out last night on the back of the bathroom door. I ran the shower and steamed it so you're going to look extra pulled together." Claire poured herself another coffee and topped Jean's off, too. "Go get dressed—I want to take a picture before you leave."

Jean nodded and moved to the bathroom, where a plum cashmere sweater and a pair of sharply tailored charcoal pants hung neatly waiting for her. She dressed and brushed her teeth. She looked closely at her hair in the bathroom mirror. It was still short but cut neatly in a much more flattering frame around her face.

Claire waited outside holding a leather messenger bag in one hand and a silver digital camera in the other. "Here, put this on and stand by the door. I'm so proud of you, Jean." Claire grinned and posed her carefully. "Okay, don't smile too much. You're going to be a doctor in like three hours, so try to have a bit more gravitas."

Another rush of memory, like some galloping herd, of hours in a library, study sessions with Alan, asking Dr. Goldstein to be her thesis advisor. "Oh God," Jean whispered.

"Oh God nothing! You're going to kill it—I'll see you at the party tonight. Okay, Dr. Smith?"

"Don't jinx me!"

"You're too prepared for any jinx to get in the way. Oh hey, have you listened to that new Weathermen album yet? You can borrow my iPod if you want something to keep you calm on the train."

"Oh—that's really generous of you. No, I haven't listened to it."

"It's not generous at all. I have that audition later so I need to focus. Get in the zone." Claire pressed her fingers to her temples. "Here," she said, grabbing her iPod from the coffee table. "Good luck, Dr. Smith." The girls hugged in the doorway, and Jean popped the earbuds in as she ran down the steps.

Down on the sidewalk, her body took over, remembering where she was supposed to go. The world around her grew clearer, crisper, with every step. Every breath in her lungs steadied her, until she paused on the south corner of Union Square. She stood, waiting to cross the street, when a bus rumbled and belched past her. Iggy's enormous aging face was plastered across the outside, a row of slim, suited young men lined up behind him. THE WEATHERMEN in gilded capital letters drifted over their images like a banner.

The Iggy she had known was receding, already replaced by this older Iggy whose voice filled her ears. The realization didn't startle Jean—instead it washed over her in warm, natural waves, like a visit to the ocean. Jean understood, finally, that good things didn't have to be hard-won. Iggy had known that, too—he had embraced the life that embraced him back. And now his face was on buses and his music flooded speakers across the world. Jean had always fought and struggled to maintain a feeling of normalcy, to create a holding pen of stability. But the truth was, the best life in any timeline was the life you let fully in. Jean boarded her train to Dr. Goldstein's office, where she knew she was going to defend her dissertation. She flooded her consciousness with Iggy's warm, worn voice and bobbed uptown. His voice encouraged her, like he—and only he—knew what she was coming back to.

Every song Iggy sang was like a personal high five just for her. She smiled, remembering him in a full bloom of happiness up on the rooftop overlooking the old city. Jean knew that she could feel that happy, too, and her mind hummed with everything she wanted to say to the panel of Dr. Goldstein and her professors.

She got off at her stop and climbed the subway steps into the gold light of morning. The park glinted on her left, and it felt like a benediction. "Jean!" Alan called from where he waited in front of the Majestic. "Are you ready for this?" he asked. Jean watched him closely, looking for the outline of the young guitarist she'd seen on a makeshift stage in Chelsea. The smile she had seen onstage, the smile that had made her heart somersault in her chest, was the same smile he beamed at her now. Whatever had happened to Alan between then and now, Jean knew that he was genuinely happy, standing here, waiting for her.

"Of course." Jean accepted the paper cup of coffee in his outstretched hand. "You're an angel, thank you. Are you ready?"

"I think so." Alan tapped his foot on the sidewalk nervously, but with the same cool precision that gave away his former life as a rock star.

"Okay, Dr. Grudge," Jean said, beaming. "Let's do this."

"Let's do this, Dr. Smith." They linked elbows and strode through the door together.

Marcus greeted them with a wide smile. "Good luck today, you two! Not that you'll need it." He rummaged under the desk. "One second, I have a little something for you." Marcus handed each of them a small disposable camera wrapped in Congratulations Graduate! cardboard. "I know it's not exactly a graduation, but I figured, close enough."

"Aw, Marcus." Jean reached across the desk for a half hug. "Thank you."

"I'm proud of you, Jean." He shook hands with Alan. "I'm proud of you, too, Mr. Grudge. Promise me you'll take lots of pictures to celebrate, okay?"

Alan placed an open palm over his heart. "Thanks, Marcus. We will."

Jean and Alan presented their dissertations and joint research to the panel assembled at Dr. Goldstein's office. The university agreed to allow the defense in the unorthodox location as an accommodation for Dr. Goldstein—she had developed advanced mobility problems as well as worsened vision. Jean was surprised by her frailty in this new time, but pleased to see that Dr. Goldstein's mind was as sharp as ever. The most difficult of the panel's questions came from her.

"So, Jean," Dr. Goldstein began. "A lot of people would question the veracity of a patient's statements regarding their dreams. Things change so swiftly in a single dream, even as you've noted in the research you just presented. How can you be sure of the accuracy of the information they present?"

Jean nodded, pleased to elaborate. "Well, ultimately accuracy isn't what matters. It's the way a patient interprets and synthesizes the information from a subconscious experience. We get important clues about what frightens them, or energizes, or intrigues them. The accuracy of their reporting isn't what helps us treat them. The fact that they're talking to us about something that is real and significant for them, that is what helps us make meaningful breakthroughs."

Dr. Goldstein gave her a shrewd look and Jean's mind clicked—away from ambiguity, from the blurriness she had felt all morning. Her brain and body snapped fully into the space she stood in, among the colleagues she spoke to, under the brand-new degree she was about to be conferred.

"Very nice, Jean. Very good work." The home advantage seemed to imbue both Alan and Jean with extra confidence; they had conducted most of their research under Dr. Goldstein's guidance in the same room.

Jean spoke with fluid confidence, and Alan brought the same compelling swagger to his talk that he had brought to the stage. It went so well that Jean was a little sad when it was over. Dr. Goldstein glowed with pride as the panel filed out. "You two are my stars, you know that?" She clasped their hands and her eyes glistened.

"We couldn't have done it without you, Dr. Goldstein," Jean said.

"Your parents would have been so proud," Dr. Goldstein said.

Jean nodded, content, and believed Dr. Goldstein was right.

"Come up to my apartment," Dr. Goldstein said. "I have a little surprise for you both, and it may or may not involve caviar and presents."

"You shouldn't have, Dr. G.," Alan said.

"I'll be right up. I'm just going to put away our files," Jean said as she gathered the stacks of their supporting documents into matching manila folders.

"That can wait, surely, Jean," Dr. Goldstein scolded.

"No, no, no." Jean shook her head. "I want it all to be official."

"Alright. We'll see you up there. Take my arm, would you, Dr. Grudge?"

Their murmured conversation flowed sweetly and slowly out

the door. Jean smiled, filled with grateful warmth for her supportive friends and colleagues, underscored by a rush of triumph. Jean had never felt so proud or so happy. She switched the lights off in Dr. Goldstein's office and carried the files into her tiny old office, where the filing cabinets waited cold and silent. She slotted Alan's file under the G's with a bolt of satisfaction and then pulled open the drawer for the S's.

Jean thumbed through the rainbow rows of folders tucked inside, pushing past one tab labeled SELESTRON in neat, square capital letters. A single emerald green folder was nestled there. Jean couldn't tell why a sudden twinge of unease disrupted her goodwill, but tucking her SMITH, JEAN–labeled file and sealing it in with the rest of Dr. Goldstein's records dispelled the moment of discord. Once again, Jean felt better than ever, like the sun was rising inside of her body, like nothing could be better.

★ ★ ★ ★ ★

Acknowledgments

I don't know if it's just me, but the thank-yous feel very different now, in 2022, than they did the last time I acknowledged anyone in writing. I didn't think I could feel any more thankful back then, but guess what? In any event, I find it eternally reassuring to know I can change.

This book was such a delight to write, not least because I had the best publishing support system in the business. Laura Brown is one of the smartest, most compassionate editors I have ever worked with. Every writer should be so lucky. I was swept off my feet by the cover design from Gigi Lau and Elita Sidiropoulou, and by all of the wonderful work from the Park Row team. Randy Chan, Katie-Lynn Golakovich, Sophie James, Leah Morse, Rachel Haller, Erika Imranyi, and Nicole Luongo are actual stars. I am also deeply indebted to—and in awe of—the eagle eye of Tracy Wilson.

I count my blessings every day for Kate Johnson, Rach Crawford, and everyone at Wolf Literary for their enduring support and guidance.

I would not have been able to write this book without living parts of Jean's incredibly hectic, chaotic, and wild life in the city. Thank you to every single beautiful and generous person I met along the way. There are too many of you to name, but I promise I have not forgotten a single one of you. As I excavated and reflected on many of these friendships and experiences, I couldn't help but think about all of the wonderful people who were so loved and lost, from Ben Chappel to Sam Jayne. Thank you to Lizzy Goodman for writing *Meet Me in the Bathroom*, a brilliant resource that I consulted many times throughout the writing of this book to refresh or confirm my memory, and to Joey Ramone for inspiring Alan Grudge.

Thank you to all of the amazing and creative people in my life now (as an ancient middle-aged person) who encouraged this project in so many ways. The generosity of other writers always astounds me; thank you especially to Amy Jo Burns, Margarita Montimore, Morgan Jenkins, Emma Straub, Naima Coster, Rachel Yoder, Kimberly King Parsons, Jami Attenberg, Kyle Lucia Wu, Chelsea Bieker, Erin Khar, Jessica Valenti, and Liv Stratman. I am so lucky to work with Nonie Brzyski and many other brilliant people on the Freya Project, a collaboration that never ceases to restore and inspire me. Thank you to David Gooblar for everything always, and Giancarlo Vulcano for the door men. Thank you to Betsy Nadel, my guide to some of the coolest places I've ever been in this town.

Thank you to my colleagues and co-workers over the years, but especially our pandemic-era teams at Elsa and Ramona. Thank you to the world's best friend and neighbor, Zeb Millett.

A million thanks to my family, especially Milya Burian, Irka Zazulak, Scott Schneider, Arnie and Nancy Schneider, and Lis Schneider.

And speaking of Lis Schneider, amazing first grade teacher

at the East Village Community School, thank you to all of the teachers out there for making the world feel less scary and more normal for our kids in these last difficult years.

Thank you to my own beloved children, Vi and L.J.; I could not imagine two more wonderful, imaginative heavy metal hearts to beat alongside mine in the apartment we were all trapped in for most of the writing of this book.

And finally, the biggest, baddest thank-you to my partner in all things, Jay Schneider. The idea for this book started with your suggestion to set something in the early 2000s with secret passages in the back rooms of the city. Your thoughtfulness, moral clarity, anxieties, and weirdness are all of my favorite songs. (And thanks for lending your aunt Jean's name to this protagonist!)

Thank you to everyone who ever said anything nice to me about anything.

And thank you, wonderful person holding this book and getting this far (extra love and thanks to every bookseller and librarian who helped put this book into your hands).